D0356854

forbidden

SYRIE JAMES & RYAN M. JAMES

HARPER TEEN
An Imprint of HarperCollinsPublishers

HarperTeen is an imprint of HarperCollins Publishers.

Forbidden
Copyright © 2012 by Syrie James and Ryan M. James
www.epicreads.com

——

Library of Congress Cataloging-in-Publication Data
James, Syrie.
  Forbidden / by Syrie James & Ryan James. — 1st ed.
    p. cm.
  Summary: As sixteen-year-old Claire's newly-revealed psychic abilities bring unwelcome
attention from Watchers, Alec, a Watcher grown tired of having to eliminate descendants
of his angelic forefathers, has fallen in love with Claire while hiding out at her school,
unaware that she is a Nephilim, a half-angel.
  ISBN 978-0-06-202789-4
  [1. Angels—Fiction. 2. Supernatural—Fiction. 3. High schools—Fiction. 4. Schools—
Fiction. 5. Psychic ability—Fiction.] I. James, Ryan. II. Title.
PZ7.J15443For 2012   2011019364
[Fic]—dc23   CIP
                                                                             AC

——

Typography by Michelle Gengaro-Kokmen
11 12 13 14 15   CG/BV   10 9 8 7 6 5 4 3 2 1
❖
First Edition

To our loving spouses and family,
for putting up with our
long hours at the computer,
all our brainstorming and
shop talk at family gatherings
(when we were supposed to be
paying attention to everyone),
and for being so supportive of this,
our first published collaboration . . .
thank you.

And especially to Jeff,
who was the inspiration
and the voice in our heads
whenever we wanted
our characters to say—or do—
something funny.
You are the Pirate King!

one

It had been a really crappy morning.

Things can only get better, Claire Brennan thought as she flipped on her turn signal, struggling to concentrate on the road despite the throbbing ache in her head.

"Claire! Get over, you're going to miss the exit."

Claire sighed and cast a sidelong glance at her mother, Lynn, in the passenger seat. "I'm trying to, but that Beamer needs to move its ass."

The car in question finally zoomed forward. Claire pressed hard on the gas and yanked the wheel, lurching their aging white Toyota Camry into the exit lane of the 405 freeway. Out of the corner of her eye, she saw her mom's right foot stomp on the floor.

"Stop pressing the imaginary brake, Mom! I've done this at least three hundred times, okay? I know how to drive."

"Sorry, honey. I was just . . . reacting instinctively."

Claire merged onto Sunset Boulevard and joined the morning lineup of BMWs, Lexuses, Volvos, and flashy

SUVs waiting at the light to turn left toward her high school. She could feel her mom's gaze on her and suddenly felt a little self-conscious. Her mom had a way of looking at her sometimes that was really intense, as if she was inspecting her for some imperfection, or seeking something that wasn't there.

Claire often wondered if it was because she didn't look anything like her mother. Her mom was blond, blue-eyed, and beautiful—and way younger than any of her classmates' parents. Claire had long, dark brown (translation: boring) hair, and hazel eyes. She was of medium height and somewhat curvy, while her mother was paler, shorter, and slighter. Clearly, Claire thought, she must take after her father—a man she had never met. A man her mother never spoke about.

"Why are you staring at me?" Claire asked.

"I'm not staring." A brief silence ensued as her mother quickly glanced away. "Honey, are you sure you feel all right?"

So that's it, Claire mused. "Mom: You've been hovering over me ever since breakfast. You're blowing things way out of proportion! To be honest, I don't feel so great, but sooner or later every girl goes through this, okay? I'll survive."

"I just . . . I want to make sure you have everything you need today—"

"Mom, I'll be fine. You should be relieved. *I* am. It

means I'm not a freak of nature after all. Now I can be normal like everyone else."

"Is that what you want, honey?" her mom said with a loving look. "To be just like everyone else?"

"Of course." Privately, Claire added, *That's not the only thing I want.* She wanted a home. To stay in one place for more than a year or two. To put down some roots. For her mom to finally settle down and be happy, maybe even remarry. With that kind of stability, Claire might be lucky enough to find a boyfriend herself. But what were the odds of that happening, with a restless, paranoid free spirit for a mother?

"Now that I have my license," Claire teased, "the only other thing I need to be like everyone else is my own car."

Her mom immediately went on the defensive. "Just because all the other kids at this school got a shiny new car for their sixteenth birthday, it doesn't mean we can afford one. Even with your partial scholarship, the cost of tuition alone—"

"I know, Mom. I was just kidding."

Claire shot her mom a reassuring smile and then focused on navigating the steep, curving driveway that led down the hill toward Emerson Academy. It was Book Day, the Friday in early September before the school year officially began. Claire felt her spirits lift, as they always did when she arrived on campus. She knew how lucky she was to go here.

Emerson Academy was a prestigious private school, grades seven through twelve, with only one hundred students per grade. The campus—located in Brentwood, an upscale neighborhood at the base of the Santa Monica Mountains—was beautiful, with Spanish-style redbrick-and-stucco buildings nestled into the side of a steep hill landscaped with shrubs, palms, and eucalyptus trees. The gymnasium, Middle School, and state-of-the-art aquatic center, football field, and baseball field sprawled across the valley floor below. A series of concrete ramps and railroad-tie staircases snaked their way up through the manicured hillside to the Upper Campus classrooms, creating nooks and terraces where students could hang out in the Southern California sunshine year-round.

Claire loved everything about the school: the beauty of the campus, the rotating weekly schedule that kept things from getting stale, and the challenging classes. At this school, you either respected your teachers and peers, or you were kicked out. Grades were everything. Claire was one of the top students in her class, but only because she worked really hard to keep her scholarship. After two years at a place as special as Emerson, she couldn't bear the thought of going anywhere else.

Claire passed the junior parking lot and pulled to the curb of the drop-off circle, shifting the car into park. "All I have to do is get my picture taken and pick up my books. I should be done by noon."

Her mom checked her watch with a frown. "I have a really busy day. I don't know what time I'll be able to come get you."

"Okay, no problem." Claire grabbed her backpack from the backseat. "I'll ask Erica or Brian to bring me home."

Her mom was about to protest when Claire cut her off. "Don't worry, Mom. I'll make sure I wear my seat belt, that they don't go over the speed limit, play loud music, or text while driving, and that they aren't under the influence of alcohol or narcotics."

"Thank you. Call me when you get home, so I'll know you're safe." Her mom thumbed through her laptop bag, seemingly unaware of the good-humored sarcasm behind Claire's words. "Oh God. I forgot the disclosure form for the Redman account. Where the hell did I put it?" Claire's mom had become a Realtor shortly after they moved to Los Angeles and seemed to be pretty good at it.

As Claire wedged her way in between the bag and her mom for a good-bye hug, something strange happened. A shudder passed through Claire's body—like an electric shock in her veins—followed by a woozy feeling. Then a crystal clear image flashed into her mind: *her mother's hand stowing a page in her bag*. Without thinking, Claire blurted out, "It's in the outside zipper pocket."

Her mom stared at her. "What? What are you talking about?"

Claire blinked twice. "That form you're looking for.

Check the pocket of your laptop bag."

Claire's mom slipped her hand into the pocket and pulled out a printed form, looking confused. "I must have put this in there yesterday at the office. How did you know that?"

"Just a lucky guess. You squirrel things away there all the time, Mom." *Weird*, Claire thought, as she exited the car and her mom slid into the driver's seat. *Where did that thought come from? Was it déjà vu? And why do I feel so dizzy?* Claire's knees were wobbling, and sweat beaded on her brow. She turned away quickly, readjusting her fitted white top and short floral skirt. "Gotta go, Mom. See you tonight. Love you."

"Love you, too."

The Camry entered the stream of departing parents. Claire cut over to the steps leading up the hill, grateful that her mom hadn't noticed Claire's light-headedness or the flush she could feel heating her face. *The symptoms must come with the territory*, Claire decided—but it was better not to mention them. You could never tell what would set Lynn Brennan off. The least little oddity in Claire's health or behavior, the tiniest hint of a problem at school, even a wrong-number phone call in the middle of the night, could send her spazzing. Before Claire knew it, they'd be packed up and moving. *It'll be safer here*, her mom always promised. Safe from what? Claire could never figure that out.

"Claire Bear! Wait up!"

She knew that voice. Claire turned, happily returning her best friend's hug. "Hey, gorgeous! When did you get back?"

"At two a.m. I am *so* jet-lagged." Erica Fischer was tall and willowy, with stunning, shoulder-length red hair. Claire always felt like Erica's clothes—today it was an embossed aqua-blue spaghetti top, pencil-thin designer jeans, and an assortment of funky jewelry—cost three times as much as her own. They probably did. "You look pale, Claire. Did you ralph this morning or something?"

"No." She darted Erica a meaningful look as they started up the central stairs toward the Upper School. "*It* started today."

Erica's eyes widened. "*It?* Are you serious? Wow, finally!"

"I know, right? I was starting to think I was a space alien."

"Do you need any Midol?" Erica shoved her hand into her purse and held up a packet, smiling like a spokesperson in a TV commercial. "It's one of the only sanctioned drugs on campus. Guaranteed to relieve cramps and bloating!"

Claire grinned. "Thanks, but my mom already gave me some. She totally freaked when I told her. For some reason, she seemed really upset."

"My mom was the opposite when it happened to me: *über* jazzed. She was all"—Erica adopted her most annoying, sunshiny voice—"'Welcome to womanhood, sweetheart!

This is *so* wonderful! Someday when you have children, it will all be worth it!'"

Claire cringed. "I don't know which reaction is worse." They passed the central landing, where two crisscrossing stairways met, and continued up toward the South Quad. "So tell me about the South of France, and how desperately you missed me."

"Oh, you wouldn't have wanted to be there," Erica insisted melodramatically. "There were long stretches of sand-and-pebble beaches, endless supplies of chocolate éclairs, and lots of tall, dark men hitting on me who didn't know the meaning of the word *statutory*."

"Did your dad beat them off with a stick?"

"Sadly, yes. I drowned my sorrows in wine. No one in Europe seems to care about your age." Erica thrust out her wrist, exhibiting a dangly silver charm bracelet. "My mom bought this from a flea-market gypsy in Aix-en-Provence. What do you think?"

"I think she's gonna hunt you down for swiping it."

"She'll never notice it's gone. She's too busy shuttling my brother around today."

They reached the top of the hill and headed into the quad, where two lines of juniors were waiting outside classroom doorways to have their photos taken. "Let's get this picture over with, shall we?" Claire said with a nervous sigh. She never liked any of her school pictures and found the whole experience somewhat demoralizing.

A hand waved to them from near the end of a line, and they moved to join Brian Yao—a cute, short boy with spiky black hair and a ready smile—whom Erica had known since seventh grade. Even though Brian's parents had plenty of money, he always wore the same ancient pair of sneakers, held together at this point by willpower and duct tape. The duo had welcomed Claire when she'd arrived at Emerson two years ago, and they'd been close ever since.

"Hey, Bri!" Erica scampered over to give him a hug. "Good to see the evil summer internship didn't sap your good looks."

"Oh, they tried. My dad's a taskmaster! I had to wear a suit and tie, even though I spent most of my time filing. But everyone was nice." Brian hugged Claire. "Sorry I've been MIA all summer, CB. Did you end up slaving at Peet's again?"

"*And* two summer school courses. Try not to be jealous." Claire's eyes were drawn to the guy standing in line behind Brian. She'd never seen him before, but he was staring at her—and not, she thought, in a friendly way. "Don't worry, we're just saying hello," she said quickly. "We're not cutting, I promise."

The guy instantly ducked his head and busied himself fiddling with an antique-looking gold pocket watch that he pulled from his Levi's. "You're already here. Might as well stay."

He spoke with a charming Scottish accent that was more *Braveheart* than *Trainspotting* (i.e., you could actually understand what he was saying). He was pale but very attractive, with a lean, muscular build, messy, dirty-blond hair, and dark green eyes. His jeans and black T-shirt were complemented by battered army surplus combat boots, while his backpack was casually slung over one of his broad shoulders.

"Nice watch," Claire said. "You're new, aren't you? Are you from Scotland?"

He seemed to consider his words before answering, "Aye."

"Cool." Brian grinned. "Are you an exchange student or something?"

The Scottish guy shook his head, his handsome face unreadable as he put the watch back in his pocket. Claire couldn't tell whether he was stuck-up, rude, or just uncomfortable being the center of attention. "No. Just moved here."

They all stepped forward as the line advanced. Erica shot Claire a silent, wide-eyed look that conveyed *exactly* how hot she thought the new guy was. Whirling back to stare at him, as if she'd just found a shiny new toy, Erica gasped, "Say something else!"

"Something else?" he said tentatively.

Erica giggled and clapped her hands with delight.

Claire rolled her eyes and grinned apologetically.

"Ignore her. She's always been a sucker for anyone with a foreign accent."

Rather than return Claire's smile, the guy glanced away again. His eyes scanned the quad as if determined to look anywhere but at her. *Well*, Claire thought, *so much for trying to be polite.*

Brian, unruffled, stuck out his hand. "Hi, I'm Brian. These two harpies are Claire and Erica. Allow me to personally welcome you to the City of Angels."

"Alec. MacKenzie." He shook Brian's hand and cracked a stiff smile.

Claire wondered how much longer they were going to have to endure this one-sided conversation. Despite how good-looking he was and his cool Scottish accent, he seemed like a pain in the ass. Thankfully, the line had moved quickly and they were next. "Bri, get in there. You're holding us up." Claire shoved him playfully toward the open classroom door.

Brian turned back to them and bowed. "Reflect, ladies and gentleman, on the seriousness of this moment. This picture is no mere ID photo. It will hang all year long on the Student Life Center wall for everyone to see, trapped in the class collage. And it will last for time immemorial in the yearbook, to embarrass us and entertain our grandchildren."

Erica looked at Alec with a laugh as Brian strode into the classroom. "I know what you're thinking, and no, he's not crazy. Brian and I are both . . . theater people." She whispered *theater people* mischievously, as if it were something delightfully sinful.

"I figured," Alec said, still doing his best impression of a statue.

Claire hoped they were done with him. But Erica had other plans.

"Mr. MacKenzie," Erica continued with a melodramatic, mock English accent, "you simply *must* join our little group after your photograph. Books are distributed in the gymnasium down the hill, and we would not wish you to become lost on your first day here."

Alec paused again, as if taking great pains to weigh the decision. Finally, he answered quietly, "Sure."

Great, Claire thought with an inward sigh. *Won't this be fun.*

two

Alec cast a glance at the girl beside him as they made their way down the hill. It was all he could do to keep his face impassive, to retain his usual calm and collected façade. He hoped she couldn't tell how fast his heart was beating, or guess the effect she had on him.

He couldn't stop staring at her. Sunlight glimmered on her long, lustrous brown hair, bringing out its hidden highlights. She had stunning hazel eyes with intriguing golden sunbursts. She was curvy without being too voluptuous; just right, to his way of thinking. But although her beauty had caught his attention, it wasn't the only reason he was attracted to her. He was well trained in the art of reading people, and although he'd barely heard her speak more than a few sentences, she radiated intelligence, confidence, and vulnerability all at the same time—a combination he found extremely compelling.

Clearly, he thought, Claire wasn't experiencing the same magnetic pull that was wreaking havoc on *his* mind and pulse rate. If anything, he sensed that she didn't much like him—that he'd made a poor first impression. As they walked along, she laughed effortlessly with her friends and directed the occasional comment his way, but she was clearly doing it more out of politeness than real interest. He did his best to nod and smile, but he felt awkward, as if his tongue was glued to the roof of his mouth.

Get a grip, Alec silently chided himself as they left the stairs and crossed the main street of the campus toward the gym. It was so unlike him to react this way. Over the years, he'd become adept at taking on whatever role was needed, while at the same time hiding his feelings and talents. But in the past there had always been an ulterior motive to his interactions. Now, for almost the first time in his existence, he had an opportunity to truly be himself—but without a specific goal, he found himself floundering. He wasn't sure what to say or how to act.

For eons, he'd fantasized about making friends— wasn't that one of the reasons he was here? It went against everything he'd been taught, and he knew he wasn't really prepared for it; but he couldn't help himself. As long as he remained hidden, as long as he didn't cross any lines, and as long as none of the others found him, he should be safe—right?

Still, these *feelings* had happened much faster than he'd anticipated. He'd barely just settled in, accepted as a last-minute entry based on his stellar entrance exam test scores—legitimate—his flawless transcript—not so legitimate—and a substantial financial contribution from "his uncle Gregory." He'd scoped out the school as a visitor several times, and today was supposed to be the final stage of recon. Assess the population. Gather more data. Remain inconspicuous. Instead, this friendly group seemed to have adopted him—and here he was, struggling to hide an immediate, overpowering attraction to a girl he'd just met.

"Check your schedule, Alec." Erica's voice jolted him back to the present as they entered the brightly lit gymnasium. The space was packed with students lining up at tables for their textbooks according to grade and subject. The bleachers were collapsed against the side walls beneath a patchwork of red, white, and blue banners representing sports victories that went back over thirty years. It was warm and stuffy inside, the rafters echoing with conversation and laughter.

"If you're in an honors class, be sure to mention that to the teachers, because the books are different," Claire explained as they approached the juniors' English table.

Say something, Alec mentally instructed himself. He'd barely strung more than three words together since he'd met these people. They must think him a half-wit. He studied his class schedule. "I think most of my classes are honors."

"Are you serious?" Brian said. "I barely placed into honors physics."

"Sounds like you and Claire will be in a lot of the same classes." Erica put her arm around Claire, smiling like an affectionate parent. "Claire's the class brain. We're so very proud of her."

"I am *not* a brain," Claire insisted, rolling her eyes modestly.

Claire showed him her schedule, her hand nearly touching his as she stood beside him. It turned out they were indeed in several classes together. Her proximity—and the knowledge that he'd be seeing her throughout the school day—sent his heart racing again. *Focus*, Alec reprimanded himself. *Stop acting like an idiot.* They all got their English books and moved on to the history table. "So," Alec asked in a deliberately casual tone, even though he was well aware of the answer, "how does this rotating schedule work again?"

Claire glanced at him with raised eyebrows, as if surprised to find him capable of coherent speech. "There are seven tracks, A through G—six classes per day except Fridays, when we get out at one thirty instead of having a lunch break."

"It sounds confusing, but I swear it's not—every morning they post which track you begin with," Erica chimed in. "It's a cool system because it means you never have a class at the same time every day. So you won't always have a post-lunch food coma during French, or be half-asleep in early-morning pre-calc."

Alec pulled out his cell phone and started typing, as if this information was new to him.

"Careful with that come Monday, dude," Brian cautioned. "Cell phones are banned on campus during school hours."

Before he could reply, Alec suddenly found himself at the front of the line. Shoving his phone in his pocket, he glanced at the history teacher's name on his schedule. "Mr. . . . Patterson?"

A tall, broad-shouldered man in his late thirties turned in Alec's direction. Despite his handsome features, the man projected irritation and condescension. Without looking up from his list, he barked, "Name?"

"Alec MacKenzie."

Checking his name off with a pencil, the teacher motioned toward one of the stacks of thick hardcover texts on the table. "Take a book. Only one. Move along."

"As if we'd *want* more than one," Claire whispered behind him.

Alec couldn't help but smile.

After the others got their history books and they moved off together, Brian muttered, "God, what an ass. I heard Patterson actually locks the door to his classroom the minute the bell rings."

"*I've* heard he gives lots of pop quizzes," Erica added. "He might make even *your* life a living hell, Claire."

"Fantastic." Claire frowned.

Suddenly, two arms clapped around Erica's and Brian's shoulders. "Hey, you two. How's it going?"

At the sight of the tall, lanky, good-looking guy standing behind Erica and Brian, Claire's eyes lit up. Alec turned to examine the object of her interest. He had golden-brown eyes and dark, wavy hair, and seemed like the easygoing type who claimed not to care about primping but always looked great anyway.

Erica gave the newcomer a big hug. "God, Neil, I think you grew another six inches over the summer!"

"Three, actually. Did you hear? Mr. Lang wants us to sing the *Messiah* this Christmas."

Brian and Erica gasped. They immediately launched into shoptalk about choir with the new guy and ignored Alec and Claire completely. Alec noticed Claire's gaze lingering on Neil's face. For the first time since he'd met her she seemed nervous, as if she was secretly, desperately wishing that Neil would look in her direction.

Alec turned to Claire, searching for something appropriate to say, seized by a need to capture her attention. "I take it those three are all in choir together?"

"Not choir—that's a different class. They're in Concert Singers, the elite choral group. It's Brian's pride and joy—and his only other honors class."

"An honors class that you're *not* in?"

To Alec's dismay, Claire visibly winced, as if the question stung a little.

"Sorry," he added quickly. "That was an attempt at humor that clearly failed."

"It's okay—I shouldn't be so sensitive. Really. It's just that I'd give anything to be able to sing well enough to get into Concert Singers."

Right. Alec frowned, irritation prickling through him. Because it would give her a chance to spend time with Neil—who was now cluelessly saying good-bye to his friends, without a word for her. *What is this guy—blind or stupid? Or both?*

As soon as the thoughts entered his mind, Alec scolded himself for being uncharitable. He didn't know a thing about Neil, or about Claire for that matter, and he had no business making judgments about either of them. "I take it you like music, then?" he asked Claire.

"I *love* music. But sadly, I inherited tone deafness from my mother. I tried piano lessons when I was nine but wasn't very good at that, either."

The foursome left the gym a while later—sans Neil—their backpacks bursting with books. As they crossed the paved drop-off circle and headed for the south stairwell, they passed under a section of construction scaffolding that crawled up the face of a nearby building. A sign in black and red lettering warned, CAUTION: WORKERS ABOVE.

"What's going on up there?" Erica asked.

"I heard they're remodeling the theater lobby and putting in new windows or something," Claire answered.

"They'd better be done soon," Erica muttered as they marched up the stairs, "'cause I plan to be the first junior to get the lead in the school musical."

"Which one are we doing this year?" asked Brian.

"I don't know. Does it matter?"

"If they do *Twelve Angry Men: The Musical*, you're screwed." Brian grinned.

Erica swatted him on the shoulder. "Claire, you should really grow some balls this year and try out."

"No way." A blush bloomed in Claire's cheeks. "How about you, Alec? Do you sing?"

Alec paused. The fact that Claire had a crush on a guy who could sing was not lost on him. With a small smile, he said, "A bit. But not in public."

They all exited the stairwell onto an open-air upper terrace, where a short stretch of beige lockers was tucked beneath an overhang beside the back entrance to the library.

"Here's my locker," Brian said, moving up to test his combination. Erica's locker was in that grouping as well.

Claire checked the sheet with her assignment. "Anybody know where locker 302 is?"

"On the other side of the library. Mine's 308. I'll show you," Alec responded. As soon as he said it, he wished he could take it back. Would it seem odd that he knew these things?

As if on cue, Claire glanced at him in surprise. "You're the locker tour guide now? I thought you were the new guy."

Alec hesitated, then said honestly, "I . . . stopped by to look the place over the other day. I always like to be prepared." He turned and started walking.

"And do you always like to think for about twenty minutes before you speak?" Claire asked as she followed him.

"Sometimes longer. I guess I don't think as fast as you do."

"Somehow I doubt that, Mr. All-My-Classes-Are-Honors," Claire said with a smile.

The teasing warmth in her eyes made his stomach do a somersault. They reached the front of the library, where two long rows of freestanding lockers faced each other in a covered, open-air pseudo-corridor. Several other students were shoving in their new books. Claire found her locker and opened it while Alec moved to his.

"What's that?" Alec asked, pointing to a contraption that Claire had pulled from her backpack.

"A LockerMate." Claire knelt on the concrete and began to unfold and assemble the unit, hooking the corners of what looked like two painted metal shelves onto the four legs. "It's a little rusty and rickety, but the shelves make the locker a lot more organized."

"Would you like a hand?"

"Thanks, I'm okay. I've had this since sixth grade."

He watched Claire carefully lift her assembled LockerMate into her locker. Loosening the wing nuts in the center of both shelves, she pushed against the unit's legs, as if trying to widen it to fill the space—but it wouldn't budge. She pushed again. No luck. With a frustrated sigh, she turned to him with lowered eyes and mumbled quietly, "Help?"

Alec grinned and moved to her side. "What do I do?"

"The shelves have to expand, but they're stuck. You'll have to shove hard."

"Will do." Alec slipped his hands inside Claire's locker and gave the LockerMate an easy sideways thrust in both directions.

BAM! The sound echoed dramatically in the passageway. He heard Claire gasp. Heads spun in their direction. Alec stared down in embarrassment. His arms were wedged against both sides of Claire's locker, which were now horribly bowed, and the door was bent at a funny angle.

"Shite." Alec shrank back, mortified.

"What the hell?" Claire exclaimed in astonishment. "Did you just break my locker?" She tried unsuccessfully to shut the crooked door. "Well, *that's* never gonna close again."

Alec felt his face turning red. How could he have made such a boneheaded mistake? "Sorry. You said to shove hard." Gesturing toward his own locker, he added quickly, "Would you like to take mine?"

"I couldn't do that."

"Please, I insist. I'll take yours. It's the least I can do."

"No, no, really." Claire looked down at the heavy bag of

books at her feet and said reluctantly, "If you don't mind, I'll just stash my books in your locker for now—until they fix mine."

"Not a problem. I was thinking of bringing my books home today anyway. Here, let me give you my combination." Alec handed her his locker assignment sheet.

"Don't you need the combination to get back in?"

"I've already got it memorized. Have a good weekend. See you Monday." With a brief nod, Alec hefted up his backpack and dashed off down the corridor, his cheeks still burning.

three

❧

"I can't believe MacMuscles actually *broke* my locker," Claire said as she crossed the junior parking lot with Brian and Erica. "What a freak."

"He must be Superman!" Brian exclaimed.

Claire shook her head with a sigh. "More like Clark Kent. Superman's the suave one."

After Brian waved good-bye and moved off to his car, Erica sidled up closer to Claire. "You've got to admit, even though Alec's shy and klutzy, he's totally gorgeous. Plus that Scottish brogue? It's to die for."

"He *is* good-looking," Claire admitted. Alec was even more handsome than Neil Mitchum—the star of stage, track, and soccer field, the athletic demigod whose singing voice had been melting Claire's heart since ninth grade. "But Alec seems kind of rude sometimes—or he's a total introvert, I can't tell which—and he doesn't have much of a sense of humor. I think I only saw him smile once."

"Don't be so judgmental," Erica said with a dismissive

wave of her hand, as she unlocked her car. "He's new. He's nervous. And I'm sure he feels terrible about your locker." There was a sudden clink on the pavement. "Oh! My bracelet!"

Claire bent down to pick it up. As soon as her fingers came in contact with the cool metal, she was overcome by the same weird, woozy sensation she'd felt earlier that morning. Then she felt really hot, as if she'd stepped under a heat lamp. Perspiration broke out on her brow, her stomach lurched, her knees began to buckle, and—

WHAM. A series of vivid images flashed into her head:

She was driving a car. Glancing down, she saw she was wearing a long-sleeved red blouse and had a wedding ring on her finger. A sudden flash of movement brought her eyes back to the windshield. Another car was heading straight at her! She gasped in terror and stomped on the brake, her arm flying out to protect a young boy in the passenger seat beside her—a boy she recognized. It was Erica's brother.

There was the sound of a sickening crunch.

"Claire? Are you okay? Claire?"

Erica's voice cut through the fog that enveloped Claire's mind. Claire took a deep, steadying breath, grabbing the hood of Erica's shiny black SUV to keep from sinking to the ground. What on earth was going on? Was she going crazy? Was she hallucinating?

"Claire, what's wrong? Are you sick?"

Struggling to find her voice, Claire said, "I'm . . . fine.

Is . . . where's your mom? And your brother? Are they okay?"

Erica stared at her in surprise. "What? Why?"

"I don't know. I just . . . Never mind." Claire thrust the charm bracelet at Erica as if it was a hot potato, glad to be rid of it. "Where'd you say you got that thing?"

"At a flea market in France." Just then, Erica's cell phone rang. Still eyeing Claire with bewilderment, Erica dug it out of her backpack. "Hello?"

As Erica listened, she gasped in alarm and asked frantic questions. When she hung up and turned to Claire, she was on the verge of tears.

"That was my mom. She and Henry were just in a car accident."

"So they're both all right?" Claire leaned back against the headboard of her bed a few hours later, her cell phone clutched to her ear.

"Just a little shaken up," Erica's voice assured her on the other end. "Some guy turned left in front of them at a yellow light. Mom swerved and crashed into the curb, but she and Henry walked away without a scratch."

"Thank God." Claire had been so worried, ever since Erica had screeched out of the parking lot and left her to scramble for a ride home with Brian. All afternoon, her thoughts kept drifting back to that moment right before the accident, and what she'd *seen*. It was so bizarre, the way those images had popped into her mind the minute she'd touched that bracelet. Was the accident happening at that exact moment? Claire wondered. Or had it happened a few minutes before? The most unsettling part was how she seemed to see the whole thing through Erica's mother's eyes. Weird, weird, weird.

"Erica. What's your mom wearing today?"

"What's she wearing? I don't know. Black pants and a red blouse, I think. Why?"

Holy shit, Claire thought. Was she a certified nutcase, or had she just had a psychic experience? She'd never had one of those before. Maybe it wasn't her, though. Maybe it was that bracelet. Didn't Erica say her mom had bought it from a gypsy?

"Why do you care what she was wearing?" Erica repeated. "And why did you ask if they were okay earlier, in the parking lot? That was *before* my mom called."

Claire heard the front door open. "I'll . . . explain later. My mom just got home. Can I come over tonight?"

"Sure. I'm stuck here babysitting while The Parents pick up a rental car."

"I'll call before I leave. Bye." As Claire hung up, she heard her mom's laptop bag thud against the entryway table downstairs.

They lived five miles south of school in a small, two-bedroom, townhouse-style apartment. As far as she could tell, she was the only person at Emerson (except maybe some of the teachers) who didn't live in a huge, gorgeous, art-filled, extravagantly furnished mansion with a pool. Claire didn't need anything *that* upscale to be happy—but every time she walked in the door and saw the cream-colored walls and carpet (in other words: bland), and few personal items on display, she was reminded that they never stayed in one place for long. Ever since she could remember, her mom had insisted that they keep their possessions to a minimum and all the important stuff in one place, so they could move at a moment's notice. When she was little, Claire had thought of it as a kind of game: *Let's see how fast we can pack up this time!* But even though they'd been here two years, their apartment didn't really feel like a home. Claire was too embarrassed to have anyone but her two best friends come over.

Claire left her room and padded down the stairs. "Are you a burglar?" she called out.

Her mom was in the kitchen, unloading a bag of groceries. "Hi, honey. What a day! I showed the Wangs six houses, and I think they're really interested in one of them." Digging something out of a bag, she extended it to Claire. "I got you some fruit leather. Cherry, strawberry, and apricot. Try not to eat it all in one sitting."

"*Gracias*, Mom!" Claire snatched the booty, immediately ripped the plastic wrapping off the dried apricot strip, and commenced scarfing. "You're the best. I was totally starving."

"Did you eat lunch today?"

"Not really."

Claire's mom studied her with concern. "Is something wrong? When I called, you said everything went okay at Book Day."

"It did."

"Then why do you look so worried?"

Claire hesitated. How to answer? No way could she tell her about the weird vision she'd had, or whatever it was. The last thing she needed was for her mom to go into freak-out mode. "Because Erica's mom and brother were in a car accident. I just heard, five seconds ago, that no one was hurt."

"Oh—thank God."

"Yeah." Claire helped unload the groceries. "Mom, is it okay if I go to Erica's after dinner?"

"Sorry, honey. I need the car. I'm meeting a client tonight."

"Can you drop me off at Erica's first?"

Her mom shook her head. "I don't have time to drive all the way to the Valley and back in Friday traffic."

"Maybe I can get Erica to pick me up and drive me home."

"You know how I feel about you riding in other people's cars at night. Anyway, I don't want you going over there. You'll be up talking until all hours, and God knows what time you'll get home."

"I can sleep over at Erica's, then."

"No. The last time you slept over at Erica's, boys were there."

"*A* boy. *Brian.* Our best friend, whom neither of us is even remotely interested in."

"That doesn't mean he's not interested in you, dear."

Claire groaned in frustration. "He isn't, I promise. What do you have against boys, Mom? Don't you trust me?"

Her mom paused. "It's not that. It's just . . . Erica's mom doesn't supervise her kids the way she should."

"You mean she doesn't hover over them every second, and never lets them go anywhere or do anything?"

"I don't do that," her mom said defensively.

"Yes, you do." Claire's stomach tensed with rising anger. "I swear, you're the most uptight, paranoid hippie who ever lived."

"Just because I don't believe in bank accounts or use credit cards, that doesn't make me a hippie."

"Yes, it does! You're all: 'Who needs a permanent mailing address, when you can have a P.O. box?'" Claire mimicked her mom's voice and shrug.

Her mom slammed a cabinet door and whirled on Claire, eyes flashing. "Don't you take that tone with me, young lady. Everything I've done is for a good reason."

"What reason? You say that every time! What was so wrong with Chicago that we had to leave? Why have we lived in seven different cities since I was born? What are you running from? Does it have anything to do with my father? It's like we're in the goddamned witness protection program!"

Her mom averted her gaze, a grim look on her face. "What does this have to do with boys, Claire?"

"See! There you go again! Always changing the subject."

"I repeat: What does this have to do with boys?"

Claire sighed, giving up her line of questioning. "It just sucks. *You* don't date. All men are off-limits for you—and you expect me to follow the same rules."

Her mom looked at her, a hint of apprehension in her eyes. "Since when do you even care about dating?"

"I'm sixteen, Mom. Of course I want to date. Not that I've ever even had a boy look at me yet. But I *hope* it's gonna happen. And just because I'm now *physically* able to get pregnant, it doesn't mean I'm gonna end up a high school dropout with a newborn and a guy who ditches me—like you did!"

Claire's mom's eyes widened with sudden pain, and she didn't reply.

Turning, Claire left the kitchen and stormed up the stairs, slamming her bedroom door behind her. She threw herself on her bed, her frustration and anger dissipating as her stomach knotted in guilt. Why, oh why had she said that? She hated these rare fights with her mom and wished she'd kept her thoughts to herself.

It was a truly horrible end to one hell of a strange day.

four

❧

*I*diot. *Moron. Half-wit.*

Alec shook his head in disgust as he drove home. He'd spent the past few hours on his favorite local rooftop, watching the sun set as he struggled to regain his normal sense of calm. He was still struggling. The last thing he'd wanted today was to call attention to himself. Then he'd mangled a locker—something no average teenager would ever be capable of. What had come over him?

He knew the answer, of course. It was because of Claire.

Alec pulled his '69 Mustang into his parking space and crossed the small concrete lot. He'd felt a brief connection with Claire just before they found their lockers. In that moment, he'd thought that maybe, just maybe, she didn't *completely* dislike him after all. Then he'd ruined everything with that ridiculous, clumsy move. Not that it mattered. She was obviously more interested in the Choir Boy.

When it came down to it, Alec had no business pursuing his interest in *her*, anyway. It was dangerous, not to mention forbidden. In the few similar cases he'd heard of, the punishment exacted had been instantaneous and unforgiving.

But he didn't care. He'd left his old life for good—which meant the old rules no longer applied. For more than a century, he hadn't been allowed to indulge in anything remotely pleasurable. There were so many human experiences that had been denied to him—high school among them. Even though human beings often spoke of high school as if it was hell on earth, Alec had always strangely longed to try it for himself. Despite his youthful appearance, he'd never infiltrated a school before—his elite training had prepared him for more complex assignments.

If the plan was going to work, however, he was going to have to try harder to fit in.

You need to smile more and stare less, he reminded himself. *And your reaction time in conversation was too slow.* These things had never mattered before, but they did now.

Setting these concerns aside for the moment, Alec entered his first-floor studio apartment and closed the front door behind him, all senses on hyperalert. He flipped the three locks in quick succession, set down his backpack, and withdrew a black metal knife from his boot, whirling to search for any sign of intruders. Without opening the blackout curtains, he carefully cased the dark, starkly furnished space. Nothing behind the couch. No one in the shower. Kitchen: empty. Weapons cabinet: undisturbed.

With a relieved sigh, Alec glanced at the light switch. It blinked on.

He sank down on the couch, resheathed his knife, and removed his boots. Unable to relax, he unzipped his backpack and dumped everything out onto the coffee table. One by one, he began scanning the contents of each textbook, curious to see what juniors in high school would be learning this year, to understand what he was—and wasn't—supposed to know.

The academics would be easy to handle. Other than socialization, he had only one real worry. He'd spent decades planning his escape and had taken every precaution to cover his tracks—but even so, there was still a chance he could be found. He wondered who they'd assigned to search for him.

He would never—*could never*—go back. He was committed to making this work, no matter what. Not that they'd take him back even if they did find him. If he was lucky, he'd be tried and imprisoned for life at a mountaintop monastery in Tibet.

If he was unlucky?

The penalty was death.

five

ꙮ

"Are you kidding?"

"No, I'm serious." Claire leaned forward on the table, cupping her grande soy vanilla latte in her hands. "I felt nauseous and light-headed, and suddenly it was like *I* was the one in the car, like I *was* your mom, reaching out to hold Henry back and everything."

Erica stared at her. "Oh my God."

"I know, right?"

The aroma of brewing coffee wafted out to the coffee shop's shady garden patio where they sat. It was that quiet period after the Sunday morning crowd had left and the afternoon rush had not yet begun.

"So . . . what?" Erica's eyes narrowed. "Are you, like, psychic or something?"

"If I am, it's news to me. Nothing like this has ever happened to me before."

"Never? Are you sure?"

"Yes." But then Claire remembered something. "Oh,

wait. There was this one other thing, Friday morning."

"The same day as the accident?"

"Yeah. My mom was all worried about some document she couldn't find for work, and as I was hugging her good-bye in the car, the same weird feeling came over me—and suddenly I knew exactly where it was. It was like the image popped into my head. I saw my mom's hand putting the page into her bag."

"You *saw* it? Like you were watching your mom doing it?"

"No, it's like I *was* her, seeing it from her perspective."

"Wow. Trippy."

"I didn't think much about it at the time. After your mom's accident, I thought the thing I saw had something to do with her bracelet. Like it was cursed or magical somehow."

"It's just a bracelet, Claire. I've worn it a dozen times, and I've never gotten any visions. No, this is all about *you*."

Claire tried to shrug off the suggestion. "I did some research on the internet last night about psychic abilities and phenomena. There are ten million sites about ESP, clairvoyance, telepathy, telekinesis, and all kinds of weird bullshit from ghosts to Atlantis and killer fog. It all looks so cheesy, I couldn't take any of it seriously."

"Maybe you should." Erica sipped her coffee, then looked up with an eager expression. "What am I thinking right now?"

"I have no idea. That I'm a lunatic?"

"No, no, no. What am I *thinking*? Use your new mojo."

"I can't read minds, Erica."

"How do you know? Try it."

Claire stared at her friend for a moment. "This is stupid."

"Oh, wait, wait, wait! Maybe it's not a telepathy thing. What if it's a touch thing? You hugged your mom and got a vision through her eyes, right? Then you touched my mom's bracelet and saw something about her."

"Huh. Okay, so?"

Erica grabbed Claire's hand and plunked it against her arm. "Tell me what you feel. Are you getting any vibes about me?"

"Yeah. I'm rethinking which one of us is the lunatic."

Erica sighed and sat back on her stool. "You're such a disappointment. It would be so awesome to have a best friend who's psychic. You'd be able to tell me who my next boyfriend's going to be, where I can find a pair of ankle-wrap, blue suede, Jimmy Choo sandals in size eight, what questions are going to be on my pre-calc tests, even which colleges to apply to."

Claire shook her head. "No, the stuff I saw had already happened. I think."

"Good point. Well then, you're definitely useless."

They sat in silence for a long moment.

"Maybe I was just suffering from an iron deficiency that day," Claire mused.

"Maybe you're having hallucinations induced by your mom's drug-taking days, a brain defect passed on at birth."

"As far as I know, my mom never took drugs. She's a free spirit, yes. But she's devoted to clean living."

"Okay. If you're not psychic, then how else would you explain it?"

"It defies explanation."

"I guess you'll just have to wait and see if it happens to you again."

"God, I hope it doesn't." Claire let out a nervous breath, then finished her coffee. "In the meantime, promise not to tell anyone, okay? Especially my mom. We had a fight on Friday. I apologized, and I think she forgave me. But I don't want to give her any more fuel for liftoff."

Erica gave her a two-finger salute. "Copy that. Don't tip off the crazy hippie lady."

Crap, Claire thought, as she stood before her locker early the next morning. She'd forgotten that it was busted. She'd have to report it to the office later so they could assign her a new one. *What a great way to start the year.*

She stepped over to Alec's locker, got out the combination, and opened it. She stopped short. A shiny, brand-new LockerMate had been installed. Her books were neatly arranged on the shelves, but none of Alec's books were in sight. Instead, a bulky, black metal lockbox took up the entire bottom space.

What the hell? Claire thought. She stared at the box. What on earth was he keeping in there? Blackmail photos? A rare comic book collection? His mother's haggis recipe? Porn?

The first bell rang. She had ten minutes to get to class. Claire grabbed her honors history book, slammed the locker shut, and raced to the farthest end of the school. She joined the small herd of students filing into class, then paused just inside the door. The desk you chose on the first day of school was important. It usually ended up being the seat you were in for the whole year, and it gave the teacher an impression of who you were. Claire didn't want to sit in back with the slackers or in front with the brownnosers. The only spot left in the zone she wanted was right next to Alec, who was settling into the second-row seat against the wall.

Alec glanced at her with an awkward grin. Claire briefly returned his smile as she sat down next to him. She studied the walls of the room. They were hung with maps of the United States during various historical periods, an American flag, and a large poster that read:

NO CELL PHONES
NO TALKING
NO FOOD
NO GUM

NO DISRUPTION
NO DISRESPECT
NO WHINING

The sign did nothing to soothe Claire's fears about her new history teacher. Her gaze fell on the backpack at Alec's feet. It was bursting at the seams. "Do you have all your books in there?"

He nodded. "I wanted to make sure you had enough room in the locker."

That was chivalrous of him, Claire thought. His bag must weigh a million pounds. She'd forgotten how charming his accent was. The way he rolled his *R*s was actually quite enchanting. "Thanks for setting up those shelves," she said gratefully, with a genuine smile this time. "It was really nice of you."

Alec started to respond when the eight a.m. bell rang, announcing the start of first track. Mr. Patterson strode in, slamming and locking the door behind him. He dropped his briefcase beside the mahogany desk at the front of the room, and without even a cursory glance at the students, he turned and began writing his name on the whiteboard.

"Good morning. As you may notice, that door is now closed. And locked. As it will be at the start of every class period." He whirled to face them, focusing his attention on cleaning his eyeglasses. "If you are late, don't bother to knock. Our session will have already begun, and those who care about this class will be busy learning. You may spend your new free period in the library or doing whatever you wish, but you will receive a zero in participation for the day."

Well, Claire thought. *He certainly lives up to his reputation.* She glanced at Alec, who silently acknowledged their mutual doom.

Mr. Patterson finally raised his gaze. "Before we begin, does anyone have any questions?"

A hand shot up. "What does that sign mean?" The student pointed to a wooden plaque above the door that read ESCHEW PROLIXITY.

"Any honors English students in the room?" Mr. Patterson responded. A third of the class raised their hands. "Any of you know what it means?"

Claire saw every hand return meekly to its place, including her own—save one. Alec's.

Mr. Patterson gave Alec a nod. "Enlighten us, young man."

"Avoid boring verbosity," Alec replied.

Of course Alec knows that one, Claire thought, impressed.

The teacher seemed surprised, but said nothing whatsoever to acknowledge Alec's answer, immediately pressing on. "This phrase will be your guiding star when writing papers in this class. Which you are going to start doing tonight. I want a five-page paper on my desk Wednesday morning, detailing your impression of any single event in our country's history, and how it has affected you as an individual." Over the chorus of groans, he continued, "If I assigned it for Friday, you'd just put it off until the last minute anyway. So I'm making *now* the last minute."

Without missing a beat, he launched into his opening lecture. Claire began scribbling notes furiously. It was all she could do to keep up. She was relieved when the class ended. Her next three classes—honors Spanish, AP bio, and honors calculus—had teachers who were less strict than Mr. Patterson, and passed by in a blur.

At lunch, Claire stopped by the administration office to explain about her locker before working her way through the crowd of students to the bustling cafeteria. As she entered the room, the delectable, mingled aromas of baking pizza and chocolate chip cookies enveloped her, making her mouth water.

Erica, Brian, and Alec were just getting into line together. As Claire joined them, she noticed a pair of freshman girls in the next line over eyeing Alec appreciatively and whispering among themselves—but he didn't seem to be aware of it.

"Hey, CB!" Brian greeted her. "Alec said Patterson assigned you a paper already. Due on Wednesday!" He laughed mockingly.

"Are you still sorry you're not in the honors track?" Claire responded dryly.

"Only because it means I'll probably never make it into Harvard," Brian sighed.

"Alec," Claire said, "I didn't want you to get in trouble, so I reported that my locker was broken when I found it."

"Thanks."

"They're going to assign me another one by the end of the day. So I'll be out of your hair before you know it."

Alec looked disappointed. "All right." Now at the front of the line, he turned and studied the food on offer.

The hairnetted man behind the counter smiled patiently. "Pepperoni pizza or the works, take your pick. Otherwise, it's salad bar."

Alec hesitated. "I'll take salad bar."

Claire stared at him. "Are you nuts, or just a vegetarian?"

"Neither."

Claire waited, but he didn't elaborate further. "Eschew prolixity. Your personal motto, right?" she teased.

Alec grinned and gave her a nod. Claire caught Erica eyeing them intensely with that *Aren't you two cute?* look. Was she jealous or amused? Claire couldn't tell.

Brian brashly inserted himself in front of Alec before the counter. "Ignore this man, he's new and hasn't had his meds today. He'll take a slice of each, please."

"Wait—" Alec began.

"You can have rabbit food any day," Erica agreed, "but trust us: Pizza is the best thing this cafeteria has going. They bring it in from a New York–style restaurant in Brentwood Village, just off campus."

Alec didn't offer up any more arguments. After they all got two slices and their cartons of milk, Claire paused before the snack bar, where an assortment of goodies were for sale. She saw that Erica and Brian had already each bought a freshly baked chocolate chip cookie, but Alec had not, so she grabbed two.

The foursome made their way across the South Quad, past the tables crowded with the popular, athletic kids. Claire spotted Neil standing by one of the tables. A gaggle of seated girls stared at him dreamily while he chatted with Gabrielle Miller—the star of the girls' volleyball and tennis teams, and one of the prettiest girls at school. As usual, Gabrielle was wearing an outfit that was worth more than everything in Claire's closet combined—and looked absolutely great with her olive skin and long, perfectly highlighted chestnut hair.

As they left the quad, Claire felt a stab of envy. Not for Gabrielle's money or beauty, but because of the way Neil had been looking at her while they talked. It wasn't outwardly romantic, but he did seem to be hanging on her every word. What would it feel like, Claire wondered, to have a guy interested in *her* like that?

She shook her head, determined not to think about it as she and her friends tromped down the stairs to the small outdoor terrace beyond the library. At the far corner, a lone wooden picnic table with attached benches overlooked the landscaped hills and Middle School below and the football field beyond.

"Nice spot," Alec said, admiring the view as they all sat down.

"This table was handed down to me at the end of eighth grade by my senior drama friends after we did *Peter Pan*," Erica explained. "I was one of the Lost Boys. See? Here's where we carved our initials."

"Hooligans. Shameful of you. Defacing school property!" Brian said through a mouthful of pizza.

"Brian's initials are right here," Claire added, tapping the spot on the table with a pointed look.

Alec laughed.

Score! Claire thought. She had actually made the guy laugh! As she dug into her pizza, however, she noticed Alec staring at the slices on his plate, looking a bit uncomfortable. "Something wrong?"

"No."

"Then why aren't you eating?"

"I will. It's just . . . this may sound strange, but I've . . . I've been on a kind of strict diet for a really long time. And I haven't—"

Claire exchanged a look with her friends. "Don't tell me that pizza is against your religion or something."

He grinned. "No, nothing like that."

"Why in hell would *you* be on a diet?" Brian asked. "Did you used to be fat?" As Erica swatted him forcefully, he cried, "Ow! What?"

"I was raised to eat healthfully, and pizza has always been off-limits."

"Are you serious?" Claire gasped. A bite of her own pizza caught in her throat and she coughed, her eyes watering.

"Are you saying you've *never tasted pizza?*" Brian cried, pounding Claire on the back until she could breathe again.

Alec shook his head.

"Holy shit!" Erica dug into her backpack and withdrew her cell phone, glancing about to make sure no one was watching. "Screw the rules. I have to document this moment for posterity." Placing the phone in camera mode, she aimed it at Alec with a grin. "What are you waiting for? *Bon appétit.*"

Alec took a deep breath, picked up his large slice of the works, and deliberately folded it in half. He paused, glancing at them, then took a bite and began to chew. The look that crossed his face—*If there's an expression that mirrors attaining nirvana,* Claire thought, *this is it.*

"I think he like*s* it," Brian decreed with satisfaction, as Erica proudly displayed the photo.

Alec was mostly silent through the rest of lunch. When it came to dessert, it was the same thing all over again—he practically devoured the cookie Claire gave him. She was beginning to change her opinion of him. It seemed that Alec wasn't rude or totally introverted after all. He was just quirky, and . . . new.

After school, Claire picked up her new locker assignment.

"It's the last one available," the lady from the administration office explained as she wrote down the new locker number and combination on a card. "You're lucky we even have this one."

Claire thanked her and hurried up to Alec's locker, where she removed all her books and folders, stuffed them into her backpack, and then lugged them up the hill to her new locker. Passing through an arched brick entryway, Claire found herself in a narrow, dark corridor that culminated in a dead end. To her dismay, the locker they'd given her was at the very end of the passage, in the bottom corner, where a pile of dead leaves and filth had accumulated. She hesitantly entered the combination, opened the door, and shuddered in dismay. Every surface inside was caked black with dust, grime, and cobwebs. She slammed the door in disgust and heaved a sigh.

Better to share with a food-impaired Scotsman than be stuck with The Locker That Time Forgot, she thought.

Moments later, she was back at Alec's pristine locker, returning her books to their shelves. She hoped he didn't mind sharing. He *did* break her locker, after all.

She was headed for the stairs nearby when she heard the music. Someone down below was playing the guitar. The melody was gentle. Haunting. And beautiful.

For as long as Claire could remember, she'd always

been drawn to guitar music, although she couldn't quite explain why. She especially loved anything acoustic. She followed the sound to an enclosed space at the bottom of the stairwell, just outside the rear entrance to the theater, where she was stunned to find the music's source—Alec. He sat on one of the small wooden boxes left over from former stage productions, strumming a guitar with his eyes closed. His dirty-blond hair was brushed back off his forehead in smooth waves, framing his handsome face. Claire couldn't help but notice his muscular arms as his long fingers moved along the guitar's strings. She stopped and leaned against the wall, closing her own eyes. For a long while, she stood there listening in wonder, transported to another time and place.

The music stopped. Ripped back to the present, she opened her eyes to find Alec looking at her.

"Please don't stop," Claire said quickly. "You're amazing."

He shrugged modestly. "What would you like to hear?"

"Anything. What *was* that?"

"A flamenco lament."

"Then more of the same! Or—whatever you feel like playing." She grabbed a wooden box and sat down across from him.

"Ladies' choice."

"I don't know the names of anything classical like that. Can you . . . do something by the Beatles?"

Without missing a beat, he began playing "You've Got to Hide Your Love Away"—one of Claire's favorites. As Alec began to sing, Claire's heart leapt. He had the voice of an angel, far more beautiful than Neil's, which she had thought impossible.

After the first verse, the singing stopped, but Alec went on playing.

"Keep singing," she prodded.

"Only if you sing with me."

A knot formed in Claire's stomach. "No. I don't—"

"—sing, aye, so you said. But how about if we both try something new today?"

Claire shook her head, horrified. "Trust me. You don't want to go there."

"Come on. There's no one else around. What have you got to lose?"

"My dignity?"

"Dignity's overrated."

There he went, rolling those *R*s again. It was charming but so distracting. Alec began strumming again, his eyes holding hers as he launched into the second verse.

As Claire listened to him sing, she felt mortified by the notion of mingling her sorry excuse for a voice with his. It was akin to Rembrandt inviting a kindergartner to paint on the same canvas. But embarrassed as she was, she couldn't ignore the playful challenge in his eyes. She inhaled deeply and tentatively forced herself to join in.

Claire sang a line, then froze in astonishment. Was that really *her* voice?

Alec smiled with his eyes and kept going, silently urging her on. Claire continued singing, amazed to find that—for the first time in her life—she was not only perfectly in tune, but she actually sounded good. Great, in fact. How was that possible?

They finished the duet. Claire couldn't stop grinning. "Wow. Wow. *Wow.*"

"You're right," Alec teased. "You're terrible. Like fingernails on a chalkboard."

"I don't get it. I've never been able to sing like that before."

"Maybe you never really gave yourself a chance. Or maybe your voice is like a fine wine: It just needed time to mature."

"Maybe." She smiled, still overwhelmed by what had just happened. Glancing at his guitar, she said, "Where do you keep that all day? It wouldn't fit in our locker."

"*Our* locker?" he asked with a grin.

"Yeah. I hope you don't mind. The one they assigned me was filthy and in Siberia."

Before Alec could respond, the backstage door swung open and Neil peered at them eagerly. "Was that you guys singing?"

Claire sprang to her feet. Her heart skipped a beat as she nodded wordlessly.

A slow smile curved the edges of Neil's handsome mouth, and there was a twinkle in his eyes. "I could hear you all the way from the lobby. You're both awesome."

"Thanks," Alec replied, abruptly packing up his guitar.

Claire's voice was still firmly lodged in her feet.

"What a drag that we don't have a guy's spot left in Concert Singers this year," Neil said, before turning his gaze toward Claire, "but Brennan, guess what? We're short a soprano."

Claire could hardly believe he was talking to her, or that he knew her name. She struggled to unearth some words in response. "I—"

"Do you know how to read music?" he asked.

Claire nodded.

"Great! We *need* you. I'm sure if you audition for Mr. Lang, he could petition to squeeze you in. We meet B track. Do you have a free period at all?"

"Um, yes. But—" *Damn it!* She sounded as uncommunicative as Alec.

"You might have to shuffle your schedule a bit, but please say you'll do it?"

Claire paused, dumbfounded. Was this really happening? Was Neil actually insisting that she join Concert Singers? Or was this another hallucination? "When . . . could I audition?"

"You're already warmed up. Why wait? Lang's in the music room right now."

"Okay. Well—" Her heart racing, Claire turned back to Alec to make her apologies and say good-bye.

But Alec was gone.

"I'll tell Mr. Lang not to leave yet." With that, Neil raced off.

Claire felt a sudden stab of guilt. Why had Alec left? She hadn't been talking to Neil that long. But in that brief interval, she'd completely forgotten Alec was there. Did he notice how she'd been drooling over Neil? *God, how embarrassing.*

But there was no time to think about it now. Mr. Lang—and Neil—were waiting for her.

six

Spanish III was Alec's first class the next morning. As he took his seat, he couldn't shake the image of Claire, sitting across from him on that crate yesterday, singing her heart out. She had been so shy and self-deprecating about it, and then it turned out she had a spectacular voice. For a little while, it was as if a quiet bond had formed between them.

Then Choir Boy had shown up.

Alec glanced at Neil, who was sitting on the far side of the classroom. If Neil had sat closer, Alec would have asked him about Claire's Concert Singers audition. For her sake, he hoped they had accepted her.

A twinge gripped Alec's insides as he recalled Claire's reaction to Neil the afternoon before. Alec frowned, cursing himself for falling into a cliché. A few other girls had made overtures in his direction since school started—perfectly nice girls, from what he could tell—but he had no interest in any of them. He hadn't expected the whole dating question to come up so soon, but it was one of the parts of this human experiment that intrigued him the most. He *wanted* to try it.

So why did he have to fixate on the one girl who clearly had no interest in him?

He heaved a sigh. This situation, which he'd worked so hard to set up, and had looked forward to for so long, might end up being nothing but an exercise in frustration. He'd be forced to see Claire not just in his other classes every day, but at his locker as well—*their* locker.

At that moment, to his complete astonishment, Claire herself darted into the room, out of breath and looking flustered—but still beautiful. Her dark brown hair shimmered with tones of red and gold, even beneath the harsh coolness of the fluorescent lights. He found himself staring at her again, just as he had on the first day they met.

Claire's gaze immediately fell on Neil, and a shy, delighted smile crossed her face. Alec pressed his lips together, the twinge in his insides tightening like a vise. There were lots of empty seats. Presumably, she'd sit next to Neil.

A warmth filled him as Claire sank into the empty chair beside him. "What are you doing in this class?" she asked, sounding just as surprised to see him as he was to see her. "I thought all your classes were honors."

"The rest of them are," he admitted. "This was the only foreign language class that fit into my schedule."

Not that it really mattered *what* language he took. "What about you? I saw your schedule, you were listed in honors Spanish."

"I had to change it. That class was the same track as Concert Singers." She darted him a hesitant look. "I tried out yesterday afternoon. And got in! Can you believe it?"

Alec smiled, hoping to convey how genuinely pleased he was for her without betraying his inner turmoil. "Of course I believe it. You deserve it. You have a beautiful voice."

"Thanks. I still can't get over it. I had no idea. And I never would have known about it if not for—"

Claire was interrupted midsentence as their teacher, Señora Guiterez, a plump, dark-haired woman, rapped sharply on her desk for attention. *"¡Hola, clase!"* The class quieted and focused their attention up front as she continued speaking in Spanish, explaining that everyone was required to do so for the entirety of the period.

To Alec's amusement, after a brief introductory lecture, the class was subjected to an episode of an old Spanish soap opera. *Is this really the way high school students learn languages?* he wondered. When the TV clip was done, Señora Guiterez asked the class to describe what they'd just seen. After several students gave their impressions, the teacher fixed her gaze on Neil.

"Señor Mitchum," she said in Spanish, "in the scene on the balcony, why was Julio so angry?"

Neil looked baffled, replying in halting Spanish, "Because he wear so ugly a sweater?"

The classroom erupted with laughter. Even Señora Guiterez couldn't hold back a chuckle. Alec's stomach burned as he watched Claire gaze at Neil with an admiring smile. What did she see in him? Other than his stunning good looks and charming personality, that is?

As the laughter continued, Claire never took her eyes from Neil's face. A pressure began in Alec's chest that rose through his throat to throb at his temple. Every muscle in his body tensed. The air he was breathing suddenly felt thinner, as if he were on top of Mount Everest. Without further thought, Alec leapt to his feet, crossed the room in the blink of an eye, lifted Neil from his seat, and flung him through the classroom window in a hail of splintering glass. The sound of Neil's helpless scream was intensely satisfying.

Alec blinked as the laughter in the classroom brought him back to reality. Neil still sat in his seat, undamaged, not a lock of hair on his head out of place.

Is this what jealousy feels like? Alec wondered. If so, it was an emotion he didn't care for.

"*Sí, sí.* It *was* an ugly sweater," the teacher was saying. "But besides that, *señor?*"

Neil tried again. "Because . . . Maria. And Julio. The girlfriend, she. They are. They were—" He trailed off, at a loss for words.

The teacher's eyes swept the room. "Anyone else know the answer?"

Claire looked like she was struggling to formulate a reply. No one responded. Alec shook his head, frowning. It was so easy. Here, he realized, was his opportunity to show Claire the difference between himself and the Choir Boy. His hand shot up like a rocket. The teacher pointed at him.

"Julio was furious," Alec replied promptly in pitch-perfect Spanish, "because his cousin Guillermo had just revealed that Maria is not just his girlfriend. Julio's father, before he went to law school twenty-three years ago, had met Maria's mother in a hotel bar in Tierra del Fuego and spent the night with her, making Maria his half sister."

The teacher's jaw dropped. His classmates turned to stare at him. Alec darted a look in Claire's direction. Her eyes were wide and she was smiling at *him* now, as if to say, *Wow. That was good. Really good.* Alec grinned triumphantly.

"Well said, *señor*," asserted Señora Guiterez. "Are you sure you need to be taking this class?"

Alec paused, his smugness instantly fading. *Shite*, he thought. What had possessed him? Showing off wasn't his style. Had he jeopardized his cover? In broken Spanish, he backpedaled, "*Sí*. No. Sorry, *señora*. I live in Spain two years as child. My grandfather watching this soap opera. I see this episode before."

As the teacher nodded and patiently corrected his grammatical errors, Alec secretly breathed a sigh of relief. Hopefully, people would forget all about this by tomorrow and go back to laughing at Neil's jokes.

He wasn't sure that Claire bought his explanation, though. For the rest of the class, he felt her eyes on him, as if she sensed that there was something strange going on. Alec kept his own eyes fixed on his textbook, and as soon as the bell rang he darted out of the room without looking back.

seven

That was weird, Claire thought, as she finished washing her hands in the girls' bathroom during break. It was obvious that Alec was practically fluent in Spanish. Why was he trying to cover it up? He'd said it was the only class that fit into his schedule, but she doubted that was true. He could have probably taken French I or Japanese I instead. She shrugged, taking out her brush and running it through her hair. Maybe Alec just wanted a class he could skate by in. If so, she could understand that. This school was hard enough, and all honors and AP classes only made it harder.

She wished she'd had a chance to talk to him after class, to thank him for encouraging her to sing with him yesterday, and to apologize for unintentionally ignoring him afterward. She still felt guilty about that. But he'd rushed out of class so fast just now, she hadn't been able to catch him.

Claire returned her brush to her backpack and was

zipping it up when a sudden flush and wave of dizziness came over her. *What the hell?* she thought fearfully. It had been four days since her last "episode." She'd started to think—hope—that the whole thing had just been a fluke. Apparently not. A deep heat, which seemed to be emanating from her core, now coursed up through her body like a raging inferno. She broke out in a sweat, her stomach churned, her knees quivered, and she slammed back against the bathroom wall, crying out in pain. *Thank God no one else is here to see this*, Claire thought frantically, as she slowly slid down to the tile floor.

All at once, an image appeared in her mind:

A silhouetted figure stood before her, lit from behind by a bright golden light, surrounded by inky blackness.

"Claire!" *cried a raspy, whispering voice.*

A long series of garbled words followed—an attempt at speech interspersed with static.

Only one part—the final sentence—came through loud and clear: *"Don't tell anyone."*

Then it was over. Claire gasped, struggled to her feet, and stood there for a long moment, gripping the counter for support.

What the hell was that?!

It was totally different from the other psychic episodes she'd experienced. It felt incomplete, like she could hear someone talking *to* her, instead of seeing through their eyes. Was she going batshit crazy? Or was this really happening?

Was someone trying to contact her telepathically?

In the staticky section, the only words Claire had been able to understand were "danger," "gift," and "help." Who or what was in danger? What gift? Was she supposed to help someone? Then there was the kicker: *Don't tell anyone.*

Don't tell anyone *what*?

Claire sighed. How was she supposed to figure this out on her own?

"I can't wait to hear the voice that bowled Mr. Lang over," Erica said a few minutes later.

"Yeah, why've you been holding out on us all this time, CB?" Brian asked.

"I wasn't holding out," Claire insisted. "I never used to be able to sing. I'm just as surprised as you are."

Claire followed her friends into the music room, past the grand piano toward a semicircular row of chairs, each of which had a music stand in front of it. She'd been so excited about this class. But how was she supposed to relax and enjoy herself after that bizarre mental episode in the restroom?

"Bass section sits on that end," Erica explained, before leading Claire toward their own seats. "Then tenors and altos. Last but not least, sopranos—that's us."

"I told you you'd make it, Brennan," Neil said, striding up with a smile. "Congrats and welcome." He placed his hand on Claire's bare shoulder and gave it a squeeze.

The instant Neil's hand made contact, a dizzy heat began to engulf her. Claire had a fleeting thought: *How pathetic are you? The guy barely touches you and you swoon?* But as her head began pounding and her knees trembled, that thought was immediately replaced by another: *Oh no. Not again! Not now!! I just barely got over the last one!* And then—

WHAM.

She was in her Spanish classroom. The person sitting next to her was . . . her.

Señora Guiterez laid a corrected quiz facedown on her desk.

Nervous, Claire flipped over the paper with hands that were not her own—hands that were larger and more masculine. She saw three things. First, the date on the paper. Second, a big red F. Third, the name scrawled at the top of the page:

Neil Mitchum.

Claire blinked and found Neil still standing in the flesh before her, eyeing her with concern. "Brennan? You okay?"

"Fine!" Claire manufactured a smile as she quickly wiped sweat from her brow. "Shouldn't have had that latte at break, I guess." She hurried off to the soprano section and sat down next to Erica, heart pounding.

Erica shot Claire an intensely curious look. "You just *saw* something, didn't you?" Erica whispered urgently. "When Neil touched your shoulder?"

Claire nodded as she lowered her eyes. Thankfully, no one else seemed to have noticed anything.

"See! I *told* you it was a touch thing. Was it a vision about Neil?"

Claire nodded again and leaned in to Erica's ear. "It was a vision of the *future!*"

"Really? Are you sure?"

"I saw Neil get an F on a Spanish quiz. It was dated next Wednesday."

"An F? But Neil's a good student."

"Apparently not in Spanish."

Claire's brain was going a mile a minute. Was all this somehow connected to the garbled message she'd gotten just before class? *Danger . . . gift . . . help.* Suddenly, the whole thing made sense. *She was supposed to help Neil—who was in danger of flunking Spanish.* For some reason, she was supposed to keep it a secret. But Erica already knew everything that was going on with her. Surely, she could tell Erica about it.

"And guess what?" Claire went on softly. "I had a separate vision a few minutes ago. I think I've just been charged with a mission: to help Neil pass that Spanish quiz."

Erica raised an eyebrow, incredulous. "Who would send you on a mission?"

"I have no idea. What should I do? Is it okay to meddle with the future?"

"Of course it is!"

"But if I help Neil get an A, it might change the course of history. There's a cause and effect for everything. If

Hitler had gotten into art school, there might have been no World War II."

"Did you just liken Neil to Hitler?"

"They're both vegetarians."

Erica rolled her eyes. "Claire, come on. How can you sit back and do nothing? If you'd known about my mom's accident beforehand, I would've totally wanted you to warn me."

Before they could continue, Mr. Lang breezed into the room, sat down at the piano, and began playing scales with a flourish. An elegant man with a neatly trimmed auburn goatee, Mr. Lang's no-nonsense, down-to-business attitude was complemented by an upbeat, positive inner energy. Everyone began to warm up, singing along with the piano. Claire tentatively joined her voice to the chorus of sopranos. She had no clear idea what she was doing, but somehow it all seemed to come naturally to her—and thank God, since she was finding it impossible to concentrate. Her thoughts were consumed by the task ahead of her.

Claire would have to initiate a conversation with the guy she'd had a major crush on for the past two years—the guy every girl in school had a crush on—and the one person she'd always been too shy speaking *around*, let alone *to*. And of all things, she had to somehow convince him that he needed *her* help. Could she do it?

She had to at least try.

❧

As they exited class, Claire strode quickly after Neil. *You can do this*, she told herself.

When she caught up to him, she put on her most cheerful smile. *"Señor Mitchum."* Her voice cracked, her mouth had gone dry, and her heart was pounding so hard it threatened to leap out of her chest.

"Brennan." Neil casually returned her grin. "How's it going?"

"Good." The single word came out like a squeak. Claire cleared her throat. "You know," she said slowly, straining for calm, "you did me a huge favor by getting me into Concert Singers. I'd like to perform a service for you in return."

Neil looked at her. "I'm not quite sure I get your meaning," he said hesitantly.

Claire was suddenly aware of the innuendo in what she'd said, and felt her face grow hot. "I meant . . . that is, I was just wondering . . . if . . . you might like some help with Spanish."

His smile faded. "What makes you think I need help with Spanish? Just 'cause I don't get soap operas?"

"No, that's not it," Claire replied quickly. *"I* didn't know how to answer that question either, even though I saw the episode last year. But . . . I couldn't help noticing that you were struggling with verb tenses, which are super hard. I finally understand all that stuff, and I just thought . . ." Her voice trailed off.

Neil glanced aside, clearly uncomfortable and reluctant.

Before he could openly refuse, Claire blurted, "Neil. The thing is, after what you did for me, I'm beholden to you."

His eyes returned to hers, and he shrugged, his grin back. "All right, Brennan, you're on. We'll try it and see how it goes. But only because you said beholden."

At lunch, Claire finally had a chance to talk to Alec. They were sitting at their usual table on the upper terrace with Brian and Erica. Alec was tense and quiet, concentrating on his chicken stir-fry.

"Alec," Claire said apologetically, "when I was telling you earlier about getting into Concert Singers, I didn't get a chance to say the most important part. It never would have happened if you hadn't encouraged me to sing with you yesterday. I'm really grateful to you for that. I really enjoyed it. Singing with you, I mean. And I'm sorry if I abandoned you afterward when we got interrupted. I didn't mean to."

Alec looked at her in surprise and seemed to relax a notch. "Don't worry about it," he intoned softly.

"Claire said you have a great voice, Alec," Erica put in. "I hope you try out for the Homecoming assembly."

"What? They're having musical acts this year?" Brian asked. "How do you know?"

"Because . . . drum roll, please?" Erica said with

a dramatic pause. "I have just signed up to be on the Homecoming Committee."

"You?" Claire retorted. "On a committee? Are you on crack?"

"College admissions people place a great deal of emphasis on extracurricular activities," Erica said. "And it sounds fun. Homecoming is only a month away, and we just had our first meeting. We decided to have performances at the assembly, along with the usual carnival, football game, and . . . dance. Which—might I add—I insist we attend this year."

"Go to a *dance*?" Brian made a face. "But we've avoided those so successfully thus far."

"Brian, you only hate dances because you don't have the nerve to ask anyone," Claire said.

"Oh, like you're the expert," he retorted. "How many have you been to?"

"Zero," Claire admitted, blushing a little. "But only because no one ever asked *me*."

"Wait. Could someone please explain this to the foreigner?" Alec inserted. "Isn't Homecoming supposed to be for visiting alumni? What's this dance about?"

"The dance is the one thing that's for *us*," Erica explained. "It's our first opportunity of the year to agonize about getting a date, buy an expensive dress, cheer as the most popular kids get crowned king and queen, and dance to ridiculously loud music in a gym filled with helium balloons and crepe paper."

"Well, I wouldn't want to miss *that*," Alec said with a smile.

It was the first time Claire had seen Alec smile all day, and she realized he was suddenly gazing at her. The look in his eyes was so warm, it made her stomach flutter, as if a rush of a hundred butterflies had taken wing. She smiled back, wondering what she should say to get Alec talking more. Just then, she heard a voice over her shoulder.

"Brennan? So this is where you four hide out for lunch. Nice spot. Great view."

Claire sprang out of her seat. "Neil! Good timing. I just finished eating." To the others she said, "Excuse me, guys. I'll catch up with you later. Neil and I are going to work on Spanish. Where do you want to sit, Neil?"

"You're the boss. Would you prefer a cubicle in the house of knowledge?" Neil gestured to the library. "Or as they say in Spain, tutoring alfresco?"

"Over there will do just fine," Claire replied, pointing to a nearby bench on the terrace, "and alfresco is Italian, actually."

Neil shrugged with a light, self-effacing chuckle. As he and Claire walked off, she thought she caught a look of frustration and disappointment on Alec's face—or did she imagine it?

The tutoring session went well. Claire coached Neil on

all the things the teacher had promised would be on next week's quiz. By the time they finished, he seemed to have a better grasp of the material.

"Thanks, Brennan," Neil said as they put their notebooks away. "I'm glad you twisted my arm about this. It pisses me off that I suck at Spanish, since I'm halfway decent at everything else."

"Aw," Claire responded lightly as she zipped up her backpack. "He's as modest as he is pretty." The moment the words left her mouth, Claire thought she'd melt into the ground with embarrassment. Had she actually said that out loud? She felt a tug on the end of her ponytail, and glanced up to find Neil grinning at her with a mischievous glint in his eyes. She'd seen that look before with people he was close to and was thrilled that he was using it with her now.

"Pretty, eh?" He chuckled.

"Well, *studly* seemed a bit over the top." She couldn't believe she was talking to him like this, as if they'd been friends for years.

"Fair enough," he said with an approving nod. "I'll take pretty. *You* can be studly."

Had Neil just implied that he thought she was *pretty*? As Claire struggled for some kind of witty reply, the bell rang, ending the lunch period. They both stood up from the bench.

"What do you say we do this again tomorrow—*after*

school?" Neil added. "Maybe in the Student Life Center?"

"Sure. I usually have to wait about an hour for my mom to pick me up, anyway."

"Cool. See you later." Neil waved as he headed off.

As Claire watched him go, she felt another tug on her ponytail, causing her to jump.

"Isn't there a law," Erica said, "against tutors fraternizing with their students?"

Claire gave her friend a faux shocked look. "We were hardly fraternizing."

Erica just smiled. "If you say so."

Over the next couple of days, Neil showed vast improvement during their after-school tutoring sessions. Claire grew more and more comfortable around him and wasn't tongue-tied anymore in his presence. She loved Concert Singers. Her year of piano lessons helped her to sight-read the music with ease, and she fit right in with the more experienced students, as if she'd been doing this for years. She found herself singing in the shower and while doing the dishes. If only she'd had the nerve to try her voice years earlier, instead of being so shy about it!

To Claire's disappointment, however, Alec was quiet and standoffish. He didn't sit at their table at lunch, and when she saw him in class, he didn't speak to her. She didn't run into him again with his guitar, and he was never at their locker at the same time she was. Was he just the loner type, or was he angry and purposely avoiding her? When she'd apologized that day at lunch, she'd thought—*hoped*—she'd smoothed things over with him. His behavior hurt more than she cared to admit.

Alec wasn't the only one acting peculiar that week. Twice, while Claire was doing homework in her room, her mom stopped in the doorway to silently stare at her, then walked off without a word.

On Thursday night, her mom finally spoke. "So! Claire . . . how was your day?"

Claire glanced up from the calculus problems she was working on. "Fine."

"How's choir going?"

"Good."

Silence ensued. Why was her mom looking at her like that? Claire wondered self-consciously. She felt like a piece of produce her mom was inspecting for possible defects before purchase.

"You've seemed a little . . . preoccupied the past few days," her mom said at last. "Is there anything you'd like to talk about?"

"No."

"Has anything . . . unusual been going on lately?" Her mom was clearly fishing.

Claire sighed. It wasn't like she could tell her mom, of all people, about the weird visions she'd been having. "Mom, I've got a lot of homework."

"Okay! Just . . . keep studying. I'll call you when dinner's ready."

Friday was a shorter day at Emerson. Although Claire had been dreading the week culminating in another one of Mr. Patterson's belittling lectures, there was no way she could've anticipated what would happen at the end of the period.

In her hands, she now held her history paper—the paper she'd stayed up most of Monday and Tuesday nights writing—which Patterson had already graded and returned with lightning efficiency. It was littered with red marks, and at the top of the paper was a thick, rosy D, accompanied by a note: "Eschew prolixity."

D. Claire felt the hot threat of tears behind her eyes. She'd never gotten anything below a B in her life. Patterson couldn't find fault with her grammar, she knew, or her historical accuracy—but clearly he thought she'd been too wordy. Entire paragraphs had been red-lined, and the pages were full of comments like: "Awkward," "Why?" "Unsubstantiated," "Get to the point."

"I figured," Mr. Patterson drawled as he finished handing out the papers, "since I gave you only two days to write these, it was only fair to return them two days later. You're welcome."

The bell rang, signaling the end of the school day. Claire stuffed her book and paper into her backpack, her lips trembling. How would this grade affect her scholarship?

She felt Alec's eyes on her but was too mortified to look in his direction. She hurried up to the front of the room. "Excuse me, Mr. Patterson. Can I talk to you for a second?"

Mr. Patterson didn't even turn to face her. "No time. Week's over. See you Monday." Abruptly, he left the room.

Shocked by his coldness, Claire trudged out the door. To her surprise, Alec was waiting for her.

"I saw your grade. I'm sorry," he said gently.

It was the first time he'd spoken to her in days. The sympathy in his voice and the kind look in his eyes—which she hoped implied that he wasn't angry with her anymore, if he ever had been—unleashed the tears that Claire had been holding back. "I worked really hard on that paper," she said brokenly as she and Alec moved down the path. "It wasn't Shakespeare, but it didn't deserve a D."

"A lot of kids got Ds. The guy behind me got an F."

"Really? What did you get?"

Alec looked self-conscious. He silently formed an "A" with his fingers.

His admission cheered her somehow. "You must be the only human being alive who's embarrassed about getting an A."

"I just feel bad." He shrugged. "Mr. Patterson seems to think he has to humiliate students to get results."

"Ds are so confusing. It's like you didn't pass, but you didn't fail, either." Claire wiped tears from her cheeks and took a deep breath. "Please don't think I'm crying because I'm some übernerd who needs to get As on everything to feel validated. It's because of my scholarship. It requires a 3.8 GPA."

"3.8? Wow. That must be difficult to maintain."

"You have no idea. I have to work my ass off. I'm not a genius like you."

"I'm not a genius," he protested.

"It's not open for debate. I've heard you in class. Calculus, English, history, whatever. You always know the answers to everything. You speak Spanish better than Señora Guiterez."

He blushed. "Maybe I . . . should've taken a different language."

"You think?" Claire teased. They'd reached their locker now. As Alec dialed the combination, she continued, "Anyway, all the hard work is worth it. I love it here. I'd do anything to stay at Emerson. That's why I basically have no life. Well, that and the fact that my mom is an overprotective worrywart who watches over my every move."

"That doesn't sound so bad."

"What? That my mom never lets me go anywhere?"

He opened his mouth to reply, but just then Brian and Erica descended on them.

"Whassup, peoplez?" Brian crowed. "Anybody hungry?"

"You'd better be," Erica chimed in. "It's Friday! I'm taking us all to Venice Beach for empanadas, *maintenant*. That's French for *now*, in case you were wondering."

"Neil's coming with us," Brian added. "He's waiting down by the circle."

Claire saw Alec's smile fade at the mention of Neil's name, but he didn't comment.

"Have you ever had an empanada?" Claire asked Alec, as they finished retrieving their books and headed toward the library stairwell.

"Are we always going to play the 'Has Alec Eaten This?' game?" he asked quietly.

Claire worried that she'd offended him, until she saw a good-natured smile tug at his lips. "I'm just curious. I mean, after the pizza thing—I've never met anyone before who hadn't—"

"Let's put it this way," Alec interjected. "If it's fried, fattening, caffeinated, alcoholic, or high in sugar content, it's safe to assume that I rarely eat it—or have never tried it."

Claire stared at him. "Why?"

"Are your parents fitness freaks, or do they just hate you?" Erica said.

Alec stiffened visibly. "They just followed a healthy lifestyle, which I continue to embrace. But they . . . died when I was young."

Erica went red in the face. A silence fell.

"Way to go, Erica," Brian said, clapping. "That was awkward."

"I'm sorry." Claire felt terrible.

"Me too." Erica looked at her feet.

"Thanks, but . . . don't worry about it. It's okay."

Now Claire understood Alec's earlier comment about her mom. *No wonder he's often so quiet and moody,* she thought, her heart going out to him. It was bad enough to grow up without a father. But to have no parents at all? That was too awful to contemplate. She'd assumed Alec had moved here with his parents because of a job transfer or something. *Who does he live with?* she wondered. *A grandparent? An aunt or uncle?* She wasn't sure this was the right moment to ask.

They neared the bottom of the stairs, where the construction crew was still working atop a three-tiered scaffolding tower. Claire spied Neil standing just beyond it by the drop-off circle. He waved at them and shouted something Claire couldn't hear over the annoying beeping noise of a truck backing up.

The four of them passed underneath the scaffolding, heading toward the circle. They were halfway through the makeshift corridor when Claire heard the sudden, loud roar of an engine. To her horror, the truck was speeding backward toward them. Before she could think or move, the vehicle collided with the base of the scaffolding with a devastating crash.

The screech of tearing metal ripped through the air as the entire structure overhead began to collapse.

A huge wooden platform barreled down directly at them.

Claire screamed and ducked, a single thought popping into her mind: *I'm going to die.*

eight

᠁

Frozen in terror, Claire fixed her gaze on the heavy wooden platform hurtling toward their heads, which was a split second away from crushing them all.

But it never did.

Somehow, impossibly, the platform seemed to hover for a fraction of a second in midair. Alec stood tall above her, one arm extended, fingers splayed, as if magically holding up the platform by sheer willpower. She heard screams and shouts from above as suddenly the whole board tilted to one side. In her peripheral vision she caught sight of three men landing safely on the pavement nearby.

Before Claire could blink, Alec's arms were wrapped around her and their friends and then they were airborne. They landed heavily and painfully on the concrete, out of harm's way, as the entire scaffolding tower smashed to the ground beside them in an explosion of dust, screeching metal, and splintering wood.

The thundering clatter echoed in Claire's ears as they

all lay in a heap. Dust stung her eyes, but as she blinked it away her gaze briefly locked with Alec's. Then, just as suddenly as he'd tackled them, Alec was up on his feet and gone. Claire struggled to regain her senses, her ears ringing. Erica and Brian moaned beside her.

"Oh my God." Claire's voice sounded strange and muffled, as if she were underwater. "Are you guys all right?"

Her friends sat up, choking. "What the hell just happened?" Brian shouted, grimacing in pain as he rubbed his left arm. The dust coating his spiky black hair made it look almost gray.

"We almost died!" Erica cried just as loudly. Then she burst into tears.

Numbly, Claire wrapped her arms around Erica and held her. Everything sounded so muted, making her feel detached from the world around her.

"Where's Alec?" Brian said.

"I don't know." Claire craned her neck, trying to see over Erica's shoulder, but the truck that had caused it all was buried in the debris, blocking her view—and no doubt blocking everyone else's view of them.

"What happened?" Brian said again. "Did Alec just save our lives?"

"I think he did." Claire pulled herself dizzily to her feet, as the sounds around her slowly returned to normal volume. "I'll be back in a sec."

As she carefully made her way through the rubble, she

noticed that the cab of the pickup truck was empty. Where was the driver who'd caused the accident?

A crowd was gathering in the drop-off circle just ahead, all chattering loudly and staring at the gigantic mess. Mr. Lang and Neil ran up to her.

"Claire! Holy shit!" cried Neil. "I saw the truck hit that thing, and then it all came down. . . . I thought you guys were dead!"

"No, we're okay."

"Thank God," said Mr. Lang.

"How the hell did you get out of the way in time?" Neil asked.

"Alec tackled us. He—" Before Claire could finish that thought, she spotted Alec talking to some of the faculty and construction workers, who looked just as befuddled as she was. She couldn't understand a word they were saying. "What language are they speaking?"

"Who?" Neil said.

"The construction workers."

"Somebody said it was Korean," answered Mr. Lang. "That student over there is translating, so the teachers will know what to tell the paramedics."

Korean? Stunned, Claire turned back to where Alec had been standing just seconds ago—but he had disappeared into the throng.

Sirens blared. Two police cars and an ambulance charged down the hill and pulled up to the scene. As Erica and Brian joined Claire, a bevy of concerned teachers, students, and parents descended on them.

The next four hours felt like twelve. The paramedics examined everyone involved in the accident, except Alec, who had vanished. Brian had dislocated his shoulder, and one of the workers had twisted his ankle, but everyone else, including Claire, escaped with only minor cuts and bruises. Neil stood patiently by her side during everything, making sure that she was comfortable, and bringing everybody bottles of water. He even stuck around while she, Brian, and Erica were questioned by the police.

"So you're saying this other student, Alec MacKenzie, pulled all three of you to safety when the scaffolding fell?" asked a tall, gray-haired police officer as he jotted down notes.

"Yes," Brian replied, adjusting his arm sling.

"Is Mr. MacKenzie here?" the cop asked.

"I think he already left," Claire said.

"And he's a friend of yours?"

Claire nodded.

"Do you have his contact information?"

Claire hesitated. "We . . . just met Alec a few days ago." She was embarrassed to admit that they knew so little about him. "I don't know his phone number, but it should be listed in our school directory."

"It isn't," Erica chimed in. As Claire shot her a curious look, Erica added, "What? I checked. Alec's not in there.

Maybe they didn't have a chance to add him yet, because he's new."

"What about the pickup truck that ran into the scaffolding?" the policeman inquired. "Did any of you see who was driving it?"

Erica and Brian shook their heads. Claire said, "When I walked by right after the accident, no one was in it."

"What was up with that guy, anyway?" Brian interjected. "Was he high or something?"

"We won't know that until we find him," the cop replied. "Thanks for your help. If I need anything else, I'll be in touch." With that, he turned and walked away.

"What did he mean, 'We won't know until we find him'?" Erica said.

It was Neil who explained. "There's this mystery about the truck driver. I was listening while Alec translated for the teachers. Two of the construction workers claim their fourth man called in sick today, but no one can get him on the phone. The third guy insists he saw the missing dude climb into the truck just before the accident."

"He must have fled the scene," Claire mused, "probably afraid he'd be fired or arrested."

"Or deported," Brian added, taking a swig from his water bottle.

"But why did *Alec* leave in such a hurry?" Neil said with a frown. "I swear, he was right next to me, and then he was gone."

Claire wondered that herself. Just then she heard her mom's voice.

"Claire!"

Lynn raced toward her, leaving her car parked in the jumble of vehicles beyond the police blockade. She was at Claire's side in seconds, her face a mixture of panic and relief as she threw her arms around her. "Claire! Oh, honey."

"It's okay, Mom. I'm all right. Really." Claire relished the warmth of her mother's embrace, grateful to have a mom to hold and comfort her . . . and grateful to be alive. She knew most people didn't walk away from such a serious accident—which brought her back to the question: *How the hell had Alec saved them like that?*

Claire wondered if Erica or Brian had seen Alec's strange hand gesture when the scaffolding seemed to hover briefly in midair, instead of falling straight down on them. Neither of them had mentioned it, and Claire didn't want to bring it up with all the adults around. The police would probably say she'd imagined it.

But Claire knew what she saw.

"Do you think Alec is a vampire?"

It was Saturday afternoon, and Erica, Brian, and Claire were sitting on a bench at the end of the Venice pier, chowing down on the empanadas they'd missed out on the day before. It was an uncharacteristically foggy day, with a cool breeze rippling across the surface of the gray-blue ocean below. A handful of fathers and their kids were fishing off the edge of the pier nearby.

"A vampire?" Erica laughed. "What brought that on?"

"I know this sounds insane," Claire said, "and you may think I'm totally crazy. But Alec is different from the rest of us. Sometimes, he doesn't even seem human to me."

"You're right!" Brian steadied the cardboard food tray on his lap as he tried to eat one-handed. "You do sound crazy."

"Hear me out, will you?"

"We're listening." Erica looked at Claire, chewing patiently.

"First off, Alec's really strong. I mean, the first day we met, he broke my locker by barely pushing on a LockerMate."

"So he works out," Erica replied. "Have you seen his biceps? He looks like he could break *me* in half."

"What about yesterday?" Claire insisted. "The way he lifted all three of us at the same time?"

Brian shrugged. "It was a crisis situation. You've heard all the stories: mothers lifting up cars to save their babies, blah, blah, blah."

"But did you see what he did *before* he tackled us?" Claire persisted.

"You mean in that split second when I cringed and shut my eyes?" Erica asked.

"My eyes were open. Alec was standing above us with his arm raised like this." Claire stretched her hand skyward and swung it outward, demonstrating. "That platform was falling *straight down* at us. It should have smeared us on the pavement. Instead, I saw it *pause* for a split second, like Alec was somehow magically holding it back, and then it tilted and crashed off to the side instead."

"That's ridiculous," Brian scoffed. "The scaffolding just collapsed in stages, that's all, and fell sideways, which gave Alec time to save us."

"I don't think so. And what about the construction workers? They were on top of a three-story tower, but somehow they all slid safely to the ground. People said it was a miracle they weren't all badly injured."

"What are you suggesting?" Erica asked, shaking her head. "That Alec guided them all down to the ground with the Force?"

"Maybe."

A pair of seagulls squawked overhead, then swooped down and snapped up some invisible tidbits from the heaving sea.

"Okay, even if that did happen, it doesn't mean Alec's a vampire." Erica grinned. "It means he's from *a galaxy far, far away.*" She and Brian glanced at each other and laughed.

Claire frowned. "Come on, guys. I'm being serious here."

"CB, Alec is not the next Obi-Wan Kenobi. Trust me," Brian insisted with patience and mock solemnity, as if he was trying, once and for all, to convince a deluded grown-up that there was no Santa Claus. "And even if vampires *did* exist—which they don't—there's no way Alec is one. Think about it: He walks around in broad daylight, and he doesn't (a) burst into flames, or (b) sparkle like a disco ball."

"Have you read *Dracula*?" Claire asked. "Sunlight didn't affect him at all."

"Yeah, and *he* wasn't real *either*," Brian retaliated.

"Alec *eats*," Erica pointed out emphatically. "Vampires don't eat food, remember?"

Claire shook her head. "They did on *Buffy*. They just didn't like the way it tasted."

Brian snorted. "You've switched sources now from a hallmark of Victorian literature to a cult TV series?"

"Alec *loves* food!" Erica went on. "Have you forgotten his chocolate-cookie orgasm, or the way he inhaled that bowl of mac-and-cheese like it was manna from heaven?"

"Yeah, but don't you think it's weird that he'd never eaten anything good before he got here?"

"Not really," Erica replied. "He said he grew up on a strict diet."

"Okay, fine, but Alec has skills that should be beyond people our age," Claire continued. "He's a total prodigy at classical guitar. He got an A from a teacher who apparently only hands out Ds. And he seems to be fluent in both Spanish and Korean."

"So he's a brilliant guy who grew up abroad, probably

moved around a lot, and knows a few languages," Brian said. "Big deal. That still doesn't make him a vampire."

"I suppose you're going to say he's pale because he's from the UK?"

"Exactly!" Brian and Erica cried simultaneously.

"So if he had nothing to hide yesterday, why did he run off before anyone could question or examine him?"

Erica shrugged. "I don't know. I wish we knew where he lives or at least his phone number, so we could call and check that he's okay."

Claire stood and twisted her hands together, perplexed. "Something just doesn't add up, guys. Even if you can explain away all those other things, the fact is, I saw those platforms hover for a moment in mid-fall before they tipped. I'm telling you, Alec *held them up*—*somehow*—*with his mind*, and he *made* them fall to the side. He may not be a vampire, but I think he's . . . I don't know . . . telekinetic."

"Telekinetic. Huh." Erica nodded pensively as she crumpled up her cardboard food tray and tossed it into a nearby trash can. "Well, Claire, if *you* have ESP, I suppose it *is* possible that Alec has some kind of mental super-power, too."

"Erica!" Claire shot her a silencing look and then glanced worriedly at Brian.

Brian blinked several times, staring at them. "*Exqueeze me?* I bacon your powder?"

Erica heaved a sigh. "Claire said not to tell anybody, but

she's been having some weird psychic episodes ever since Book Day."

"*Erica!*" Claire cried again, irritated and embarrassed.

"You almost passed out in the girls' bathroom the other day!" Erica retorted emphatically. "I think he should know!"

"Hold the phone," Brian said. "Are you guys serious?"

Ignoring him, Erica continued, "Speaking of which, Claire, why didn't you know in advance that the scaffold was going to fall on us?"

"I'm not an oracle. I've only had one vision of the future. One! I have no idea how this works, or when the visions are going to come."

"You're having visions?" Brian sounded stunned, talking mostly to himself. "How did I miss that?"

"So," Claire said to Erica, "returning to my original question: Alec. What is he?"

"He could be an alien possessing a human's body," Erica suggested. "Or a visitor from the planet Krypton."

Claire rolled her eyes. "So—vampires are improbable, but *aliens* are believable?"

"At least they're scientifically *possible*."

Brian sat stupefied, sucking up the dregs of his soda through his straw. Shaking his head, he mumbled, "The truth is out there."

Yes, Claire thought. *And I'm going to find it.*

nine

❧

Alec was running. Fast. His combat boots made a clacking sound on the stone steps beneath him.

He was in a Japanese garden. But where? In Los Angeles? No, it wasn't Los Angeles—and, he realized suddenly, it wasn't a garden. It was a graveyard.

In the moonlight's glow, he recognized the stairs sloping sharply down the hillside in front of him, ringed by hundreds of red, centuries-old funereal gates. He'd been here many times before. This was the Fushimi Inari Shrine in Kyoto. It was isolated and quiet at night—the perfect time and place to finish a job outside the public eye.

He ran on, his labored breathing growing shallower with every step. His quarry was nimbler than Alec had expected. Alec leapt down the steps two at a time, then three, but the man still maintained a good ten yards' lead. With the agility of a cat, his target turned a sharp corner at the base of the stairway and began to clamber up another one. Alec swerved to follow, trying to sight the retreating form along his silenced pistol, but he was visible only intermittently between the row of tightly packed, archlike gates lining the pathway.

The figure darted into one of the small cemeteries on the wooded hillside and Alec dashed after him, cursing silently. A firearm was useless here. The thick mist in the air obscured visibility, and the claustrophobic jumble of slender gravestones, many of them six feet in height, gave the man too many places to hide.

Alec paused, catching his breath as he holstered the gun and drew two long, curved daggers from his belt. Treading as quietly as he could from one row of headstones to the next, he readied himself to lunge at the first moving object. The tinkling of a pebble on the cobblestone in the fifth row set him on hyperalert and he darted forward, steeling himself for action.

What he encountered around the corner, however, stopped him dead in his tracks. It wasn't the middle-aged Japanese gangster he was after. Instead, a tall Caucasian woman with platinum-blond hair was walking silently toward him, her blue eyes blazing with fury.

What the hell? Alec thought, lowering his blades and stepping backward in confusion. He recognized the woman—and he remembered her crime—although he couldn't recall her name. But how was this possible? *She couldn't be here. She was dead.* Alec wanted desperately to turn and run, but his legs were rooted to the ground. All at once, the hairs prickled on the back of his neck. He spun, weapons raised again.

The mobster he'd been chasing stood just a few yards away. But he wasn't alone. To his left stood a well-dressed, elderly businessman; to his right, a stocky, nondescript man in military fatigues. Behind them stood several other figures, all people Alec recognized, people whom he knew, with a certainty, no longer existed on this earthly plane. How was it that they were still alive? As one, the group slowly stalked toward him, now joined by more people of various ages and descriptions, all glowering at Alec with the same fierce glare of contempt.

"What do you want?" Alec cried out, brandishing his daggers. "Why are you following me?"

But he knew why.

Alec's throat tightened in fear and guilt. He was trapped, with nowhere to run. The large man in uniform suddenly pounced. Alec deftly swept him to the ground with a low spinning kick, then knocked another assailant away with sharp strikes of his elbows. But they just kept coming. More and more people, all faces he'd seen before, all as silent as the graveyard around him. Someone snatched both blades from Alec's grasp and jabbed them sharply into his abdomen.

Alec jerked back and screamed, but no sound came from his throat.

He awoke with a gasp to find himself back in his studio

apartment in L.A., trembling with relief, his body coated in sweat.

The nightmare again. He'd been having that same dream, in one version or another, over and over for years now. Would he ever be able to forget?

Too agitated to go back to sleep, Alec rose from his couch and—desperate for some distraction—crossed to the weapons cabinet. He concentrated on the lock, heard the tumblers move, and stood back as the heavy door unlatched and swung open. From the array of blades and firearms racked within, he yanked out a broadsword. Sinking down on the sofa, he mentally summoned his whetstone, rag, and bottle of oil and set to work sharpening the blade.

The recurring dream, Alec knew, was the least of his problems. As he worked, his mind drifted back to the far more pressing concern that had been haunting him for the past two days: the incident at school.

Except for the mishap with Claire's locker on Book Day and that one lapse in Spanish class, he'd managed to keep a low profile at Emerson. That is, until Friday, when he'd been forced into using his abilities in the most blatant of displays—a move that was regrettable on so many levels.

He'd done his best to tilt the scaffolding and save those workers and his friends in a manner that was physically explainable. No one at the scene had seemed to question it, and he was pretty sure Brian and Erica hadn't seen anything. He wasn't so sure about Claire. He'd glimpsed an odd look on her face when he pulled her to safety. Did she suspect something? He hadn't waited around to find out. He dreaded going to school tomorrow, fully expecting her to give him the third degree. But it wasn't only Claire he was worried about.

The simple use of his powers wouldn't show up on the grid. But what if another one of his kind had happened to be nearby, looking for an aura? As far as Alec knew, there was no reason for the local Watcher to be at Emerson; however, Alec had been out of the loop for months. Anything was possible. If Zachariah had spotted Alec, he was screwed. He'd spent the past two days sweating it out, expecting a knock at his door any second with a warrant for his arrest—but it had never come.

Alec passed his sword methodically over the whetstone, heaving a long sigh. Maybe he'd been lucky and was still flying safely under the radar.

His thoughts were interrupted by a deep voice.

"So this is it? Your secret hideaway? Your *Bat Cave?*"

Alec gasped and leapt up in alarm, his heart pounding, holding his broadsword at the ready. A figure stood before him—and it wasn't Zachariah. The man was over six feet tall, broad-shouldered but thin, with ebony skin and a mischievous grin. His head was shaved and he wore a dark gray suit with a crisp blue shirt.

"I must say," the visitor went on, surveying the room

with distaste, "it's very quaint and . . . spartan."

Alec's stomach tied itself in knots. Perspiration broke out on his brow. He lowered his weapon and asked quietly, "What are you doing here, Vincent? How did you get in?"

"I'm not *here*, actually." Vincent motioned toward the front window. "I'm outside. But I thought this illusion might prove more entertaining than knocking. Now, go open the door and let me in." With that, he vanished.

Aware that he had little alternative, Alec resheathed his sword and directed his attention toward the door, which unlocked and opened itself. Vincent entered, in the flesh this time. Alec mentally slammed and relocked the door, hovering between relief and fear as he tried to gauge Vincent's mood. "Did the Elders send you?"

"They did."

Alec's heart sank, his worst fears realized. Was this it? Was it all over?

"You should see that as a compliment," Vincent continued. "When you went AWOL after that assignment in Johannesburg, they knew it would take their best Watcher to locate you. Even so, it took some heavy persuasion on my part to convince them that I could be impartial, considering our relationship."

"I thought I'd left a vapor trail to nowhere."

"Close. It took me three months to piece it together. By that time, I was pretty sure you were in L.A., but it wasn't until I remembered one of the surnames you used as a child that I finally tracked you down."

"So," Alec sighed, "your finding me has nothing to do with the scaffolding accident."

"Of course not. That was a stupid but understandable exhibition of your powers that you covered up well. No, I've been watching you for twelve days."

"Twelve days?" He'd been under surveillance for almost *two weeks* and hadn't even realized it? Was he losing his edge? But then he reminded himself, this was *Vincent*. Vincent, who could have been a fly on the wall and Alec wouldn't have had a clue. "Have you reported me?"

Vincent blew out an impatient breath. "Do you think I'd report my own godson?"

A flicker of hope rose within Alec. "Then what are you going to do?"

"I'm still trying to figure that out." Vincent sat down on the couch and regarded Alec with intense dark eyes. "I *know* you, Alec. I raised you. I *trained* you. You've always been a good little soldier like the rest of us. I think you're just . . . confused right now. A bit misguided."

"No, I'm not."

"You should know better than to argue with me, son. *A high school student?* Alec, *really?* Of all the human experiences you could have tried, you gave up everything, risking your own life and the safety of billions, to choose something so *banal?* A period of life that most humans look back on with distaste and abhorrence? There are so many other places you could be spending your time."

Vincent snapped his fingers. Suddenly, they were no longer in Alec's dingy apartment, but in a box at the Teatro alla Scala in Milan, one of the most magnificent opera houses in the world, watching a performance of *Don Giovanni* with a beautifully dressed crowd. "Isn't this an improvement?"

Alec shook his head, aware that the change of scenery was just an illusion Vincent had projected into his mind. "I'm not looking for entertainment. I wanted an identity and a place I could fit in," he called out over the operatic score. "I don't look old enough to teach at Harvard. I had to go with what was believable."

"Yes, but couldn't you have used a little more imagination?" In the blink of an eye, they were on a tropical beach with bikini-clad waitresses offering them cocktails.

"Knock it off, would you?" Alec said, annoyed.

Vincent took an elaborate drink from a tray and held it up toward Alec. "Mai tai?"

"You know I never drink."

"What? You're still following the Code? I knew you were a stickler for the rules, but now you've flown the coop! You're off the grid! You can do anything you want. Isn't that the point?"

"Some habits are harder to break than others."

Vincent shook his head, removed the umbrella from his drink, and took a sip. "You used to be so much more interesting. Your thirst for vengeance gave you such passion and fire for what we do. Now, you bore me."

"A hundred years is a long time to do *what we do*, Vincent. I was loyal, I did my job, and I believed in it for a long time. But . . . it caught up to me."

"What caught up to you?"

"The . . . memories. Too much blood on my hands. I had to get out."

"No one *gets out*, boy. We have our orders and our duties. And you are neglecting yours with this self-indulgent fantasy. What's your plan, anyway? Do you really think you can live among them forever, pretending to be one of them?"

"Aye, at least . . . that's my hope."

"Hmmmph." Vincent snorted and with a snap of his fingers returned them to Alec's apartment—keeping his mai tai.

"I like it here, Vincent." Alec struggled to keep the desperation out of his voice. "I need to do this. Please. Tell the Elders you couldn't find me."

"I suppose that's one option . . . ," Vincent began, but then just sipped his drink in silence for a long moment, frowning.

Alec's pulse raced. His fate was in this man's hands. Vincent had been his father's best friend and had made good on his vow to take care of Alec after his parents died. Vincent cared deeply for him—Alec felt certain of that—and the affection and respect went both ways. Still, he wasn't sure what to expect. Vincent was known for his high principles. Would he turn Alec in or let him go?

"The thing is . . . there's been a development," Vincent continued finally.

"A development?" Alec asked, puzzled by this tangent.

"Something interesting happened a week ago. It turns out it's a good thing I was here."

"What do you mean?"

"There's an Awakened at Emerson Academy."

"*What? At Emerson?*" Alec sank down beside Vincent on the sofa, astonished and upset. The first time an Awakened used their gift, it caused a brief shock wave of metaphysical energy that allowed the Elders to discern the individual's approximate age and location, but not who they were, their gender, or the nature of their powers. That was when the hunt began—the hunt that was one of the things Alec had walked away from forever. "Shite! Of all places, it has to be the school I chose?"

"What's that old saying—'Trouble follows you wherever you go'?"

Alec's heart clenched with worry. Surely, he'd be discovered now. "Does Zachariah—?"

"Relax, boy. Zachariah's been sent elsewhere. To protect you, I convinced the Elders to assign this particular Awakened to me instead, since I was here anyway."

Alec blew out a relieved yet surprised breath. "Thank

you. But how did you convince them of that?" He and Vincent had usually been called in to take care of much older, higher-level targets. "A newly Awakened is a little beneath your skill set, isn't it?"

"From the surge that showed up on the grid, it appears to be a very unique individual." Vincent paused for dramatic effect as the mai tai disappeared from his hands. "We have reason to believe it's an actual Halfblood."

"A *Halfblood*? Are you serious? Shite. When's the last time one of those came along?"

"It's been eons." Vincent's expression darkened. "You know what they did to the last Halfblood, don't you?"

"I've heard about it, aye." Alec swallowed hard and glanced away, his concern for his own safety overshadowed by this new, potential threat to one of his classmates. Was it anyone he knew? If so, Alec felt sorry for them. Turning back to Vincent, he said, "So besides stalking me, I suppose you've been hanging around the school all week, looking for an aura?"

"Yes."

"Posing as who?"

"Whoever is convenient. I served you mashed potatoes in the cafeteria on Thursday."

Alec cringed and stood up, still grappling with this unwelcome news. "That's nothing short of creepy."

"Unfortunately, the target's been very difficult to identify. At first I thought it could be the case I've been working on for the past sixteen years."

"Oh. That one." Alec nodded slowly.

"However, now I'm not so sure. Although the boy I've set my sights on hasn't used any abilities while I've been around, he doesn't appear to have both of the talents I'd expect." Vincent heaved an irritated sigh. "And to make matters worse, of all times, I have to leave town."

"Where are you going?"

"There's a situation in New York that also requires my expertise and may take a week or more to resolve. The timing couldn't be worse. I *hate* to put this job on hold."

Alec sensed what was coming with rising dread. Striving for a casual tone, he said, "What's a week, more or less? If this Halfblood has just Awakened—"

"Depending on their power, a Halfblood could be a dangerous anomaly—and a prime threat if recruited by the other side. *They* may have made contact already. You know I can't let it wait. I need someone to handle this while I'm gone." Vincent fixed Alec with his gaze. "And there's only one person I can trust."

Alec backed away several steps, shaking his head vehemently. "No. *No.* Forget it, Vincent. I'm here to get away from all that."

"So you said." Vincent rose and crossed his arms over his chest. "You *also* said you want to stay here at Emerson. And you want me to keep quiet about it."

"Aye. But Vincent . . . I just can't."

"What would you rather?" Vincent asked, eyes blazing. "That I bring Zachariah back? He'll certainly discover you when he searches the school. And he won't be as understanding as I am. If you don't run and hide—more successfully this time—he'll turn you in. They'll incarcerate you for eternity with a bunch of monks, if they don't sentence you to death."

"Isn't that what they're going to do to the Halfblood, if we find him?" Alec said, his pulse racing. "I can't exchange someone else's life or freedom for my own."

"We don't know what the Council will do. Maybe they'll be more lenient this time. Unless, of course, we don't get to him first. They'll have no choice if he's already been corrupted. All I'm asking *you* to do is to identify him and make sure he doesn't get into any trouble until I get back. Do that, and I won't report you to the Elders."

Alec hesitated, frowning. "That's it? You just want me to . . . watch over him?"

"That's it. I'll take care of the rest when I return." Vincent looked at Alec, his dark eyes full of meaning. "Do me this one favor and I'll grant your wish. As long as you don't break any laws, or do any more foolish things—no matter how noble—you can stay here and play human for as long as you like."

Alec silently debated Vincent's offer, deeply conflicted. Did he want to do this—spy on his own schoolmates and condemn someone—however dangerous—to a dubious fate? Absolutely not. It felt like a deal with the devil. But if he didn't do it, Vincent would eventually find the Halfblood on his own anyway. And at this point, did Alec really have any alternative? He was lucky that Vincent was granting him this out. He took a deep breath.

"Okay. It's a deal," Alec said.

"Splendid." Vincent removed a postcard-size electronic tablet from his jacket pocket and set it on the table. "Here's a recap of everything I've done so far. Just pick up where I left off."

Alec stared down at the tablet, the gravity of their agreement starting to sink in. He barely noticed as Vincent walked to the door.

"Don't look so despondent, Alec. When all this is over, you will thank me. Happy hunting."

ten

%

When Claire's mom dropped her off at school on Monday, the debris from the scaffolding accident had all been cleared away, and it looked as if construction had been halted. Claire scanned the crowd but didn't see Alec anywhere. As she crossed to the stairs, a group of girls came up to her, concern written all over their faces.

"Claire! Oh my God! Are you okay?" asked the leader of the pack. It was Gabrielle Miller, the athletic goddess she'd often seen talking with Neil.

"I'm . . . fine." Claire was taken aback. Gabrielle had only talked to her twice in her life—once to welcome her to Emerson, another time to invite her to watch a varsity tennis match—and Gabrielle's clique had never so much as glanced in her direction. So why were they talking to her now?

"We heard you were, like, almost crushed to death by that scaffolding on Friday!" cried Ashley, the curly-haired blonde at Gabrielle's side.

"We were at lunch in the Village and missed the whole thing," put in Courtney, the third girl. "Everybody's talking about it. They said you were interviewed by the cops!"

"Is it true that Alec MacKenzie dragged you out from under the wreckage?" Gabrielle asked.

"Well, he . . . he didn't actually *drag* us, it was more like he tackled us, and—" Claire began.

"Oh my God!" shrieked Ashley. "I would so *love* to be tackled by Alec MacKenzie!"

"He is *so* hot!" agreed Gabrielle.

"I'd give anything to have *him* save my life," Courtney swooned. "He's that quiet, loner type, which is *so* sexy. And he has such an awesome accent."

"*So* awesome . . . ," echoed Ashley.

Just then, Erica and Brian joined them.

"Whassup, peoplez?" Brian said in his typical cheerful fashion.

Gabrielle's group whirled on them en masse, gasping at the sight of Brian's sling. "Oh my God!" Gabrielle exclaimed. "Is your arm broken?"

"No, it was just dislocated," Brian said.

"It's a miracle that you guys survived!" cried Courtney.

"Are you, like, having nightmares and shit?" asked Ashley.

"Well, it *was* terrifying," Erica admitted.

"It would have totally sucked if you'd died." Gabrielle shuddered. "I mean, school's just barely started! That would have ruined the whole first semester."

"Everybody's so freaked about it," added Courtney, "saying, 'It could have been me.'"

Gabrielle shouldered her backpack. "Brian, my dad's a doctor, so let me know if you need any painkillers."

"Thanks, but I'm already well supplied," Brian returned with a grin.

The three girls waved and dashed off. Claire glanced at her friends with eyebrows raised as they headed up the stairs in the group's wake. "That was strange."

"Not really. We're famous now." Erica smoothed back her shiny red hair, a huge smile on her face.

"Have you seen Alec?" Claire asked.

"Not yet," Brian answered.

"He's usually right on time." Claire was getting worried now. "I hope he's okay."

"He looked fine on Friday," Erica said.

Claire frowned. "Maybe he's avoiding school so we can't grill him about what happened."

"You just keep telling yourself that, Detective," Brian said, shaking his head.

All day long, the scaffolding accident was the major topic of conversation at school. So many people came up to ask Claire if she was okay—most of them people she'd never talked to until now—that it made her head spin. She'd never been the center of so much attention before. Admittedly, it was exciting—but at the same time, she felt uncomfortable. She hadn't really *done* anything, except not die. Alec was the one who deserved the recognition, but he was absent all day. Where was he?

After school, as Claire was grabbing her books from their locker, her eyes were drawn to the bulky, black mystery box sitting at the bottom. What *was* that thing, anyway? she wondered. Could any of her questions about Alec be answered by what was inside?

The box was locked tight, with a digital keypad on the lid. A thought occurred to her: Even if she couldn't open it, maybe she could put her new ability to some practical use and try to get a reading off the box—the same way she had with the bracelet. She knew this was prying, but her intense curiosity overcame her feelings of guilt.

Taking a deep breath, Claire extended her right hand over the lid of the box, then pressed her palm down onto it, concentrating on the feel of the cold, textured surface.

Nothing happened. Nothing at all.

Just then, she heard the sound of laughter and approaching footsteps. She quickly slammed the locker door and hurried off with a disappointed sigh. *It figures*, Claire thought, frowning. Nothing about her supposed ability had ever been predictable or convenient. If she was going to learn anything about Alec, it'd have to be the old-fashioned way.

That is, if he ever returned to school.

The following morning, traffic was so bad that Claire

arrived at school with only two minutes to spare before classes started. She made a beeline for history in the North Quad, arriving breathless just as the second bell rang.

To her astonishment, Mr. Patterson's door slammed shut in her face. Claire stopped short, speechless, then quietly tried the door handle. It was *locked*.

Claire had *never* been locked out of a class! It was bad enough that she'd received a D on her first history paper. This would only further jeopardize her grade—and, ultimately, her scholarship. Fighting back a wave of panic, she wandered around the side of the building. Through the classroom window, she could see Mr. Patterson already lecturing. She was about to head to the library to study when she noticed Alec sitting in his usual seat.

So he's back—and he's okay, she thought. A surge of intense relief swept through her. A second, lesser thought followed: Maybe she'd finally get a chance to talk to him today, and find out what planet he was from. Her cell phone vibrated in her pocket, signaling a new text message. *Crap!* she thought. She'd forgotten to turn off the damn thing when she arrived on campus. She yanked the phone out and glanced at the screen, fully expecting the text to be from her mom.

Instead, it was from an unknown number. All it said was:

Don't panic.

She glanced up and saw Alec secretly working his cell phone beneath the cover of his desk. Another message arrived:

I'll share my notes. —A

Claire smiled. That was nice of him. She was putting her cell phone away when the sharp rap of knuckles against glass brought her eyes back to the classroom window. She froze in horror. Mr. Patterson opened the window, his eyes fixed on her, Alec's cell phone in his hand.

"Congratulations, Miss Brennan," he said with a derisive smile. "You and Mr. MacKenzie have just earned yourselves detention tomorrow."

eleven

Alec stared at the green wad of gum that was stuck to the underside of the cafeteria table just inches from his face. What possessed these kids, he wondered, to engage in such a repulsive, germ-spreading habit? From his awkward position, seated cross-legged on the tile floor, he raised his weapon—a butter knife.

"I'm sorry I got you into this mess." Alec began chiseling away at the offensive lump.

Claire smiled, similarly employed beneath a nearby table. "It's okay. Getting EMD will help defuse my rep as a goody-goody."

The administration at Emerson apparently believed that it was best for student growth to focus their time after school on athletics, the arts, and other extracurricular activities, so detention—instead of being after school—was served *before*. Hence the name Early Morning Detention, or EMD. As demeaning as this task was, Alec didn't mind being here—both because he was with Claire, and because it was a welcome distraction from the assignment that had been weighing on him ever since Vincent's visit. Alec knew he was supposed to be keeping an eye out for the Awakened at school—he should have started looking yesterday—but so far, he hadn't been able to bring himself to even glance at the data on Vincent's tablet. Thankfully, at least Claire was out of the running, since the target was male.

He glanced at her as she concentrated on removing a particularly difficult piece of gum. Even at seven in the morning, crouched beneath a cafeteria table, she looked bright and beautiful, and best of all, blissfully unaware of it. He wondered what she was thinking. The whole school seemed to be talking about the scaffolding incident, and he felt certain it was still fresh in Claire's mind. Vincent believed Alec had covered up the use of his powers well, but Alec was unconvinced. He'd been so reluctant to talk to Claire that he'd deliberately cut school Monday, but he couldn't keep that up forever. She hadn't said a word about it yesterday after history. Maybe—just maybe—he'd imagined that look she'd given him after he tackled them, and she didn't suspect a thing.

They worked in silence for a few minutes, accompanied by the sounds of clanging metal pans and fervent chopping from the nearby kitchen. Alec was trying to decide how to begin a conversation when, thankfully, she did it for him.

"I've been meaning to tell you," Claire said with a cautious glance in his direction, "after what happened on Friday, we were . . . *I* was worried all weekend."

His pulse quickened. *Shite. Here it comes.* "Worried?"

"Yeah, I was afraid you might have been hurt in the accident."

"Oh." Was that all that was worrying her? Relief curled through him. Alec popped off a wad of pink gum, dropped it into a trash bag, and scooted along the floor to the next table. "No, I'm fine. I was really sorry to hear about Brian's shoulder, though—and I'm glad you and Erica weren't hurt."

"Thanks. We all felt bad that we couldn't call you or anything. Did you know you're not listed in the Emerson directory?"

From the expression on her face, he could see that she was dying to probe further—just as he was dying to change the subject. "I like to keep that information private." Alec hoped his tone sounded casual.

"Why?"

"Because I live by myself." He was grateful that he could at least answer that question truthfully. "The administration is okay with it, but I thought it'd seem strange to others if a student was listed without any parents or guardians."

"How'd you pull that off? I thought it was against the law for minors to live alone."

"I'm emancipated." He'd told this story so often over the past month—to school administrators, his landlord, the guy he'd bought his car from—it was starting to feel as if it had really happened. "Last year, I moved to northern California to live with my uncle Gregory. Unfortunately, he turned out to be a raging alcoholic, so I petitioned the court to let me live on my own—but he still pays my tuition."

"Wow. That must have been hard. But don't you have any other relatives you could live with?"

"Not really, no." It was the perfect opening: He could slip in a few tidbits to address his previous mistakes. "At first, after my parents died, I lived with my grandfather in Spain—but he's an anarchist, and they threw him in prison. Then I stayed with an aunt who's a missionary in Korea, but her boyfriend wasn't too keen on having me there, and neither was the aunt with seventeen cats in Edinburgh." *That should tie things up nicely—if she buys it.*

Claire frowned, sliding to another table, where she began de-gumming its underside. "Brutal. I don't envy your family reunions."

He laughed.

"But at least you *have* some family," Claire continued. "I don't know where any of mine is. My mother is the only relative I have."

"Really? Why? Is your mother the black sheep of the family? Did she run away and join the circus, or marry someone they didn't approve of?"

Claire shrugged. "I wish I knew. She refuses to talk about it. All I know is they got married, had me, and then he left."

"Do you even know who your father is?"

"Nope. I like to think he was a Nobel Prize–winning scientist who had to return to vitally important, top-secret work, and then died rescuing his lab workers from a fire. Or the emperor of some small island nation forced into hiding when a coup took over." She sighed. "But the truth is, I think he's just some deadbeat who knocked up my mom at seventeen and bailed."

"I'm sorry. I know how hard it is, growing up without a father."

"How old were you when your parents died?"

"Ten." The truth, again—although age ten had been so long ago for him, he could barely remember it.

"Now it's my turn to say I'm sorry."

"It's okay."

Claire fell silent once more as they continued scraping. Alec felt her eyes on him, and he sensed that she was drumming up the courage to ask him something else.

"By the way," she said hesitantly, "about Friday . . ."

He froze. "Aye?"

"I haven't thanked you properly for the whole . . . saving-my-life thing."

"Oh. That." His heart pounded. "Don't even think about it."

"I can't help thinking about it. Alec, what you did, it was amazing. You *saved us*. But then you left without a word. I get that you like your privacy, but why did you disappear like that?"

Okay, Alec thought. Still a harmless enough question that he could deal with. "I'll tell you the same thing I told the police when they called me. I just didn't want the attention."

"Because of what you did?"

Alarm flickered through him. "What?"

"That scaffolding was going to hit us—we were all toast. But I saw you raise your arm as if you were pushing it away, and the whole thing wavered and crashed off to the side. Then you lifted us to safety and vanished like a superhero in a comic book. How did you do it?"

Well. There it is, Alec thought. *She did see, after all—and she certainly isn't beating around the bush about it.*

The first bell rang, giving him the reprieve he desperately needed. "I don't know what you mean, Claire. I didn't do anything," he said quickly, as they both stood up. "Maybe I held up my hand protectively for one confused second, but then I just acted on instinct to get us all out of danger."

Claire nodded slowly. His reply clearly disappointed her, but she seemed to accept it. "Okay." Before she could say more, the kitchen supervisor appeared. He signed their detention slips, releasing them. They dropped their bags of gum in the trash and made their way to the door, where Claire paused, turning to him.

"Well, whatever happened, Alec, thank you again for what you did. I'm really, really grateful." Unexpectedly, she wrapped her arms around him and gave him a hug.

The action caught Alec totally off guard, and he froze again, his heart going wild. No one had *ever* hugged him before—except his parents, and that had been so long ago, he'd almost forgotten what it felt like. "You're . . . welcome," he stammered, raising his arms and awkwardly hugging her back.

When she drew away, their gazes met briefly. He saw that her cheeks were as flushed as his felt, and there was a new expression on her face that seemed to mirror his own confusion.

"Bye," she said quickly. Averting her eyes, she darted off without another word.

twelve

Claire hurried down the ramp toward her first class, her pulse pounding in her ears. What had just happened?

She didn't believe Alec's version of the events on Friday—there was no way he or anyone else was going to explain them away as natural—and there were so many other things about him that still didn't fit. But that wasn't the uppermost thing on her mind at the moment.

All she'd intended was to give Alec a quick, friendly hug, but while she was in his arms, the feelings that had risen within her had taken her completely by surprise.

Through the thin layer of Alec's T-shirt, she'd felt the rapid beat of his heart. In response, her own heart had begun to race so fast, she'd felt as if it might suddenly burst out of the too-confined space of her chest. The firm touch of his hands against her back, the sensation of his body in contact with the length of hers, had caused a heat to rise deep inside her that—as far as she knew—had nothing to do with the psychic weirdness that had been happening lately. When the hug ended, she'd been so self-conscious, she could hardly look at him.

She recognized these feelings; she had them—or used to have them—in a somewhat less intense fashion whenever she was around Neil, or was thinking about Neil. Why was she feeling like this now, with Alec? Was she attracted to him? If so, when the hell had *that* started, and why hadn't she noticed it before?

Claire was still mulling the questions over later that morning when she entered the theater building for Concert Singers.

"You hugged him?" Erica grinned when Claire brought her up to speed. "That's a clever tactic. Did you get a vision off him?"

"What? No! It wasn't a tactic," Claire insisted, blushing. "I'm just grateful to him. I wasn't even thinking about visions."

"Did you touch his skin when you hugged?" Brian chimed in. "Or just his clothes?"

Claire thought for a moment. "Just his clothes."

"You must be right," Brian told Erica. "Her powers operate strictly by skin-to-skin contact. Except, on rare occasions, when she's touching an object whose owner is involved in a traumatic—"

"Will you please stop talking about me like I'm a lab rat?" Claire interrupted, annoyed.

"How did Alec react to this hug?" Erica was still smiling. "I'll bet he swooned."

"Why do you say that?" Claire's blush deepened despite herself.

"Because"—Erica rolled her eyes—"Alec is clearly nuts about you."

Claire stared at her. "What?"

"You mean you didn't know that, CB?" Brian shook his head. "I swear, girls are so clueless sometimes."

Claire took her seat and warmed up along with the rest of the class, processing this news. Was it really possible that Alec liked her? The thought was so new and unexpected, as were the feelings rioting inside her, that she wasn't sure what to believe.

Out of the corner of her eye she saw Brian surreptitiously scribbling on a scrap of paper. Folding the note into a tiny square, he silently passed it to the boy on his left, nodding in Claire's direction. The note made its way down the row, finally arriving on Claire's music stand.

Still singing along with the choir, she covertly opened it and read:

So, when you hugged—did you feel Alec's heartbeat?

Claire stifled a laugh. She looked at Brian from her seat and nodded emphatically, patting her chest one-handed with a rapid drumbeat. He grinned triumphantly and made a motion with his hand for her to turn the note over. She did. It read:

See. Told you. He's not a vampire.

thirteen

❧

A lec sat in his car, watching as the other students vacated the junior parking lot. All day, he hadn't been able to stop thinking about the hug he'd exchanged with Claire in the cafeteria.

The sensation of Claire's warm body pressed against his—her arms locked around him—her face nestled against his shoulder—the fragrance of her shampoo—it had all been so incredible and so intoxicating. He'd been distracted ever since, unable to concentrate in class, much less on the assignment Vincent had given him. He sensed that Claire had felt it, too, but he couldn't be sure.

At least Claire seemed placated enough after their conversation to stop asking questions about the *incident*. Alec sighed and leaned back in his seat. It was time, he reminded himself, to stop thinking about Claire and focus on the task at hand. His very freedom depended on it.

Vincent's digital tablet felt heavy in his hand. Alec still dreaded the thought of turning it on. Once he started a hunt, it became all-consuming, and he knew he wouldn't feel comfortable at school anymore—or with himself. It wasn't just the idea of going back to work that bothered him, however temporarily. It was the possible consequence that awaited the target, especially if he was actually a Halfblood. The Council's decision, however, was out of his hands—and would occur whether or not Alec got involved. In fact, it would be much worse for the Awakened if Alec didn't find him before the Fallen did.

Reluctantly, Alec pressed the tablet's power button. The screen lit up, and with one click Alec restored it to the last file Vincent had opened: a series of detailed notes with bullet points culminating in a surveillance photograph of Vincent's prime suspect. Alec almost dropped the device in astonishment.

It was Neil Mitchum.

Alec leaned on the rooftop railing eighteen stories above the sleeping city, watching the ribbons of empty, illuminated streets stretch away westward toward the distant, endless expanse of dark ocean.

Could it be true? Was Choir Boy the Awakened that Vincent was looking for? If so, it would make sense.

Everybody said Neil had a beautiful singing voice, which of course came with the territory. Apparently he was the fastest sprinter in the school and a superstar soccer player—that could be a sign. Plus, the kid had unbelievable charm and influence—a definite potential talent. Somehow, Neil had managed to convince a music teacher to add an untested singer to an exclusive honors choir at the eleventh hour. And Alec couldn't forget how incredibly shy and tongue-tied Claire had been around Neil on Book Day, or how swiftly that shyness had evaporated under Neil's influence in the two weeks since. The last time Alec had been around someone with such presence, it was his mark in Panama five years ago. Who knew what other hidden abilities Neil might possess?

Alec shook his head, frowning, and leaned against the wall, his back to the city. Taking his guitar from its case, he began plucking away at the strings, filling the air with a melody of his own creation.

It *could* just be the jealousy talking, Alec admitted to himself. It seemed that every time Claire had expressed even the remotest flicker of interest in Alec, Neil had shown up and diverted her attention. If Neil really was the Halfblood, it would be very convenient. In one fell swoop, his competition for Claire would be gone.

Alec's blood ran cold at the thought of what the Council might do once Vincent turned Neil in. Alec wouldn't wish that fate on anyone, not even Neil. But Vincent was right. Humanity was probably safer if the Halfblood was in the custody of his own kind. He'd give Vincent what he wanted. He'd identify the Awakened, protect him during Vincent's absence, then turn over the information and be done with it.

Alec's mind worked on his strategy as he played faster and faster, a musical frenzy, like a train racing down a track. It wouldn't be enough to just keep a lookout at school. The Fallen made it their business to corrupt the innocent. If they'd caught wind of this fledgling, they were likely to descend at any time to sway him to their side. Generally, they favored meetings in public places, where—with so many onlookers—it was difficult for someone like Alec to exercise any overt protective powers. Alec doubted, however, that they would dare to make an appearance at a closed campus like Emerson Academy, where they'd probably stick out like a sore thumb. *No,* he thought, *they'll choose some other location to make contact.*

Alec struck a final chord, the note reverberating in the stillness of the night.

He'd just have to be on hyperalert, and keep a particularly close eye on Neil.

fourteen

❧

Muted sunlight filtered down gently through a canopy of tall trees, which sheltered Claire in a realm of delicious coolness. She was strolling through a forest, wearing a beautiful, filmy white dress that reached her ankles—a dress she'd never seen before. The ground, strewn with pine needles, felt springy beneath her sandaled feet. From somewhere not too far off she heard the crash of ocean waves and the cry of a seagull, and when she inhaled, she smelled the salty tang of the sea.

What is this place? Claire wondered. *How did I get here?* She'd never been in a forest so close to the ocean before. She was possessed by the need to find something—or someone—but she didn't know who or what.

About ten yards ahead, a soft golden light emanated from between the trunks of two trees. She ran toward the light, which seemed to be calling to her. As she drew nearer, a figure appeared: a dark form surrounded by an aura of gleaming yellow.

Claire stopped, crying out in astonishment. *It was Alec.* He glided closer, until he stood immediately before her.

"You wondered what I am?" Alec said gently, his voice echoing as if they were inside a cathedral. "Go ahead. Find out." He opened his shirt, grabbed her hand, and pressed it to his beautifully sculpted chest.

As their skin made contact, the light surrounding Alec increased in intensity, growing so bright that she was forced to shield her eyes with her other hand. Claire gasped again as a sizzling heat ran up her arm and spread through her entire body. Trembling, she saw that *she was now glowing, too*—although the light around her wasn't yellow. It was a shimmering emerald green. She felt as if her very blood were on fire—but it was a delicious sensation, an electric intensity more exhilarating than anything she'd ever felt in her life.

Alec's eyes were filled with undisguised affection as he took Claire firmly in his embrace. *"Now you know,"* he whispered, his face just inches from hers.

"But . . . I don't know anything." Claire's heart drummed in her chest as his lean body molded against her own. Was he going to kiss her? Suddenly, desperately, she yearned for it.

Alec lowered his head closer, until their lips nearly touched. . . .

Claire awoke with a start, sitting up and breathing hard, her pulse thundering.

My God, she thought. That was the most vivid dream she'd ever had. Scooting back in bed, she collapsed against the headboard as she struggled to return to reality.

Where did all that come from? she wondered. Why was Alec *glowing* in her dream? Why had *she* been glowing? *What in the world did it mean?*

She'd been so focused on Neil for the past two years that she hadn't noticed any other boys, or considered that anyone else might like her. Neil was finally showing a hint of interest in her, but at the same time, here was this other gorgeous, intelligent boy with whom—she couldn't deny it—she felt a genuine connection. Ever since their hug in the cafeteria, she hadn't been able to stop thinking about Alec.

Claire knew she should be excited. But Alec was such an enigma. It'd be one thing if he was just a normal guy who was maybe a little secretive about some things. However, despite his protests to the contrary, something *definitely* was different about him, and no one could explain it away to her satisfaction. She had never seen anyone glow in real life, but after the way Alec had saved their lives on Friday, she was beginning to believe he was capable of it, and maybe a whole lot more. Whoever—or whatever—Alec was, he was sexy, powerful, brilliant, fascinating . . . and frightening . . . all at the same time.

Claire's thoughts were interrupted by the sound of her door quietly opening. Her mother stood silhouetted in the doorway.

"You all right, honey?" her mom said. "I thought I heard you call out."

"I just had a weird dream."

Her mom crossed the room and sat down on the bed beside Claire, regarding her in the slice of light shining in from the hall. "What was your dream about?" she asked, brushing back Claire's hair from her eyes.

Claire felt her cheeks grow warm. She sometimes told her mom about her dreams, but she didn't want to share the details of this one. "I don't remember much. Just that I was lost in a strange forest."

"Well, you're safe now." Her mom hugged her tightly.

There she goes again, Claire thought. *Always talking about being safe.*

Her mom's voice broke as she continued, "All week, I've been so upset about that horrible, horrible accident. I keep thinking about how I almost lost you."

Claire returned her mom's intense hug. "I'm totally fine, Mom."

Her mom sat back, wiping the corners of her eyes. "Are you? Are things okay at school?"

"They're great," Claire reassured her. "Even history is starting to look up. So many kids got low grades on that first paper that my teacher said it wouldn't count. He devoted a whole class period to the basics of the analytic writing style that he wants, and how to avoid overwriting. I think I get it now."

"I'm so glad."

"How are things with you, Mom? You okay?"

"I am. More than okay, actually. Work is going great. And . . . well . . . I wasn't sure whether or not to mention this, but—"

"What?"

Her mom took a breath, and despite the low light in the room, Claire thought she saw a blush creep up her cheeks. "I thought about what you said the other day. About me living like a nun. And how maybe it's time for me to start . . . going out a little."

Claire's jaw dropped in surprise. "Did you meet somebody?"

"Yes. Well, sort of. It was at Peet's Coffee Shop on Sunday. I was just leaving, and I forgot my laptop bag on the table. This handsome man came running after me to return it, and after I thanked him, we chatted for a few minutes. His name is Dennis and he was . . . nice."

"Mom, this is major!" Claire cried, ecstatic. "Did he ask you out?"

"He asked me to meet him for coffee sometime and gave me his email address. I didn't want to do anything, though, until I'd talked to you first, to see how you'd feel about it. All these years, it's just been the two of us—I want to make sure you're comfortable with the idea."

"Of course I am! It's just a coffee date, Mom. Say yes, for God's sake! Go! Have a good time."

"Thanks, honey. Maybe I will. Go back to sleep now." She kissed Claire's cheek, hugging her again, and then stood up and moved to the door. "I hope you have better dreams."

"Good night, Mom." Claire settled back beneath the covers, closing her eyes. She couldn't stop smiling. It'd be great to see her mom have a boyfriend. Maybe she'd lighten up and let Claire date, too.

More importantly, it might keep them in L.A. a little longer.

"It's Thursday, people," Claire announced as she smashed the Ping-Pong ball across the table toward Brian. "Do you know what that means?"

"That tomorrow's Friday?" Brian returned the ball with a swing of his good arm.

"Oh!" Erica gasped from her spot on the sidelines, clearly getting Claire's meaning. "Thursday! Did you get your Spanish quiz back?"

"Yep." The three of them were relaxing in the Student Life Center after school. Aside from them, the place was deserted.

"So how did Neil do?" Erica prodded.

Claire smiled proudly. "B minus."

"Wow," Erica noted. "That's a *huge* improvement from what you saw."

"When he gets here for your little study session," Brian

asked, "we don't have to be all after-school-special, do we? With the thumbs-up and the encouraging grins?"

"Please, no. Just keep a low profile. I think Neil already feels self-conscious enough about the tutoring."

As Brian nodded, Erica held up a Ping-Pong paddle like a microphone and quipped in her announcer voice, "Congratulations, Claire Brennan! You have proved, without a doubt, that the future is not set. And that the voices in your head are clearly aligned with the forces of good. Now, which man are you going to choose: Neil, your long-time crush, or Alec, an even more handsome and brilliant guy, who has a crush on *you*?"

Claire blushed. "I don't want to choose anyone. At least not yet, until I get to know them both better."

"Ah, a ménage à trois," Erica mused. "That's an interesting approach."

"Erica!" Claire protested, her blush deepening in dismay.

Just then, Brian slammed the ball to the right corner. "Success! Yao beats Brennan, twenty-one to fifteen. One-handed, no less!"

"Oh, that was fair," Claire grumbled, extending her hand for a conciliatory shake.

Brian stowed his paddle in his sling and reached out to accept, but then recoiled. "Whoa, CB, are you crazy? I'm not gonna have you spelunking through my psyche and foretelling my future. *No touching!*"

Claire sighed, retrieved the ball, and propped her paddle on it atop the table. "Great, now I'm a leper."

"You're not a leper," Erica said, trying to be reassuring. "But I know what Brian means. I'd love to know what my future holds, if I could be sure it'd be *good*. But what if it isn't? And the idea of you touching me and maybe seeing something through my perspective—*that's* creepy. What if it's something I'd rather keep secret?"

"Fine," Claire muttered, tugging at the sleeves of her hoodie until they reached down to her fingertips. "I'll keep my hands to myself from now on."

"Good plan." Brian turned to Erica and said in a humorous accent, "So, Miss Fischer, do you dare to challenge the Ping-Pong *Master*?"

Erica grinned cockily and took Claire's place at the foot of the table. As the two began to play, Claire crossed to the activities bulletin board, which was littered with brightly colored sign-up sheets. Her attention was drawn to one entitled "Homecoming Assembly Entertainment Auditions." She scanned the list of student names scrawled on it. There were some solo acts, some duets, and even some trios. Claire suddenly remembered Erica's suggestion that Alec should try out, but his name wasn't listed. She'd have to remind him about that. He had a great voice and deserved a chance to show it off.

That was when the vision hit.

Heat infused Claire's body, and she began to tremble,

her knees giving way beneath her. She fumbled dizzily onto the nearby couch and closed her eyes. *Why is this happening to me now?* she wondered, alarmed.

She heard Erica cry, "Oh my God, she's having another one."

Then Claire's mind emptied of thought, replaced by an image—the same image she'd seen in that weird episode a week ago.

A shadowy figure stood surrounded by inky darkness, lit from behind by a bright yellow light. The face was indistinguishable, but an arm was stretched out toward Claire, beckoning, accompanied by a whispering voice.

"Claire! Claire!" The voice was weathered and raspy, as if it required great effort to speak. The ensuing words were distorted and filled with gaps, like a radio transmitting on a bad frequency. But this time, Claire recognized a decidedly feminine timbre in the speaker's voice, and a British accent, and she could understand more of the warning than before:

"You're in danger . . . because of your special gift. Only . . . can protect and help you . . . Come to Twin Palms . . . Helena."

It finished with the same eerie pronouncement: "Don't tell anyone."

Claire gasped aloud, her eyes blinking open as the voice and image disappeared from her mind. Her heart pounded with anxiety as she struggled to ground herself in reality once again. Brian and Erica stood over her with confounded expressions.

"Wow. Was that what I think it was?" Brian asked.

"What did you see?" Erica cried, excited.

Claire mopped the sweat from her brow with a shirt-sleeve. Should she answer? It was the second time she'd been told not to tell anyone. But they both already knew! And she desperately needed their help to figure this out. "It was that same weird vision again with the raspy voice, the one I got last week in the bathroom."

"Yeah, the one that told you to help Neil," Erica said.

"I think I was wrong about that." Claire shook her head slowly. "I heard more words this time—it was definitely a woman, and I think she was trying to tell me that *I'm* the one who needs help."

"You? Why do you think that?" Brian asked.

"She started off saying, 'You're in danger . . . because of your special gift.' Then it cut out again, but I caught: 'can protect and help you.'"

"Wait a minute. I thought this gift of yours was all about touch," Erica said. "What did you touch?"

"Nothing. I was just standing here."

Brian pursed his lips, thinking. "When you had this vision before, were you touching anything or anyone?"

"No."

"So it was a female voice that said the exact same thing as before, only more clearly?" Brian asked.

Claire nodded.

"Maybe it's Claire's own subconscious that's warning

her," Erica suggested.

"I doubt it," Claire replied. "The voice had a British accent."

"*Interesting,*" Brian mused. "Claire, I think you've got two different psychic phenomena going on here."

"What do you mean?"

"I think the visions you get when you touch people or things are one type. But this one's not a vision at all. It's a *message.*"

"A message?" Claire repeated, intrigued.

"Yeah, like that alien signal in *Contact,*" Brian continued. "A repeated warning, sent from somewhere else, *by someone else.*"

"He could be right," Erica exclaimed. "You're seeing a figure talking *to you,* instead of being inside someone's body."

"Oh—that's true." Claire shook her head, puzzled. "But who is it? Why is she sending the message? Why does she want to help me, of all people?"

"Good question." Brian scratched his head.

"And *what* is she warning me about? What could I possibly be in danger from? Death by meteor? Am I going to be hit by a bus? Do I have a brain tumor?"

"You're joking, but I'm deadly serious, Claire," Brian said. "If you're really in danger because you're psychic and there's someone who can help or protect you, we'd better find out who it is."

"And *fast*," Erica added, frowning with newfound worry.

Fear sparked through Claire's veins. "You're right. But how are we going to do that?"

"Did the voice say anything else?" Brian asked.

"Yeah. It said, 'Don't tell anyone.'"

They all laughed nervously. "Too late for that," observed Erica.

"It also said two other things. 'Come to Twin Palms.' And 'Helena.'"

"Twin Palms?" Brian asked. "You mean like the mall in the Valley?"

"I don't know. Maybe. Do you think her name is Helena?"

"Could be." Erica whipped out her phone and browsed the mall's website. "Maybe Helena is a psychic, and she's waiting to talk to you at the Twin Palms Mall."

"Let's go check it out," Brian suggested.

"I'm all for being proactive," Claire intoned dubiously, "but how would we find one particular person named Helena at a mall?"

"Maybe she'll find you," offered Brian.

Erica, focused on her phone, added, "We can come up with a plan in the car. I say we head up to the Valley right now and check this out."

"Who's checking out what now in the Valley?" Neil had popped into the room and was looking at them all questioningly.

The three of them froze.

"Um . . . ," Claire stammered, embarrassed that in all the excitement, she'd completely forgotten her study date with Neil. "We're checking out . . ."

". . . whether or not they still have this awesome pair of boots on sale at Twin Palms!" Erica finished for her, flashing an advertisement on her phone.

Neil's face fell. He glanced at Claire. "Wait. You guys are going to a mall? In the *Valley*? I thought we were gonna study Spanish."

Claire was flattered by the look of disappointment on Neil's face. She hesitated. She didn't want to cancel on him so last minute, but she couldn't tell him the truth, either. "You did so well on your quiz, Neil. I think we should postpone this till tomorrow, take a day off, and celebrate. Come with us."

"I didn't do *that* well, Claire," Neil responded.

"It's a matter of perspective, amigo," Brian said with an overenthusiastic smile and a thumbs-up. "You could have failed that quiz, but you didn't!"

"Yeah!" Erica said brightly, flashing a covert, reluctant look at Claire. "Join us. It'll be a field trip. We can speak Spanish in the car."

"Don't you take French?" Neil asked, as they herded him out the door.

"Whatever," Erica replied. "*¡Vamanos!*"

Claire and Erica pretended to browse in the Boot Shack for ten minutes, then left the guys at a video game store and strolled out into the crowded shopping center.

"What were you thinking?" Erica said in a low, exasperated voice. "Why did you invite Neil? It makes this all so complicated!"

"It would have been rude to just ditch him. We can do this, even with him here. Let's just make a plan."

"It was your vision. *You* make the plan."

"*You're* the one who said we should come to the mall and look for someone named Helena!" Claire hissed.

"It sounded easier in theory, I admit. God. There are hundreds of people here, and three stories of shops. Where are we supposed to start?"

"Maybe Brian was right. Maybe we don't need to do anything. Maybe whoever sent the signal can sense that I'm here and will come to me."

Erica popped a piece of gum into her mouth. "I'm always a fan of doing nothing."

They stood there, eagerly watching for any glimmer of interest from the stream of female shoppers passing by, but no one in particular glanced their way. After a few minutes of that, Erica said, "This is weird. I feel like a hooker. A lesbian hooker."

Claire's eyes were suddenly drawn to a large fixture on the mall floor six feet ahead of them. *Oh my God,* she thought. *How could we have missed it?*

"What?" Erica said, noticing Claire's stunned expression.

Claire strode forward and pointed to the mall directory and map. Under Specialty Stores, it listed a shop on the second floor called Helena's.

"Holy crap," Erica said. "We've been so short-bus about this."

"So where are we going next, amigos?" Neil asked, carrying a bag from the video game store as he and Brian caught up to them.

Claire gestured toward a spot on the map. "Helena's."

"Helena's?" Brian repeated. "Why do we need to go there?"

Claire and Erica shot him a silent glare of death.

"Oh! *Oh!*" Brian cried, his eyes widening with comprehension. "I've . . . heard about that place. I've always wanted to go there!"

"Why? What do they sell?" Neil asked.

Brian stared at him blankly, like a deer in headlights. "Uh . . ."

"We don't want to spoil the surprise," Claire said, boldly taking Neil by the arm. "You'll see when we get there."

Five minutes later they stood outside the shop, its name emblazoned in metallic purple script: HELENA'S. The shop windows were stuffed with New Age and occult trinkets, from crystal balls and pentagrams to Ouija boards and funky-looking candles in every shade of the rainbow.

"This is the shop you were all so excited about?" Neil asked Brian curiously.

"No . . ." Brian feigned surprise. "I thought it was the *other* Helena's, the one that sells . . . cookies."

"Well, we're going in," Claire said emphatically. "How about if you guys go do something else for a few minutes?"

"Great idea," Brian and Neil responded in unison. They took off like a shot.

Claire and Erica pushed open the glass door, triggering a motion sensor that chirped melodiously. Soft, atmospheric music drifted from speakers above. Sun-, moon-, and star-shaped ornaments of all sizes hung from the ceiling, and several shelves of books stood at the back.

"Okay. This is . . . ," Erica began.

"Lame?" Claire finished under her breath.

"I was going to say *cool*."

"You're into this kind of stuff?"

"Not really. But I'm trying to get into the spirit of things. This could be promising! It's much more likely that you'll find a psychic here than in a clothing store or a cookie shop."

They moved to the long glass counter, where silver jewelry was on display, and a middle-aged woman with frizzy red hair and flowy clothing was affixing price stickers to a stack of glittery picture frames. Claire smiled at her. "Nice store."

"Thank you."

Claire deflated a little as she realized the woman didn't have a British accent.

"We just opened a couple of weeks ago," the woman continued with a smile. "I'm still trying to get things in order. Are you looking for anything in particular?"

"No. We're just browsing," Erica said.

"I'm curious, though," Claire added, "about the name of the store. Are you Helena?"

"Oh, no. Helena is my kitty." She gestured behind the counter to a basket at her feet, where a large calico cat was resting.

Claire and Erica exchanged a look. Was this what had brought them here? Claire wondered. A psychic cat?

"Can I pet her?" Claire asked.

"Sure. My Helena loves people."

Claire scooted behind the counter and crouched down by the cat's basket, then hesitated. What would it be like to get a vision off an animal?

The cat stared back at her. As Erica knelt down beside her, Claire tentatively extended her hand and began stroking the animal's soft fur. It purred contentedly.

"Anything?" Erica whispered.

"Nothing," Claire whispered back. "I think it's just a cat."

"Maybe we were wrong. Maybe it's not a person—or animal—named Helena after all. Maybe it's the *store itself,* at this mall, that you were supposed to visit. There might be something here that's important."

"You think?"

"Why don't you try touching some other stuff and see what happens?"

Claire stood up, remarked how beautiful the cat was, and began wandering around the shop. She picked up merchandise randomly but didn't get a reading off anything.

The entry chime sounded as Neil and Brian entered. "So, have you two found anything cool?" Brian asked, eyeing them meaningfully.

Claire shook her head. "Just a nice cat. Named *Helena*."

"Ah," Brian responded with a nod.

The entry chime chirped again. Claire turned and couldn't help but stare at the new arrivals: two guys and a girl who looked to be in their early twenties, all of whom had a bunch of piercings and tattoos. It was as if the whole atmosphere in the place changed with their presence. They reminded Claire of rock stars. They exuded confidence, and for some reason she felt drawn to them.

The trio glided into the store and instantly separated, like fighter planes breaking formation. As the two guys browsed, looking a bit bored, the girl strolled in Claire's direction, nodding at her with a friendly but commanding smile. "Hey."

"Hey," Claire responded. The girl was tall and breathtakingly beautiful, with long, inky black hair that flowed down her back. She wore a tight, red plaid dress over black leggings, dark lipstick, heavy eyeliner, black nail polish, and lots of dangly silver jewelry. The girl casually studied the merchandise, pausing when she reached Claire's side. Feeling self-conscious that she'd been staring, Claire glanced away.

The girl plucked a small, silver dream-catcher pendant from a display. It was decorated with turquoise beads and tiny silver feathers. "Have you ever used one of these?" Her voice was soft, rich, and elegant, like molten chocolate. And it was decidedly British.

Claire's pulse leapt. She darted a look at her friends, who seemed equally mystified that this goddess was chatting with her. "No," she answered.

"They're like spiderwebs," the girl replied, twirling the pendant in her fingers. "They trap your nightmares, so only the good dreams filter through. When the morning sun hits the net, all your bad dreams are instantly burned to ash."

"Like a vampire net?" Brian said.

"Kind of," the girl replied with a raised eyebrow, as if she considered that a strange question.

"That's cool." Claire nodded.

The girl fixed her eyes on Claire for a long beat, almost studying her. "I think you should buy this. I think it will help you."

"Why do you say that?" Claire asked, taken aback.

"You look like a very intuitive person. Like someone who dreams a lot—even when you're awake. This would protect you."

Claire almost gasped. Protect her? *Oh my God*, she thought. This must be the person she'd been searching for! She had a British accent and everything! It wasn't as raspy as the voice in her vision, but that warning had been very garbled. Did she have a message for her? Claire exchanged a look with Erica, who was clearly on the same page and silently acknowledged her excitement. Before Claire could respond, however, Neil piped up brightly, "You are definitely the most persuasive salesperson I've ever met. Do you work here?"

The girl laughed politely. "I don't believe in work."

The two boys joined them, flanking the group on either side.

"How're you guys doing?" one of them asked with an inviting smile. He was tall and broad-shouldered, with colorful tattoos covering his neck and forearms, his shoulder-length black hair pulled into a ponytail. A heavy silver chain dangled from the studded belt that held up his strategically ripped jeans.

"Celeste, who're your new friends?" added the other. He was shorter and stockier, with a shaved head and bushy goatee, and piercing dark eyes in a bulldog face. Both guys wore black T-shirts stretched across their muscled chests.

Celeste? Claire thought. Then she realized it didn't

matter what the girl's name was, if Helena's was just the place where they were supposed to meet.

"We haven't been properly introduced yet," Celeste said with a slow smile, as she replaced the dream catcher on the jewelry rack with a smooth, manicured hand. "I'm Celeste. The tall one's Javed. The other one's Rico."

"I'm Claire. This is Erica, Brian, and Neil."

"So what are you guys doing later?" Javed asked, still smiling.

"Do you like hockey?" Rico added.

"We won seven rink-side seats to a Kings exhibition game tonight, and four of our friends just bailed," Celeste explained. The threesome spoke in such quick succession, it was as if they were completing one another's thoughts.

"Oh, wow!" Brian exclaimed.

"I've always wanted to see the Kings!" Claire heard herself say. She glanced at Erica, sensing that she understood how important this could be. If she was in some kind of danger, and these people knew something about it, it made sense for her to go with them—didn't it? She couldn't explain it, but even though they'd just met, she somehow felt connected to all three of them. They had a carefree, casual manner, but still seemed genuine and sincere. On the other hand, she didn't know a thing about them. Why didn't she feel more nervous?

"I'm sorry if we're coming on a little strong," Celeste said, as if noticing Claire's wary expression. She grinned, flashing her perfect white teeth. "You guys just seem cool."

"If we left right now, we'd make it downtown in time for dinner," Rico added.

"They make great nachos at Staples Center," Javed chimed in.

"What do you think, Erica?" Claire said slowly. "You're our chauffeur."

"I'd love to go," Erica replied cautiously. "We probably need to check with our parents first—school night, and all. But I'm sure they'll all be cool with it."

Yeah, as if my mom would ever be cool with it, Claire thought.

Surprisingly, Neil reached over and put his arm around her with a warm smile. "It all sounds great. How about if we follow in our car?"

Before Celeste could answer, the door chimed yet again, this time accompanied by the sound of heavy footsteps. Claire's eyes widened in surprise.

Alec strode toward them, halting only a few feet from Claire and Neil. He was wearing a hooded black leather jacket that fell midway to his knees. It hung open to reveal an olive green army surplus vest, its multiple pockets full of—something. His black canvas guitar case was slung across his back like a knapsack.

And he looked really, really pissed.

fifteen

"What are you guys doing here?" Alec asked quietly. Fury simmered within him. He'd followed Neil, waiting for a glimpse of an aura. He'd hoped that nothing would happen, but had geared up just in case. It had been bad enough to be forced to witness Claire hanging on to Neil's arm as they made their way up the escalator, and to find them here in a similar pose. But now *this trio*, of all people, had to appear and complicate things.

Celeste had a knack for smelling out the newly Awakened, and they were particularly susceptible to her charms. Alec knew in his gut that Celeste was out trolling for one now. Had she gotten wind that a possible Halfblood was on the loose? Is that why she'd zeroed in on this group?

"We're just . . . browsing," Claire said hesitantly. "What are *you* doing here, Alec?"

"I wasn't talking to you," Alec replied. He saw hurt and surprise in Claire's eyes and quickly refocused his gaze on Celeste and her cohorts.

"Alec?" Celeste said nonchalantly, her voice dripping honey, just the way he remembered. "Long time no see."

"We knew Vincent was here," Javed added with undisguised interest, "but didn't expect to see you."

"Out on a little shopping spree, are you?" Alec pressed calmly. If he was lucky, maybe they'd reveal who they were after. It occurred to him that it could be Neil *or* Brian; they were both talented singers.

"Alec, how do you know these guys?" Claire asked. "Is something wrong?"

Before he could reply, Celeste interjected, "Don't mind him. We've known Alec for years—and he's never been any fun at all." To Alec, she added innocently, "Stop scowling, would you? You're scaring our new friends."

"MacKenzie, what's your problem?" Neil asked, baffled, his arm still around Claire. "These guys have tickets to a hockey game. We're meeting them there."

"Great," Alec replied stonily. "I'm in the mood for hockey." To Celeste he added, "Let's go outside. I can ride with you."

Celeste's eyes darted to the guitar case slung over Alec's shoulder, and she frowned.

"Hey, kids," the owner of the shop interrupted, moving out from behind the counter with concern. "What's going on? Is everything all right?"

Celeste turned to Claire with a little sigh. "I'm sorry,

sweetie. I just remembered, our tickets are for tomorrow night. Maybe we'll run into you again sometime."

"Don't even think about it," Alec said, his tone threatening.

"Whatever." Celeste waved her hand as if shooing a fly, then swirled up to him and whispered privately in his ear, "I can't *believe* the great and powerful Vincent had to call *you* in as backup to rein in one little filly, even if it *might* be half-thoroughbred."

A cold feeling stirred in the pit of Alec's stomach. *Filly?*

"Ciao." Celeste exchanged a sharp look with her two counterparts. "Boys?"

The trio sauntered out the door, leaving a deathly silence in their wake. Alec's heart lurched as the terrible truth dawned on him. *Filly?* They were after a *girl?* From the way Celeste had been cozying up to Claire, it wasn't hard to guess which one it was.

"Dude, what is up?" Brian muttered, perplexed. "Did you used to bang that chick or something?" As Erica swatted him, Brian added defensively, "What? She was hot."

Claire broke away from Neil and marched up to Alec angrily. "Alec! What just happened? What did you do that made those guys leave?"

"Be glad they did," Alec replied, struggling to keep his voice even. "Believe me, they're not the type of . . . *people* you want to associate with."

"What kind of . . . *people* are they?" Erica asked,

mimicking Alec's tone and emphasis.

"They're extremely dangerous," Alec replied tersely. *Dear God. Claire.* He'd been so focused on looking for a boy, it hadn't once occurred to him that Vincent might be wrong about the target's gender. And yet, he realized now, Claire had always been more likely than Neil, who'd been in choir for years. Claire's newfound ability to sing just days after a surge on the grid would be a startling coincidence, if it wasn't a full-blown sign.

"How do you know they're dangerous?" Claire demanded. "Just because they had some tattoos and a few piercings?"

"Their appearance is irrelevant," Alec said.

"I wanted to talk to that girl!" Claire insisted. "Now she's gone and I didn't get her number or anything!"

"Listen to me," Alec warned. "Should that girl—or either of the others—ever approach any of you again, promise me you'll walk as fast as you can in the opposite direction."

"Why?"

Alec's eyes locked with Claire's. A wave of deep anguish and concern swept through him, so powerful that his voice cracked when he spoke. "Because . . . I may not be here to protect you the next time."

Claire gave a little gasp. Her anger seemed to fade, replaced by confusion and vulnerability. "*Protect* me?" she murmured quietly.

Alec nodded, not trusting himself to speak further. With an apologetic smile for the shopkeeper, he turned and left without looking back.

From the rooftop of the Twin Palms Mall, Alec watched as Celeste and her lackeys climbed into their sleek yellow Humvee and roared out of the parking lot into the night.

Thank God he'd been here. Who knows what would have happened if he hadn't defused the situation?

Every day, the ranks of the Fallen increased in number. Individually and in small groups, they ignored and abused the rules of society. If they ever banded together, they'd be too strong for any human law enforcement agency to control—that was his kind's greatest fear—yet he and his colleagues were not allowed to touch them unless they committed a blatant criminal act.

Celeste had been Alec's assignment about six years ago—one of those rare instances where he'd been sent in to search for an Awakened. Unfortunately, before he found her, she'd been enticed into joining the two reprobates she was with now. It was one of his few failures, and it had bothered him ever since.

If only he'd spotted Celeste a few minutes earlier today, he could have stopped her before she'd descended on Claire and her friends. Now he'd have to explain away more odd behavior. The prospect exhausted him, but there was nothing he could do about it.

Was Claire the Awakened? Alec's throat tightened with worry. If so, was she truly a Halfblood? It was starting to look that way. Celeste not only knew about Vincent's assignment, but she'd said her quarry "might be half-thoroughbred."

Claire. Claire. In silent agony, Alec's heart went out to her. If it *was* Claire, it would mean that the relationship he longed for was even more dangerous and taboo than if she were a normal human girl. But that was the least of it. His own feelings for her aside, he couldn't bear to think about the consequences in store for *her*. Somehow, he had to protect her—to convince *Vincent* to protect her. But first, he needed proof of her identity. He needed a controlled environment in which he could run some basic tests—eyesight, hearing, reflexes—to get her guard down so she'd be forced to reveal her hidden paranormal ability, if she had one. Of course, Claire could have any number of talents which were difficult if not impossible to test for, but at least it would be a start.

An idea presented itself: a way to get what he needed. It shouldn't be too hard to pull off. Claire would no doubt have a million questions for him after his behavior just now, and she'd be all too happy for a chance to grill him about it.

With a sigh, Alec crossed to the far side of the roof, where he glanced down at the dark, deserted loading dock several stories below. He was anxious to be on his way.

Fortunately, no one was around, and tall trees obscured the alley from any probing eyes, making it safe to move in his most expeditious manner.

Stepping up to the very edge, he vaulted out into the abyss.

Feeling the weight of his body in his mind, Alec concentrated to slow his descent as he dropped through open air. *Please*, he prayed silently, *let me be wrong. Don't let it be Claire.*

Because if it *was* Claire—if she was a Halfblood—it meant that, through no fault of her own, her life as she knew it was about to implode.

sixteen

Claire's bedside clock digitally ticked the hours away as she tossed and turned, replaying the events at the mall in her mind.

She'd been so sure Celeste was the person who'd been sending her the psychic messages. Then Alec showed up, pissed as hell and dressed like something out of *The Matrix*, and had somehow scared Celeste away. Claire had been furious with him at first, but now she was just confused. What was Alec so mad about? Had he been following them? How did he know Celeste and those guys, and why did he insist they were dangerous?

Claire had to admit, there *was* something strange about them. Claire and her friends had been totally up for going to that Kings game, and none of them even *liked* hockey that much. It was almost as if they'd been hypnotized.

Of course, there was definitely something strange about Alec, too. Claire still couldn't shake the deep certainty that he had some kind of supernatural abilities. But if so, what was he doing at her high school? What had he meant when he said *he* could protect her? The expression on Alec's face and the tremor in his voice as he'd pronounced those last words continued to haunt her. It felt as if he'd been looking straight into her soul, and she knew he'd spoken from the heart.

Erica and Brian insisted that Alec liked her. Claire was beginning to think it was true—and she could no longer deny that she was attracted to *him*. There was no way she could pursue these growing feelings, however, until she knew the truth about who or what Alec was. Somehow, Claire decided, she was going to have to get answers.

But the next day at school, although she felt Alec's eyes on her everywhere she went, every time she turned to start up a conversation with him, he was either looking the other way or was gone.

It was a typical short Friday, and she'd agreed to tutor Neil during lunch after school. They met at a corner table at Maria's Restaurant in Brentwood Village, a short walk away at the top of the hill, and shared a mushroom calzone while going over the intricacies of the preterite tense.

The session went well. The whole time Claire was coaching Neil, however, she found her thoughts drifting back to Alec, wishing she was having lunch with *him*, contemplating how and when she could get Alec alone for a private chat.

When an hour had passed, the calzone had been

decimated, and they'd finished the chapter in question, Claire said, "You've got this, Neil. I'm really impressed."

"Thanks." He eyed her warily across the table. "But . . . why do I hear a 'We have to break up' tone in your voice?"

A flash of guilt warmed her cheeks, but she willed it away. She hadn't been planning to end their study sessions, but it suddenly became clear to her that she wanted to— and there was no reason for her to feel guilty about it. "You said you were bad at Spanish, but that's not true. I think you were just rusty after spending the whole summer surfing. You don't need me anymore."

"Oh, but I do." Neil reached out and lightly gripped her forearm, his hand warm even through the soft fabric of her long-sleeved shirt. "I'm never gonna remember all this stuff on my own. It's only because you keep drilling it into my head. And when you talk, I don't mind listening."

Claire could feel the weight of sincerity behind his words. But his grin didn't cause her stomach to flutter the way it used to, and his touch on her arm felt friendly instead of causing sparks. "Tell you what, Neil. Let's ease off next week and see how you do. I'm not abandoning you, I promise. If you still need my help, I'll be here."

Neil leaned back in his chair and sighed. "Okay. If you insist." With a smile, he added, "But tell me one thing."

"What's that?"

"Even though you're bailing on the Spanish thing, will

you still be beholden to me?"

Claire couldn't help laughing. "Always."

Claire waved good-bye to Neil in the junior parking lot and raced up the school stairs to get her books for the weekend. When she turned the corner to her locker, her pulse skittered. Alec was standing there, digging through it.

Claire strove for nonchalance as she walked up. "Hi."

Alec smiled. "Hi. Just the person I was hoping to see. I wanted to ask you something."

"Oh?" His dark blond hair was disarmingly tousled. "I . . . have something to ask you, too. Can I go first?"

Alec finished getting his books and stepped back, giving her access to the locker. "Okay."

Claire took a deep breath as she exchanged several books and folders from her backpack. *Be ballsy and go for it,* she told herself. "Alec, you seem to have been avoiding me all day."

He opened his mouth as if to reply, then shut it again.

"I figure it's 'cause you didn't want me to ask about what happened at the mall yesterday. Brian and Erica and I have been arguing about it ever since. So instead of asking straight out, I'm going to give you our two running theories. Let me know if we're warm, or way off."

After a brief pause, Alec nodded with a hint of a smile. "I suppose that's fair."

Claire plunged in. "One: Those people at the mall were vampires and you're a Slayer. Two: You used to date Celeste, and she broke your heart."

Alec laughed in surprise. "I wish it were as amusing as the first, or as simple as the second. But it isn't."

"And?" She waited.

He glanced away, a troubled look now crossing his face. "And . . . that's all I can say. I'm sorry. Can we leave it at that?"

Claire sighed, zipping up her bag. What had made her think he would admit anything? "Whatever. I get it. Like you said, you 'like to keep that information private.'" An awkward silence fell. Claire looked at him. "You said you had something to ask me?"

"Right." His eyes flicked back to hers. "I hope you won't be upset. But . . . I really enjoyed singing with you last week. I was afraid if I asked you about this you'd say no, or I'd chicken out. So I just went ahead and did it."

"Did . . . what?"

"I signed us up for an audition to sing together at the Homecoming assembly."

Claire stared at him in astonishment. That was the *last* thing she'd expected. "Are you serious?"

"They're going to pick the three best acts. I think we might have a shot at it."

"A shot? *You* have more than a shot." Yesterday in the Student Life Center Claire had wanted him to do this very thing, sign up for the auditions—but she never dreamed he'd consider letting her tag along. The idea of singing with Alec again sent a buzz coursing through her that was both thrilling and unsettling. "Your voice is gorgeous. But I don't know about me. I've never sung in front of an audience before."

"Neither have I." Alec's voice was soft and deep.

"Really?" Claire could hardly believe it.

"Really." A warm sparkle danced in his green eyes. He took a step closer.

Claire could feel the heat emanating from his body. Suddenly, all she could think about was that moment in her dream when he'd almost kissed her. He was looking at her now in the same way. The fear and doubt she'd been harboring began to trickle away. Whoever Alec was— *whatever* he was—Claire realized she wouldn't mind if he *did* kiss her. *Control your hormones*, she commanded her brain. *Concentrate.* He'd asked her to sing with him and was waiting for an answer.

This could be a good thing, she told herself. It would require them to rehearse together. The alone time would give her a chance to learn more about him, hopefully satisfying her burning curiosity—so if he ever *did* kiss her, she wouldn't have any lingering questions about him.

"All right. I'm in," she said. "Where and when do we start?"

He looked both happy and relieved. "It's your call, but

I suggest my place, tomorrow morning."

Wow. His place? "Fine, but I don't know where you live, and I don't have a car."

"I'll pick you up at eleven."

Claire sat on the low front wall of her apartment complex, cell phone in hand as she waited. She was a bundle of nerves. "My mom's working all day, but if for any reason I don't hear my cell, she'll probably call you to check in on me."

"Don't worry, I've got you covered," Erica said on the other end of the line. "I'll tell her we're doing our nails and you can't come to the phone."

"Thanks, Erica. Next time you go to a guy's apartment alone—especially an emancipated guy who might be a vampire-slaying alien—I'll return the favor."

"I bet there's someone on Craigslist with that exact description."

Claire laughed, a little shiver running through her. She was both excited and intimidated by what she was about to do. She'd never even been on a date with Alec, but here she was going to his apartment, alone. Hell, as a result of her mother's rigid rules, she'd never been *anywhere* alone with a boy—unless you counted Jackson Spencer, who'd walked her home from sixth grade every day for a month until her mother found out and started picking her up again from school.

"You have to tell me what his place is like," Erica said.

"All he said was that he lives on his own, and that it's nothing special." Claire heard the roar of an engine and looked up to see a cool, vintage, dark blue car pull up to the curb, with Alec behind the wheel. "Holy shit. He drives a Mustang."

"I know. He parks near me every day, and I keep wanting to steal it. Anyways, good luck! Come home a virgin!"

"Thanks, Mom!" Claire dropped her phone in her bag and hopped off the wall as Alec reached over and opened the passenger door from inside.

Claire bent down and looked in over the top of her sunglasses, her heart doing a flip-flop when her gaze met Alec's. The morning sunlight fell across his face, bringing out the strands of gold in his hair. He took off his own sunglasses and smiled at her, giving her a full view of his beautiful green eyes. He wore the black leather jacket and dark jeans she'd seen before, but this time he sported a crisp, striped, button-down shirt. He looked so gorgeous, she was suddenly less embarrassed that she'd spent over an hour getting dressed, settling on her favorite peasant top, denim skirt, and brown suede boots.

"Hi. Nice shirt." Claire returned his smile as she climbed into the car and shut the door. "You clean up nicely."

"You should see me in a tux," he joked, but his expression told her that he thought she looked great too.

"I'm sure you put James Bond to shame," Claire teased, "except for the Scottish accent."

"The most famous screen Bond was a Scotsman, Miss Brennan," Alec replied, in a deep Scottish burr that Claire recognized as a perfect imitation of Sean Connery.

Claire laughed. "I forgot about that." Glancing around at the gray leather interior and chromed instrument panel, she added, "Wow. I officially have car envy."

"Do you want to drive?"

"Do I? *Yes!*"

"Okay, then." Alec unbuckled his seat belt and leapt out of the car, moving around to the passenger side. He opened Claire's door with a gentlemanly flourish. "She's yours."

Claire quickly scooted out of the car. "*She?*"

"All vehicles are women. From the *Santa Maria* to the Starship *Enterprise*."

As Claire settled into the driver's seat, her eyes fell with alarm on the gearshift lever in the center console. "Oh no. Is this a stick shift?"

"Of course. Don't you know how to drive stick?"

"No. My mom drives a Camry."

"Ah. Want to learn?"

"I'd better not. I might break your car."

"You won't, it's easy. I promise." Alec pointed to the three pedals at her feet. "See that pedal on the far left? That's the clutch. Press down on it with your left foot.

Right foot does gas and brake like always, left foot helps you change gears."

Claire followed his instructions through the tricky process of letting out the clutch as she gave it gas. The first time she tried it, the car lurched forward, sputtered, and died.

"That happens to everybody. Try again."

It took three tries, but Claire finally got the hang of the clutch, eased the car away from the curb, and merged into traffic. The car jerked every time she had to shift gears or start up at a light, but it was fun to drive. When she pulled into the small parking lot behind Alec's building and killed the engine, she heaved a sigh of relief. "Thank God you don't live too far away from me. I shudder to think what might have happened if I'd had to take the freeway."

"You did great. I think the car likes you."

They got out, and Alec led her past a patch of scrubby bushes to a nearby door tucked beneath an exterior stairwell. The gray stucco building was boxy and nondescript, a stark contrast, she thought, to the flashy automobile she'd just driven.

Alec withdrew a set of keys from his pocket and proceeded to unlock a series of deadbolts. Claire couldn't help but notice a hint of tension in his shoulders.

"Why do you have so many locks?"

"Keeps other people out." Alec opened the door. With

a pleasant smile, he added, "Wait here a moment." Then he slipped inside.

That's odd, Claire thought in sudden apprehension. Why did she get the feeling that Alec was working just as hard as she was to appear casual? She watched curiously through the half-open door as he darted from corner to corner, as if looking for something. Maybe checking to make sure his place wasn't too messy? The heavy curtains were shut, and it looked completely dark. How could he see anything?

Alec returned to the door and opened it wide, motioning for her to enter with a cheerful, *"Bienvenida, señorita."*

His jacket was gone, and in his fitted shirt he looked particularly handsome. *If only I didn't like him so much*, she thought, her pulse racing. *That would make everything so much easier.*

She walked inside and Alec shut the door, leaving the three locks alone. "Put these on the table, would you?" Unexpectedly, he tossed both his car keys and house keys to Claire.

She fumbled in the dim light, trying to catch them, but missed. "Sorry, I can't see anything." Claire scooped up the keys from the carpet. "Can you turn on a light?"

"Aye, got it." Alec flicked a switch and then quickly opened the curtains.

Wow, Claire thought, glancing around the austerely furnished studio with its blank, off-white walls. He hadn't even put up a poster. It reminded her of every featureless place her mom had moved her into over the years—except a lot smaller. It was weird to think of a sixteen-year-old living here all by himself. Her glance fell on his sofa.

"Do you . . . sleep on your couch?"

"Aye."

She suddenly felt very self-conscious, knowing that this was the room where Alec slept—and that they were together and alone. Alec moved into the tiny kitchenette, muttering something under his breath.

"What?"

Alec returned to the doorway. "I asked if you want anything to drink."

"Sure." He seemed to be studying her intently, as if he was waiting for something . . . although she had no idea what it was.

"Anything in particular?" he asked.

"Do you have iced tea?"

Alec's eyebrows lifted, as if her answer conveyed some deep, inexplicable meaning to him—and then shook his head. "Sorry. No."

Why is he acting so weird? Claire wondered. She felt like she was going through some sort of social obstacle course. "Water's fine." He disappeared into the kitchen again, and she heard the sound of ice cubes popping out of a tray.

Claire wished she could use her psychic powers to find out what Alec was thinking, but sadly they didn't seem to work that way. *Whatever you do*, she instructed herself, *keep your hands off him*. The last thing she wanted right now was to get a vision and fall dizzily to the floor.

Claire sat down on the comfy sofa, plunking Alec's keys onto the rectangular wooden coffee table. She glanced around, desperately searching for some detail to quiz him on. The only other items in the room were an end table with a single lamp, Alec's guitar on a stand, and a large metal storage cabinet with a sturdy handle and a keyhole. *He has a thing about locks*, Claire mused, recalling the mysterious box in their locker.

Alec emerged from the kitchen with a tall glass of water rattling with ice.

"What do you keep in there? Gold?" Claire gestured toward the cabinet, hoping her tone sounded like witty repartee and didn't betray her intense curiosity.

"No, strictly uncut diamonds and vials of plutonium."

"So you really *are* James Bond."

"I like to think of myself more as the Jason Bourne type." He grinned.

Claire smiled and sat forward on the sofa as Alec crossed the room with her drink. Here was the perfect opportunity, she realized, to conduct a little test, to see if he had any extraordinary abilities. He offered her the glass. She reached out, wrapped her fingers around it, and then deliberately let the wet glass slip from her grasp.

"Oh!" she cried—anticipating the impending crash—but

before the word had even left her mouth, Alec's hand shot out in a blur and caught the glass in midair.

They froze, their faces barely a foot apart, gazes locked. *Busted!* Claire thought, her heart thundering. *His hand had moved at the speed of light!* Alec's wide eyes betrayed a sense of anxiety that Claire pretended to ignore.

"Sorry," Claire said softly. "It was slippery."

"Can't believe I caught it in time," he responded with forced cheerfulness.

"Yeah, nice reflexes." As she stared into his green eyes, adrenaline rushed through her, and it was all she could do to maintain a calm demeanor. She was right! Alec *did* have some kind of special powers.

And he was close. So close. And they were so very alone. It was scary and intoxicating all at the same time. Part of her wanted to yell at him, *What the hell are you?!* And the other part (even knowing full well that it was the *last* thing she should do) wanted him to take her in his arms and kiss her.

Neither of those things happened. Alec tore his eyes away and carefully set the glass down on the table. Methodically, he lifted his guitar off its stand and brought it back to the couch, where he sat down beside her. Tension filled the air.

Claire's forearm and bare thigh below her short denim skirt were dangerously close to Alec's hand. She wanted more than anything in the world to reach out and touch him. Instead, she tugged her skirt down and edged over a bit on the couch.

Alec noticed her sideways move and frowned. "What's wrong?"

"Nothing."

Looking unconvinced, he strummed a few random bars on his guitar. "What should we sing?"

"You signed us up. Didn't you have a song in mind?"

"No."

He went quiet, turning to face her again. To her surprise, she saw fear and yearning mingled in his gaze, a mirror of her own bottled-up feelings. What was *he* afraid of? He reached up toward her cheek. Should she stop him? She felt certain that if his fingers came in contact with her skin, she would *melt* (for one reason or another)—but she was paralyzed. *I don't want to stop him*, she thought. *Can't I have this normal, simple moment, like any other girl?*

Alec's hand brushed gently against her cheek. "Claire—"

As his fingers trailed along her cheekbone and paused at the corner of her mouth, his touch seemed to ignite a delicious warmth that spread across her face and down her neck, to burn like embers within her chest. But it was a thrilling sensation, totally different from the all-consuming heat that preceded a vision.

Claire took a sharp breath. He'd touched her. And it was okay. It was more than okay. Relief flooded through her, washing away all her questions and worries. Alec's eyes locked with hers, tentative yet smoky with desire. Claire could barely hear herself think over her thundering pulse.

She said softly, "Just kiss me, you idiot."

Alec needed no further invitation. He set the guitar on the table, his other hand sliding around her back, drawing her close until her upper body molded against his. Claire slipped her own hands up the length of his arms to settle between his shoulder blades. She could feel every contour of his chest pressing against hers through the thin layers of their clothing. Suddenly, his lips were on hers. The gentle touch was exhilarating, wondrous—everything she'd ever imagined a kiss would be. She felt herself shudder as his lips moved softly against hers, exploring, lingering.

And then, despite herself, Claire felt a dreaded, familiar blaze building deep inside her.

Please, no! Not now! her mind screamed, trying to will the heat away, but every inch of her body seemed to burst into flame. Her stomach churned, her head spun, and a rush of images poured into her brain.

seventeen

*S*he was looking at Alec's face. In a mirror. Through his eyes. He looked a couple of years younger, his hair slicked back but disheveled, his face bruised and bloodied. He wore a black leather bomber jacket and a bloodstained T-shirt. She felt the anger and adrenaline that was rushing through him.

A hand clamped down on her shoulder—Alec's shoulder—and spun him around. A gun was aimed at his face. The man who held it glared at him with hateful eyes. They were inside an auto shop full of cars from the fifties and early sixties, but all shiny and new. The signs were in French. A calendar on the wall gave the year as 1962.

"Give it up, hunter," the man spat out in French, but somehow she understood him.

Alec kicked the gun from the man's hand. The two exchanged a flurry of violent blows. Blood splattered on the concrete. Alec's fist hit his opponent square in the chest. The man flew backward as if hit by a battering ram, slamming into a hydraulic rack, and crumpling to the oil-stained floor beneath it.

Alec's right hand thrust out deliberately, stretching his fingers toward the car on the rack above. She could feel an invisible flow of energy course through his arm and surge outward, wrapping itself around the vehicle. Then, as if he was moving nothing more weighty than a textbook, he sent the car hurtling downward, toward the man. The victim's scream was cut short by the crash of the impact.

With a gasp of horror, Claire blinked and came back to herself, sickened, perspiring, and breathing hard. Instantly, she shoved Alec away and leapt to her feet. What had she just seen? The world was still spinning, the air shimmering like heat rising from a desert road. Looking down, she saw that her entire body was surrounded by an emerald-green glow that rippled off her skin like flames—*just like she'd seen in her dream.*

"Oh my God! What's going on?" Claire cried, staggering back in terror. "I'm on fire!"

"You can see that?" Alec returned her stare, unmoving. For some reason, he didn't look too shocked—more . . . disappointed, if anything. "*Shite.* It *is* you. I really hoped I was wrong."

Claire dropped to the floor and started to roll to put out the flames when they dissipated as if by magic into thin air. She stared at Alec. "What did you *do?*"

"What do you mean?"

Overcome by a surge of nausea, Claire curled into the fetal position, dry-heaving, and then lay there, struggling to breathe. As her stomach settled, she started shivering uncontrollably. Alec moved to the carpet beside her, but she shrank away from his touch. "I saw you!" she cried, her eyes wet with tears. "You killed that man, didn't you?"

"Who?" Alec's expression was unreadable.

"Who are you?" she whispered, staggering to her feet.

He sighed. "Don't move." Getting up, Alec strode to a built-in cupboard near the bathroom and swung it open.

Claire panicked. What did he have stored in there? Whatever it was, she didn't want to find out. Grabbing his car keys from the coffee table, she bolted for the door.

"Claire! Wait!"

There was an odd whooshing sound and suddenly, impossibly, Alec was standing right behind her, reaching for her arm. If she'd had any doubts about his abilities before, they evaporated in an instant. Claire screamed and shoved the door back at him as she slipped through. It met his face with a heavy blow. Alec cursed as she raced away. She was at his car in a flash, her hands shaking as she fumbled with the key. As she yanked his car door open and jumped in behind the wheel, she heard that odd sound again, like a faint rush of wind, and all at once Alec stood outside her car door.

Claire gasped in terror and slammed her fist down on the door lock.

Alec stared in at her through the car window, bleeding from a gash in his forehead. "Claire, get out of the car," he said calmly. "You don't know what you're doing."

Claire didn't wait to hear more. She stuffed the key into the ignition, stomped on the clutch, and gunned the car into reverse. It lurched and groaned and then slipped into gear. As Alec leapt out of the way, she backed the car out of the parking space and with a screech of tires swerved around toward the street.

Incredibly, the car began to falter. Claire stomped harder on the gas pedal. The engine was roaring—and yet for some reason the vehicle slowed down even further. *What the hell was happening?* Claire floored it, causing the car to lurch forward. But then it jolted to a complete stand-still, slamming Claire into the steering wheel and then back against the seat.

Crying out in pain, her foot still pressed hard on the gas, Claire looked over her shoulder. Her eyes widened in terror. Alec was standing just a few yards behind the car, his arm extended toward it, a look of deep concentration on his face. *He was stopping the car with his mind.*

Alec's eyes bore into hers from beyond the glass, blood running down his face. The car slowly started to inch away from him. At the same time, she saw his feet slowly slid-ing forward along the pavement. Was the car pulling him? Was its weight and power more than he could handle? Claire faced the steering wheel again, refusing to let up on the gas. In the rearview mirror, she saw Alec's face tighten and his arm start to tremble from the continued stress. At last, with an exasperated look, he lowered his arm. The car roared forward unhindered into the street. The tires squealed as Claire yanked the wheel hard, struggling to maintain control as she made the sharp turn at full throttle. Glancing back, she saw Alec standing in the driveway behind her, shaking his head.

Claire drove to a supermarket parking lot about five miles away, where she waited, blinded by tears, until Erica pulled up in her SUV. Only when she saw her best friend's face did Claire feel safe enough to unlock the door and get out.

"Thank you for coming to rescue me," Claire said, leaping into Erica's vehicle and hugging her tightly.

Erica pulled back and stared at her, a worried look on her face. "Tell me again, what happened with Alec? You were talking so fast on the phone, I could hardly understand you."

Claire sank back against the seat and heaved a sigh as she buckled up. "Just take me to your place, *now*. I want to get as far away from here as possible."

"So," Erica said slowly. "You're saying that you saw Alec murder a man with a car. In a memory. Of his. *Fifty years ago*. But he only looked maybe fourteen."

"Yes."

They were lying on Erica's four-poster bed, staring up at the ceiling of Erica's spacious room, surrounded by lavender walls, designer curtains, and classy hardwood furniture cluttered with stacks of books and tchotchkes from Erica's various travels. The cartons from their take-out salad lunches sat on the floor.

Claire was finally beginning to feel normal again. Her neck ached slightly, but she'd refused medical attention, insisting that all she needed was an ice pack for the mild bruises on her upper chest from the seat belt and steering wheel.

"And then," Erica continued, "when you tried to escape in Alec's car, he magically held it back for at least a minute."

"Yes."

Erica rolled over to face Claire on the bed. "Tell me you're at least kidding about the last part."

Claire took a pillow and put it over her head, batting it with her fist in exasperation. "God, are we still debating this?" She ripped off the pillow and hurled it at Erica, who ducked just in time. "It was just like what I saw underneath the scaffolding! He reaches his hand forward like this—" Claire demonstrated the action again. "And he can move things—push or pull them—without touching them. I told you! *He's telekinetic.* And I know what it feels like. *I was in his head today.* It was like I mentally grabbed that French car myself and pulled it down off the rack—as if it weighed almost nothing."

"Holy crap." Erica sat up now, wide-eyed, grabbing her boba milk tea. "Well, I guess that confirms all the alien superpower stuff you were obsessing about before."

"*Finally*, she believes me." Claire set the ice pack aside with a relieved sigh.

"There's one thing I still don't get. If the memory happened fifty years ago, how was Alec alive? And how could he have been only fourteen?"

"I don't know. *Whatever* he is, I think he ages way differently than we do."

"Neat." Erica sipped her drink slowly, deep in thought. "How did you get the vision? Did you touch him? Or his guitar?"

"No." Claire realized she'd left out that detail. "It . . . um . . . happened when he . . . kissed me."

Erica's eyes bugged out. "WHAT? He kissed you? And you conveniently forgot to mention it?"

"I was getting to it," Claire said defensively.

"How was it?"

"How was what?"

"The kiss."

"Are you kidding me?" Claire stared at Erica, incredulous. "I barely escape with my life, and you're asking if Alec's a good kisser?"

"Claire, we don't know that your life was in danger. Did Alec make a move to hurt you?"

"Well, no, but—"

"But nothing. You got a scary vision, freaked out, and ran—totally understandable—but that doesn't necessarily make Alec a bad guy."

"Erica, I saw him *kill a man*."

"Alec might have had a good reason." Erica set her drink down on the nightstand and faced Claire crossed-legged on the bed. "Maybe the guy was an evil vampire. Or a dangerous double agent. Or both."

"So what are you saying? That Alec *is* a Slayer—or a telekinetic spy?"

"It's possible. Or he *could* be genetically engineered. Never discount the sci-fi angle."

"This is all insane." Leaning up on one elbow, she drew invisible circles on Erica's quilt with her fingertip. "It's too much, Erica. Everything that's been happening since Book Day—all these weird psychic episodes and danger warnings, and at the same time, I meet a guy with superpowers of his own—what am I supposed to make of all this? Is Alec the reason I'm in danger, or not?"

Erica shook her head, frowning. "I don't know—but you need an answer, and fast."

"No problem. I'll just call Merlin. Or Dumbledore. Get my phone. I have them both on speed-dial."

"Claire Bear." Erica met her gaze affectionately. "You already have a wise wizard to consult with: the person who's sending you that warning."

"Assuming it really *is* a person, and not just a voice in my head. But even if that's true, how am I supposed to consult with someone who sends random, incomplete messages?"

"Brian said it's probably the same message being broadcast over and over. We just have to figure out how to help you hear the whole thing."

"*Great*," Claire replied sarcastically. "Let's call I-800-PSYCHIC, and ask them to patch me through to the sender."

"There *are* ways for you to get in touch with whoever's talking to you." Erica reached under her bed and withdrew a thick, oversize paperback book called *So, You're a Psychic?* "I bought this last week, and I've been reading a little every night, to see if I could learn something useful."

Claire glanced at it dubiously. "And . . . ?"

"I know it sounds crazy, but there's all kinds of fascinating stuff in here. According to this, you need to try some combination of astral projection and channeling."

"I've read about that stuff online," Claire replied, still doubtful. "It said astral projection is about going somewhere with your mind, and channeling is about contacting spirits. How does either one help me?"

"Think big picture, Claire. Astral projection isn't just about finding some *place*; it can be used to find *someone*. Channeling is about listening to someone *who's talking to you*. Somebody is out there traveling the psychic moors, calling out your name. Your job is to either meet them on the moors, or to bring the moors to you."

Claire stared at her. "You've been reading *Wuthering Heights* again, haven't you?"

"Just go with the metaphor."

Claire sighed. "What do I have to do?"

Erica adopted her most sagelike tone, clasping her hands dramatically. "We have to put you in a trance."

Claire sat in the lotus position on the plush carpet, propped up against Erica's dresser with a large throw pillow as a backrest. It was after dinner now, and the sun was going down. The curtains were drawn, leaving the bedroom in near darkness. Erica sat across from her, methodically lighting a semicircle of candles around them.

"Love-you-too-Mom. Bye." Claire hung up the phone. "Miracle number one: Mom is fine with me staying over. Miracle number two: She's meeting that guy for a coffee date."

"Wow," Erica said. "She's really coming out of her shell fast. I mean that in a good way."

"Yeah. Now that she thinks I'm fine, she's easing up on me and starting to think about herself for a change."

"Which is rather ironic, since, for the first time ever, you're not really fine at all."

"Hey. I thought you were supposed to be helping me *relax.*"

"Sorry! Forget I said that." Erica lit the last candle and then touched the match to some incense she'd placed between them. A strong herbal fragrance began to permeate the room. "*Now,* my child," Erica intoned as she picked up the psychic book and opened it to a particular page, "are you ready to begin?"

"As ready as I'll ever be." Claire leaned back against the pillow and closed her eyes.

"Take several slow, deep breaths," Erica said calmly and quietly. "Choose an image that you associate with the voice you've been hearing, and focus on it alone."

Claire nodded silently. She called to mind the silhouette she'd seen each time the voice had called to her: the amorphous, faceless figure, rimmed by glowing yellow light, against a backdrop of inky darkness. "Okay, I see it."

"Good. Now be silent. Concentrate on your breathing. Every time you exhale, try to release all your other everyday thoughts and emotions, including any anxieties or skepticism. Hold on to that image, and just . . . be."

As Erica continued, Claire followed her instructions.

Claire kept the silhouetted image before her closed eyes, but despite her best efforts, she couldn't feel anything. The sounds around her were too distracting. She heard the tick of a clock. The swoosh of a car passing on the road outside. The muffled explosions of a video game from Erica's brother's room next door. She concentrated harder. *See it*, she commanded herself. *Feel it.* Suddenly— to her surprise—the silhouetted image seemed to grow a bit sharper, its edges more defined. Claire could now make out that the figure had a feminine frame. Her pulse quickened in excitement.

A phone rang loudly. Claire's eyes snapped open, the spell broken.

"Crap!" Erica snatched up her phone, glanced at the caller ID, and barked into it, "Brian! Not now! We're doing psychic stuff!" She quickly ended the call and turned to Claire. "Sorry, I should have shut it off before we started. Did it work? Did anything happen?"

Claire nodded eagerly. "I was just starting to see something when the phone rang. I think it was a woman."

"Crap!" Erica said again.

"It was really hard to focus. Maybe we should try this later, when it's quieter—after everyone goes to sleep."

Erica looked disappointed. "Okay." They blew out all the candles and the incense, leaving the room shrouded in murky darkness. "Let me dump the ash, and then we can go downstairs and have dessert. My mom got Mochi ice cream, two flavors."

"Yum."

Claire stood up, stretching, watching as Erica carefully carried the tray with the incense across the room. Erica paused in her bathroom doorway to flick on the light switch, and for a brief moment was backlit by the bathroom light—a moment which, Claire realized with a start, bore an eerie similarity to the blurry image Claire had just been trying to bring to focus in her mind. Erica disappeared inside.

Then something strange happened. All the distracting sounds around Claire went silent. She couldn't even hear her own breathing. *Whoa,* she thought, glancing around her. *What's going on?*

The room—the floor, the ceiling, everything—had disappeared. Claire was surrounded by black nothingness. Although she still felt her own body, she seemed to be floating in the void, as if in zero gravity. The only visual cues left, inexplicably, were the bathroom doorway hovering before her and the glow that emanated from within.

"Erica!" Claire whispered insistently. "Something's happening!"

"What?" Erica sounded like she was a million miles away.

The light inside the bathroom doorway began to shift and change. A faceless, silhouetted, female figure appeared—the same figure Claire had seen a few minutes earlier. The light was coming from her, a glow of shimmering golden flames that radiated around her body.

"I see it!" Claire said quietly. "It's definitely a woman, and she's glowing!"

"Oh my God!" came Erica's distant voice, filled with wonder.

Then Claire heard the same raspy British voice that had invaded her head twice before: "Claire. Your life is in danger."

The figure moved forward. Claire saw her more clearly now: She was a stunningly attractive woman in her early sixties, with gentle crinkles beside her kind, hazel eyes, and a small beauty mark on her right cheek just above her mouth. Her chin-length, stylishly coiffed hair was pale blond, almost white. She wore a chic, formfitting navy-blue dress and a delicate necklace sparkling with tiny, floating diamonds.

"Oh! She's beautiful!" Claire whispered in mingled awe and trepidation. "She's smiling at me." The woman seemed so real, Claire felt as if she could reach out and touch her. With a shiver, she reminded herself that the woman wasn't really there.

Claire felt a sound coming up through her chest and out of her mouth—but it wasn't her own voice. It was still raspy, but it was a perfect, cultured, British accent, as if the woman were now speaking directly through her:

"Someone wants to kill you because of your special gift. You are one of the Nephilim."

I'm one of what? Claire thought, confused and alarmed.

"Only one person can protect and help you. Alec."

Oh my God, Claire thought. Alec? Alec's my protector?

"Alec is a Grigori, as am I. Come to Twin Palms. I will explain everything. My name is Helena."

The woman brought a finger up to her lips in a silencing gesture as she repeated the familiar, final phrase of the eerie message:

"Don't tell anyone."

The light became so blinding that Claire had to close her eyes. When she reopened them, the woman was gone and she was back in Erica's room. Erica was standing in the bathroom doorway, staring at her in openmouthed amazement.

Claire had the oddest sensation, as if she were still floating. Glancing down, she gasped in astonishment. She hadn't just been floating in her mind. She was actually *suspended in the air*, about a foot above the floor. "Holy crap!" Claire cried. With that exclamation she dropped straight down, landing on the carpet with a thud.

"Wow!" Erica cried. "Claire, are you all right?"

Claire nodded, touching her throat, which felt hoarse and dry. "I need a glass of water."

Erica brought her a glass from the bathroom, rushing up to kneel beside her. As Claire drank it Erica enthused, "That was so cool! You rose up like some kind of divine being and were hovering the whole time!"

Claire was still in a daze. "Who *is* she?"

"I don't know, but I think she was talking *through* you! You sounded just like Helen Mirren."

"Did she actually say that someone wants to *kill me*?" Claire asked, her insides constricting in fear.

"She said they want to kill you because of your *gift*," Erica said solemnly. "Which I guess is this whole psychic thing."

"*Who* wants to kill me? How do they know what's been going on with me? And why do they care?"

"I have no idea. But at least we now know what's going on with *Alec*. He's not here to hurt you."

Claire nodded. "This is all so . . ." *Weird. Scary. Mind-boggling.* She shivered, unable to finish the sentence.

"I know, right? You were totally channeling that lady's spirit, Claire. It was like you were talking to someone beyond the grave!"

"That doesn't make sense. If she were dead, why would she say 'Come to Twin Palms, I'll explain everything.'"

"Oh. Okay," Erica agreed. "But if she's alive, why doesn't she come to you? Why is she doing all this psychically?"

"Maybe she lives really far away and can't travel right now," Claire mused as she set the empty water glass aside. "I still don't get who she is or why she's trying to help me. But whatever the reason, I say we try to find her."

Two hours later, Claire and Erica were still huddled over Erica's laptop, researching *Twin Palms* on the internet. There were over five hundred thousand hits on Google for Twin Palms—a whole cornucopia of places all over the world: the mall they'd visited, a former restaurant in Pasadena, a nail salon in Texas, a publishing house in New York, three hospitals, a stretch of condominiums in Florida, and multitudes of hotels and apartments from northern California and Arizona to the Caribbean and Thailand. It was even the name of Frank Sinatra's original estate in Palm Springs.

"There is no way we are ever going to find this woman," Erica complained. "Without her last name or some more identifying information, it's impossible to narrow this down."

"She said, 'Come to Twin Palms.' As if it were the name of a city. But it isn't." Claire sighed in frustration and leaned back against the headboard of the bed. "If someone is really trying to kill me, you'd think she would have given me a better way to find her! Like an address maybe?"

"If you're in danger, we can't keep searching for this mystery woman forever." Erica opened up a new tab in her web browser. "Let's attack this from a different angle. When she talked about your gift, she used a word I've never heard before, like you were special in some way. What did she call you? A Nefah-what?"

"I don't know exactly. But I remember what she said Alec was—a *Grih-gore-ee*."

"I've never heard that before, either." They searched a few alternate spellings of the term, beginning with *Gregory* and ultimately landing on *Grigori*.

Two million hits came up when they Googled *Grigori*. The very first title listing contained two words that nearly made Claire's heart stop:

Watcher.

Angel.

eighteen

§

"Alec's an *angel*?" Brian stared in disbelief as he plopped into the corner chair in Erica's bedroom twenty minutes later.

"Apparently." Stunned, Claire paced back and forth at the foot of Erica's bed. They'd just filled him in on what had happened at Alec's apartment that morning and had given him the gist of Claire's vision.

"If that's true, why doesn't Alec have wings and a halo?" Brian asked.

Erica gestured at the computer on her lap. "Well, according to what we read on the web, the angels in the Bible never had wings or halos. Those are just visual symbols used in illustrations to help the illiterate masses identify the beings as superior to man."

"Oh." Brian shook his head in rising awe. "Wow, this is epic!"

"We're not sure how big it is," Erica retorted matter-of-factly. "We don't even understand most of it yet."

"All we have to go by," Claire added, "is what the woman said in my vision. But just because *she's* supposedly an angel, too, that doesn't mean (a) she's a credible source, or (b) I wasn't hallucinating the whole thing."

"I seriously doubt you'd hallucinate words you've never heard of before," Brian pointed out. "She never actually said *angel*, right?"

"No," Claire admitted. "She said Grigori."

"Is that singular or plural?" Brian asked.

"Apparently it's both. Like *fish* or *moose*," Erica explained, glancing at her computer screen. "At least, according to Wikipedia."

"Another credible source," Claire added with a roll of her eyes.

"The Bible says that the Watchers, or Grigori, are a group of angels sent to watch over humanity," Erica continued, undaunted. "But before the great flood, they began to lust for human women. It's all in Genesis, Chapter Six. Look."

Erica turned her laptop around, and Claire read aloud from the screen:

> Now it came about, when men began to multiply on the face of the land, and daughters were born to them, that the sons of God saw that the daughters of men were beautiful; and they took wives for themselves. . . . The Nephilim were on the earth in those days, and also afterward, when the sons of God came

in to the daughters of men, and they bore children to
them. Those were the mighty men who were of old,
men of renown.

"So Nephilim are hybrid angels and humans," Brian
mused when Claire had finished reading.

"And supposedly, I'm descended from one of those
'hybrids,'" Claire said doubtfully.

"No shit?" Brian's brown eyes grew as wide as saucers.
"She said that? You're part *messenger from God?*"

"I *might* be," Claire insisted. "*If* any of this is true, it
must go way, way back. I might have, like, a drop of angel
blood in me."

"Might?" Erica scoffed. "Claire, two hours ago you
were floating above my bedroom floor!"

"*Floating?*" Brian shook his head. "I gotta give you
credit, CB, you are never boring."

"Am I the only one who finds all this hard to believe?"
Claire frowned. "Do you guys really think Alec—or anyone else—could actually be an *angel?*"

"Why not?" said Erica. "You were totally ready to
believe he was a vampire."

"That's different. I don't know why, but I can accept
that *vampires* could be real. But angels? If angels exist,
doesn't that mean that God and the devil exist too?"

Brian shrugged. "Maybe they do, but angels aren't
proof either way."

"I always thought angels were beings of pure goodness and light," Claire went on, "so why did I have a vision of Alec killing someone?"

"The Bible also has warrior angels who carry swords and smite the wicked," Erica pointed out. "Maybe that's what you saw."

Claire nodded, cringing. "He was definitely *smiting* someone." She threw up her hands with a sigh. "None of this proves that *I'm* descended from an angel. How did it happen? Was one of my mother's distant ancestors a Grigori? Or does the bloodline come from my father's side?"

"You don't know anything about your father, right?" Brian asked.

"Absolutely nothing. Except that he vanished not long after I was born."

"Well, whichever side it comes from," Erica said, "I think it's real. It must be responsible for these weird psychic powers you have—and be the reason someone wants you dead."

"Wonderful," Claire added quietly, sinking down on the bed with renewed trepidation, "and the person who's supposed to protect me is *Alec.*"

Claire didn't sleep a wink that night. Although Erica, beside her, nodded off minutes after her head hit the pillow, and Claire could hear Brian snoring in the guest room across the hall, Claire tossed and turned all night long, too astonished and frightened by everything they'd just learned to even contemplate sleep.

On the one hand, the whole thing seemed impossible and ridiculous. Claire tried to convince herself that there was some other explanation for Alec's incredible powers and for her freakish mental episodes. But the more she thought about it, the more convinced she became that it might be true.

All her life, her mom had been so secretive and neurotic, watching over Claire like a hawk, packing up and moving at the slightest indication of impending trouble. Was it possible her mother knew something about all this? Did her mom suspect that Claire might have inherited angel blood? All these years, had her mom been worried that Claire might come into some kind of weird, part-angel powers, and that somehow it would spell her doom? If so, it would explain a lot. But did it mean that the angel blood came from her mom's side or her dad's side? And why would somebody want to *kill* her? What possible threat could *she* be to anyone?

At breakfast the next morning, Claire sat silent and bleary-eyed as Erica and Brian made small talk with Erica's family. Afterward, Claire picked up Alec's car from the parking lot where she'd left it the day before and tried to return it, with Erica and Brian following in Brian's silver Accord. When they got to Alec's apartment, however, his curtains were drawn and he didn't answer her knock. Since the car keys wouldn't fit in his mailbox slot, she left him a note instead.

Alec,

I'm sorry I stole your car in a panic. I'm keeping it safe at my place. Please call me so I can bring it back to you.

Claire

P.S. We have to talk. Now.

Claire dropped the note in the box. As they headed back to their cars, Brian said, "Want us to follow you home and stay for a while? Just to make sure you're safe?"

"Thanks, but no." Claire slipped into Alec's car. "I'll be fine." In truth, she didn't feel fine at all. She was overwhelmed by fear and exhaustion, her mind was still in a whirl, and every nerve in her body seemed to be standing on end—but she was dying for some alone time. "I haven't seen anybody lurking in the bushes yet," she added, striving for a light tone. "Thanks again, guys, for everything. I'll see you tomorrow."

The drive back to her place was mercifully uneventful.

"Mom! I'm home," she called out in her cheeriest voice as she unlocked the front door and entered.

There was no answer. Claire saw a sticky note resting

on the entryway table. It read:

> *Claire—*
> *I have two showings this morning and an open house until*
> *5. Please take the lasagna out of the freezer and pop it in the*
> *oven at 4:30. See you for dinner!*
> *Love, Mom*

Claire sighed with relief, grabbing the note and bringing it upstairs as a reminder. She'd assumed her mom wouldn't be home—her mom almost always worked on the weekends. Although Claire was desperately curious to ask her mom a few things, she wasn't ready to talk about this just yet. She looked forward to taking a hot shower and dropping into her own bed where, hopefully, she'd finally be able to sleep.

Sticking the note on her door, Claire entered her room, dumped her purse on her dresser, and kicked off her boots. With both hands, she grabbed the hem of her peasant top and was about to yank it up and over her head, when suddenly a calm, deep voice sounded from behind her.

"Wait."

Claire yelped in alarm and spun, her fists still gripping her shirt.

Someone sat in her desk chair, his eyes on the floor. Someone looking as red-faced and sleep-deprived as she was.

Alec.

nineteen

"How the hell did you get in here?" Claire cried, shrinking back and grimacing as she banged into her dresser.

Alec winced in sympathy. "I'll explain in a minute," he responded quietly.

To Alec's relief, Claire didn't appear to be terrified at the sight of him—just tired and astonished—although she blushed furiously, crossing her arms over her chest, as if she felt exposed even though he'd stopped her before she took off her shirt. "I'm really sorry I startled you, Claire," he continued, "but I had to talk to you. I was afraid you wouldn't let me in if I came to the door."

After everything Claire had seen yesterday, he had no idea what she was thinking or feeling, or what she imagined him to be. But to his chagrin, there was no longer any doubt about *her*. Claire was definitely the Halfblood Vincent was seeking. Alec still didn't know what her true power was, or why she'd reacted so violently when he'd kissed her, but he'd seen her emerald aura, a color so rare he'd never witnessed it in his entire life—and had only heard about it in old legends.

"How long have you been here?" Claire asked, her hazel eyes wide.

"A few hours. Since your mom left this morning." Alec noticed several small purple bruises on her chest above the neckline of her blouse, and he cringed inwardly. "You're hurt."

"Your car doesn't have air bags. No big deal, they're just bruises."

"I'm sorry, that's my fault," he said again with deep sincerity, not moving from his chair. She was staring at him tensely, as if she might bolt at any second—and any movement on his part might trigger her flight. "There's a lot to say, Claire. But the most important thing is: I'm not here to hurt you."

"I know."

"You do?"

She nodded, her wariness now giving way to what looked like a mix of awe and fascination as she studied him. "Every time I've asked you what you are, you've avoided the subject or made me feel like I was crazy. Are you here to tell me the truth?"

He took a deep breath and let it out slowly. Now that he knew what she was, it wasn't against the rules to discuss this with her. In fact, it was encouraged. "Aye."

"Finally." Then, with confidence and conviction, she said, "So, you're a Grigori?"

The question was so unexpected that Alec nearly fell out of the chair. "How do you know that word?"

"Just answer the question: Are you or are you not a Grigori? A Watcher? *An angel?*"

His heart pounded in a frenzy and he glanced away. He couldn't believe it: *She knew.* How was it possible? No one had *ever* asked him that question point-blank before. It felt strange not to broach the subject himself with a reluctant or skeptical subject.

Alec returned his eyes to hers again. "I don't like the term *angel*. None of us do. But—yes. I am a Grigori."

"Okay. Okay." She looked like she was about to hyperventilate now. "And *what am I*? Am I really a Nephilim?"

If he'd been surprised before, it was nothing to this. He'd had a speech all prepared, but apparently it was unnecessary. All he could do was nod, dumbfounded.

Claire reacted in equally stunned disbelief. "Wow. This is . . . really . . ." Her voice trailed off, and it took a long moment before she looked him in the eye again. Then they were just staring at each other.

He broke the silence. "How do you know all this, Claire? Can you read minds?"

"Not exactly." Claire shook off her exhaustion with a deep sigh. "It's a long story. I'll tell you all about it, and I have about a million questions to ask you. But I've just spent the past twenty hours cooped up in Erica's bedroom, and with what I know now, being alone here with you is kind of . . . nerve-racking, to say the least."

"I understand."

"Do you mind if we go somewhere else to talk? Someplace *outside* that maybe has one or two other people around?"

Alec rose to his feet, his lips twitching with repressed amusement. "As in, a quiet location with a few potential *witnesses*?"

"Something like that, yeah."

"It would be my pleasure."

Alec took her to one of his favorite spots: the Venice Canals, a unique and peaceful neighborhood in West Los Angeles just five blocks from the famous Venice boardwalk, where paved sidewalks meandered alongside intersecting water channels covered by arched bridges, past long rows of beautiful homes with small, landscaped gardens.

"I can't believe I live only a few miles from here and I didn't even know this place existed." Claire gazed about with a tense smile as they strolled along, listening to the ducks splashing in the canal and the chirping of birds in the nearby trees.

The hot sun baked Alec's shoulders and was reflected so brightly in the dark greenish-blue of the canal that he wished he'd brought sunglasses. They passed a mom pushing a baby in a stroller, a couple working in their yard, and several people walking their dogs on the other side of the canal, but otherwise the area was quiet and serene.

"Some people live in L.A. their entire lives and never find out about it," Alec said. "I hoped you'd find it the perfect blend of visibility and solitude."

"It is," Claire agreed, although she still looked nervous and wary.

As they walked, Claire told him what had been happening to her over the past two weeks—that she'd been receiving weird visions through touch, revealing random glimpses of people's past or future—and how she'd actually changed Neil's future by tutoring him in Spanish.

"So *that's* your gift," Alec mused. "A form of second sight."

"It doesn't feel like a gift. It feels like a curse. The visions make me sick, and I have no idea when they're going to come."

"We call each of our abilities a gift or talent. You'll learn to control yours in time." Alec sent her a look that he hoped was reassuring. She looked so pretty and vulnerable, walking beside him, the sunlight glinting off her hair. How much did she really know about her own situation? Was she aware of how much danger she was in, if she was found? He wanted more than anything to take her hand in his—both to offer her comfort, and for the joy her touch would bring him—but in light of her newly awakened abilities, that didn't seem like a good idea.

Hesitantly, he asked, "What happened yesterday, when we . . . kissed? You said you saw something. Did you get a vision about me?"

Claire nodded. "I saw you drop a car on a man and kill him. In 1962. I think it was in France."

"Oh shite." Alec felt his cheeks grow warm.

He vaguely remembered the incident in question. *Of all things for her to have seen. Although it could have been worse.* "No wonder you ran off in such a panic."

"Is that just a typical day in the life of an angel?" Claire's hands clenched as her eyes challenged him. "You go around smiting people?"

Alec's blush deepened. He shook his head. She deserved an honest answer—although he wasn't ready to go into all the details of that just yet. "There are multiple classes of Grigori," he admitted, "Elders, Guardians, and Watchers, to name a few. I'm one of the latter."

"A Watcher?"

"Aye. We've all become so severely outnumbered by Earth's exploding population that it's difficult to do our jobs, but we still try. Watchers rarely kill anymore, and only with good reason."

"Well, I'm glad to hear *that*."

"And as I said before," he added, "we don't really think of ourselves as *angels*."

"Why not? Grigori *are* angels, aren't they?"

"We don't really know *what* we are. We've been living a certain way, entertaining certain beliefs, and following a certain set of rules for thousands of years, all completely on faith—similar to the followers of most human religions, if you think about it. We just do what our Elders tell us to do—but not even *they* know the truth of our history."

"Tell me what you do know."

"Okay." Alec led the way up onto a white wooden bridge arching gracefully over the canal and paused halfway across, leaning on the rail. "We know that we're born of other Grigori and raised on Earth."

"So you're not from heaven?"

"No. There's a theory that we originated in heaven—wherever and whatever that is. But as far back as any of us can remember, we've been earthbound. We live among humans and age at the same rate they do for the first thirteen years or so, until we reach puberty. After that, we age much more slowly, about one year for every twenty human years."

"So that's why you didn't look that different in the vision I had. How old are you?"

Alec hesitated. "By human standards I'm about eighteen years old, even though I can pass for sixteen."

"No, how old are you *really*?"

"A hundred and thirteen, more or less."

She gaped at him. "Well, you look really good for your age."

He couldn't help but smile. "Thanks."

Their eyes caught then and they both laughed, which seemed to release some of her built-up tension. A quiet moment passed as they leaned on the wooden rail, staring down at the dark, still water below. Then she glanced at him again and said, "I'm sorry about yesterday, when I . . . freaked. I caught you pretty good with that door."

"It's okay. I understand why you were scared."

Her eyes narrowed. "Your forehead was bleeding—I saw the gash. But now there's not even a mark."

"We heal a lot faster than humans."

"Are you immortal?"

"No. We *can* be killed. And we do die eventually."

"Do you all have the same powers?"

"Not at all. Our gifts are very diverse, and passed on from generation to generation, in the same way that humans pass on blue eyes or red hair. For example, you inherited a mental power that is very different from mine."

"Oh." She looked at him. "You're telekinetic, right?"

"Yes. From my father."

"But that's not your only power? You can move really fast?"

He nodded. "I also have my mother's strength and speed."

"I knew it!" She grinned. "I knew I didn't hallucinate about the scaffolding."

"Most Nephilim have a hard time understanding

and accepting the Big Picture, or where their particular, extraordinary abilities come from. But you seem to have it all figured out already."

"Well, I had all night to read up on it and think about it."

"But how did you know to search for the word *Grigori*?"

She shrugged with a sigh. "Would you believe an old lady told me?"

As they crossed the bridge and ambled down the narrow sidewalk lining the other side of the canal, Claire launched into a vivid description of the series of psychic messages she'd been receiving. "The woman is beautiful, looks like she's about sixty, and has a British accent," Claire said as she concluded her story. "She claims to be a Grigori, and her name is Helena. Do you know who she is?"

"No. I've never met her."

"Well, she definitely knows who *you* are, and that I'm a Nephilim."

"Actually, Nephilim is plural. It's Hebrew. The feminine singular is *Nephila*, masculine is *Nephil*."

"Whatever." Claire waved a hand impatiently. "Am I right that Nephilim are descendants of the Grigori—the result of your species interbreeding with humans thousands of years ago?"

"Yes. Every legend you've heard in the history of the world—not just about mythical heroes and gods, but monsters like the Sasquatch, wizards, werewolves, prophets, or demons—pretty much all of them are based on encounters with Nephilim. Most look like humans, but are more gifted."

"Do all Nephilim have powers?"

"No. For those who do, their inherited talents become more and more diluted with each ensuing generation, and the powers don't manifest until puberty, when the individual Awakens."

Claire's eyes widened now as if she was struck by a sudden realization. "*Puberty*," she whispered, her cheeks turning crimson. "Oh! So *that's* why . . ."

Alec could guess what she was thinking—it was common enough—and he felt bad that she was embarrassed. An awkward silence descended. He was relieved when Claire finally spoke.

"Is that why I'm able to sing so well now?"

"All of us can sing."

"Choir of angels, huh?"

He shot her a displeased look.

"Sorry. I'll stop using the *A*-word." Claire shook her head as if in wonder. "So what exactly do the Grigori do?"

"In general, we keep to ourselves, hiding our abilities, and silently watch over the Nephilim. If and when they use their powers to the detriment of others, we're obliged to step in and instill in them a sense of responsibility."

"What happens if they aren't responsible?"

Alec lowered his eyes briefly. "We call them the Fallen.

That's the group that lower-level Watchers have to police, and the Elites—like I was—are *sometimes* obliged to eliminate."

"Eliminate," she repeated slowly. "That's what I saw you do . . . in France?"

He nodded.

"So . . . the Grigori's job is to police the hybrid descendants of their forefathers?"

"Basically. We're not allowed to meddle in human affairs unless they are threatened or compromised by the actions of the Fallen."

A thought seemed to occur to her. "That Goth group at the mall . . . the people you insisted I stay away from . . . are they Fallen?"

"Aye."

Claire frowned. "But they're rare, right? Not all Nephilim are evil?"

"Most awakened Nephilim use their gifts in non-destructive ways. In fact, some of the most brilliant, productive, and influential 'human beings' in history were Nephilim."

"Huh. So . . . was Leonardo da Vinci a . . . Nephil?"

"Aye. Mozart and Shakespeare, too."

"Benjamin Franklin?"

"I believe so."

"Einstein and Elvis?"

"Absolutely."

"Michael Jordan?"

"Nah, he was that good on his own."

Claire laughed. "Good to know there are still *some* of us who are just naturally talented."

"Actually—I hate to remind you, Claire—you're not *one of them*. You're not a human being."

"Right, right. But I'm *mostly* human, aren't I? I mean, come on, I've got, what, like a couple of drops of Grigori blood in me? And by the way, since you seem to know all about it—which side of the family did I get this from? My mom or my dad?"

Alec looked at her, startled. Clearly, Claire wasn't aware of her true nature after all. "When Helena spoke to you, didn't she tell you what you are?"

"Yeah. She said, 'You are one of the Nephilim.'"

"Aye, but you're not a typical one." Alec frowned, wondering how he should break the news. He didn't want to frighten her—but he couldn't hide the truth, either. They rounded a corner and headed down the adjoining lane, past the tightly packed, magnificent houses bordering the canal. "Claire, where were you born?"

"New York."

"I thought so." Alec shoved his hands in his jeans pockets as they walked. "Seventeen years ago, a Grigori conceived a child with a human mother in New York, and then disappeared. I think that was your father."

Claire blinked. "My father is . . . a *Grigori*?"

"He is. Which makes you a Halfblood."

Claire stopped in her tracks, staring at him, speechless.

"We were fairly certain to begin with," Alec went on, "but now I've seen your aura—Grigori have golden auras, Nephilim's are blue—and yours is green. There's no question, Claire."

Her hand went to her mouth, and she drew in a long breath, clearly thunderstruck. "I'm *half* angel?" she whispered.

"Aye."

"Oh my God."

"I'm sorry—all this time we've been talking, I thought you knew. You seemed to know everything else. . . ."

"So you know my father?" Claire asked, suddenly eager.

From her tone, it was clear she had no clue how serious her situation was, or the deadly consequences that might lie in store. Alec's heart wrenched, knowing that he was going to have to shatter her world.

"No, but I know *of* him," Alec replied slowly. "I don't know all the details, but a colleague of mine has been searching for him, the mother, and," he went on, glancing at her, "their Halfblood child all these years."

"Why has he been searching for us? Why did my dad disappear? Did he do something wrong?"

"Aye."

"What did he do?"

Alec paused, a flurry of sadness and frustration welling

up within him. If only he could put off the answer to that question, or at least find some way to soften it. "He conceived you," Alec answered quietly.

"Why was that a crime?"

"Because, since the proliferation of the Nephilim began, it's been prohibited for Grigori to associate with human beings *or* Nephilim—let alone procreate with them."

"Wait, wait, wait, wait, wait. You're saying my birth was . . . *illegal?* That my entire *existence* is . . ."

"Forbidden," he responded, his chest constricting at the look of pain on her face. Gently, he added, "As far as we know, Claire, there hasn't been a true Halfblood for over a thousand years."

"A thousand years?" Claire backed away, clasping and unclasping her hands, which were now visibly shaking. She stopped at the side of the canal, where she stood for a long moment, staring at a moored rowboat where a trio of white herons were roosting. "So that's why my father disappeared," she whispered hoarsely. "He had to hide."

"Aye."

A sudden thought seemed to occur to her. She whirled and stared at him, her eyes glistening with sudden tears. "You said it's forbidden for Grigori to associate with human beings *or* Nephilim?"

He nodded grimly.

"So then . . . is it against the law for *you and me* to . . . ?"

Alec's teeth clenched. "Aye. Technically, any relationship

between us is against Grigori law. *If* the Elders discover us—which I hope they never will."

A tear slid down her cheek. "What about me and my mom? You said they were searching for us." Her eyes flickered with fear. "Helena said my *life* is in danger. Does that mean the Grigori plan to . . . get rid of me? Or get rid of both of us?"

"I don't know." Alec heaved a bitter sigh. He'd hoped he wouldn't have to spring this grim fact on her yet, but he couldn't lie to her either. "The truth is, the last time there was an offspring of this nature, there was a lengthy and convoluted trial. The Elders saw the Halfblood as a great risk, and the parents as the perpetrators of that risk. The Grigori mother, human father, and Nephila child were all executed."

"Oh my God." Claire turned away, brushing away another tear. Her hands were shaking.

"But that was such a long time ago," Alec continued quickly. "I believe the Council would be more open-minded today."

Claire's knees seemed to give way. She sank down onto a low brick wall edging a garden, crying openly now. It cut him to the quick. *Damn this touch thing,* Alec thought. He sat down on the wall beside her and took her in his arms, pressing her tightly against him, desperate to reassure her. "If the Grigori or anyone else mean you or your mother harm, I'll watch over you," he vowed solemnly against her ear. "I'll do everything in my power to protect you, Claire."

She pulled out of his embrace to look up at him, wiping tears from her eyes. "Why would they see me as a risk? *Why* was my birth such a sin?"

Alec ran his fingers through his hair, resisting another strong impulse to take her hand in his. "You're as close to a Grigori as a Nephila can get, Claire. You have the potential to be more powerful than any Nephilim on the planet."

"All I do is get visions," she protested.

"Visions of the past and future. A future you've proven you can *change*. It's a mighty gift. Not to mention that you've just Awakened. Your gifts will grow in strength as you age, and you may even develop other abilities."

"What other abilities?"

"Your father would have had a second talent, but I don't actually know what it was. Any new abilities you've inherited will reveal themselves in time. But a true seer is very rare. In the wrong hands, a person with great mental powers could bring a nation to its knees."

"The wrong hands? Like who? What are they worried about? That I'll become a spy?"

"I realize this is a lot to take in all at once," Alec said patiently. "Suffice it to say that, without any ties to bind you to the Grigori, they'll see you as a loose cannon. My guess is they'll want to keep you—and possibly your mother—someplace where they can monitor you closely."

"Keep me?" Another tear ran down her cheek. "You mean imprison me."

"If they find you."

"What do you mean? You *have* found me. Wasn't that your job? Isn't that why you're here?"

"No. I've just been standing in for the Grigori Watcher assigned to find you. His name is Vincent. He was called out of town for a while, and asked me to keep an eye out at Emerson. When he returns later this week, I'll tell him about you—without giving away your name. And I'll assure him that you pose no threat."

Claire looked at him with half fear, half hope. "And he'll believe you? He'll take me off the wanted list? My mom and I will be safe?"

"Vincent is my godfather and my mentor," Alec answered resolutely. "He taught me everything I know. I'd trust him with my life."

Alec hoped he could trust Vincent with *her* life as well.

twenty

❧

"A re you okay?" Alec regarded Claire with concern as they paused on her threshold.

"Not really," Claire replied honestly.

She felt overwhelmed, both mentally and physically—and as if she were a completely different person than she had been the day before. But in fact, she reminded herself, she was not a *person* at all. She was this paranormal . . . *being* . . . who shouldn't even exist.

Nothing was simple anymore. Her relationship with Alec was illegal. Her birth—her very life—was illegal. Some supernatural police force she'd never known existed might decide to imprison or execute her the minute they found her—just because her father was an angel.

"It's a lot to digest," she added, "and it's all . . . terrifying."

"I'm sorry."

"I still have a lot of questions. Like, who is Helena? If she's a Grigori and she knows who I am, isn't she supposed to turn me in? Do you think she already has? But if so, why send me all those warnings?"

"I don't know. But unless she contacts you again and gives you more information, there's nothing we can do about it. Meanwhile, you're exhausted and so am I. Right now I think we should get some sleep."

"I hope I *can* sleep. Two weeks ago, my biggest concern was how to fit in, how to be normal. Now I know that's never going to happen and instead I'm afraid for my *life*."

"Normal is overrated, Claire. And as for your life . . . I swear, I won't let anything happen to you." A weighty pause followed and then a gentle smile lit his handsome face. "After all, I don't want to sing at the Homecoming assembly all by myself, do I?"

Claire could tell that behind Alec's smile he was still very worried about her—but the affection in his voice, and the way he was looking at her, made her heart skip a beat. She matched his playful tone, hoping to ease some of his concern. "I forgot all about that. I owe you a rehearsal."

"How about tomorrow, after school? In the music room?"

"Deal," she answered, realizing she was looking forward to it.

He fell silent. Claire glanced up at him, catching a sudden, uncertain look in his eyes. She wondered if he was thinking the same thing she was. Here they were, standing just a few feet apart, at her front door. Were they supposed to kiss good-bye?

Remembering their kiss yesterday—at least before it turned disastrous—made her tingle in anticipation. But, she reminded herself, she wasn't just a girl with a crush, and Alec wasn't just a boy she had a crush on. There were bigger things at stake now. Did she dare kiss him again, knowing what might happen? And of far greater consequence: If their entire relationship was against Grigori law, what would happen if they pursued it?

"Alec, even if you can convince them that I'm not a threat," she whispered, her heart seizing, "what would they do if they found out about . . . us?"

"I don't know," he answered, staring at his shoes. "At the very least, I imagine they'd sever all ties between us and send me away. At the worst . . ." His eyes lifted to hers again, fiercely determined. "Let's not think about the worst. I believe that anything worth having is worth fighting for. Don't you?"

"Yes," she replied emphatically.

They moved into each other's arms then for a quick, intense hug. Through the thin fabric of her blouse, Claire felt the warmth of Alec's hands as they pressed firmly against her back. It made her feel comforted, reassured . . . safe. And then he was stepping back and carefully shoving his hands in his pockets again.

"See you at school tomorrow?" he said softly.

All she could do was nod as he turned and walked away.

Claire undressed and turned on the shower, gratefully stepping beneath the comforting warm spray. As she washed her hair, she tried to calm herself, but her mind was in a whirl, her thoughts consumed by all that she'd just learned.

Was her mother aware of her father's true identity, and the dangerous heritage he'd passed on? Did she dare ask her about it? Claire frowned, nixing the idea. Whatever her mom *did* know, she was finally happy, and she'd even had a coffee date the night before. Alec had insisted he was going to do his best to defuse the situation. What would be the point of disrupting her mother's newfound harmony? Besides, the woman in Claire's vision had been so emphatic: *Don't tell anyone.* Claire had already screwed that up. Twice.

It'd be best, Claire decided, to wait a few days until Alec talked to his godfather. When Alec came back with a report that they were safe, then, hopefully, it would be okay to talk about all this with her mom.

However—her mother's peace of mind notwithstanding—Claire was still dying to know the truth. Who *was* her father? How and when did they meet? As Claire dried off from her shower and finished dressing, she wondered if she could find proof that he was a Grigori.

She had been tempted many times to look through her mother's things for some clue to her father's identity, but she'd always talked herself out of it. Back then, her father had just been a man who'd abandoned her and her mom. Now, he was something else entirely—a Grigori in danger who had to flee to protect them. She just *had* to know more.

Stifling a wave of guilt, Claire opened her mother's bedroom door and snuck in. The room was as starkly furnished as Claire's: just a double bed, an end table, and a dresser strewn with a few knickknacks. Matted and framed posters of Paris, London, and other far-flung locations hung on the walls, offering the only hint at her mother's personal interests.

Claire spent several minutes going through her mother's drawers. Not finding anything special, she moved to the collection of little boxes on her dresser, which contained an assortment of costume jewelry. Then she remembered that her mom kept her best jewelry hidden in a shoe box in her closet.

Claire methodically searched through every shoe box on the closet shelf, but to her disappointment, she found nothing but shoes. *Come on*, she thought, *there has to be something in here*. As her hand grazed a pair of blue pumps, Claire felt a sudden tingle rush up her arm. She gasped and dropped the shoe instinctively. She'd forgotten her new ability could be triggered by an object and not just a person. Brian's theory was that it had only worked because the bracelet's owner—Erica's mom—was having a traumatic experience, but maybe he was wrong. Maybe if she concentrated really hard, harder than she had with Alec's lockbox, she wouldn't have to rely on physical evidence alone to find out more about her dad.

She paused, bracing herself, and then wrapped her fingers around the shoe she'd dropped. *Speak to me*, she implored with her mind, repeating the phrase over and over. To her satisfaction, the tingle grew stronger, and then came a brief flash of a vision: *She was in a store, trying on those very shoes, and admiring the way they looked on her feet. Her mom's feet.*

Claire let go of the shoe with a smile and returned the shoe box to the shelf. Any item in this room *might*, if she was lucky, give her the information she was so desperately seeking—and that last vision hadn't made her feel woozy at all.

On the floor beneath the clothes were a few more shoe boxes. Claire dug behind them and found another box, buried in a deep corner of the closet. When she saw what was inside, her heart leapt. It was the hidden jewelry stash—the one Claire's mother had shown her once or twice when she was younger—an assortment of tiny boxes and pouches containing various pieces of precious jewelry.

Claire fingered every piece, admiring them and hoping for a vision. One tiny, old box contained a beautiful, antique-looking gold ring with a large, emerald-cut amethyst. Claire had never seen it before. Even in the dim light of the closet, the stone reflected a pure, deep purple light.

She took the ring out of the box and studied it. The band was engraved on the underside: TO L, WITH LOVE, R.

Could it be an engagement ring, engraved with a message to her mom? She slipped it on. The ring was so small, it only fit her little finger. *Strange*, she thought. Her mother's hands were the same size as her own.

Then she felt it. A vision was coming. Claire blinked, and then—

She was sitting at a wrought-iron table set with a bone china tea service, on the back porch of a large brick mansion, overlooking a green expanse of garden.

The amethyst ring sparkled on the slender ring finger of her right hand as she sipped from a cup. The tea was warm and fragrant, and it relaxed her.

The sound of a little girl's laughter caught her attention. A golden-haired child, perhaps four years of age, sat at her own miniature table across the lawn, serving tea from a tiny teapot to a group of dolls and stuffed animals.

"Lynn!" The womanly voice that issued from Claire's mouth was concerned but not angry. "Be careful not to spill any tea on your dress."

"Okay, Mommy," the little girl replied.

With a rush of sound and light, the images disappeared.

Claire caught her breath. The child—Lynn—must have been *her mom*. And the body she'd inhabited must have been her mom's *mother*—the grandmother Claire had never met. Tears sprang into Claire's eyes as she carefully replaced the ring and returned the shoe box to its hiding place. She'd just seen where her mother grew up! She'd felt what it was like, for a fleeting instant, to be her own grandmother!

For the first time, she had an inkling of what Alec had meant when he said she had a potent gift that might make others wary. This power she had, it was truly amazing . . . incredible.

With no boxes left to go through, Claire sifted quickly through her mother's clothes. She made sure to deliberately touch each garment, but nothing happened. She was about to slide the closet door shut, when her eyes fell on a garment bag hanging at the far end of the rod. It occurred to her that—even though she'd touched the bag—she hadn't looked inside. In fact, although Claire had seen this old garment bag every time they'd moved, she'd never seen her mother open it. With a sudden, eerie sense of premonition, she took the plastic bag out of the closet, lay it on the bed, and unzipped it.

A brown corduroy sport coat that looked older than she was—and was obviously meant for a man—was inside. Claire's heart raced. *What was her mom doing with a man's blazer?* She extended her hand toward the jacket, her fingers trembling. It seemed as if the room was filled with an electric charge. Slowly, gently, she placed her hand on the rough corduroy lapel and waited. And waited.

Nothing.

Nothing?!

Claire frowned, annoyed, refusing to admit defeat.

She wrapped her fingers tightly around both lapels. "Breathe," she said aloud, trying to reproduce the trance Erica had put her in. "Focus." She stared at the jacket lying on the bed and mentally begged it to speak to her.

"Whose jacket are you?" Claire implored quietly. *"Who do you belong to?"*

A wave of dizziness consumed her, along with a mild twinge in her stomach. Claire felt a sudden, strange sensation of loss and distance, as if this coat had been separated from its master for a long time, dimming whatever memories it contained. She had to fight to stay upright and to hold on to the jacket.

"Tell me!" she insisted.

All at once—

Claire's ears were assaulted by the sounds of traffic. A city in motion came into focus around her. She was walking down a crowded sidewalk. On one side, she was flanked by tall buildings that reached to the sky. Across the street was a huge green park dotted with trees bursting with autumn color. In the street, a line of yellow taxicabs honked and inched slowly forward.

It looked like the New York City she'd seen depicted in every TV show, movie, and picture postcard.

Someone was holding her hand. It was a woman, blond, and shorter than she was. It was a younger version of her mother! She looked about seventeen years old and radiantly beautiful in a bright blue turtleneck and scarf.

Looking at her mom, the person that Claire was inhabiting felt a surge of warmth and happiness, a feeling so intense that it nearly took her breath away. Claire glanced down to discover that she——or whoever she was——was wearing the brown blazer. She heard herself speak. But it was a man's deep voice that issued from her throat.

"Lynn, you look cold."

In one smooth motion, the man shrugged out of the jacket and wrapped it lovingly around her mother's shoulders. It was at that moment Claire noticed the gentle swell of her teenage mother's belly. She was pregnant.

"Don't be an idiot, Tom. You'll freeze," her mom replied with a gently reproving look.

Tom, Claire thought. Was that her dad's name? My God, this was incredible! She was experiencing a precious moment from her mom's past—a moment her mother had never shared with her. Claire desperately wished her mom was wearing reflective sunglasses, so she could see the man's face.

A new sound entered Claire's consciousness, louder than even the New York traffic: the thump and vibration of the front door closing. She blinked and came back to the present with such force that she almost fell backward. The sounds of her mom dropping her bag and keys on the table downstairs filtered upward.

"Claire?" came her mom's voice. "Are you here?"

Claire quickly zipped up the garment bag and stuffed it back in the closet. She shut the closet doors and double-checked that the room was in the exact same state in which she'd found it.

"Claire?" Her mom was starting up the stairs now.

Claire tiptoed down the hall into her own room, where she dove onto the bed, jammed earbuds in her ears, and snatched up a textbook from the floor. Her mom appeared in the doorway. Claire kept her eyes on the text, pretending to read.

"Why are you reading in the dark?" her mom said, flicking on the light switch.

Claire gave her mom her most innocent, surprised look, as she tugged loose one earbud. "What?"

"Hello to you, too. Why didn't you turn a light on?"

"It was, like, totally sunny five minutes ago."

"Well, now the sun is setting. Thanks for putting the lasagna in the oven—it'll be ready in ten minutes. I'll make the salad. Come down and set the table."

"'kay. Just let me finish this paragraph."

Her mom nodded and headed briefly into her own room. Claire held her breath, listening, waiting. A few seconds later, she heard her mom return downstairs, apparently not having noticed anything out of the ordinary.

Dodged that bullet, Claire thought, heaving a sigh of relief.

Throughout dinner her mom was uncharacteristically quiet. Which was just as well, since Claire's thoughts were preoccupied by the strange couple of days she'd had and all the questions that were burning in her mind. Like: What had her mom's childhood been like? Where was that palatial house? Not to mention the whole angel thing. Tom *had* to be her father. Her mom was pregnant at the time. Why else would her mom have kept that jacket all those years, unless she loved him very much—and missed him? Still, did her mom really know who and what Tom was, and that Claire was a Halfblood?

And oh yeah: Am I destined to be vaporized by a Council of celestial beings?

This wasn't the right time to bring any of this up. She'd stick to her plan and say nothing. For now.

Thankfully, however, Claire *could* talk to Brian and Erica. She spent several hours on video chat that night, telling them about her dad's jacket vision, and detailing everything she'd learned from Alec.

"Fascinating," Brian said, in a dead-on impression of Mr. Spock, when she'd gone over all that she remembered. "And frightening." He insisted he'd been paying full attention, even though his eyes were glued to the video game he was playing—and winning—simultaneously.

"I sure hope Alec knows what he's doing," Erica added, "and can get you off the hook."

"You're not the only one," Claire agreed.

"What I want to know is, what's Alec *doing* here?" Brian said.

"What do you mean?" Claire asked.

"He said the Grigori watch over the Awakened and police the Fallen—but that he wasn't assigned to you. So what *is* his assignment?"

"Huh. That's a good question," Claire said. "We'll have to ask him tomorrow."

Mr. Patterson faced the class, swinging his right hand up forcefully against his left fist, an action that propelled a tiny wad of paper up with a resounding *pop*. "Okay! Pop quiz, everyone."

The class groaned. Claire stifled a yawn. After the late-night chat with the gang, she'd been up until two in the morning doing homework. That, compounded by her lack of sleep on Saturday night, made her so groggy that she'd barely been able to drag herself out of bed that morning.

"Clean sheet of paper, name at the top," Patterson commanded. "Question one: Name three things that Benjamin Franklin invented."

Claire leaned toward Alec, who sat beside her. "How about, name the true source of Franklin's genius," she whispered with a covert smile.

Something whizzed past her head and hit the wall behind them—a small, pink rubber eraser. Claire started up guiltily to find Mr. Patterson glaring at her.

"I'm sorry, Miss Brennan, I seem to have dropped

something back there," Patterson intoned flatly. "Would you mind bringing it back to me? Or would that interrupt your conversation?"

Claire flushed and was struggling for a reply when Alec scooped up the tiny eraser and stood. "It was my fault, sir. I wasn't sure I heard your question properly, and Claire was just repeating it for me."

"Next time, Mr. MacKenzie, raise your hand and ask *me* to repeat it."

"Yes, sir." Alec walked to the front and calmly set the eraser on Patterson's desk.

Claire hid a grateful smile. Mr. Patterson continued with the oral quiz. After class, she waited for Alec outside.

"Thanks for taking the blame," Claire said as he emerged.

"I told you I'd protect you."

She returned his grin as they headed off together toward their next class. She was bursting with questions for him, but first she was eager to share her news. "I have something to tell you."

"What?"

"I found my father's jacket last night."

Alec's green eyes widened as Claire told him the whole story, from the thing with her mother's shoe, to her grandmother's ring, to the vision about her mother and Tom.

"For a few minutes, I *was* my own father—at least, I'm pretty sure it was him. I didn't feel sick or hot during any of those visions, either. Why is that?"

"Your body is getting used to your mind being displaced to another time and location," Alec explained. "But there could be more to it. They were pretty gentle visions, weren't they?"

"They were all lovely."

"And the sickest you ever felt was when you watched me . . . ?"

Claire nodded.

"It's possible that the more violent a vision is, the greater the toll it takes on your body."

"Fun," Claire muttered sarcastically.

"This is really significant, Claire. You should be proud. You made all those objects talk to you. That level of control doesn't always happen this quickly." Alec reached out hesitantly, as if to take her hand.

Claire flinched away just inches from contact as their eyes met. She swallowed hard. "We probably shouldn't . . ."

"Right," he said, lowering his hand and shoving it in his pocket. "Better not to take any chances."

"This is so frustrating," she groaned, "being so afraid to touch anyone."

Alec gave her an encouraging smile. "It won't always be this way."

"It won't? How do you know?"

"I don't—not for sure. But look how much progress you've made already. Something tells me you'll learn how to control your abilities, Claire Brennan, and it will happen sooner than you think."

twenty-one

&

"Erica, you're staring," Alec said, amused.

The four of them were sitting at their usual lunch table. It was a blue-skied, sunny afternoon, the late September air as warm as summer, and Brian and Erica were gazing at him in a kind of silent awe, not even touching their food.

"Sorry, but I'm still trying to get used to . . . I've never eaten lunch with"—Erica glanced around, lowering her voice even though they were alone on the terrace—"an *angel* before."

"Yes, you have." Alec speared a piece of lettuce from the Caesar salad that filled half his tray and took a bite. "Lots of times. You just weren't aware of it."

"Oh. I guess that's true."

"And you've been hanging out with Claire for a couple of years now," Alec reminded her. "And she's half . . . *you know.*"

"Alec doesn't like the *A*-word," Claire explained,

sipping her chocolate milk.

"You're gonna protect Claire, right?" Erica persisted. "From whatever dark celestial forces might frown upon her existence?"

"You have my word on that."

"Good." Erica leaned her elbow on the table and rested her chin on her fist, studying him. "'Cause even if she is only half human, we still think of her as one of our own."

Brian was still staring at Alec, his eyes wide and unblinking. "How did they find out she's a Halfblood, anyway? Is there, like, a group of Grigori sitting in a control booth in heaven, staring at a radar screen and waiting for blips?"

"I wish I knew. All I was told is that when an Awakened shows up on the grid, an Elder is alerted, and he or she in turn alerts one of us."

"How do they alert you?" Claire asked.

"We communicate with each other through meditation."

"The same way I connected to Helena?"

"It sounds like it."

"Wow, that beats cell phones." Brian dug into his turkey sandwich. "No roaming charges."

"There's a more important reason. Anything we say over the regular airwaves might be picked up by the Fallen. There are hundreds of thousands of them, everywhere, with every imaginable kind of ability. Although they exist in small, local groups, like gangs or Mafia families, many of them share information globally, and infiltrate every level of the world's infrastructure."

Erica finally took a bite of her own salad. "If the Fallen are so powerful, why haven't we heard of them before?"

"They—like us—keep their existence secret," Alec explained. "Humans have always seen anything different from them as a threat. If mankind knew about them and made a concerted effort to wipe them out, they'd probably succeed."

"Why don't the Grigori just take them out?" Brian asked.

"We're only allowed to eliminate those Fallen who commit serious crimes unpunished by society, the ones whose actions pose a danger to mankind. But we have to be careful. If we kill too many, they might strike back in large numbers, and it could escalate into a full-scale global conflict—a true Armageddon. Not only would they overwhelm us, they'd take many innocent human beings in their wake."

"So how many Grigori are there?" Claire asked.

Alec shrugged. "Hundreds, I think? Perhaps a thousand?"

"Wow, you really are outnumbered." Erica frowned.

Brian munched on his potato chips, gazing at Alec pensively. "Claire said you're a Watcher Ange—Grigori. That sometimes you monitor the Awakened, but your main job is to track down the Fallen who turn to the dark side and knock them off. Is that right?" He grimaced as Erica kicked him beneath the table. "What? That's what she said."

Alec winced at this blunt assessment. "I guess that's it in a nutshell—aye."

"You must be pretty good at . . . killing people," Claire observed, a quaver in her voice.

Alec shrugged and concentrated on his food, thinking it best not to reply.

They ate in silence for a while. Alec saw the threesome exchange a silent look. He anticipated what was coming next—it was a topic he'd avoided with Claire earlier but knew was bound to come up today.

Sure enough, as soon as Brian polished off his sandwich, he said, "So, dude, who's your current assignment? Who are you here to kill?" This time it was Claire who kicked him. "Hey! You were all thinking it, weren't you? I think we have a right to know."

"You don't have to answer that, Alec, if you don't want to—or aren't allowed to," Claire said quickly.

Alec felt blood rush to his cheeks. "It's all right," he answered quietly. "The truth is, I'm not on assignment at all."

"You're not?" Claire blew out a relieved breath. "I'm so glad." Then her brow knitted in confusion. "So why are you here?"

"I quit."

"You *what*?" Erica blurted, astonished.

"What do you mean, you quit?" Claire asked.

"I mean, I left. I've basically—how does your military phrase it? I've gone AWOL."

"Why?" Brian asked.

"We're taught that what we do is right and just, that our actions *save* lives in the end. And perhaps they do. But I'm tired of spying on people. Tired of being responsible for choosing who lives or dies. And tired of *taking* lives. For more than a hundred years, I ate nothing but rabbit food, did my job, and spent all my free time training. I was always alone, with no family or friends. After so many decades watching people from afar, I longed to try it for myself—to be *free*—to be one of you."

"I don't blame you." Claire's voice was deep with empathy. "That sounds like an awful way to live."

"It's like being a monk and an assassin, all rolled into one," Erica observed.

Alec nodded grimly. "With all the responsibilities, and none of the benefits." He had never had such a frank discussion with anyone before—much less with a group of humans. He felt raw and exposed—but at the same time, it was as if a weight had been lifted from his shoulders. He was glad they knew—particularly glad that Claire knew.

Claire's eyes widened suddenly. "What's the penalty for going AWOL?"

Shite, Alec thought. He'd been hoping she wouldn't ask that.

"If there are all these rules for everything," Claire went on, "I'm assuming you aren't allowed to just walk off the job anytime you want to. What will they do if they find you?"

Claire's face was so creased with anxiety, Alec couldn't bring himself to burden her further. She had enough problems of her own without worrying about his. "That's up to the Council to decide," he replied, which was as close as he wanted to come to the truth. "And I think that's enough questions for one day." He set his fork down on the table, looked around to confirm that they were still alone on the terrace, and smiled brightly. "Watch this."

Alec gazed fixedly at his fork, wrapping his mind around the implement. He then sent out a stream of energy, mentally lifting the fork until it hovered a few inches above the table.

"Oh!" Erica cried, amazed.

But Brian was disappointed. "That's it? Claire said you held back *a car* with your brain. Can't you levitate something bigger than a fork?"

"One thing at a time, Brian." Alec smiled. "Claire, keep your eyes on me. I want to teach you something."

Claire looked directly at Alec. "What am I looking for?"

"It's like looking for a hidden image in a 3-D picture."

Alec made the fork spin in the air. "Look just past me, Claire, over my shoulder. It should come into focus."

"Whoa!" Claire gasped suddenly. "You're glowing!"

Alec beamed. "You can see it?"

"See what?" Brian said, sounding like he felt left out.

"There's this glow of golden light all around him," Claire said excitedly.

"It's my aura. Its intensity correlates to the level of power being used at the time."

"I don't see anything." Erica frowned.

"That's because you don't have Grigori blood. Erica, are we still alone?"

"Yep."

"Excellent. Watch quickly, Claire. I don't want to draw too much attention, just in case." Alec concentrated until he felt the weight and breadth of the picnic table in his mind. "Everybody, hang on."

The benches began to shudder and creak beneath them. Startled, the others grabbed on to the table. Alec felt a surge of determined energy ripple through his body, up and outward, as he raised the table with its attached benches and occupants a few inches into the air, the fork jumping even higher and spinning above it.

Erica and Brian gasped.

Claire gasped even louder. "You're right—your aura is even brighter now. It's like fire radiating off you!"

Alec slowly returned the table to its former setting with

a gentle thud. The fork dropped with a clatter.

"*That,*" Brian said, his mouth agape, "was totally awesome."

Erica sat in stunned silence, still gripping the table as if her life depended on it.

Alec smiled at Claire. "It usually takes months to learn to see an aura—but then, I've never met a true Halfblood before. Now you know what to look for, Claire. You might find it handy one day."

As soon as school let out, Alec met Claire outside the theater building with his most cheerful smile. "Ready to sing?"

"You know it."

Alec was still surprised by how alive he felt when they were together, and overjoyed that she seemed to feel the same way. But knowing how complicated a relationship between them would be, let alone the possibly fatal consequences, he couldn't help worrying that she might eventually gravitate toward someone more normal, like Neil.

Alec willed himself to put all negative thoughts out of his mind. It was going to be fun to further test the limits of Claire's abilities, and just being with her now was like a gift in itself.

"When *are* auditions for the assembly, anyway?" Claire asked.

Alec yanked open the heavy exterior door and held it for her. "Friday after school."

"That's only four days away! We'd better practice every day, if we're going to be ready."

"Okay." He repressed a chuckle. While he'd like nothing better than to spend that time with her, he was pretty sure practicing wouldn't be necessary.

"What?" She glanced at him, her eyes narrowing as they moved down the corridor. "Why are you smiling?"

"No reason."

The music room was thankfully empty. Alec tried the handle on the closet door where the orchestra kept their instruments, but it was locked.

"Mr. Lang must be gone for the day." Claire frowned. "How are you going to get your guitar?"

"Like this." Alec laid a hand on the doorknob and stared at the lock intently, until he could sense the pins inside. With his mind, he carefully slid them into their proper configurations. After the tumblers clicked, he turned the handle and the door opened.

Claire stared in awe as he retrieved his guitar from the closet. "Is that how you got into my apartment yesterday?"

"Aye."

"That's much cooler than regular lock picking."

"It does have its uses." Alec grabbed two music stands and placed them in front of a pair of chairs. Claire sat down next to him as he took his guitar out of its case, then withdrew two sets of sheet music and handed one to her. "I was thinking we could sing this."

Claire glanced at the sheet music, puzzled. The song was titled "Stick with Me Baby." "I've never heard this before."

"No? It's one of my favorites. The best version was sung by Robert Plant and Alison Krauss."

"Alison Krauss?" Claire let out a nervous laugh. "I've barely started to learn how to sing *classical* music, and you want me to sing like *her*? I think that's a little out of my league."

Alec's lips twitched with the effort to hold back a smile. "I don't think so."

"Will you sing it through once for me first? Mr. Lang always does that."

"No need. It's not a complicated song. I'm pretty sure you can do it."

She made an impatient noise. "I'm honored that you have so much faith in me, Alec, but I'm still really new at this. I can't sing something I've never heard."

"Let's just give it a shot."

Claire threw up her hands. "Whatever you say, maestro. You've been warned."

Alec played the opening riff and plunged into the vocals. Claire took a deep breath and hesitantly began to sing along. As he'd expected, her voice was instantly in tune and in perfect harmony with his own. She was able to translate the notes on the page into song instinctively, just as he did—as if she'd been familiar with them all her life.

The look of astonished delight on Claire's face as she sang almost made him laugh out loud. By the final chorus, the harmony between them was perfect. The joy he felt seemed to reverberate throughout the room. Alec strummed the last chord with gusto and shot Claire an exuberant smile. "Bravo."

"Holy crap!" Claire leapt up from her chair with excitement. "Did I really just do that?"

Alec let go the laugh that had been building inside him. Seeing her this happy made him feel lit up from within, something he'd rarely experienced before. "Just like I knew you would."

She stared at him, ecstatic. "How did you know?"

"I told you before—we can *all* sing. My kind can take it one step further and sing anything, even if we haven't heard it before. You're closer to us than anyone else alive, so I figured there was a good chance you could do that as well."

"Wow. Wow. *Wow.* I guess that means we don't need to rehearse at all?"

"Nope." Alec grinned as he began packing up his guitar.

"But when I mentioned it just now, you didn't say a word!"

"I thought it'd be more fun for you to figure it out for

yourself," he answered, dropping his guitar case inside the storage closet and relocking it by touch. He turned to find Claire standing right in front of him, arms crossed.

"I blocked out the whole afternoon to work on this. I told my mom you'd drop me off at six thirty."

"Great." Alec withdrew his pocket watch from his jeans and clicked it open, glancing at the timepiece's antique face. "That gives us almost three hours before she expects you. What would you like to do with that time?"

Claire fell silent, her eyes on his. "Well, I guess we could go to the library and study. I have a ton of homework. . . ."

He nodded in agreement, although he had no interest in studying at the moment. "There's reading for English, a worksheet for Spanish, twelve problems for calculus, three chapters for history. . . ."

"A lab write-up for bio . . ."

A lock of hair fell forward into her eyes. Alec smothered his impulse to reach out and brush it back. "Twenty equations to solve for physics . . ."

"Physics must be a cakewalk for you," Claire teased. "Or maybe not, since the laws don't really apply to you."

"So, homework it is?" As Alec's eyes locked with hers, his heart beat faster, hoping she wouldn't say yes.

"We could always . . . do it later."

"But then we'd be forced to go someplace fun," Alec said jokingly.

Claire opened her mouth to reply, but he cut her off,

remembering her caveats last time.

"I know, I know. It has to be outside, and full of witnesses."

Claire shook her head, smiling. "That isn't a requirement anymore, Mr. MacKenzie. In fact—shouldn't we be worried about going to a public place? I mean, in light of the rule about relationships with Nephilim? What if we're spotted by another Grigori?"

"Don't worry, Vincent is the only Watcher who's looking for us, and he's on the East Coast at the moment. Plus he doesn't know *you're* the Halfblood."

"Well that's good, because the place I was thinking of *does* just happen to be outside and chock-full of people."

"Where's that?"

She smiled. "How do you feel about Ferris wheels?"

twenty-two

❧

Claire savored the last bite of the crisp, cinnamony churro Alec had bought her as they wandered down the Santa Monica Pier past fast-food restaurants, portrait artists, and vendors selling sunglasses, jewelry, I HEART L.A. T-shirts, and other tourist memorabilia. She loved being with Alec. With him at her side, her fear of the Grigori Council was beginning to dissipate. Claire felt invulnerable. Happy.

And excited. Every time she stole a glance at Alec's handsome face, and caught the warm glimmer in his green eyes, her heart rate sped up a little.

"You've told me a lot about the Grigori, but I'd love to know more about *you*," Claire said. Seagulls cried overhead as the pair headed to the amusement park in the middle of the pier. "Are you really from Scotland?"

"Born and raised." Alec finished his own churro, and they paused to drop their napkins and wrappers into a trash can.

"Do you really have an aunt in Korea and an uncle Gregory who pays your tuition?"

"No. I made them up—sorry."

"How do you know Korean, then?"

"I've been able to understand every language on the planet since the day I was born. Every Grigori can do that."

"Are you serious? You can speak Swahili? Mongolian? Basque?"

"*Every* language. It's like our singing talent. I don't necessarily *know* I can speak or read a language until the situation presents itself. When I hear someone talking, I automatically understand what they're saying and can respond just as easily."

Claire was impressed. She tilted her head toward a young couple nearby who were conversing quietly in what clearly wasn't English. She lowered her voice. "Okay. What language are they speaking?"

Alec slowed his footsteps, then leaned in so only Claire could hear him. "Farsi, I think."

She could feel his breath, warm and sweet, on her cheek. It made her skin tingle. "Have you ever spoken Farsi before?"

"No, only Arabic."

"What are they saying?"

Alec stopped to listen, keeping his eyes averted. "The guy's saying that they've known each other a long time, and he knows he should ask her father about this first, but—"

Alec's eyes lit up. "Oh, this is good. I think he's getting ready to propose."

"Really?"

Alec's face was just inches away, his arm and hand nearly brushing hers. Claire longed to feel the warmth of his touch, wished desperately that he would take her hand in his—but she knew he was as worried about her getting an unwanted vision as she was. Reluctantly, she pulled back and they kept moving. When they were farther away, Claire turned to look behind them.

As Alec had predicted, the young Persian man was down on one knee, whipping a tiny red velvet box from his pocket, which he opened to reveal a ring. The woman gasped and began to cry with joy.

"That is so cool," Claire said. "It's like magic. Maybe it goes back to the Tower of Babel, when all the world spoke one language."

"Maybe."

They passed through the entrance of the amusement park.

"So if you used to travel the world, policing all the bad Awakened, how did you pay for it?" Claire asked. "Did you have a safety-deposit box full of passports and stacks of cash, like the CIA?"

"We had access to bank accounts around the world, but it wasn't like a salary. We took what we needed for each job."

"Where'd you get the money to come here?"

A cautious expression crossed his face. "I . . . slowly put that money aside, a wee bit at a time."

"Isn't that kind of like embezzling . . . from *God*?" Claire asked in faux shock.

Alec shrugged and grinned at her good-natured teasing. "Honestly, I don't know where the money comes from. But I worked hard for it and like to think of it as saving meticulously."

They'd reached the ticket booth for the Ferris wheel now. It towered above them, stopping intermittently to pick up passengers. After Alec bought their tickets and they'd moved into the waiting line, Claire asked more seriously, "How long did it take you to save?"

"Thirty years."

"Wow. You've been planning this since before I was born?"

Alec glanced around them a little uncomfortably, but the only other people in line—a young mother tending to a couple of children—were paying no attention to them. He continued under his breath, "Aye. For a long time, this whole thing was just a dream I was toying with. By the time I mustered my resolve, I had saved enough to afford a place like Emerson."

"Well, I'm happy you did."

Handing over their tickets, Claire and Alec climbed on board the bright red gondola and sat down facing the ocean.

"Do you really find this kind of thing fun?" Alec asked dubiously as the wheel lurched them forward into the air, high above the pier.

"Yes! Whenever I ride one of these, I feel like I'm flying—something I've always wished I could do."

Alec nodded with a small smile. "Oh, I see. That *would* be an attraction."

The breeze felt cool against Claire's face. Sunlight sparkled on the deep blue ocean below. Since it was a Monday afternoon, the wide expanse of pale sand was nearly devoid of people, except for the occasional stroller and a few surfers in wet suits, charging out with their boards to conquer the waves. Claire leaned back against the gondola seat, very aware of how close her jeans-clad thigh was to touching Alec's. "What made you pick Emerson, specifically? Was it because of our lovely Los Angeles weather?"

"Partly. And because it's a school where students seem to actually enjoy learning. I thought—I hoped—that it would help me fit in and remain inconspicuous."

"So you had no idea I was here, or that I was a Halfblood?"

"Not until Vincent told me. If I *had* known, I would have chosen someplace else, for fear of being spotted by the local Watcher." He glanced at her. "So I'm glad I didn't know. Otherwise, we never would have met."

The look in his eyes was so sincere, it filled Claire's stomach with butterflies again. The Ferris wheel paused with them in midair, affording a panoramic view of the coastline. "Is that why you showed up at the mall the other day? Because you thought I was the one Vincent was looking for?"

"Ah. Funny story, that." Alec cleared his throat. "Actually, the first person we zeroed in on was Neil."

"Neil?" Claire started laughing. "Are you kidding? Why?"

"He sings. He's an amazing athlete. He's got a charm quotient that's off the charts."

"That's a power?"

"It can be. In its most potent form, it's called mind control. So I followed the four of you to Twin Palms, waiting for a hint of Neil's aura or to see if he'd be approached by the Fallen."

Claire shifted so she could face him. "And here I thought you followed me because you were jealous." As soon as the words left her mouth, hot blood rushed to her face. Did she really just admit that? Really?

Alec's eyes met hers. "Do you want me to be jealous?" he asked quietly.

Claire felt as if her tongue was lashed to the roof of her mouth. "I . . ."

Alec leaned in closer. "Well?"

Claire's heart skipped a beat. A shiver ran through her limbs, even though she was warm. His lips were so tantalizingly close. Her heart thundered in her chest. She wanted him to kiss her, wanted it more than anything.

At that moment, the Ferris wheel started up again with a jolt that broke the spell. Hot disappointment washed through her. Alec leaned back, a look of sudden aware- ness and regret on his face. "Maybe we shouldn't . . . ," he began. "I mean, until you learn to control your gift better. I wouldn't want you to . . ."

"You're right," she agreed reluctantly, her cheeks burn- ing. "We probably shouldn't . . ."

They fell silent. The Ferris wheel whirred around in a smooth and faster cycle. The wind was in her face again, and Claire was grateful for the breezy distraction as she willed her body to cool down and her heart to resume its natural cadence.

Alec studied her with a slow grin. "I feel like I'm under strict Grigori law again."

"What do you mean?"

"Physical contact is frowned upon in my culture."

"Are you saying . . . you aren't allowed to touch each other? Or anyone? Ever?"

Alec nodded.

"Why? That's awful!"

He pursed his lips, thinking. "How can I help you understand this? Even though we live on Earth, our culture is very removed and isolated, and more . . . well, *Vulcan*, than anything. We follow ancient laws and traditionally, we don't have families. Mating is allowed only once every five decades, at an appointed day and time scheduled by the Elders."

Claire stared at him. "You're kidding."

"I wish I were. The Elders choose the partners who are to engage in each one-time coupling. Sex isn't for pleasure, only reproduction."

"Oh. So, have you"—Claire blushed again, the heat traveling up to the roots of her hair—"ever engaged in a . . . coupling?"

"No. I'm not old enough. You have to be at least two hundred and fifty."

Claire was surprised by how ridiculously pleased she was to hear that. "So I guess with so few of those going on, there aren't many children."

"No."

"What happens to the kids?"

"Children are raised by a tutor or godparent—a Grigori who generally has no offspring of their own."

"In your case, Vincent."

He nodded. "However, my parents got tired of the rules. They secretly formed an alliance similar, in many ways, to a human marriage. Although as a young child I spent half my time with Vincent to keep up appearances, the rest of the time I lived with my mother and father covertly, in a remote corner of Scotland."

Claire felt a rush of empathy for him. "That must have been hard. From the time you were born, you've always been hiding something."

"Aye." He sighed, then added, "But then again, I *did* get to spend the first ten years of my life with parents who loved each other—and me—and who ignored the restrictions on physical contact. Although my mother did have to be careful not to crush my father and me to death when she hugged us."

"That's right! Your mother had superstrength!" Claire couldn't help but laugh.

"Funny, isn't it?" he agreed. "But I can relate to the problem. I've been afraid to hurt you in the same way."

Claire's blush deepened, and she wasn't sure what to say.

Alec's eyes found hers again. "That desire to show affection through touch—I've never forgotten it. It's something Grigori don't usually experience, as far as I know."

"I guess that explains why you, of all people—I mean Grigori—went AWOL."

He nodded pensively as the wheel slowed to a halt again. "I guess it does."

They had stopped at the very top of the Ferris wheel. The view was breathtaking, but Claire gave it only a cursory glance. Her attention was fixed on Alec. Beneath his show of quiet strength, she sensed his deep vulnerability. The thought of all he'd been through—and all the loneliness he'd endured for more years than she'd been alive—wrenched at her heart.

Her entire body trembled with the desperate need to

touch him, to offer him some comfort. She yearned to hug him, to feel his hands on her body, to feel his lips on hers.

"I want . . . ," she began.

"I know. So do I." His eyes and voice were filled with longing, but also concern. He waited, allowing her to make the choice.

Claire held her breath. His hand was resting in his lap. She reached out until her own hand hovered just an inch above his. Alec had said she could learn to control her powers. Could she do it? Did she dare?

"It's all right," he encouraged softly. "Just focus, Claire. Command your mind to stay in the moment, and not to travel."

She nodded, steeling herself. Their gazes locked. Her stomach tensed. *Focus. Focus.* Her entire body felt like a taut wire. *I am Claire*, she insisted silently. *I will stay Claire, and I will remain here beside Alec.* Slowly, gingerly, she lowered her hand until it closed over his. At first, as the gentle warmth from his skin radiated into her palm, she remained completely still, afraid to move or breathe, mentally repeating the words over and over like a mantra. *Let my mind remain here. Let my mind remain here.* To her relief, there was no dreaded, burning heat, no warning flush of a vision.

It worked, she rejoiced inwardly. *It worked!*

Alec smiled into her eyes. It felt so wonderful to touch him. Silently repeating the mantra, Claire slid her fingers around his to cup his hand, then squeezed it. Alec squeezed her hand back, his gaze never leaving hers—a wordless communion that sent a thrilling tingle up her arm and, with the speed of an arrow, straight into her heart.

Without further reflection, Claire dove across the space between them, wrapped her arms around Alec, and brought her lips to his. She sensed his initial surprise, but then he wound his arms around her, drawing her close as he kissed her back.

The kiss started slowly, a sweet, tentative searching. Alec's lips and tongue felt warm against hers, mesmerizing her. As their mouths melded with growing fervor, a sudden image infiltrated Claire's brain. She recognized it as what Alec must have experienced while gazing at her that afternoon in the stairwell when they first sang together. *No! Stay!* Claire ordered her mind, rejecting the lovely vision of how Alec saw her then, concentrating with every molecule of her being on the here and now and her own body. *Stay in the present. Be in this moment.*

The invading image fled. To Claire's relief, she was herself once more. Alec drew back slightly, his eyes searching hers, and she could hear and feel his breath coming in unsteady gasps that echoed her own.

"Are you okay?"

Claire smiled. "I'm fine. More than fine."

"Well thank goodness for that." He brought his mouth back to hers.

His kiss grew bolder and more passionate, awakening

new sensations deep within her. She melted into his embrace, kissing him hungrily, parting her lips and letting desire draw her down. She smoothed her hands over the sinewy muscles of his upper arms, then reveled in the feel of his lean, hard back beneath his T-shirt. As she pressed herself against him, straining to get closer, his hands moved restlessly up and down her back, then rose up to tangle in her hair. All the while, she repeated the mantra to herself: *Stay in the present. Be in this moment.*

She loved the way they fit together, loved the way he tasted and felt. It was as if they were two halves of a circuit suddenly connected and made whole, allowing a current of electricity to spark between them. She never wanted the kiss to end.

The wheel began to spin forward again and they broke apart, both breathing hard. Claire was stunned. The look on Alec's face told her he felt the same way. With a deep, happy sigh, she leaned her head on Alec's shoulder. His arm slid around her. They remained in that position, silently staring out at the ocean during the final revolution of the ride. It took every minute of that time for Claire's breathing and heart rate to return to something approaching normal.

When the wheel carried them down to the bottom and they had disembarked, Alec reached for her hand with a smile. "I've decided," he said as they headed back down the pier, "that I like Ferris wheels."

twenty-three

꩜

The first person Claire saw when her mom dropped
her off at school the next morning was Neil.

He was sitting on the low wall in front of the gym,
reading a book—but when he saw her, he stood up immediately and started in her direction. "Hey, Claire."

His smile was so winning that she couldn't help but
smile back. "Hey, Neil. You guys are reading *The Great
Gatsby* now?"

Neil glanced down at the book as if he'd forgotten
what it was. He let out an embarrassed chuckle. "Actually,
I finished it a week ago. I just didn't want to make it obvious that I was waiting for you." He darted her a look. It
reminded her of the way Alec had looked at her all day yesterday—the kind of look she used to long for from Neil.
Claire was flattered, but nothing more—which was a little
surprising. If this had happened two weeks ago, she would
have been over the moon.

"So," Neil said as they climbed the stairs toward

the Upper School, "have you cast your primary vote for Homecoming Court yet?"

"No. Why? When's that due?"

"It has to be turned in by the end of the day."

"Good to know. But to be honest, I've never paid much attention to the whole Homecoming Court thing."

"Why not?"

"I guess because I was never eligible before." Nominations for king and queen were restricted to seniors, and prince and princess were chosen from the junior class. "What's the point of having a king or queen, anyway, when they don't actually do anything?"

Neil shrugged as they passed the stream of students jogging back downhill from their lockers. "I think it's like all kings and queens today. They're figureheads, a proud tradition to rally the citizenry."

She eyed him suspiciously. "Is that a quote from last year's history textbook?"

"*Busted*," he admitted with a grin. "But it sounded convincing, right?"

"Like Churchill himself," Claire stated with mock reverence.

"What I was getting at," Neil went on, "is that high schools need figureheads, too. Which is why I nominated you for Homecoming Princess."

"You *what*?" Claire gasped, astonished.

"And I told all my friends to do the same."

"You have got to be kidding me! Neil, what were you thinking? No one in this school knows I'm alive."

"Where have you been, Claire? After that scaffolding accident, *everybody* knows who you are."

Claire flushed a little. "Oh—that. Still, that doesn't make me princess material."

"You're one of the most beautiful girls in this school, certainly one of the nicest, and hands down the smartest. You definitely deserve to be in the Royal Court."

"I . . . don't know what to say," Claire replied, flustered.

"How about *yes*, and you'll go with me?"

Claire's stomach clenched. Uncertainly, she asked, "Go with you . . . where?"

"To the dance?" he said hopefully.

"Oh! . . . Oh . . ."

Neil's face fell. "Okay. That's not *quite* the response I was hoping for."

They'd reached the library landing now, a few yards from Claire's locker. She stopped and tried to gather her wits. This was the moment she'd been dreaming of for over two years! But after yesterday, everything had changed.

"Neil," she began hesitantly, "I'm sorry, but . . . I think Alec and I are . . . I mean, he hasn't asked me to the dance yet, but—"

Neil cut her off, holding up his hands. "Looks like it's my turn to say 'Oh.' I knew you two were rehearsing a song, but I had no idea you were . . . Seriously, Brennan.

That's totally cool. Alec seems like a great guy . . . that freak-out at the mall notwithstanding."

Claire gave him a soft smile. "Thanks." *Crap*, she thought. He looked so disappointed. Despite her aversion to the whole Homecoming Princess thing, she still liked Neil and would love to go to the dance. What if Alec didn't ask her?

Neil's eyes were suddenly drawn to something immediately behind Claire. His mouth tightened slightly. Claire spun around to find Alec at their locker, his gaze fixed casually on the two of them. Her heart skipped a beat at the sight of him. How long had he been standing there? He looked incredibly handsome in his faded green T-shirt and black leather jacket. She hadn't stopped thinking about Alec since he'd dropped her off at home the evening before, when they'd exchanged another good-bye kiss at her door—a kiss equally as thrilling as the ones they'd shared atop the Ferris wheel.

Claire smiled at Alec, then whirled back to find Neil staring at them as if struggling to remain calm.

Tension crackled through the air. Claire couldn't believe this was happening. She'd never even had *one* boy pay attention to her before; and now *two* boys liked her at the same time?

Brian and Erica rounded the corner of the library and, caught in the awkwardness, shot questioning looks at Claire. After what seemed like forever, Alec gave Claire and Neil a friendly nod, then turned his attention back to his locker.

As if released from a spell, Neil shrugged good-naturedly. "See you in Concert Singers." With a wave to Brian and Erica, he was gone.

Claire had no idea what she was supposed to do next. Kiss Alec hello? Go talk to her friends?

The first bell rang, rescuing her from either option. "Morning!" she blurted, and then raced off to her first class. It was AP bio, which, to her relief, she shared with no one.

After bio came Concert Singers, and with that came more quizzical looks from Brian and Erica. For the entire fifty-minute period, through every note of the *Messiah*, Claire felt them staring at her, while Neil did his best to act normal.

When the bell rang at the end of class, Erica and Brian pounced on Claire.

"Tell us everything. *Now*."

"On top of the Ferris wheel, huh?" Erica nodded with approval. "That's a good make-out spot."

Claire blushed. She had quickly summarized yesterday for them as they helped Erica put up Homecoming posters during their break. Although she hadn't told them *everything*. The day before had been so special, she wanted to keep *some* details to herself.

"You had mouth-to-mouth contact, and you didn't have a vision?" Brian asked, impressed, as he grabbed a poster from the stack and handed it to Claire. "How'd you pull that off?"

"By concentrating really, *really* hard," Claire confessed.

"That's awesome!" Erica enthused. "You're making progress."

"So, are you guys official?" Brian asked.

"I think so." Claire slapped the poster up against one of the stucco walls and secured it with masking tape.

"Have you told your mom?" Erica asked.

"Not yet."

"Has he asked you to Homecoming?" Erica persisted.

"Slow down, guys! This was *yesterday*. We kissed. That's all." *Although*, Claire thought, *it had been incredible.*

Erica pulled a strip of tape from the roll that hung around her wrist like a bracelet. "Well, if you guys aren't an official item, then what was that silent pissing contest between Alec and Neil?"

"Yeah, I've never seen Neil look so uncomfortable in my life," Brian agreed.

Claire sighed. "Neil had just asked me to Homecoming. Alec might have overheard—I'm not sure."

"Oh my God!" Erica cried. "What did you tell Neil?"

"I said no, and that I'm kind of with Alec now."

Erica nodded. Brian groaned.

"What?" Claire said.

"You did the right thing," Brian said, "but that sucks. You've wanted Neil to ask you out for, like, forever."

"Yeah, so Alec *better* do the right thing and ask you to Homecoming," Erica exclaimed with authority, "or I am going to figure out what his own personal Kryptonite is, and kill him with it."

"That reminds me." Brian exchanged a look with Erica. "We, uh . . . went shopping yesterday."

Claire looked at them, confused. "What?"

"Oh yeah." Erica withdrew a small bag from her backpack and handed it to Claire. "We got you something."

The bag was from a local boutique. Claire reached inside and took out their gift: a pair of long, stretchy black gloves. "What are these for?" she said uncertainly.

"Think of them as your own personal, nonlethal Kryptonite," Brian explained. "Fabric seems to work as a barrier to suppress your powers, just like it did for Rogue in *X-Men*."

"Hopefully you can touch people now, without having to concentrate so hard," added Erica.

Claire nodded slowly, conflicted. "Thanks, guys. It's a good idea, and very thoughtful. But . . . I'll look like a freak wearing gloves to school."

"Not if you have company." Grinning, Erica pulled another pair of long gloves from her backpack—these in bright pink spandex—and pulled them on, fitting them deliberately over her fingers. "It'll be a fashion statement.

We might start a new trend."

"Or be classified as a *pair* of freaks." Claire laughed and put on her own gloves. "Thanks for the solidarity, sister." She and Erica high-fived.

"Vision?" Erica inquired, after their hands had smacked together.

"Nope." Claire smiled happily.

"Score!" Brian cried with a satisfied nod. "But keep in mind, CB, they'll only help with the hand-touching thing. If you go around kissing people, you're on your own."

twenty-four

꩜

Alec spotted Claire on her way to history class and hurried up to her. She looked great in her pin-striped hoodie and formfitting jeans, her hands shoved in her pockets as she walked along, her face glowing in the late morning sunlight.

The previous afternoon had been so amazing, he'd barely been able to sleep all night. He'd spent the time replaying the events and wondering how and when he should pose a particular burning question. When he spotted Claire with Neil that morning by their locker, he'd been filled with dread that he might be too late—but Neil's look of disappointment had renewed his hopes.

"Hi there." Alec smiled down at Claire, hoping he appeared more calm than he felt.

Claire returned his smile a little awkwardly. "Hi yourself."

Shite, he thought, his heart drumming in his chest. *Why does she look uncomfortable?* Had he misunderstood Neil's expression? *Get on with it*, he told himself.

"About this morning," he began tentatively.

"Yeah?" She wasn't looking at him.

"Did . . . Neil ask you to Homecoming?"

She hesitated. "He did."

His stomach tightened. "And? What did you say?"

"I said no."

Relief cascaded over him like a wave. He still had a chance. But her expression was unreadable. Would she turn him down, too? Maybe she had no interest in school dances. He took a deep breath. "Well, I had *hoped* to be the first," he said, striving for a light tone. "But I was wondering if you'd like to—"

"Yes!" Claire burst out, beaming. "I'd love to!"

Alec let out a long sigh, unable to stop the huge smile that followed, thrilled when Claire suddenly stopped and threw her arms around him. He hugged her back fervently. They stood in each other's tight embrace for a long moment, heedless of the rush of students swerving around them. When Claire drew away slightly, he saw his own happiness mirrored on her face.

"After yesterday, how could you even doubt that I'd say yes?" she asked softly.

He was too filled with emotion to reply. Stepping back, he slid his hands down the length of her arms, caressing them affectionately through her sleeves, reminding himself that he had to stop before he reached her bare hands—but she boldly took one of his hands in hers. He started at the feel of the silky texture covering her fingers, and glanced down at their clasped hands in surprise. "Gloves?"

"They were Brian and Erica's idea. Now I can relax when I hold your hand, without repeating a mantra like a crazed monk."

He grinned as they walked on together. "Why didn't I think of that?"

"You're the first boy I've ever brought home," Claire said to him two days later, as they walked up to the front door of her apartment.

"And this is the first time I've ever been *brought* home to meet anyone's mother," Alec replied with a chuckle.

When Claire told her mom that a boy had asked her to Homecoming, her mom insisted on meeting him first. So here they both were, about to make the introductions—and Alec just prayed he could pull it off with aplomb.

He was nervous—and fully aware of how ironic that was. He thought about the thousands of assignments he'd undertaken over the past century—the cultures he'd studied, the many and varied personas he'd created, the populations he'd infiltrated—and he had to smile. Most of those situations had been fraught with danger; in some cases, he'd come close to losing his life; yet none of them had made him feel as anxious or uncertain as the one he was about to undertake.

"Be prepared, my mom might act like a total spaz. I told her your emancipation story, but nothing else."

"Okay."

Claire removed her gloves, stuffed them into her backpack, and unlocked her front door. The delicious smell of curry wafted out from somewhere inside.

"Hey, Mom!" Claire called out as they entered. "This is Alec."

A pretty, pale, slender blonde was working at a computer desk in the front room. When she crossed the room to greet them, Alec could detect a slight mother-daughter resemblance in their faces, but that's all. Clearly, Alec thought, Claire inherited her darker hair and complexion from her father.

"Hi." Claire's mom gave her daughter a quick hug, then extended her hand to Alec, her blue eyes wary as she sized him up. "Nice to meet you, Alec."

Alec shook her hand firmly. "It's a pleasure to meet you, Ms. Brennan."

"Ooh, you were right." She grinned at Claire. "He does have a luscious accent."

"Mom!" Claire blushed.

To Alec, her mom added, "Please, call me Lynn. Come in, have a seat."

Lynn sat down in an easy chair, gesturing for them to sit across from her. Claire and Alec did as instructed, perching awkwardly on the sofa beside each other.

"So, Claire tells me you just moved here from Scotland, and that you live alone."

"Aye, mum," Alec returned politely.

"That must be difficult. How do you support yourself?"

He and Claire exchanged a glance. They'd talked this out in detail before coming, and he'd prepared himself to be quizzed. Still, Alec hated to lie to this woman. It was obvious how much she adored her daughter. He suspected that she'd also dearly loved Claire's father. Alec could easily imagine the kind of boy Lynn would want Claire to date: a smart, decent, straitlaced young man from a good family—who was 100 percent *human*.

"I've worked every summer for years," Alec replied. That, at least, was completely true. "And I have a small trust fund." Also true—in a way.

"I was very sorry to hear about your parents. Claire said they passed away when you were very young?"

"Aye. I was ten." The truth again.

"I'm so sorry," she repeated.

"Thank you." Alec steered the conversation in a new direction. "I miss them very much, and I think about them every day. They'd be so happy to see where I am now, and how lucky I am. I love living here, and Emerson is a great school. Did you know that Claire and I are auditioning tomorrow to sing in the Homecoming assembly?"

"So she told me." Lynn looked at Claire with a somewhat awestruck expression. "I admit, this whole choir thing has taken me completely by surprise. I haven't heard Claire sing in years."

"Well, that's a shame, because your daughter has an amazing voice, and we're going to kick arse at the audition tomorrow."

Lynn laughed. "I hope you do."

Alec darted a look at Claire, wondering why she wasn't saying anything. She seemed to be holding her breath. The look in her eyes told him she was thrilled by how well this was going.

"The assembly's a week from Friday," Alec added. "If we're chosen, I hope you'll come and watch."

"Yeah, Mom," Claire blurted out. "You should totally come. If we get in, that is. They're gonna post the results on Monday morning."

"I wish you luck." Lynn stood and gestured toward the kitchen with a smile. "Alec, I don't claim to be a fabulous cook, but I've had chicken curry in the Crock-Pot all day. Will you join us for dinner?"

Claire beamed, nodding enthusiastically in Alec's direction.

"I'd love to," Alec responded. "Curry is one of my favorites. Thank you."

After they'd taken their seats at the kitchen table and Alec had swallowed his first bite of curry—which was spicy and delicious—Lynn turned and fixed him with her gaze. "Alec, Claire tells me that you invited her to the

Homecoming Dance, and she's accepted?"

"Aye."

"That's very sweet, but you know I can't in good conscience allow you to take her to the dance until I've asked a few more questions."

"Mom!" Another blush bloomed on Claire's cheeks. She covered her face with her hands, looking as if she wished she could disappear.

"Of course. This is your daughter we're talking about. It's your job. So go ahead, grill me."

Lynn smiled. "Thank you for humoring me. According to Claire, you're an excellent student with no disciplinary record. She insists that you don't have any of the usual vices that a parent worries about—"

"Kill me now!" Claire moaned.

"Is it true that you don't drink? Alcohol, I mean?"

"It is."

"Do you take drugs?"

"Never have, never will."

"How old are you? Sixteen?"

His first lie. "Aye."

"You can't have been driving very long?"

"I got my permit earlier than most. My car is the most expensive thing I own, so I keep it well-maintained and drive very carefully. Your daughter is safe with me."

"I hope so."

Lynn began peppering him with questions about his

past. Alec launched into his prepared answers, smoothly talking his way through and around everything she asked. He told amusing stories about his supposed aunts and uncles that were full of realistic detail. Ultimately he appeared to set her mind at ease, and managed to leave the dinner table feeling only somewhat guilty.

"I'm so glad we had this chance to talk," Lynn said as she gave him a warm, maternal good-bye hug at the front door.

"So am I." He thanked her for dinner. She wished him good luck at their upcoming audition again, then thoughtfully returned to the kitchen, giving him and Claire a moment alone. The minute she was gone, Claire grabbed him by the arm and drew him out onto the front step into the mild evening air.

"Oh. My. God," she said tensely, after the door shut behind them. "I cannot believe she put you through all that."

"It's okay, Claire. Really." Alec took her in his arms and pressed his lips briefly against her hair. "I think it went quite well, all things considered. She's a lovely woman. But I'm glad it's over and that she seems to approve."

Claire hugged him tightly. Her breath felt warm and inviting against his neck. In a low tone, she added, "When did you say Vincent will be back?"

"I expect him tomorrow or the next day. Why?"

"Because I can't wait for you to straighten everything

out with him. I'll feel so much better when I can finally tell my mom what's been happening to me, and who you are."

Alec pulled back slightly to look at her. "Do you really think that's a good idea, Claire? I don't like to keep deceiving your mother, but I don't see that we have any choice. Even after I get Vincent's approval and the danger to you both is removed, how do you think she'll take it—the fact that you're dating a Grigori?"

He felt her shrug in his arms. "I don't know. I'm trying not to think about it. But if you can somehow convince my mom that we're safe, I'm pretty sure we'll be all right."

"Your safety is my number-one priority," he promised.

"Thank you." Her arms tightened around him again.

The feel of her body against his was exhilarating, driving all rational thought from his head. "All right, prepare yourself, Claire Brennan."

She looked up at him curiously. "Prepare myself for what?"

He gazed at her affectionately. "Repeat your mantra, or whatever it is you do. Because I'm about to kiss you."

twenty-five

"What a nice young man," Claire's mom said later, as she and Claire did the dishes together.

A wet plate almost slipped from Claire's hands as she stowed it in the dishwasher. The memory of Alec's delectable kiss was making it difficult to concentrate on the task at hand, much less uphold her part in a conversation. Still, she couldn't help but smile at her mom's comment. "Yes, he *is* a nice . . . *young* man." How old had her Grigori father been when her mom first met *him*? Claire wondered suddenly. Would she ever find out?

"Obviously, Alec's very good-looking and polite," her mother was saying. "The accent's charming. He's had an unusual upbringing and he tells great stories. But . . . ."

"But?" Claire's full attention snapped back to her mom.

"It's the handsome, independent ones who often . . . don't stick around," her mom uttered softly. "Just . . . be careful."

"Mom," Claire said, striving to sound light and airy, "we're just singing a song together and going to a dance."

"I know. But I was in high school once too. And at sixteen, it's easy to fall for the first boy who takes an interest in you. It doesn't mean he's your one true love, or that it's forever."

"I'm not in love with Alec," Claire replied quickly. But her cheeks grew warm, and a jolt of insight made her doubt her own words. "I've . . . only known him for a few weeks," she added uncertainly.

Her mom glanced at her carefully, but didn't reply.

They finished the dishes in silence.

Claire's heart beat erratically as she climbed the stairs to her room, her mom's words still reverberating in her brain. *It doesn't mean he's your one true love, or that it's forever.* They stayed with Claire as she started her homework, the math problems and science passages interweaving with an elaborate parade of images and sensations in her mind: the look in Alec's eyes at the door, the deep, pure happiness she felt in his presence, the glorious sound of his singing voice, the feel of his strong arms around her, the sweet pleasure of his lips on hers.

She was still thinking about it all hours later as she lay in bed on the verge of sleep.

The jumble of intense feelings that had slowly been building up inside her over the past few weeks suddenly assembled themselves, taking on new meaning.

She was falling in love with Alec. Falling in love with an angel, just as her own mother had before her.

Friday started with a bang, and never really let up. In a good way.

Claire arrived at school fifteen minutes before her first class. She'd just reached the top of the central stairway when she saw a big group of students crowded around the general notice board outside the library, chattering excitedly. She couldn't see what they were looking at, but figured it was probably some kind of sports announcement.

She had just passed by the group and was en route to her locker, where she hoped to find Alec, when Gabrielle Miller's head whipped around.

"Claire!"

She stopped. Gabrielle unexpectedly separated herself from her pack of friends and descended on Claire, wrapping her in a hug. "Congratulations! This is so exciting!"

Claire—at first too stunned to reply—was relieved that she'd had the good sense to wear a long-sleeved shirt and her gloves today. "What's exciting?"

Gabrielle drew back and stared at her, tucking a perfectly highlighted lock of hair behind one ear. "You mean you haven't heard?"

"Heard what?"

"We've both been nominated for Homecoming Princess!" Gabrielle squealed.

Claire's jaw dropped. "You're kidding, right?"

"Don't be so modest." Gabrielle laughed. "This is so cool. I mean, come on, for two years, none of us really got to know you. It sucks that it took you almost *dying* to bring you out of your shell, but now here you are, center stage, and I'm so excited for you!"

Claire couldn't believe her ears. Homecoming Princess? She'd been shocked enough that Neil had conspired to get her name on the primary ballot . . . but for her to make the final five? It was inconceivable!

Gabrielle was still talking. "If you need any help or advice about where to go to print posters and buttons, or how to run a campaign, just call me. My sister was Homecoming Queen two years ago, and I helped her with everything, so I'm totally in the know."

Claire was too bewildered to utter more than a stammered, "Thank you."

"By the way, I *love* the gloves. It's a way cool look," Gabrielle said in parting, as she flitted off to join her clique.

Claire suddenly felt a lanky arm wrapping around her shoulder and pulling her close.

"You've always been a princess to me," Alec murmured in her ear.

Claire felt herself beaming. "Thanks, cheeseball."

She wanted to turn and melt into his embrace, but he added softly, "Enjoy the moment. You deserve it." Then he vanished into the crowd.

Students continued to jostle past her on their way to class, offering Claire their enthusiastic congratulations. When she was finally able to make her way up to the notice board herself, she had to admit it was thrilling to see her name listed as one of the five finalists under Homecoming Princess. She quickly scanned the names on the other three lists—for Homecoming Queen, King, and Prince—and was delighted to see that Neil had made the cut for prince.

That was when she heard his voice over her shoulder. "Way to go, Brennan."

Claire whirled and looked up into his smiling, golden-brown eyes. "Neil! Congrats to you, too. How can I ever thank you?"

"Me?"

"My friends and I total exactly four votes. This never would have happened without you. Whatever you did—whoever you blackmailed, arm-twisted, or otherwise coerced—you pulled off the impossible."

Neil shrugged modestly. "I told you, you *belong* on that list. So I've been making phone calls like a madman for the past three days."

Claire laughed. "Well, thanks. I know I won't win, but just to be one of the final five is a real honor. You know, this is twice that you've done something amazingly awesome for me this year."

"All I did was open doors, Brennan. You did the rest yourself. See you in Spanish." With one last warm smile, he turned and raced off.

Wow, Claire thought, feeling a little guilty as she grabbed her books from her locker and hurried to her first class. Neil had done all that for her, even knowing that she was with Alec. It was good to know that the guy she'd had such a massive crush on for the past two years was truly such a great person.

All day long, people kept congratulating Claire on her nomination, many of them people she didn't even know. Brian, Erica, and Alec could talk of nothing else during break.

"Did Gabby Miller really hug you?" Erica said, amazed.

"I think she's just excited because she knows I'm no competition for her. With me taking up space, there are only three other girls fighting for her tiara."

"I think you could win, Claire." Alec shot her an admiring grin, taking her gloved hand in his and squeezing it.

"*You* are biased," Claire pointed out. She'd been dying for a moment alone with him today, but it hadn't happened. Ever since her revelation last night, her mind had been soaring on some alternate plane. Did Alec feel the same way about her as she did about him?

"He's not wrong, though." Erica's voice broke into Claire's thoughts. "You definitely have a shot at princess, Claire. It's all about politics." Erica chewed on the end of the ballpoint pen she held in her pink-gloved fingers as she spoke. "Whoever puts up the most posters and hands out the most buttons and cookies always wins."

Claire cringed. "I can't imagine going to all that effort to promote myself. I'd feel like such an egomaniac. And with all this supernatural, life-altering stuff going on, I can't really take this princess thing very seriously."

"That's exactly why you *should* take it seriously," Erica insisted. "It will take your mind off that other crap for a while."

"I doubt it. Anyway, you guys deserve to be on the ballot more than I do. I nominated all three of you."

"Well, I'm glad I'm not on the ballot." Alec shrugged.

"You only missed it by three votes, Alec," Erica said.

"And Erica and I weren't allowed to be on it," Brian added, "so, Claire, you owe it to us to at least *try*."

Claire looked at them, puzzled. "Why couldn't you two be on the ballot?"

Erica sighed, exchanging an awkward little glance with Brian. "Okay. This wasn't how I planned to bring this up, but . . . according to school rules, no one on the committee can be in the running . . . and neither can their date."

"Their date?" Alec repeated, surprised. "You guys are going to the dance together?"

"We just decided yesterday." Erica blushed.

"We figured, why not? *You've* got this guy." Brian pointed at Alec. "So we couldn't exactly go as a group."

Claire couldn't decide how she felt about this. Their

group had been so perfect up to now. If they started pairing off romantically, it might get a little weird. But admittedly, things had already changed between them since she and Alec were together. Trying to put all worries from her mind, she gave her friends a genuine smile. "That's great! But we can still all drive there together, right?"

"Of course." Erica leaned forward eagerly. "We now have two important things to plan, Claire: what we're going to wear to the dance, and what kind of campaign we're going to run for you. We'll all pitch in and help. Am I right, guys?"

"You bet," Brian said.

"Whatever you need, Claire," Alec agreed, "I'm there."

"Thanks for the support, everyone," Claire said steadily, "but no thanks. It's nice to be nominated, and I'm looking forward to the dance, but I'm not running a campaign. I'm just going to concentrate on maintaining my scholarship, and"—with a smile at Alec—"on today's audition for the Homecoming assembly. Which is the one thing I think I—*we*—really have a shot at."

Before Claire knew it the school day was over, and she was sitting tensely on an upholstered bench in the theater lobby with Alec and another duet, waiting for their chance to audition. The windows of the lobby were still masked by plastic, an unsettling reminder of the scaffolding accident that had occurred two weeks before.

"Those guys have listened to way too much Nirvana,"

Alec said, shaking his head at the steady beat emanating from the music room.

"What's wrong with Nirvana?" Claire asked.

"Nothing, but I think grunge rock is way too dark for the adult judges. That makes us a sure thing."

Despite Alec's obvious confidence (which, she had to admit, was sexy), *her* stomach was full of knots. They had only practiced the song that one time, on Monday afternoon. The past few nights, she'd had nightmares about choking at this audition, and she just hoped they hadn't been visions of the future.

She said quietly, "I'm terrified. I don't even remember the song we're about to sing."

"Don't worry," he whispered back. "When I play the first note, you will."

Claire was still dumbfounded that anything could work that way. "This is so nuts." She leaned closer and whispered into Alec's ear, "Are we cheating?"

"What?"

"Isn't this like the Flash entering a footrace? Or Colossus entering a weight-lifting competition?"

"I suppose the morality is kind of fuzzy," he whispered back with a grin. "But we're using our natural-born gifts, Claire, just like everyone else. And we're only using them to entertain people, not for financial gain."

Claire conceded silently. Just then, the music in the other room ended. She heard the murmur of voices and the shuffle of feet. A minute later, a trio of boys dressed in plaid flannel and denim emerged, followed by Erica, holding a clipboard.

"You guys ready?" Erica asked enthusiastically, pointing to Claire and Alec. "You're up."

As Erica ushered them into the room, she announced loudly, "Don't think this is a slam dunk just 'cause I'm on the committee. I've promised the other judges to be very objective when it comes to you two, so you're going to have to work hard to impress me."

Alec took a seat and gave his guitar a confident strum. "We'll try our best, Your Honor."

Erica nodded to Alec in a businesslike manner, then secretly darted Claire a quick grin as she took her seat behind the table. The five judges beside her—two students and three teachers—all looked a bit weary.

Claire took her position, standing at Alec's side. Sure enough, as Alec strummed the opening chords of their song, it was as if a light had switched on in her brain. They began to sing, their voices weaving together, and she saw the faces of all six judges, including Erica's, light up with astonished delight.

Claire's heart soared along with the music. Alec's voice sounded amazing, as always, and she had to admit that it complemented her own perfectly. When they reached the first chorus, Claire saw Alec glance at her warmly. She tried to keep from grinning too widely—Mr. Lang insisted that smiling during singing distorted the quality of sound the mouth produced—but she was so happy, she couldn't help herself.

She suddenly realized she didn't care if they won the audition—just the experience of singing with Alec, here and now, was all that mattered. She lost herself in the joy of the moment and sang her heart out.

"To my favorite singing partner." Alec raised his glass of iced green tea to hers.

"To my favorite singing teacher," Claire responded, as they clinked glasses and drank.

They were at an upscale Japanese restaurant in Westwood, where Alec was treating Claire to a celebratory dinner. The walls around their black leather booth were exposed brick, and the ceiling was open-beamed and airy. The gentle sounds of an indoor fountain, along with soft piped-in music, made a pleasant backdrop for their conversation and the delicious sushi meal.

The audition, they agreed, had been a resounding success. The results wouldn't be posted until Monday, but the reaction from the judges when they'd finished their song—the beaming delight on their faces, the clearly evident reining in of a joint impulse to burst into applause—seemed to guarantee them a spot as part of the Homecoming assembly entertainment.

"Alec," Claire said suddenly, as a fresh concern invaded

her mind, "is there any chance that Vincent will be at the Homecoming assembly?"

"I don't know. Why?"

"You said when Vincent comes back, you're going to ask him to take me off the wanted list, without giving away my identity."

"Aye."

"What if he doesn't agree? Won't he just keep searching for me himself? And if he hears me sing—won't that be a pretty big clue that I'm his Halfblood?"

Alec fiddled absently with his chopsticks. "Just because you can sing, Claire, it doesn't prove anything. He has to see your aura, and that only generates when you use one of your unique talents—in your case, visions."

"Oh."

"Give me a chance to talk to him, all right? I have high hopes that this will work out."

"Okay." Claire popped a shrimp tempura roll in her mouth and savored its delectable blend of flavors. When she'd finished chewing, she said, "Why do we have to wait for Vincent to come back, anyway? Can't you just call or text him?"

"Well, conventional means are out, because of the Fallen. And telepathy is not an option, at least if I wish to remain hidden."

"You mean if you *log on*, the Grigori Council will know where you are?"

"Instantly. Anyway, for all I know, Vincent's already here and just hasn't made his presence known yet."

"So, you don't know where he's staying?"

"No, I mean, he could be *right here*. In this room. At this very moment. And I'd have no idea."

Claire stared at him. "What? Can he turn invisible?"

"Sort of. But his talent is far more versatile. He's a master of illusions."

"Illusions?"

"He can make you see and feel whatever he wants, just by projecting it into your mind."

"Are you serious?"

Alec nodded. "He could be anyone or anything: our waiter, the woman at that table over there, or the bamboo plant by the front door. If he wanted, he could make us think the walls were bleeding, or that we were sitting in a cabin in the Alps eating fondue."

"Holy shit," Claire said, nearly dropping her chopsticks.

"And since he's telling you what he wants you to see, he can hide his aura when he uses his powers, making it impossible for even most Grigori to detect him."

"That's scary."

"It can be. It can also be fun. Vincent used to amuse me as a kid by taking me to impossible places in my mind, like the top of Mount Everest, the bottom of the ocean, or a crater on the moon. Hanging out with Vincent can be quite an adventure."

"Wow. Like what Merlin did for Arthur, before he was king."

"I suppose so."

"Very cool . . . but I still say: *scary*. I'm glad you trust him."

"He was my parents' best friend, and kept their secrets—even after they died. Then he took me under his wing until I was ready to go out on my own. He's promised to keep my secrets, and I'm certain, by extension, he'll agree to keep yours."

For the second time that day, Alec's quiet confidence allayed Claire's fears. She fell silent for a moment, remembering everything he'd told her about his parents. "I hope you don't mind my asking, but how did your parents die?"

"They were murdered by the Fallen."

"Oh my God." No wonder Alec saw the Nephilim as so dangerous, Claire thought. "Were you there?"

Alec nodded almost imperceptibly. "It was a Saturday evening. I was playing chess with Vincent. We lived so far off the beaten track, I have no idea how they found us. My parents were just returning from a moonlight stroll. They were attacked at the front door, dead before they even knew what hit them. I'd be dead too, if Vincent hadn't spirited me away in time."

"I'm sorry."

"It was a long time ago."

"Were you really, actually, *ten* at the time?"

"Really, actually."

Claire did a computation in her head. "So you've been on your own, living like a monk, doing that horrible job—for over a hundred years?"

"Aye."

She reached across the table and laid her hand on his forearm, squeezing it tenderly through the fabric of his shirt, aching with empathy for him. "I'm sorry," she said again.

"Don't be. I channeled my frustration and rage into my work for years. And now I'm done."

After dinner, Alec snuck Claire into the service elevator of the building next door and took her up to the roof, twenty-three stories above.

"This is one of my favorite places to come and think," Alec said, taking her gloved hand and drawing her to the wall at the building's edge.

The roof was nothing special in and of itself (just a big, gray, open expanse dotted with air-conditioning ducts) but Alec had promised her that the view would be spectacular, and it was.

Below them, a million lights twinkled through the darkness, from downtown in the east all the way to the pitch-black ocean in the west. The only sounds were the wind in her ears, the hum of the AC units, and the

281

drone of the city far below. People as tiny as ants scurried along the sidewalks, while red and white lights pulsed from the halting flow of traffic on the streets and freeways.

"It's beautiful," Claire said softly.

"In the past, I loved to watch the people down below. Now I like it even better, because I'm one of them."

"Let's make sure you keep it that way."

Alec drew her into his arms and held her close against his chest, his handsome face and dark blond hair bathed in moonlight. "That's my plan."

Claire's stomach fluttered at the look in his eyes, which was infused with emotion. Alec lowered his head and brought his lips close to hers. "Ready?" he murmured softly.

Claire nodded, her heart jumping. As she wrapped her arms around him, she closed her eyes, willing her mind to stay in the moment and reciting her mantra. But at the first touch of his mouth on hers, all thoughts fled like leaves on the wind. She became immersed in the exquisite joy that spread through her as his body pressed tightly against hers. It was wonderful. Magical. Effortless. Visionless. She felt as if she was floating.

I love you, she thought, her heart so full, it seemed as if it might overflow or burst from her chest. *You are my universe. I want to spend the rest of my life with you.* If only she had the nerve to say the words aloud.

Even though she couldn't read Alec's thoughts, even though he'd never given voice to his feelings, she sensed from the way he'd looked at her and the way he was holding her that he felt the same way. In his arms, she felt both strong *and* desirable for the first time in her life.

When Claire opened her eyes and met his gaze, she couldn't help but smile, which inadvertently interrupted the kiss. The breeze brushed through her hair, and she felt her skirt fluttering against her legs. *How can that be?* Claire wondered, with the part of her mind that could still think. How could the wind pass through the low wall beside them?

In her peripheral vision, she suddenly caught sight of something strange—the rooftop was several yards below them.

Below them?

Claire gasped. Looking down, she discovered that they were hovering in the air in each other's arms.

"Oh my G—" she began.

"Shhh," Alec cautioned swiftly. "I'm concentrating. You wanted to fly, didn't you?"

Claire's heart pounded wildly as she reveled in Alec's protective embrace. She held on to him even more firmly, soaking in the twinkling lights of the city all around them as they slowly began to spin.

And spin.

And spin.

Letting all her fears go, Claire brought her lips back to his.

twenty-six

❧

Alec hummed to himself as he closed his front door. He tossed his keys onto the coffee table, slipped his knife from his boot, and went through his usual coming-home ritual. Lock on the weapons cabinet: check. Under the sofa: check. Bathroom: check. Kitchen: check. Area secured.

He was still humming as he set his knife down on the kitchen counter and pulled a root beer out of the fridge. Popping the top off with his fingers, he started whistling.

He'd never been allowed to love before, but he knew that was what he was feeling now—what he had been feeling for weeks, ever since he and Claire first met. When they were apart, he thought of her practically every minute. When they were together, he never wanted to be anywhere else. And he knew that her happiness and safety were more important to him than his own. It was an exuberant feeling, love. He finally understood why people couldn't stop talking, writing, and singing about the emotion. He truly felt as if he was glowing.

Alec couldn't wait to see Claire again, to speak with her. Would it be too soon to call her right now, considering that they'd spent so much of the day and evening together? She'd said she was going shopping with her mother tomorrow to buy a Homecoming dress. But what about after that? They could make plans for Saturday night.

His musing—and humming—were interrupted by the sound of his front door slamming open, and a familiar voice bellowing, "Will you please *cease* that infernal racket?"

Alec started in alarm, dropping his root beer bottle to the floor with a crash. Vincent strolled into the apartment and leaned against the kitchen doorway, clicking his tongue disapprovingly. "You're getting sloppy, Alec. Three locks on your front door, and you didn't even secure one of them."

Alec's face colored. *Shite*, he thought. He was getting careless. There was no excuse for it, no matter how distracted he'd been lately. Alec heaved a sigh and smiled grimly. "Good thing it was you, then. How was New York?"

Vincent opened the door to the fridge and rooted around inside, finally selecting a ginger ale. "Their new Watcher is tentative and susceptible to emotion—both cardinal sins in my book. One of the largest districts in the nation, and now it's in shambles. But let's not waste time talking about *that*. Shame you don't have any Crown Royal." He uncapped the ginger ale bottle and held it aloft. "Cheers!"

Alec grabbed a wad of paper towels and began mopping up the soda and broken glass on the floor, trying to gather his thoughts. He was about to have the most important conversation of his life, and he hardly knew where to begin.

Without offering to help clean up, Vincent strolled into the main living area and draped himself luxuriously on the sofa, feet on the coffee table. "So. Tell me. How did you fare in my absence?"

Alec rinsed his hands off, then dried them on a towel as he emerged from the kitchen. Taking a deep breath, he plunged in. "I've found your quarry," he said, hoping that his smile would appear more calm and confident than he felt.

"Have you?" Vincent sat up slowly, clearly trying to hide his eagerness. "Do tell. Was it the boy?"

"No, it's a girl . . . but first, I need to say something."

"Be my guest."

"I've already assessed and debriefed her. She's not a risk."

Vincent chuckled. "Not a risk? Is she a Halfblood?"

"Aye," Alec admitted reluctantly. "Her family history syncs with the New York runaways. Her father disappeared shortly after she was born. And her aura—"

"Is it green?"

Alec nodded. "I've never seen anything like it before."

"Fabulous." Vincent looked excited. "Talents?"

"Mental. Primarily visions of the past, and an occasional hint of the future."

"Ah." Vincent nodded. "A psychic. Just as I'd feared, it's my old case after all."

"But she poses no threat to anyone."

"How can you say that? A Halfblood with psychic abilities who can see the future?"

"*Hints* of the future."

"Sure, *now*. But you know as well as I do, there's no telling what she might be capable of. The Fallen will be all over her in a heartbeat. They'll do anything to recruit her."

"They already tried—it was Celeste and her cretins. But I was there when they approached her. She's not the type to give in to the Fallen. I promise you."

"You *promise* me?"

"Aye. This one—she's an honorable person. She's had a difficult time of it up to now, and I hate to think what her fate might be if the Council gets ahold of her. If you could, just this one time, look the other way . . ."

Vincent stared up at Alec from his seat on the couch. "Let me get this straight. Even though I've been pursuing this case for years, even though our Elders would consider her a threat of the highest level, even though the Fallen sent one of their *best* recruiters after her—you want me to . . . what? Walk away, sight unseen, and leave her alone? Report that *I* found her rather than *you* and swear there is no reason for concern?"

"Aye."

Vincent started to respond, then his jaw dropped and his eyes widened as a sudden realization seemed to dawn on him. "You've developed *feelings* for this Nephila, haven't you?"

Alec cringed inwardly, straining to maintain an unreadable façade.

"What, do you imagine yourself to be in love with her?" Vincent was incredulous. "A *sixteen-year-old girl*?"

Alec didn't trust himself to respond.

"I should have seen this coming," Vincent went on, shaking his head. "The way you were raised—your parents put impossible ideas into your head. When I found you here, I warned you not to do anything foolish. I hoped you'd come to your senses and see this absurd dalliance of yours for what it is: a mistake."

Alec swallowed hard. The conversation wasn't going the way he'd planned. He'd hoped to be able to admit the truth, that Vincent would understand, sympathize, and eventually support him. He saw now that he'd been naïve—so blinded by hope that he'd allowed himself to forget Vincent's basest instincts. "I swear to you, I'll watch over her carefully. She won't be a problem to anyone."

"Have you told her . . . everything?"

Alec nodded.

"Well. It seems that you've done my job for me."

"If you would do *this* for *me*, I'll be forever grateful."

"Are you going to give me her name?"

"If you give me your word that you won't let them touch her."

"Alec, you know I will find her on my own in any case. You are simply saving me time." Vincent's dark eyes narrowed as he examined Alec. "Oh. Wait. Never mind. I know who it is. It's that little brunette with the beguiling smile that I've seen you with—Brennan, I think her name is."

Alec flinched internally, furious that Vincent had figured it out before he could secure a promise for Claire's safety. There was no point in lying about it now that he'd fingered her. "Please," Alec pressed, struggling to rein in his emotions. "I *do* love her. She's . . . I couldn't take it if . . . I don't want anything to happen to her."

Vincent frowned. "My dear boy. You know your well-being and happiness is of the utmost importance to me. You've always been like a son to me. But this is a great deal to ask."

"Don't make me beg," Alec said quietly.

Vincent clasped his hands together, shaking his head and heaving a sigh. "All right. I'm sure I will come to regret this, but—all right."

"Give me your word," Alec insisted.

"I give you my word: I will not let the Elders touch her."

"Thank you." Relief engulfed him.

"However."

Alec's eyes flew to Vincent's. His godfather's warning tone, and the deadly serious look in his eyes, caused fear to stab through Alec like a knife. "However . . . ?"

twenty-seven

❧

The dress was blue. It was short but not too short, sexy but not slutty, and somehow managed to be classy, sophisticated, and slinky all at the same time. It was delicately beaded at the bodice, made of a clingy, textured fabric that Claire knew would hug her curves, and shimmered when the light hit it from a certain angle. And . . . it cost four hundred dollars.

Claire stared at the dress as it hung on the rack, unable to disguise her longing.

"Oh, that's gorgeous," her mom exclaimed, coming up behind her.

Claire couldn't remember the last time her mother had taken off from work on a Saturday to spend time with her in *any* fashion, no pun intended—but to shop in the department store formal-wear section? Clearly, this Homecoming Dance was important to her.

"You'd look great in that dress! How much does it cost?"

Claire flashed the price tag at her mother with a defeated sigh.

"Four hundred dollars? That's ridiculous. It's not even silk. What is it, designer?"

Claire nodded sadly. "Nothing here fits our budget."

Her mom put an arm around her affectionately. "I'm sorry, honey. It shows you how long it's been since I've bought formal wear. Let's try the junior section."

As they made their way through the store, Claire had the sudden, uncanny feeling that someone was watching her. She glanced around warily but saw nobody suspicious.

"Can you explain the gloves to me again?" Lynn nodded toward Claire's hands. "They're germ protection, is that right?"

"Yes," Claire lied. "It's an extra-credit experiment for AP bio. Erica and I want to try this for a few weeks and see if we stay healthier than our classmates. Plus, we think they're cool."

Her mom shrugged. "Well then, we'd better get you a pair for the dance, to match your dress."

"That'd be awesome, Mom. Thanks!"

They descended on the junior discount rack. "What's Alec's favorite color?" her mom asked.

"I don't know." Claire grabbed her cell phone from her purse. "Let me ask him."

She dialed his number, hoping he'd pick up. But—just like the last time she'd called him this morning—it went straight to voice mail. She'd also tried texting him once and had gotten no reply. Where was he? When they'd kissed good-bye the night before, he'd promised to call her in the morning, but he never did.

"Hey, Alec," she said after the tone, "I'm dress shopping with my mom and I have a question. Call me back." She hung up. He'd seemed so happy while they were floating above that Westwood rooftop, and later, standing by his car, it was as if he couldn't take his eyes off her. So why hadn't he called?

"He isn't answering?"

"No."

"Well, he'll just have to live with whatever we find." Her mom held up a black, one-shoulder dress with a skirt that was cut on the diagonal. "What do you think of this one?"

"I prefer symmetry." Hearing footsteps close behind her, Claire turned, but there was no one nearby. The hair on the back of her neck stood on end. Had someone been there? Or was she hearing things?

Her mom replaced the dress on the rack. "Symmetry. Got it." Noticing Claire's troubled expression, she added, "Don't worry, honey. I'm sure there's something here that's worthy of a Homecoming Princess."

Claire dropped her phone into her bag, grateful that her mom thought her worries were just about the dress. "Thanks, Mom, but I'll only be a princess if I win, and I'm not popular enough for that to happen."

"Don't say that. You have as much of a chance as anyone else. Did I ever tell you that I was Junior Prom Queen?"

"You were? Really?" Claire's mom had revealed so little about her teen years, this news came as a shock. Without thinking, Claire added, "That's so great! Did you go with Tom?"

Her mom froze, her stunned gaze meeting Claire's over the clothes rack. *"What did you say?"* Lynn's voice was charged with quiet intensity.

Claire caught her breath. Could she pass off her slipup as a lucky guess? No. There was no way on earth she could explain away the fact that she knew her dad's name. Desperate to cover it up, Claire played the moody teenager card: Crossing her arms defensively, she said, "Why are you so freaked? I just asked, who'd you go with to prom?"

"Oh." Her mom sounded visibly relieved. She glanced back at the dresses, suddenly unable to meet Claire's eyes. "To tell you the truth, I don't remember the boy's name."

Claire knew it was a lie. What little her mother had told her about her past was that she'd gotten pregnant during her junior year of high school, left school to get a job and get married, and never graduated. Claire did the math. Since her birthday was in December, that meant her mom must have been two or three months pregnant with her at that very dance. And no knocked-up girl would ever forget the boy who took her to prom—especially not if he was the child's father and the guy she married.

Desperate for a subject change, Claire grabbed two dresses at random from the rack and smiled brightly. "Can I try these on?"

"Sure." As they made their way to the dressing rooms, her mom looked like she was a million miles away.

Minutes later, they stood before the mirror studying Claire's reflection in the second of the two dresses. The first one was so skimpy and sparkly, it had made her look like a prostitute. And the second . . .

"I'm wearing a tent," Claire lamented.

"That one should go straight to army surplus," her mother agreed. "It's okay, honey. We have lots of time. If we don't find something today, we still have a whole week before the dance."

As they filtered back into the crowded mall, the weight of disappointment caused Claire's shoulders to sag. It seemed as if nothing was going right today. The dresses they could afford were hideous, Alec was mysteriously MIA, and she still couldn't shake the creepy feeling that an invisible pair of eyes was trained on her.

It was only when they stepped down onto the escalator that she saw him. He was standing across the mall, one floor above, leaning over the balcony. A complete stranger, staring at her intently. He wasn't very tall, but he was broad-shouldered, with a tanned, sinewy frame, a square jaw, bushy goatee, and a mane of platinum-blond dreadlocks.

Claire felt a chill race up her spine. Who was he? Why was he staring at her like she was a piece of meat? With a sudden rush of dread, she wondered, could it be Vincent? Could Alec have failed in his attempt to placate him? Had Vincent done something to Alec and come here to finish her off?

Just then, Claire's body began to tremble, followed by the warmth and odd sensations that preceded a message vision. *Oh God, not here! Not now!* she thought. It had been so long since she'd had one of these, she'd begun to hope they'd stopped coming. But there was no way to prevent it. Claire clutched the rails of the escalator just as her knees began to buckle, and—despite her struggle to keep them open—her eyes clamped shut.

She heard the familiar, raspy, feminine voice with the British accent:

"Claire! It's Helena. Why haven't you come? You're still in danger. Look! Look!"

A fragmented image infiltrated the blackness of her mind, like a TV with bad reception. As the image came into focus, Claire saw a young woman standing on a landscaped hillside under a canopy of twinkling stars. She recognized the setting: It was at school, just above the northern stairway. The girl turned, and she saw her face.

It was her!

She was wearing the blue dress—the classy, four-hundred-dollar blue dress. There was a rustle in the bushes nearby.

"Alec?" the vision Claire cried, worry in her voice.

Suddenly, with a loud growl, a large, tawny-furred creature leapt from the bushes behind her. It was a giant mountain lion. In a blur of teeth and claws, it hurled itself at the back of her neck, knocking her to the ground. The vision Claire screamed as the beast tore at her flesh.

Claire jerked in horror and felt as if she was falling. A blast of pain infiltrated her skull. Then everything went black.

"You actually fainted on the mall escalator?" Erica asked.

Claire lay back on her bed, staring up at the ceiling with her phone to her ear. "Yeah. I woke up on the floor, with my mom and a bunch of strangers crouched over me. It was horrible. Thank God Mom believed me when I said I tripped."

"But you're okay—mysterious dreadlocked stalker and scary vision aside?"

"Not really. Alec still isn't answering his phone. I'm worried about him."

"Claire, he's an angel. He can take care of himself."

"Then where is he? It's four p.m. He said he'd call me this morning."

"Maybe his cell phone battery died."

"He has a charger."

"Maybe he's buried in homework. I know I am. Or maybe he forgot."

"I don't think so."

"Have you guys ever even spoken on the phone before?"

"A few times. It was always pretty brief."

"Well, maybe he's one of those people who don't like to talk on the phone. I mean, he's not exactly the most chatty guy in the world."

"He has been with me . . . lately. He was supposed to see Vincent by now. Do you think Vincent said something that changed Alec's whole position about us? I mean, he *did* say it's forbidden for us to be together."

"Claire, Alec is crazy in love with you. There's no way he changed his mind about anything. Maybe he's still negotiating with Vincent, and he doesn't want to call you until he's wrapped that up."

"Maybe."

"Seriously, I'm not worried about Alec. I'm worried about *you* and this whole cougar thing on the hill. What does it mean?"

"I don't know. But it was terrifying. And Helena, who-ever she is, sounded really upset." Claire sat up cross-legged on her bed, frowning. "Maybe she's getting confused. 'Cause in the vision, I was wearing this really expensive dress I saw today, that I am *never* going to own."

"Huh."

"What am I supposed to do, Erica?"

Claire could almost hear Erica's frustrated shrug through the phone. "I don't know. But she said last time that Alec was supposed to protect you. So ask Alec."

"You mean, if he ever calls me," Claire replied with a heavy sigh.

The rest of the afternoon and evening inched by at a snail's pace. Claire plowed through her homework, constantly staring at the phone and willing it to ring. As the hours passed, her worry grew. She tried calling Alec again, twice, and sent another text message. No answer. Something was wrong—she knew it in her bones—and the only way to find out was to drive over to his place. But she knew her mom would never let her go out alone at night. It was agony waiting for her to go to bed.

Finally, when the sound of her mother's even breathing was audible from the next room, Claire slipped quietly downstairs, stealthily grabbed the car keys from the entry table, and snuck out the door.

The ten-minute drive to Alec's apartment seemed to take ten hours. Claire parked on the street. As she crossed the dimly lit lot at Alec's tiny complex, she caught sight of his Mustang in its usual spot and felt a surge of relief. He was home!

Claire sprinted up to his front door, where she stopped to collect herself, resisting the urge to hammer against it. *Everything is going to be okay*, she reassured herself. Alec would have a good reason for not calling, and together they'd figure out what to do about the latest message from Helena. She knocked quietly and waited. She heard stirring from within, and then the curtains parted slightly as someone peeked out, although she couldn't see who.

There was a pause; then the sound of the series of locks sliding.

The door creaked open.

Claire's blood froze. It wasn't Alec who answered. The man standing before her was tall, black, handsome, and clad in an expensive, gray, three-piece suit. She'd never seen him before in her life, yet his dark eyes beamed with recognition.

"Ms. Brennan!" he intoned in a deep voice, smiling as he pulled the door all the way open. "To what do we owe the pleasure?"

That's when she knew.

Vincent.

twenty-eight

❧

It's okay, Claire told herself. *He's Alec's godfather. He's going to help you.* But for some reason, her stomach refused to unknot. When she saw Alec step into view and caught the miserable look on his face, all hope died within her. He was still wearing the same clothes as last night and looked as if he hadn't slept at all.

"Claire." Alec motioned toward the tall man beside him. "This is Vincent."

"Do come in," Vincent commanded.

Claire stared at them silently, her heart beating with trepidation. Alec's eyes were full of pain and regret. Why? He'd vowed to reason with Vincent, to convince him to leave them both alone. Clearly, he must have failed. Which meant that coming any closer to Vincent could be signing her own death warrant.

Claire took two steps back. "No, I—I think I should go."

Vincent's smile widened. "Young lady, you seem

nervous. Trust me, you have nothing to fear."

"It's okay, Claire," Alec said quietly. "He's telling the truth. We've come to an . . . agreement."

Agreement? Claire thought. *What kind of agreement?* If Alec had succeeded in securing their safety, then why did he look so upset? "I shouldn't have come. It's late. I really have to go."

"Go where?" Vincent said quizzically.

Suddenly, there was a loud rumble and the concrete at her feet began to crack and fall away, creating a tremendous fissure on three sides of her. Claire screamed as she watched the destruction ripple outward, obliterating everything in its wake. She was left on the very edge of a precipice, hanging over an endless, deep chasm that rivaled the Grand Canyon. The city was gone. *Gone.* Only one structure remained standing: the single room of Alec's apartment, which glowed brightly before her.

Panicked, she stumbled backward and teetered over the abyss, still screaming.

"Vincent!" Alec cried, infuriated.

Vincent's hand shot out and grabbed Claire's arm, pulling her to safety inside the apartment. "Shhhhh," he admonished, "you'll wake the neighbors."

As Claire yanked her arm from Vincent's grasp, she turned and saw, through the open doorway, that the world outside had magically been restored to its natural state. She gasped, reeling in confusion as her brain processed this rapid distortion of visual cues.

"Was that really necessary?" Alec crossed his arms in annoyance.

Vincent closed the door and leaned his lanky frame back against it, looking down at Claire with a mischievous chuckle. "I figured it was the most efficient way to get her into the room."

Alec turned to Claire. "I'm sorry. He was just playing with your mind. Are you all right?"

Claire shook her head slowly, struggling to recover her basic faculties. She realized that the physical world hadn't changed, that the chaos she'd just witnessed had simply been a series of images projected by Vincent—that she'd been standing on Alec's doorstep the whole time. But she couldn't stop trembling. She looked at Alec, wishing he would take her in his arms. Last night, he would have done so in an instant. He would have held her and reassured her that she was okay, that *they* were okay. But Alec was still standing several feet away, and made no move to come closer.

"I'm sorry," Alec said again.

What was he apologizing for? Vincent's terrifying illusion? For not calling her today? Or—for something far worse?

"You know," Vincent asserted, gazing at her but still talking to Alec, "although unexpected, it's actually fortuitous that she's here, since we all sorely need to have a little chat."

Claire swallowed hard, backing away from Vincent again, this time farther into the room. Every instinct told her to fear this man, that she wasn't going to like whatever he said. "A chat?" she said uncertainly. "About what?"

Before she could blink, the studio apartment around them disappeared. Suddenly they were inside an elegant restaurant atop a skyscraper. A tuxedoed waiter stood beside a round, candlelit, linen-draped table, set with china, silver, and crystal for three. Through huge plate-glass windows, stars glimmered in the night sky, and the lights of a city sparkled all around them.

Claire gasped, so startled that she had to grab the back of a chair to steady herself.

"Stop it, Vincent," Alec said, exasperated.

"Stop what? You know how I feel about your spartan accommodations. There's barely seating for two, let alone three. We'll be far more comfortable here." Vincent gestured toward a waiting chair. "Please have a seat, Ms. Brennan."

Claire glanced at Alec, wondering if she had any choice. Alec gave her a silent nod to go along with it, then flicked his gaze away. Reluctantly, she sat. What did Vincent want?

Vincent took the seat across from her, while Alec begrudgingly sank into the third chair. The waiter picked up a tall bottle of sparkling water and poured glasses for Claire and Alec. When he tipped the bottle over Vincent's goblet, the liquid changed to a rich red wine.

"Thank you," Vincent said. As he uttered the words, the waiter and the bottle vanished.

Claire caught her breath. She felt as if she were stuck in some kind of dreamworld—and she was a bundle of nerves. If she wanted to leave, she didn't even know where the door was. What would happen if she drank the water? Unable to resist the impulse, she grabbed her glass and took a sip. It felt and tasted just like it should, though it didn't quench her thirst. *This is so weird*, she thought, twisting her hands anxiously in her lap. When she glanced at Alec, he looked both angry and uncomfortable.

"So," Vincent began, swirling his wine and sniffing it. "We have a *situation* here."

Claire's stomach clenched again. "A situation?"

"Yes. And apparently it's up to me to control it."

"This is not the way I wanted it, Claire," Alec interjected tensely.

"But it's necessary." Vincent took a sip of his wine. "As I told Alec last night, it was one thing when he asked me to keep quiet about his high school escapades to the higher-ups. It's quite another to expect me to ignore those escapades when—as it turns out—they break every cardinal rule in existence." His gaze fell on Claire as he added, "Consorting with a human or typical Nephila would be bad enough, when you consider the ramifications of breeding together—"

Claire's face grew hot. Did he actually just say *breeding*?

"—but consorting with a *Halfblood* is another matter entirely. And now that I've found you, it's not easy to look the other way."

"Why? Why do you care so much about me?" Claire asked. "So I'm a Halfblood, big deal. I'm not going to hurt anybody."

"You couldn't be more wrong, my dear. In truth, you are a ticking time bomb that might bring us all to war some day."

"War?" Claire stared at Vincent, astonished. "*Me?* War with whom?"

"The Fallen."

"I don't understand."

"Allow me to enlighten you," Vincent said patiently. "The Nephilim outnumber us astronomically, and too many are joining the Fallen. You've already inherited your father's gift of true sight—which, in and of itself, is enough to make you incredibly valuable to those who hate our kind. But your genes may also be hiding the other half of your father's talents."

"What other talent? What could the Grigori find so threatening?"

Vincent rewarded her with a Cheshire grin. "*That* would be telling. If you knew, you would start looking for signs of it and be tempted to explore it. But rest assured, you *are* a threat. In time, you could become stronger and more dangerous than anything we have faced in millennia."

"There have to be other Grigori out there who have this power," Claire argued.

"That's not the point. You're a *Halfblood*. *Whatever* powers you possess, you are closer to a Grigori in strength than anyone else on the planet—but you have the weak constitution of your fellow Nephilim. Regardless of any attempts *you* may make to resist, the Fallen will go to any length to recruit you to their side of the board."

"This isn't chess!" Claire retorted hotly. "I'm not a pawn to be manipulated!"

"No, quite right," Vincent agreed. "You are a queen. But we can never be certain where your allegiance will lie. If the natural order of things prevails, as it usually does, you may choose to side with *them*."

Claire's heart sank, her stomach churning violently now, and she felt the hot threat of tears. She summoned her strength. "So . . . what are you going to do? Turn me in to your hangman committee? Have me executed?"

"That's what I *should* do." Vincent finished off his wine and sighed. "But Alec has begged me to reconsider. It seems you've become so important to him, he's willing to put many lives at risk. So we've made a deal."

"What kind of . . . deal?" Claire's voice quaked.

"I'm going to grant Alec's wish. I'll report back to the Elders with a *lie*. I'll say that you've been found but are not a threat of any kind. Of course, I'll stay to watch over you, to ensure that you do indeed steer clear of the Fallen and don't misuse your gifts. But as long as you comply, I'll see to it that no Elder lays a hand on you or your mother."

Claire glanced at Alec, confused. That was good news, wasn't it? It was exactly what she and Alec had been praying for. So why wouldn't he look her in the eye?

The answer to Claire's silent query came to her in a flash. The dread that had been building inside her rose to her throat, nearly choking her. "You'll do this . . . in return for what? If you let me go, what happens to Alec?"

"Alec will come back to work, where he belongs," Vincent replied. "I'll smooth things over with the Elders. Don't worry, they won't exile or execute him."

"Execute him?" Claire cried in horror.

Vincent glanced at Alec, amused. "Oh, I guess you didn't tell her everything after all." Facing Claire again, he continued, "Yes, the penalties for leaving the fold are severe. But if I take responsibility for him for a while, he'll be back in their good graces in no time. And he will never see you again."

twenty-nine

❧

A bruptly, Alec stood and walked to the wall of plate-glass windows encircling the restaurant, where he stopped and stared down at the phantom city below. Every muscle in his body felt taut. He was so overwhelmed with helpless fury, he found it hard to breathe.

Claire shoved her chair back, leapt to her feet, and crossed to where Alec stood. "Tell me you're not really going through with this," she pleaded softly.

"I have no choice, Claire." Alec's voice broke. "It's the only way I can protect you."

Tears sprang into Claire's eyes. "There must be another way!"

"There isn't."

"You can't go back! I don't want you to give up everything for me!"

"Claire, you'll be happier without me. This is your chance to be safe, to have some semblance of a normal life."

309 ❧

"I don't want a normal life." Claire reached out to take Alec's hand. "I want *you.*"

"I want you, too." He gripped her hand tightly, his eyes welling up as he gazed at her. "But—it's not realistic. It never was."

Vincent cleared his throat sharply. "My boy, step away. You are only making this harder."

"Shut up!" Claire threw over her shoulder at Vincent. To Alec, she cried fiercely, "You said anything worth having is worth fighting for!"

He longed to kiss her one more time, to hold her in his arms, to tell her how he felt about her—but that was impossible with Vincent here. "I tried. I failed. I'm sorry. Just forget about me, Claire. Let me go. Move on."

"No. No. Please," she whispered desperately. "Don't do this. Don't go."

"I have to. I've spent my entire life pursuing justice by *ending* the lives of others. Let me do this one thing, Claire, to *save* a life. *Your* life."

She went silent at that.

Alec felt as if his chest were wrapped in a continuously constricting band of barbed wire. His heart was breaking, and he could see that hers was, too.

"When are you leaving?" she whispered, agonized.

"Now. Tonight. There's no point in prolonging this."

"Am I really never going to see you again?"

Alec shook his head. "I'm sorry, Claire. Vincent will be

watching over you from now on. He'll protect you in my stead. This has to be good-bye." He let her hand go.

A deep sob escaped Claire's throat. She whirled on Vincent, visibly seething. "Turn this thing off!" she cried as she advanced toward him. "Let me out of here!"

Vincent gave her a slight nod. Suddenly, they were back in Alec's apartment, where they'd been at the start. Vincent stood between Claire and the door.

"Now get out of my way!" Claire shouted.

Vincent obliged, opening the door to let her pass. With one last look at Alec, Claire stumbled out with tears streaming down her face.

Alec slumped against the wall in despair. "There. It's done," he choked.

"Good." Vincent nodded gravely as he stepped into the open doorway himself. "Call me when you finish packing. I'll take you to the airport."

thirty

❧

S omehow, Claire managed to drive home.
  As she headed up the walk to her apartment, struggling to contain the sobs that still shook her frame, she saw a light shining through the living room window. *Damn*, she thought. Her mother was supposed to be asleep. Claire was no sooner in the door than her mom leapt up from the couch, but the angry look on her face melted the instant she saw Claire's bedraggled state.

"Where have you been?" Her mom rushed over and took Claire in her arms. "What's wrong?"

A fresh cry issued from Claire's throat, followed by a single word, *"Everything."*

Her mom held her tightly for a long moment, rubbing her back lovingly. "Talk to me, honey," she whispered. "What is it?"

In between choked sobs, Claire managed to utter, "Alec's leaving. And I'm never. Going to see him again. Ever."

"Why?"

Claire took a deep breath, terrified to speak the next words aloud, but incapable of holding back the truth anymore. "Because he's a Grigori and I'm a Nephila."

She felt her mom tense. Then Lynn loosened her embrace and stood back to stare at her. The look on her face told Claire that she understood completely.

Claire lay on the couch with her head in her mother's lap, her throat dry from talking and her eyes swollen from crying. Her mom had made herself some coffee, and over the past hour had sipped at it slowly while Claire detailed everything that had happened since Book Day: the visions, the tactile nature of her powers, the memory buried in Tom's jacket, Alec's true identity, his heroics with the scaffolding, their feelings for each other, and the visit from Vincent, who had guaranteed her and her mother's safety—but at a terrible cost.

There was only one detail she'd carefully left out— that a mysterious messenger angel named Helena had been contacting her telepathically and had just prophesied her death.

"Ever since the day you were born," her mom said, heaving a deep sigh as she stroked Claire's hair, "I've been afraid that something like this would happen. I'm so sorry you didn't feel you could confide in me before. But even though I know this is heartbreaking for you, it's still not half as bad as I'd ever imagined. Because you're still *alive*.

And now you're going to be safe. If the Watcher who came to find you has agreed to leave you be, then all my prayers for the last sixteen years have been answered. There's nothing left to worry about."

Claire struggled to bury the image of the cougar's terrifying jaws that hovered at the corners of her mind. There was no point in talking about the vision—it would only frighten her mom, and it might never come true. "Right," Claire said aloud. "Nothing to worry about."

Her mom paused, as if catching something in Claire's tone. "Are you sure you've told me everything, honey?"

Claire sat up, nodding as she dried her eyes on her sleeve. "Tell me, Mom, how did you get through this?"

"I don't know that I ever did. I was so focused on taking care of you and keeping you safe—I think my heart scarred over instead of healing."

"Tell me about him, Mom."

Her mom hesitated again, then said, "Take my hand and close your eyes."

Claire looked at her, confused. "What?"

"You obviously inherited one of your father's gifts. So—"

"One of them?" Claire interrupted. "What else could he do?" Maybe her mom would know what frightened Vincent so much. But Lynn shook her head.

"I don't know. He never told me." Her mom took her hand and held it. "But Tom used to do this whenever I had something on my mind. Trust me, you'll see."

"Okay." Claire closed her eyes.

"I was sixteen when I met him," her mom began. "I was spending the summer in the Hamptons with my family, like we did every year. I met him at a party at one of my parents' friend's houses."

As her mom narrated, Claire began to see images of what her mom was describing, from her mom's point of view:

A party was in full swing at a swanky house. Well-dressed people of all ages were drinking from crystal goblets and snacking on tiny, expensive-looking appetizers from passing trays.

"I didn't even want to be there, and I was thinking of sneaking out when I saw him."

Across the room, a tall, very attractive man with olive skin and dark, wavy brown hair—just like Claire's—was staring intently at her, as if she were the only person in the room.

Claire's heart lurched. For the first time, she was *seeing* her father, the man she had wondered about every single day of her life. It thrilled her to realize that she looked a lot like him.

"He was older than me—in his early twenties, I guessed—but I didn't care," her mom went on. "He was the handsomest man I'd ever seen, and different from anyone I'd ever met. He was there on assignment to find an Awakened, but of course I didn't know anything about that at the time—or that he was about to postpone his mission on my account. We ended up talking the whole night, and spent the following week together. It was magical."

Claire was treated to a flash of images, showing her parents laughing at the party, walking along the beach at sunset, riding on his motorcycle, and picnicking under the stars.

"After that, he disappeared for a few months."

Claire opened her eyes. "Wow. I'm seeing it, Mom! I'm seeing it all."

Her mom squeezed her hand and smiled, then continued. "I went back to school, but I never stopped thinking about him. In November of my junior year, he showed up again outside my school. It was as if no time had passed at all. Over the next few weeks, we fell in love. Then he disappeared again. I was heartbroken. When he showed up the third time, he finally told me the truth about who and what he was, and that he was going to leave it all behind for me. I was astonished. I told him not to do it. That I wasn't worth it. That he had a duty and he should honor it. But secretly, I wanted nothing more than for us to be together, and I was relieved that I couldn't change his mind."

Claire's mom paused now, and let go of her hand. The images stopped abruptly, and Claire opened her eyes.

"I'd like to keep the visuals of this next part private." Lynn took a sip of coffee and went on, blushing a little. "One night, we . . . made love, and I soon found out I was pregnant with you. He insisted on marrying me, and I said yes. I was young, but I adored him. I wanted to spend the rest of my life with him. My parents, however, were furious and threw me out of the house."

Her mom took Claire's hand again, and the images resumed in Claire's mind. "I left high school after my junior year, and we got an apartment in Manhattan. As soon as I turned eighteen, Tom and I were married at city hall. I got my GED while working at a video store. Tom, who'd spent two centuries acquiring a variety of skills, and was not only a psychic but a master at forging the documents necessary in his former . . . occupation, got a job as a stockbroker."

Claire laughed. "He must have made zillions."

"Not really. He could predict most of the twists and turns of the market, but he had a high code of ethics. He didn't want to take advantage of his gift, and thought it best to play it safe so that no one would suspect anything. With you on the way, we rented a house in Brooklyn. We were deliriously happy for the next year and a half, even though we had to keep looking over our shoulders, worried that the Grigori would come looking for him—and you. The day you were born was the happiest day of our lives. You were so perfect, so beautiful."

Claire was treated to an image of her father playing with her as a baby. Love lit his face as he held her tiny, chubby, smiling infant self up above his head. He laughed with delight as he brought her close and covered her giggling face with kisses. The image brought happy tears to Claire's eyes.

"We tried to pretend that everything would be okay, that we were safe in our little world, and that no one would ever find us in a city with millions of people. But one day, when you were six months old, Tom didn't come home. I was in a panic. I didn't hear from him until the next morning when he called me at my job. Tom said that a Watcher had descended on him as he was heading for the subway. The Watcher insisted he didn't want to rat on a fellow Grigori, even if he had gone AWOL—the penalties were unthinkable. But he suspected Tom of a far worse crime: of being involved with a human female. If it was true and Tom gave the woman up, the Watcher said, he'd try to pave the way with the Elders for Tom to return to his calling. Otherwise, he'd turn Tom in and make certain he—and his 'spawn,' if any—faced the consequences."

Claire opened her eyes with a sense of foreboding. "That sounds like Vincent."

"Maybe it was. Tom never told me the Watcher's name. All he said was that his life—*our lives*—were all on the line. He tried to kill the Watcher, but failed, and then he ran."

"Did he ever come home?"

Her mom shook her head, tears studding her eyes as she let go of Claire's hand. "No. He said the danger was too great. He couldn't take that chance. He'd set up a bank account for us with everything he had. He told me to pack up and leave town immediately, change my name, start over somewhere else, and never try to find him. That he would come to us when he could. *If* he could. That's the last time I ever heard from him."

"And you've been running ever since," Claire said softly. "I wonder what happened to him. Where did he go? Is he even still alive?"

"I ask myself that every single day. I pray that he's all right. It's a comfort to at least know now that he was never caught." Her mom wiped away a tear that was rolling down her cheek. "I'm sorry I couldn't tell you, honey. But you can see why it had to be a secret. I kept hoping that you wouldn't Awaken, and that there'd be no need to tell you any of it."

"Well, I know everything now. And it looks like history has just repeated itself." All the heartbreak of the present returned with a crushing blow, and Claire sank back against the sofa, tears forming in her own eyes. "Mom, I'm so sorry that happened to you—to us." With a sigh, she added, "What am I supposed to do now?"

"I know it's hard, sweetheart. But the carousel of life is going to keep spinning, and you need to just hang on and move with it."

"How?"

"You have schoolwork to do, a scholarship to maintain,

friends to hang out with, and colleges to apply to eventually. And as you do all these things, you will one day meet another boy that you like."

"What? No way." Claire shook her head emphatically. "That's never going to happen."

"It will. I understand that your heart is breaking right now, but it will heal, if you let it."

"Yours never did."

"Don't make the same mistake I did, Claire. Don't shut yourself off from loving other people, just because this one relationship didn't work out."

"This *one relationship*?" Claire repeated quietly. "Mom, you make it sound so mundane and ordinary. But it *isn't*."

Her mom looked at her pointedly. "Did you fall in love with Alec because of *what* he is?"

"No. Of course not."

"Then, deep down, he's just a boy you connected with. And there are lots more of them. I know it won't be easy. But you deserve all the best that life has to offer, Claire. You are what you are . . . because of me. Because of the choices I made. It will kill me if you're denied happiness and love because of those choices. Please, honey, promise me that you'll try to keep an open mind about the future."

A brief silence fell. Finally, Claire said solemnly, "I'll try."

Her mom kissed Claire's hair and said with a small smile, "Good. I think the first step on the road to recovery is this dance on Saturday."

Claire drew back and stared at her mother, aghast. "You don't seriously expect me to go to Homecoming *now?*"

"I expect nothing. It's your call, but I hope you will. You're up for princess. I know how these things work. Someone else *will* ask you."

"I don't care. I don't want to go with anyone but Alec."

"Well then, you can always go with your friends. Just think about it, okay? You have a whole week to figure it out."

It was four a.m. by the time Claire went to bed. She cried herself to sleep, and then dreamed of Alec. They were back in the phantom restaurant Vincent had created, and Alec was holding her hand. *I'm sorry,* he was saying brokenly. *You'll be happier without me. This is good-bye.* The dream ended with her standing alone on the hillside at school, a ferocious cougar leaping out at her from the darkness. She awoke in a panic, gasping, her pillow wet with tears.

Claire slept in the next morning. She spent all day Sunday in bed, struggling to eat a few bites of the food her mom brought in on trays. She turned off her cell phone, refusing to talk to anyone. Time stood still. All color seemed to have faded from the world. Even the sky outside was dim and gray, and a light rain began to fall, as if the universe was weeping with her.

It was impossible to believe she would never see Alec

again. Knowing that he was going back to a lonely job and an existence he despised—always on the road, fitting in nowhere, a monk assassin—that he'd given up his dream of living among humans, all because of her, was too terrible to contemplate. And yet, she realized, a far more horrifying scenario might ensue. If Vincent couldn't convince the Council to go easy on Alec when he returned, Alec might be put to death—and Claire would never even know. She was consumed by misery and guilt, as if a part of her heart and her guts had been torn out, leaving her ripped and bleeding, never to mend.

Monday dawned gloomy and overcast. Claire awoke groggy and puffy-eyed, and wore sunglasses to avoid questioning looks. When she opened her locker, she saw with a jolt of fresh pain that all of Alec's stuff was still there. Maybe Vincent hadn't given him time to clear it out before making him leave. Although it was difficult to see Alec's books and the black metal box, in a way, Claire was glad; it was physical proof that Alec existed, that he had once been a part of her life. She heard Erica's voice behind her and turned.

"Claire! I called and called yesterday, but it went straight to voice mail. Where've you been?" Without pausing for a reply, Erica went on excitedly, "Did you see the list? I've been dying to tell you all weekend. You and Alec knocked 'em dead on Friday. You're singing in the Homecoming assembly!"

The news hit Claire like a punch in the stomach. "That's great," she responded brokenly, "but you can cross us off, because Alec and I won't be performing."

"Why not?"

"Because he just left town for good."

Erica let out a quiet gasp. "What? *Why?*"

Claire felt fresh tears spring to her eyes. "To save my life."

thirty-one

By the end of lunch, Claire had filled Erica and Brian in on everything, including her all-nighter with her mom. They were supportive and empathetic, but nothing they said could comfort her.

It was strange to be surrounded by people who were chattering happily and going on with life as usual. To Claire it felt as if everything she knew and loved had come to a crashing end, like the scaffolding that had nearly collapsed on her. Alec was gone, and if Helena's warning and vision proved true, his sacrifice would be for nothing. Unless Claire could figure out how to stop it, she might die anyway—from a mountain lion attack.

Claire felt hollow, empty. She took notes in her remaining classes like an automaton, without really hearing or absorbing anything. The one thing she did notice was that a dozen or more girls had shown up in school wearing elbow-length gloves. She and Erica seemed to have started a fad after all.

After Spanish—the last class of the day—Neil caught up with her just outside the door.

"I heard about Alec." There was sympathy in his golden-brown eyes.

"I think everyone has by now." Claire kept her hands in her pockets, her voice flat.

Neil walked beside her down the path toward their lockers. "Is he at least going to stick around long enough to take you to the Homecoming Dance?"

"No. He's already gone."

"That's messed up. I don't get why he's leaving. He seemed to really like you."

Sorrow gathered in her chest and throat. "It's a long story, but it doesn't matter."

"It *should* matter." Neil frowned. "I know he hurt you, and I'm sorry. But I hope you'll still go to the dance."

"You sound like my mother."

"Should I be complimented or insulted?"

"I think both. Neil, if you were in my shoes, you wouldn't want to go either."

"Don't take this the wrong way, Brennan, but I don't think I'd fit in your shoes. I'd fall on my face."

In spite of the sadness pooling within her, a small smile tugged at her lips.

"What's that? Are you smiling?" Neil craned his face down toward hers, taunting her with a goofy, bug-eyed expression. "Don't do that, Claire. Do anything but smile!"

Claire's reluctant grin grew wider. Now she understood what Alec had meant about Neil's innate sense of charm. Maybe it wasn't a superpower, but it might as well have been. With an exasperated grunt, she covered her face with her hands. "I haven't heard that line since I was in kindergarten."

"And I can't believe it still works! Claire, what you need now is a project to throw yourself into."

"A project?"

"To distract you. I say it's time to start a campaign to win that princess crown."

Claire uncovered her face and glared at him. "I'd rather crawl into a hole and die."

"Also a noble pursuit," Neil quipped. "But if you change your mind—and if you decide to go to the dance—I'd be honored to escort you."

Claire was shocked. "I thought you would have asked Gabrielle by now."

"I can't stand Gabrielle. All she talks about is herself. I just smile and nod so that I don't seem rude."

Claire didn't know what to say.

"No pressure," Neil added quickly. "Take all week to think about it if you want to, but if it's a yes, just make sure to tell me by six o'clock on Saturday, so I have time to throw on a suit before I pick you up. Five forty-five, if you want me to wear a tie."

A little laugh bubbled up inside Claire. "Thanks, Neil,"

she said, her thoughts and emotions in turmoil, "but don't wait around all week for me. You should ask somebody else."

Neil stopped and looked down at her, his eyes sincere. "I don't want to go with anyone else."

"It was nice of him to ask, but there's no way." Claire was holding a three-way video chat on her laptop with Erica and Brian as she lay on her bed that night, doodling. A progression of lop-eared bunnies was making its way across her notebook, clinging to umbrellas that floated in a cloudy sky. "I'm still in love with Alec, and Neil knows it."

"Claire, you were in love with Alec for a week," Erica pointed out, "maybe two. You've been obsessing about Neil for the past *two years*."

"You would have been thrilled to go out with Neil if Alec hadn't swooped in," Brian added. "And what if you win that crown? People will think it's lame if you don't show up at the dance."

"I have more important things to worry about than a dance, or what people think," Claire insisted. "Have you forgotten Helena's warning? The Grigori may be off my back, but Alec's not here to protect me anymore. I could be cougar chow any day now."

"Claire, that's ridiculous. There are no mountain lions in the heart of urban Brentwood," Brian said.

"One could wander down from the hills," Claire said. "That sometimes happens."

"Yeah, but they've never crossed the freeway," he countered.

"I've been thinking more about that," Erica said slowly, "and I don't see how that vision could ever come true. You don't even own the dress you said you were wearing, Claire."

"But that's what I saw."

"That lady—*whoever* she is—could be wrong."

"She was right about me, and about Alec. He *did* protect me. He gave up everything to save me from the Grigori."

"Yes, and now he's moved on," Brian reminded her, "and he told you to move on, too."

"Easy for you to say." Claire sighed. "You don't feel like you've been stabbed in the heart."

"Claire," Erica encouraged softly, "I understand how much you're hurting right now. But you said yourself, you and Alec weren't allowed to be together anyway. He made a huge sacrifice for you, but it was his choice. He doesn't want you to stop living just because he left. He would want you to go to this dance, I'm sure of it."

"You and Neil would make a great couple," Brian added. "He could be prince to your princess."

"And he's *human*," Erica put in.

Claire sighed. She felt raw inside. She had no interest in going to the dance with anyone but Alec. But her friends' arguments were wearing her down. Maybe they were right. Her mom would be thrilled about Neil's invitation, too. She'd say this was perfect timing, that Claire should accept and go and be happy.

Claire stared down at the picture she'd doodled. Beneath the floating bunnies were the toothy, gaping jaws of a giant alligator, waiting to swallow them all whole. Her life, she thought grimly, as she saw it now.

"Okay," she said in resignation, "I guess I'll think about it."

The next morning, Claire put on a smile, found Neil, and accepted his invitation. Although it had to be obvious that she was less excited about going than he was, Neil still seemed elated.

When they joined Brian and Erica for lunch, talk turned to how they were going to help Claire run a Homecoming Princess campaign. Despite her protests to the contrary, the others insisted it was important. In the end, Claire agreed that if nothing else, it might be a good distraction. Neil said he'd help bake cookies, Brian offered to Photoshop Claire's picture and have posters printed, and Erica agreed to help put them up.

"Just promise me you're not thinking of something like *that*." Claire pointed to an expensive-looking color poster on a nearby wall featuring Gabrielle Miller in a skintight tank top and long red gloves, staring out in a sexy pose.

"Well," Erica said, wrinkling her nose, "*you* don't have to get all slutty about it."

Neil suggested that he and Claire run in tandem, so they made posters featuring a photo of the two of them with the slogan, "A Winning Pair: Vote Neil and Claire." They made dozens of cookies, plastic-wrapped them with their inserted slogan, and handed them out to an enthusiastic crowd. It was time-consuming and exhausting, but somehow even all that activity didn't serve to fill the emptiness inside Claire whenever she thought of Alec.

She held conversations with him in her mind, closing her eyes and shivering with emotion as she recalled the sound of his voice, the deep green of his eyes gazing into hers, and the feel of his arms around her. She found herself searching the crowds at school, hoping to catch a glimpse of him standing in the shadow of an archway or peering down at her from a rooftop. But he was gone, truly gone.

You said to move on, she told him silently, swallowing down the lump in her throat. *And that's what I'm trying to do.*

The week crawled by. Claire tried to hide her loneliness and despair as she dealt with the routines of daily life. Take out the trash. Help make dinner. Do her homework. She and Erica staged another séance to try to communicate with Helena, but weren't able to make contact. Since there were no news reports of mountain lions roaming the streets of Los Angeles, they decided the danger must not be imminent after all. One bright note was that Claire and her mom were getting along better than ever, now that they could finally be honest with each other.

Then, on Thursday evening, her mom came home with a surprise.

"Honey, look what I found!" Claire's mom burst into her room carrying something on a hanger, obscured by department-store plastic.

"I know we planned to go shopping for your dress tonight after dinner, but I found this on my lunch hour." Her mom draped the mysterious garment on the bed and stepped back. "Tell me what you think."

Claire removed the plastic bag and couldn't hold back a gasp. It was a shimmery blue dress. *The* shimmery, four-hundred-dollar blue dress that she had admired with her mother a week ago.

"I know how much you loved it." Her mom beamed. "And it was on sale—fifty percent off. I couldn't resist."

Claire's heart thudded in her chest. Her mom was so ecstatic, an expectant look on her face. There was no way Claire could admit what was really on her mind. So she hugged her mom tightly, keeping her face averted. "Thanks, Mom. You're amazing."

When her mom left the room, Claire stared at the dress, frozen in disbelief and fear. She'd never been one to care all that much about clothing, but she *loved* this dress. There was just one problem.

She might be destined to die in it.

The school schedule was rearranged on Friday so that the Homecoming assembly was the last event of the day. Claire had just squeezed in next to Brian in the bleachers when Erica stepped up to the microphone on the gym floor.

"Thank you for casting your votes. We look forward to seeing you all after the game at tomorrow night's dance, where we'll announce our Homecoming Queen, King, Prince, and Princess. Best of luck to all the nominees."

Claire's mind was so consumed with worry about the Cougar Vision and the Dress that she didn't hear any of the prefects' announcements that followed, and was incapable of participating in the cheers for the next day's football game. Things went from bad to worse when the entertainment started. She and Alec would have been up there, if only her world wasn't such a complicated mess. Instead, the grunge band performed in their place, followed by a barbershop quartet.

Brian sent her sympathetic glances throughout the assembly, while covertly surfing the internet on his phone. His shoulder was feeling so much better now that he'd given up the sling and was able to work two-handed.

"Do you actually prefer EMD to this stupid assembly?" Claire whispered. "Put your phone away!"

"I *prefer* that you live," Brian whispered back. She'd told him and Erica about the new dress the night before, and for the first time, even Brian had seemed worried. Ever

since, he'd been searching for clues to Helena's where-
abouts. "For all we know, if you wear that dress, you could
end up in a litter box."

"Bri, I've spent weeks combing the internet, looking for
Helena. It's a lost cause. Give it a rest."

"No. The only way we can know what's up is to find
her. I still say if Helena asked you to come see her, she
must be somewhere in Southern California, close enough
that you could actually get yourself there." As he stared at
his phone, his eyes suddenly lit up. "Holy crapzores."

"What?"

He whispered, "Claire, I am a god. Not *the* God, but *a*
god."

"What are you talking about?"

"This video was posted on the internet over two weeks
ago. Look."

He handed Claire his phone, turning it sideways so that
the video filled the screen. He'd muted the sound, but it
was obviously a clip from a local news channel. Behind the
reporter was a huge white building, with a sign that read
TWIN PALMS HOSPITAL.

"A hospital?" Claire said, confused.

"Just keep watching."

A new image was superimposed on the screen: a close-
up of a pale woman asleep in a hospital bed. Although the
image was tiny, and the woman's white-blond hair hung
limply around her face, she still resembled the lady in

Claire's visions. She even had the same beauty mark on her right cheek just above her mouth. Claire's heart skipped a beat.

"You said she had pale blond hair and a beauty mark. Is that her?" Brian asked.

"It might be her. Who is she? I need to hear what the reporter is saying."

The minute the assembly let out, Claire and Brian grabbed Erica. The three of them raced to Brian's car, where they sat and watched the video several times.

"Police are still trying to identify a pedestrian who was injured in a traffic collision last Friday. She's a Caucasian, presumed to be in her early sixties, with chin-length, light blond hair. She was found wearing a navy-blue dress, but carried no other identifying information. She is stable but unable to speak, and has been transferred to Twin Palms Hospital in West Hollywood. If anyone has any information about the identity of this woman, please contact the police, or call the facility directly at the following number."

A phone number flashed across the screen, and the video ended.

"How'd you find this?" Erica leaned forward from the back seat, awestruck.

"I kept adding every search word I could think of into the Google mix," Brian answered. "When I combined *Twin Palms* and *woman* with *missing person* and *hospital,* this came up."

Erica looked impressed. "You are a *god,* Brian."

"That's what I've been saying." He beamed.

Claire's pulse raced. Was it possible that this was the woman she was looking for? "All this time that I've been getting messages, I never imagined that she might be injured or lying in a hospital bed somewhere."

"Well, if it *is* her, this explains why she's been trying to contact you telepathically, instead of coming in person," Brian pointed out. "West Hollywood is only about half an hour away with traffic. Let's go see her!"

"How am I supposed to talk to her, if she can't speak?" asked Claire.

"You were able to commune with your long-lost father's spirit just by touching his *jacket*, and now you're worried about communicating with a *live* person who happens to also be *psychic*?" Erica answered.

"Oh. Good point. Let's go right now," Claire said.

Erica's face fell. "Right now? I can't. I have to go count votes with the committee."

"Oh, too bad," Brian replied with mock sympathy. "I guess that means *I* get to do something fun for a change." He turned to Claire. "May I be your chauffeur?"

Twin Palms Hospital was an immense, modern facility bustling with activity. When Brian and Claire asked about the mystery patient, they were told to sign in, given visitor's badges, and directed up to the trauma unit on the sixth floor. Exiting the elevator, they approached the nursing station, where a woman in pink scrubs was busy doing paperwork.

"Hi," Claire began with a smile. "We saw something on the news about an unidentified woman who was injured in a traffic accident."

"Oh!" The nurse looked up with sudden interest. "Do you know her, honey?"

"It might be my aunt," Claire replied, reciting the excuse she and Brian had concocted.

The nurse checked a chart. "She's in room 643. I'll walk you over there."

As the nurse hurried down the corridor, Claire said, "They mentioned on the news that she can't speak. What happened? Did she have a stroke or something?"

"No, she suffered a severe head trauma. She's in a coma."

A coma? Claire thought. *Holy crap.*

"If she doesn't wake up, they're moving her to another facility next week." The nurse led them into a room where a pale-haired woman was lying asleep in bed, a thin blue blanket drawn up to her chest, her arms resting outside the blanket at her sides. Claire's pulse quickened.

It was her. Although she looked a bit more haggard than the woman in Claire's visions, it was definitely the same softly wrinkled, beautiful face. *Helena.*

Claire nodded covertly at Brian. His eyes widened.

"Is she your aunt?" the nurse asked.

"I'm not sure," Claire said. "I haven't seen her since I was five years old. I think I need a minute."

The nurse's pager beeped. "Okay, honey. Just let me know—or if you can't find me, you can tell any nurse on the floor."

"Thank you."

The nurse exited. Claire drew two chairs up next to the bed and sat down nervously. "I can't believe I'm finally in the same room with her."

Brian took the seat next to her, his brow furrowed. "What should I do? I've never seen this before."

"Just sit there and wait." Claire slipped the glove off her right hand, flexing her fingers. "If I start talking with someone else's voice, don't freak out."

Brian gaped. "What?"

Claire didn't feel like explaining it. She took a deep breath, then carefully picked up the woman's hand in her own. To her surprise, almost immediately, a jolt of electricity seemed to pass from the woman's body into hers. Suddenly, all the sounds around her ceased, as if she was inside an isolation chamber. The world around her vanished entirely.

She was no longer sitting in the hospital. In fact, she was no longer sitting. She was standing in a black void, similar to the one in which she'd met the woman before. Claire stared down at her arms and gasped. The green flames of her aura radiated from every pore of her body, flickering into the blackness.

Claire heard the patter of distant footsteps. A speck of golden light appeared on the horizon and slowly approached. Her heart pounded in anticipation. As the light drew nearer, it grew brighter and brighter, changing the blackness around her to a void of brilliant white. Claire squinted, as if she'd stepped out of a dark movie theater into blinding sunshine.

A figure came into focus, surrounded by a golden aura. It was the same woman, but she looked prettier and infinitely healthier than she did in the hospital bed. She wore the same blue dress and sparkly diamond necklace as in their previous encounters, her white-blond hair was once more stylishly coiffed, and her complexion was pink and vibrant—yet she was not smiling.

She stopped a few feet away and regarded Claire with a stern glare as their auras faded away. "You certainly took your sweet time getting here."

thirty-two

C laire bristled, so taken aback by the woman's prickly expression and tone that she forgot what she'd planned to say. "I'm sorry," she replied defensively. "But you didn't exactly send me GPS coordinates. It took me a while to find you."

"I thought my messages were clear," the woman replied, the raspy edge absent from her now familiar, cultured British voice. "Perhaps you did not receive them in their entirety."

"I guess not."

"That may be a reflection of my injury, or your inexperience. Most likely, it's both," the woman said crossly. "But it's of no matter now. At least you are here."

Claire stared at her. She had imagined meeting a sweet older lady, not a bitchy one.

Although Claire hadn't responded aloud, the woman's mouth crooked into a half smile. "I'm not what you expected, am I?"

"How do you know what I expected?"

"Whether you speak or think something, my dear, I can hear it. Let us begin again." She thrust out her hand. "I am Helena."

Claire took her hand and shook it. "Hello. I'm sorry you're sick."

The woman shrugged. "The body is frail, but the mind is strong."

"Why are you in a coma? I thought the Grigori heal faster than people."

"We do. Some injuries take longer to heal than others. If I were a human, I would not have survived." Helena began walking, casting a look at Claire to follow. "Come along, I need my exercise."

Claire quickly caught up to her. Every step felt weird and awkward. All around her was blank white nothingness. With no distinction between ground and sky, she had no idea where to place her feet. "Where are we?"

"A meeting of the minds. This is the place where people go when they meditate." The woman paused and looked at her. "If you're uncomfortable here, feel free to change the locale. We can be anywhere you like."

"Anywhere?"

"The only limit is your imagination. Your mind is capable of far greater things than you know. Don't be shy. Think of someplace you enjoy, and take us there."

Claire took a deep breath, trying to come up with a place. The first image that popped into her mind was the soccer field at school. Instantly, they were both there, walking across the wide, grassy expanse that spread out below the landscaped hillside.

"Wow," Claire said. "That was cool."

"Not bad for a first try." Helena gave her a polite smile.

"Where would you have gone?" Claire returned playfully.

The woman's hazel eyes gleamed. Suddenly, they were traversing the grounds of an expansive, beautifully landscaped estate on a perfect, sunny day. A magnificent brick manor home stood in the distance, surrounded by acres and acres of green lawns dotted with immense, leafy trees and bleating sheep. "I have a soft spot for English gardens."

Claire laughed. As they walked on, past high green hedgerows bordered by brilliant beds of colorful flowers, Claire was finally able to ask the question that had been burning in her mind for almost a month. "Who *are* you, and why have you been contacting me?"

"Just think of me as your guardian angel, my dear."

"My guardian? Alec never talked much about those. Is it really okay if I call you an angel?"

"I don't object to the term myself, if it helps you understand what I am."

"How did you even know about me? I thought Vincent was the one assigned to look for me."

"Yes, but your abilities are so similar to mine—albeit more diluted—that I've been connected to your mind ever since you Awakened. My accident prevented me from contacting you through normal channels."

"I see." Claire sensed that the old woman was holding something back, and she still didn't understand why Helena was helping her, but thought it best not to press the point just yet.

"My immediate concern is for your safety," Helena went on. "Since I've been incapacitated, I've sent you messages the only way I could."

That brought up the other worry brewing in Claire's brain. "Am I really going to be attacked by a cougar at the Homecoming Dance tomorrow night?"

"Yes."

Claire's pulse quickened with fear. "How do I stop it from happening?"

"My recommendation would be: Don't go."

"Don't go to the dance? But—I can't do that."

"Why ever not?"

All the pent-up emotions Claire had been holding back came flowing out in a rush. "Because my mom bought me this expensive dress and she's so excited about it, and I said yes to Neil after saying no, and it's my first dance, and there's the whole princess thing that my friends have put *so* much time into, and—"

Helena held up her hand, motioning for Claire to stop babbling. "All right. If you're going to act like a teenager about it—"

"I *am* a teenager!"

"Clearly."

"What is *that* supposed to mean?"

Helena sighed. "Well, I tell you to keep your gift a secret, and you immediately tell two friends about it—and later your mother. Then—"

"But—" Claire began.

"*Then* I point you in the direction of the one person who can protect you, and you fall in puppy love with him, despite his explicit explanation that such a relationship is against the law."

Claire's cheeks burned. To have her whole experience with Alec reduced to the term *puppy love* was insulting. At the same time, her heart ached with fresh pain just at the mention of his name. "I won't apologize for that. I love Alec and I always will—no matter what your laws have to say about it."

"Well, it was very irresponsible of Alec."

"You can't plan who you fall in love with," Claire insisted, rushing to Alec's defense.

"*He* could have. You forget that to our kind, the concept of love is entirely foreign." Helena paused in front of a large, three-tiered fountain filled with lily pads. "For more than six hundred years, I have watched humans doing the most bizarre—sometimes heinous, occasionally beautiful—things in the name of love. I still do not understand it. But Alec should have known better."

"Well, you don't have to worry about me and Alec anymore. He's gone now. I'm going to the dance with someone else."

"So I saw."

Claire sat down on the stone bench surrounding the fountain and dipped her hand into the cool water. A lump rose in her throat and she swallowed hard, struggling to hold back tears. "How far can you see into the future?"

"I can only see the crossroads which are fated to happen *next*. It is the same for you. And we can see the fate of anyone *except ourselves*."

"Okay, so if you're able to see my fate because you're not me, then what should I do about the dance tomorrow night?" Claire shook her hand to dry it as they walked on. "If I don't wear the blue dress, will I be safe? Will that keep the vision from coming true?"

"I doubt that will be enough to alter your fate. The future is a slippery thing. We are often destined to reach certain crossroads, no matter what action we take—or outfit we wear. If something *substantial* should change with regard to tomorrow evening, you will be on a new path and your destiny will change."

"Should I call animal services then, and say I saw a wildcat roaming around campus?"

"You could, but they would be woefully unprepared for this particular animal. It is no ordinary cougar."

"What do you mean?"

"Do you remember the man who was watching you at the mall?"

Claire nodded in confusion, recalling the strange, dreadlocked man who'd been staring intently at her that day. "What does he have to do with this? Does he control the cougar?"

"He *is* the cougar," Helena answered grimly. "He is one of the Fallen, and that is his gift. He can shift shapes between a human and a mountain lion."

"You mean—like a were-cat?"

"A crude term, but yes. Were-cougar would be more specific." Helena sat down on a bench beneath an enormous tree and gazed at the vista around them. "He's a well-known mercenary who will do anything for the right price. He works for both sides but has proven very useful to us on occasion, which is the only reason he's still alive. I don't know who he's working for now, or if—for a change—he's just acting on his own. Regardless, it seems that you are his target—and based on his history, if tomorrow night's attack fails, he'll try again."

Claire sat beside Helena, knotting her hands uneasily. "How am I supposed to live a normal life if the Fallen are always going to be coming after me and death is lurking around every corner?"

"Unexpected danger can strike anyone at any moment. You will get through it the same way that every human gets through their life—one day at a time. Your gifts will

345 ༄

help you. And so will I."

Claire stared at Helena. "You'll help me? Really?"

"I said I was your guardian angel, didn't I?"

"Then you're not going to report me to the Elders?"

"I *am* an Elder, Claire."

Claire felt a tiny flicker of hope. The life that lay ahead of her didn't sound pretty, but it didn't sound quite as desperate, either. Without Alec by her side, it still seemed to stretch away into oblivion like a great wave of loneliness— and she might never be out of danger. But at least now she had a psychic companion who would try to prevent the worst from happening. *One day at a time.*

"So," Claire said, deep in thought, "back to the werecougar. When I go to the dance—"

"If you *must* go," Helena interjected with a sigh.

"If it's not enough to change the dress," Claire went on firmly, "how about if I don't go anywhere near the place where I saw it happen?"

"That might be effective. And as an extra precaution, I wouldn't go anywhere on your own tomorrow night."

"Got it."

"Now promise me one more thing, Claire."

"What?"

"That afterward, you'll come back to see me as soon as you can. Once we avert this immediate threat, I will be able to see beyond it to what you might face next."

"I'll be back on Sunday morning," Claire promised.

Helena smiled. "Good. Just come back to me safely. Good-bye."

Claire opened her mouth to reply, but suddenly, in less than a blink, the mental connection was gone. She was back in the hospital room, sitting at Helena's bedside, holding the comatose woman's hand in hers. And someone else's hand was moving in circles in front of her face. Claire jumped. It was Brian.

"Whoa! Sorry," Brian said. "Just testing to see if you're conscious. Are you . . . back?"

Claire nodded.

"That was trippy." Brian blew out a bemused breath. "You never said a word, but your eyes were open the whole time, and you had this vacant, thousand-yard stare that was really creepy."

"Well, that's safer than floating. I guess I am getting better at this." Claire stood up and put her glove back on, trying to collect herself. "Let's get out of here quick."

They slipped down the corridor unnoticed and leapt onto the crowded elevator. The minute it deposited them in the lobby, Brian said eagerly, "So tell me what happened! It's *her*, right? Did you talk to her?"

"Yes to both."

"What'd she say?"

"Short version: I most likely won't die tomorrow, but every day after that is a toss-up."

thirty-three

ꙮ

Leaning close to the mirror above her dresser, Claire
added a subtle dash of glitter to her eye shadow as she
got ready for the dance. But her thoughts weren't on her
makeup—they were filled with worry about the evening
ahead.

Meeting Helena had been unnerving to say the least.
Helena claimed she was Claire's guardian angel, that she
would try to warn and protect her. Claire knew she should
be relieved—but she couldn't stop the spasm that tightened her stomach at the memory of the cougar's gleaming
eyes, the paws as big as saucers, the teeth as sharp as spikes.
Was there a chance she might die tonight? *You'll be fine*, she
told herself. She wouldn't go anywhere near that spot on
the hillside, and she wouldn't go anywhere alone.

Claire sighed and stared at her reflection. Lamplight
shimmered and danced off the folds of her dress, which
clung to every curve of her body, and the deep blue color
complemented her skin tone. She'd kept her hair simple,

just curling it a bit. She felt beautiful.

And steeped in guilt.

Her heart ached for Alec. Where was he now? In some far-flung country, utterly alone, tracking a member of the Fallen? She felt like a fraud, going to this dance with someone else, knowing the sacrifice Alec had made for her and how miserable he must be. She wondered what it would be like to know that *he* was waiting for her at the bottom of the stairs . . . what he'd look like in a suit . . . what it'd feel like to dance in his arms.

Claire shook her head vigorously, banishing those thoughts from her mind. It wasn't fair to Neil for her to fantasize about someone else. Neil was a great guy. She'd promised to be his date, and she was determined not to disappoint him.

Quickly, Claire pulled on the long blue satin gloves her mom had found her. Grabbing her shawl and evening bag, she hurried from the room. When she arrived downstairs, her mom was sitting on the sofa, talking to Neil. He was dressed in a black suit with thin pinstripes and a crisp white shirt. He had some kind of loose, narrow blue scarf wrapped around his neck instead of a tie. As usual, his dark hair was naturally groomed to perfection. Even though she saw him almost every day, Claire was again struck by how handsome he was.

Neil leapt to his feet as she approached, a smile lighting up his face. "Wow. Claire. You look amazing."

Claire blushed. "So do you. What's that around your neck? A cravat?"

"It's an ascot. I've always wanted to wear one. I went to six stores before I found this. You said your dress was blue, and I had to guess at the shade, but I lucked out—this comes close to matching."

She was touched that he'd gone to so much effort on her behalf. "It looks great. Very stylish."

"You two look perfect together." Claire's mom beamed, getting out her camera.

Brian and Erica soon arrived, looking mighty spiffy themselves. After a round of picture taking—and her mom warning Neil to drive safely for the umpteenth time—they all set off in Neil's hand-me-down Lexus, where they chattered excitedly all the way to the dance.

Claire noticed that Erica seemed a little distracted—she couldn't quite meet Claire's eyes, and seemed to be thinking carefully before she spoke. Then Claire remembered that Erica was on the committee and probably knew the results of the Homecoming Court. Did Erica's discomfort mean that Claire—or Neil—had won, or lost? Claire didn't want to ask, but Erica was clearly fidgety around them.

When they reached the gym, the foursome passed through the lobby with its glass trophy cases and doors leading to the locker rooms. The double doors to the gym interior stood wide open, and as they strolled inside, the electrified energy coursing through the room lifted Claire's spirits. It hardly looked like a gym at all. The lights were dim, casting a romantic glow over all her classmates, who were dressed to the nines and dancing to the beat of pop music pumped through enormous speakers. An arch of blue and red helium balloons framed the entryway, and dozens of other balloon clusters decorated the small tables and chairs around the room. Several teachers sipped punch by the refreshment table, while a DJ controlled the music atop a stage on the opposite side of the gym.

"I know it looks pretty standard," Erica shouted over the music, pointing to several potted trees that defined the edges of the dance floor, "but see the ficuses with the twinkle lights? *That* was me."

"Very classy," Claire commented.

"You guys did an awesome job," Neil agreed.

Erica did a mock bow, accepting the praise with relish. "Now, *entrez, mes amis.*"

The girls dropped their purses and wraps on a chair as Erica continued, "Brian, I made sure there were Rice Krispies Treats just for you. They're going to announce the winners at eight thirty. Until then, everybody *be careful.*" She darted a meaningful look at Claire. "And go nuts!"

Immediately, Erica took Brian's hand and dragged him onto the dance floor.

"What did she mean, *be careful?*" Neil asked loudly in Claire's ear.

She knew Erica was referring to the chance that Claire

351 ❧

might be attacked by a Nephil were-cougar, but she couldn't very well admit that to Neil. "She knows I have two left feet and was just warning me to watch my step when we dance," Claire shouted.

"That's okay, I wore steel-toed boots," Neil teased. He took her gloved hand and led her into the center of the room.

The DJ was blasting the newest hit singles. Some of the other dancers, Claire noticed, were gyrating to the music with no particular style. Neil, on the other hand, began to move with a fluid grace. She'd seen him perform in choreographed musicals onstage, but this was the first time she'd witnessed what he could do on his own. He was so fascinating to watch, Claire almost forgot to dance herself. The music had such energy, however, that she soon got into the swing of things, letting go of all the worries that weighed on her mind. She was getting a lot of sidelong looks—frowns from girls envious of her date, and curiosity from people she didn't know that well. A few people even came up to wish her luck in the election for princess. It felt odd, as if she were a minor celebrity for the evening.

Several songs went by before the first slow song started, at which point the mood immediately shifted. Half the students drifted off toward the refreshments or the sidelines to sit down, while those who remained moved into each other's arms.

As she wove her arms around Neil's neck, Claire silently repeated her mantra to herself, just in case Neil's hands touched her exposed upper back. As the words resounded in her brain, she couldn't help remembering how it had felt to be held in Alec's embrace, spinning through the night air. *Just forget about me, Claire. Let me go. Move on.* Her heart wrenched, and she had to suppress a sudden pang in her chest. But as she looked up into Neil's eyes, she saw such sweetness and admiration that she forced herself to focus on the present. Neil deserved that.

"Having a good time?" He smiled down at her as they moved in slow circles to the soft beat.

"Yes," Claire replied. "Are you?"

"I'm here with the prettiest girl at the dance, why wouldn't I be?"

"Was that an attempt to avoid the question?" The words came out unthinking, and Claire regretted them. Were they prompted by her own guilt?

"I'm having a wonderful time, I was just worried about you." Neil studied her face intently. "Tell me straight: Are you still thinking about *him*?"

He'd asked so gently that Claire couldn't lie to him. "A little," she admitted softly. "But I'm glad to be here with you."

Neil nodded, not looking particularly surprised or hurt. "Okay. I can accept that."

Claire smiled up at him. "Has anyone ever told you how great you are?"

"Charming is the word I generally hear," he joked.

Claire laughed. As they continued to dance, she felt the tension slowly leave her body. It was nice to be in Neil's arms, to be the center of his attention—and to actually be vision free. She hadn't felt this relaxed or normal in a long time. *Normal.* That was what Alec and her mom had both wanted for her, wasn't it? To pick a normal boy, and have a normal life?

And then she saw them—a thin, dark-haired girl clad in a short, clingy white dress and two tough-looking guys whose muscles bulged beneath their tight suits were passing through the balloon archway. Even in the dimly lit gym, Claire recognized them at once, and she stared at them in alarm.

The Fallen.

They glanced about the gym with barely concealed smirks of amusement. Claire knew they were at least four or five years too old to be in high school—not to mention that their appearance didn't mesh with the college-prep Emerson vibe at all—but no one else seemed to have noticed them yet.

Except Neil, who followed her gaze. "Aren't they those guys from the mall?"

Claire's voice was tense. "I think so."

"What are they doing here?"

"I don't know."

"Let's find out." Neil took her gloved hand.

"No, Neil, I'd rather—"

He ignored Claire's protest as he propelled her purposefully across the room through the crowd of dancers. The farther they moved from the DJ and his massive speakers, the quieter the music became, until Claire was actually able to hear herself think again.

The trio had settled in front of the refreshment table, where the tall, ponytailed guy—Claire couldn't remember his name—was chomping on a cookie. The shorter one was playing with a cell phone, while the girl sipped punch. All three of them surveyed the room intently. *Looking for me*, Claire thought grimly.

As she and Neil strode up, the girl's eyes lit up with recognition.

"Claire!" the girl cried. "I almost didn't recognize you. You look gorgeous in that dress! Do you remember me?"

"Celeste, right?" Claire's lips tightened warily—yet despite herself, she felt a friendly glow emanating from this girl, enveloping her like an invisible cloud.

"What's up, guys?" Neil said with a curious smile. "What're you doing here?"

Claire suddenly remembered that Neil had actually liked these people, and had no idea what they were up against. How on earth was she going to get rid of them?

"We came to cheer for you and Claire, handsome," Celeste replied with a flirty wave of her hand. "We heard you're up for prince and princess. That is so exciting! You make such a cute couple!"

Claire flushed, and for a moment was at a loss for words. What *else* did Celeste know about her life? And why did Celeste's smile slink under her defenses and reverberate so warmly, making her feel like a long-lost friend? The answer dawned on her—*she's using her talent on me.* Claire steeled herself, fighting back against the intrusive feelings.

"How'd you hear about that?" Neil asked, surprised. "How'd you even find out what school we go to?"

"We have a special interest in Claire," the tall guy responded, "and a high-tech, global spy network at our disposal." He fixed Neil with a shit-eating grin, and his shorter companion laughed.

Claire's mouth dropped at this blatantly candid reply. Not surprisingly, Neil took it as a joke.

"Whatever," Neil said, rolling his eyes.

Celeste oozed sympathy as she set down her plastic cup and moved closer to Claire. "Sweetie, we know things have really sucked for you lately, and it's so much harder when you're on your own. You need friends to support you. Friends who know the truth, and really understand what's going on with you."

Claire's heart skittered. *Oh my God. Do they know about Alec, too?*

"Whatever happens, we're here for you," added the shorter guy. He raised his hands. To Claire's shock, he held her evening bag in one hand and her phone in the other. "I've already put Celeste's number in your phone," he added, dropping it back into her bag and handing it to her. "You can call us anytime, day or night."

Claire snatched her purse out of his hands, stunned by his audacity. "Thanks," she said through gritted teeth. "I'll keep that in mind."

Neil looked confused. "What the hell? Claire, this guy just went through your purse and you're thanking him?"

"I'll explain later, Neil." Claire wondered how she would *ever* be able to explain. To the trio, she said, "I think you should leave."

Celeste looked taken aback. "Claire, we came here in friendship. I don't think you realize what we're offering here. We know who you are, what you want, and what you need." She took Claire's gloved hand and leaned in close, whispering in her ear. "Money? It'll never be a problem again. Your mom won't have to work such long hours any- more, you can get a house, and all the stability you need. And all those other things worrying you? Looking over your shoulder, day in and day out? We can make all that go away. We have friends . . . *everywhere.*"

No wonder Alec said they were dangerous, Claire thought, her pulse racing, as perspiration broke out on her brow. *It's like being tempted by the devil.* Thank God she'd been warned.

Suddenly, a new voice entered the mix. A voice with a Scottish accent.

"Get your hand off her, or I'll take it off."

thirty-four

C laire's heart almost stopped.
    Celeste stepped back.

Alec stood not two feet away, staring at Celeste with icy calm. He was dressed in a sharp three-piece suit and tie and his usual combat boots, his dark blond hair stylishly tousled, his guitar case slung over his shoulder. Claire barely had time to register her joy and relief at the sight of him—he was here, *really here*—when Celeste interjected sullenly, "You never know when to make a graceful exit, do you?"

The two Fallen who were flanking Celeste lumbered toward Alec like attack dogs. "Back off, cowboy, you had your chance," said the shorter guy.

"Let the filly make her own decision," the tall one chimed in.

"Cowboy? Filly? What are you talking about?" Neil asked.

"Stay out of this, Neil," Alec ordered.

"No, *you* stay out of it, MacKenzie. Claire's with me tonight."

"I'm not here to steal your date," Alec reassured him.

"Then why *are* you here?" Neil demanded.

"Alec?" Erica cried, stunned, as she and Brian suddenly appeared at Claire's elbow. "I thought you left!"

"I did." Alec's gaze flicked to Claire's. Although his lips were pressed together and his eyes were stern and forceful, his cheeks were flushed, and the muscles around his mouth twitched with the apparent effort to control them. "Looks like it's a good thing I came back."

Blood raced through Claire's veins. Had Alec returned on her account? If so, how did he know the Fallen would show up tonight? Or *had* he known? Would he get in trouble for coming back? Was he here for a minute, an hour, or a day? However long it was, Claire was so thrilled to be in his presence again, she could hardly breathe, much less speak.

Alec turned to the Fallen. "I'm going to count to three. By then, you guys are gone."

"Excuse me! Is there a problem here?" a deep voice bellowed from nearby. Mr. Patterson approached the group, looking surprisingly dashing in a brown suit and burgundy shirt and tie. He stopped in front of the newcomers. "You kids don't go to this school. Who are you here with?"

"Nobody," Claire answered, the first word she'd been able to utter since Alec appeared.

"And they were just leaving," Alec added firmly.

Celeste stared at Mr. Patterson quizzically, as if there was something unusual about the man that she couldn't quite put her finger on. Her gaze then drifted to Alec and back again. Finally, she shook her head and let out a laugh, raising her hands and stepping back in acquiescence. "O-kay. I think we've worn out our welcome at this party. *Sayonara*, and best of luck to . . . all of you."

Celeste tapped the shoulders of her two compatriots, who joined her as she ambled toward the door. Alec followed close behind, darting a look over his shoulder at Claire that went straight to her heart. His eyes betrayed a silent wealth of emotions: concern, fury, frustration, love, pain, and regret.

Before she was out of earshot, Celeste whirled around and shouted back to Claire, "Call when you need us, Claire. And you *will* need us."

A shiver ran down Claire's spine. She couldn't conceive of a time when she would ever willingly solicit or accept their help, and hoped to never see them again. As Mr. Patterson disappeared into the crowd and the trio and Alec left the gym, Claire exchanged a look with Erica and Brian.

"That was weird," Neil said.

What was going to happen now? Claire worried. Was there going to be a fight? If so, Alec was outnumbered. She had no idea what kind of talents the other three possessed.

Even though Alec was a powerful Grigori, could he successfully counter them all at once? Every instinct told her that she should follow and try to help him.

"Neil—will you excuse me a minute?" Claire's gaze involuntarily flicked back toward the gym doors. "I—"

Before she could complete her thought, the music stopped and the DJ came over the loudspeakers:

"Hey, hey, hey! It's the moment you've all been waiting for. Let's gather round the stage for the announcement of this year's Homecoming Court!"

Erica grabbed Claire's forearm and spoke fiercely in her ear. "Don't even think about it, Claire. I'm not letting you go out there."

"What could you do, anyway?" Brian added vociferously in her other ear. "They're Alec's problem now. He can take care of it."

"Don't be nervous, Claire," Neil said with a smile, completely misinterpreting her dilemma. He put his hand on the small of her back and urged her gently toward the crowd gathering around the stage. "Come on. You worked hard for this moment."

"Keep walking," Alec directed Celeste and her cohorts, as he accompanied them across the parking lot.

The past week had been the most miserable of his life. Leaving Claire was the hardest thing he'd ever done. He'd gotten as far as Stockholm, where Vincent had ordered him to log on for a mental reprimand by the Elders and the details of his next assignment—but he hadn't been able to bring himself to do it. He'd remained under the radar, festering, his innards feeling as if they'd been melted away by an acid rain, putting off the inevitable for just a little while longer.

And then a strange message had blazed into his brain, like a radio on an imperfect frequency, alerting him that Claire was in danger and needed him. He could guess who had sent it—Claire had described the experience well enough—and he'd taken the first flight back, arriving just in time, it seemed.

"We're *going*," Celeste insisted moodily, glaring at Alec. "We don't need an escort."

"I don't want to see you three here again, understood?" Alec growled.

"Oh yeah?" cried the short, stocky guy, whirling on Alec. "What are you gonna do if we come back? Hit us with your guitar?"

"Rico, don't provoke him," Celeste called out.

"Why not?" Rico advanced toward Alec and gave him a hard shove. "There's three of us, and only one of him."

Alec regained his footing, suppressing a small smirk. He'd seen these guys in action before. Their talents were physical, not cerebral, but he knew he could take them.

"What's so funny, dipshit?" Rico's eyes flashed with anger now. Suddenly, the skin on his forehead began to bulge and tear, revealing a jagged, hornlike protrusion that extended from his nose to the crown of his head.

"Rico, knock it off, I'm serious," Celeste insisted.

"I'm not afraid of this guy," Rico hooted. As he flexed his thick fingers, more short, bony spikes ripped through the sleeves of his jacket and the flesh of his knuckles. "He screwed up our party. That sweet little thing was supposed to be ours."

"The party's not over yet," Alec said quietly.

Celeste rolled her eyes. "Shit, here we go."

Rico roared and charged at Alec, spikes first. In a blur, Alec sidestepped the maneuver and delivered a hard, downward kick to the back of Rico's knee. There was the sharp, popping sound of snapped tendons as Rico tumbled to the ground.

The taller Fallen—Javed, as Alec recalled—held up his hands and rubbed them together deliberately. As he slowly drew them apart, the air in between crackled with visible arcs of electricity. Instantly, he leapt at Alec, his hands pulsing with energy.

Just before Javed made contact, Alec spun and telekinetically flung Javed's hands back against his own chest. Javed cried out and dropped to the ground, jerking spasmodically as the current passed through him.

Celeste sighed to herself. "Testosterone." She glared at Alec, pointing back at the gym. "You know, you've got far worse problems in *there* than dealing with us."

Alec frowned, uncertain what she was getting at.

Celeste let out a smug laugh. "And you don't even see it coming." She glanced down at her two cohorts. "Get up, boys, let's get moving."

The two guys groaned and stumbled to their feet, then limped after Celeste to their yellow Humvee. In a squeal of tires, it sped out of the lot and up the hill.

Alec heaved a sigh of relief, but Celeste's last statement hovered in his mind. He knew Celeste had unique powers for sniffing out the paranormal. What was she hinting at? Did she know about the were-cougar that Helena had warned him about? Or was something worse in store?

He scanned the parking lot and the bushes on the dark surrounding hillside, looking for any sign of movement, anything out of the ordinary. He'd only be able to see the creature's aura if he caught it in the act of changing forms. Then it occurred to him—the guy might still be in human form, and possibly lurking inside. Not wanting to take any chances, Alec hurried back toward the gym.

A member of the Homecoming Committee handed the DJ a sealed envelope. He ripped it open. "Ho-kay, first up is Homecoming Princess."

The tension of the moment briefly distracted Claire from her worries about Alec and the trio outside. She hadn't really acknowledged it to herself until this very moment, but deep down, she secretly *did* hope to win this, even though she was still sure it would never happen. She held her breath in anticipation, waiting, wondering, as she glanced at Erica—but Erica was avoiding her gaze.

"Everyone put your hands together for the young darling who stole your hearts and will wear this year's junior crown: *Gabrielle Miller!*"

A burst of applause followed. Claire's heart sank. Gabrielle rushed up to the stage, squealing obnoxiously as she accepted her crown. Claire politely joined in the clapping. Neil beside her let out a frustrated sigh. "It should've been you."

Brian also looked crestfallen and shot Claire a sympathetic look.

"I'm sorry," Erica said just loud enough so Claire could hear. "I knew, and I couldn't tell anyone. And it was killing me. Claire, she beat you by only twelve votes."

That made Claire feel somewhat better. "Thanks," she whispered back, reminding herself once again that none of this really mattered. Alec was outside. Had he and the Fallen gotten into a fight? Was he okay? How could she make a successful getaway?

The announcement for prince came next. "And the lucky prince who gets to dance with this lovely lady is . . . *Neil Mitchum.*" Uproarious applause followed.

Claire threw her arms around Neil. "I knew it'd be you," she said with a smile.

Neil returned her hug, then turned toward the podium,

beaming but conflicted. "I'll be back, Brennan. Don't go anywhere. I'm still your date."

Alec dashed into the gym's trophy-lined entryway. The music had stopped, and he could hear thundering applause from within. As he made a beeline for the gym doorway, Mr. Patterson suddenly appeared, blocking his path.

"Mr. MacKenzie." Patterson's mouth crinkled in an uncharacteristically warm smile. His left hand was in his coat pocket. "Did the gate-crashers depart?"

"They did."

"Good. I heard that you dropped out of school. I hope that's not true. It's nice to see you again." He reached out his right hand for a handshake.

Alec paused to shake the teacher's hand. His attention was focused on the activity inside the gym, searching the crowd for any sign of his dreadlocked quarry. In his peripheral vision, he saw a blur of movement by the side of his throat. He felt a sharp sting in his neck, and a burning sensation as if he'd just been injected with something.

"What the hell?" Alec's eyes darted up to Patterson's in shock and confusion as he stepped backward. He saw the teacher replace a syringe in his pocket. Immediately, Alec's vision began to swim, and he felt his knees buckle.

Mr. Patterson reached forward and grasped Alec beneath the armpits, pulling him close to his chest. There was an unnatural glint in his eyes as his lips curled into a wolfish sneer.

"Mr. MacKenzie, have you been *drinking*?" Patterson said under his breath, in a voice that suddenly sounded different, deeper, and all too familiar. "Let's take you someplace where you can sleep it off."

Alec's eyes widened helplessly as he stared at the man holding him up. "Vincent?" he gasped as his body grew limp.

Claire barely paid attention as the DJ crowned the winners for king and queen. *Alec is here*, her mind drummed over and over like a heartbeat. She had to find him, make sure he was okay. It might be her last chance to ever see or talk to him.

As Neil led Gabrielle onto the dance floor for the Royal Court dance, his eyes darted apologetically toward Claire. She sent him an encouraging smile. *Now*, she thought as she turned for the doors.

"Would you like to dance?" came Brian's voice from beside her. There was sympathy in his eyes. She had no time for this, and no need to be pitied.

"Thanks, Bri, but you should dance with your date. I'm going to get some air."

"Wait, you're not going outside, are you?" Erica cried urgently. "If you are, we have to come with you."

"No, please, I want to be alone for a few minutes."

367

"Are you nuts?" Brian exclaimed. "Helena said you shouldn't go anywhere alone tonight!"

Claire paused. In the excitement of seeing Alec, she'd almost forgotten Helena's warning. But if Alec was outside, she wouldn't be alone, right? Maybe the Fallen would be gone by now, and Alec would be looking for her.

"I have to find Alec," Claire insisted. "I'll just wait for him in the entryway. I promise." With a reassuring smile, she turned and made her way through the crowd.

The room slowly came into focus. Alec blinked. Where the hell was he? What had happened? His mind was foggy and sluggish, his body felt heavy, and he was unable to move.

His nose was assaulted by a damp, musty smell. The floor beneath him was cold and hard. Alec recognized the white tile and realized he was slumped in the showers of the boys' locker room. Glancing down, he saw that his hands and feet had been tied with wire.

"I trusted you to stay away," growled Vincent's voice from the body of Mr. Patterson. "I told myself that a deal, once made, was something you had enough integrity to honor. A mistake, I assure you, that will not be repeated." He was standing in full view a few feet away, over one of the benches between the rows of gym lockers, examining the contents of Alec's guitar case. "Came prepared for a fight, I see," he added, turning and holding up the broadsword that Alec had stowed within. Patterson's image flickered and changed into Vincent, who towered tall and dark above him. "Too bad you didn't come prepared for me."

Alec tried to formulate a reply, but his lips wouldn't move. He fought against the wave of sleepiness that threatened to engulf him. *Vincent was posing as Patterson?* Alec silently cursed himself for not noticing it when he first saw him. This must be what Celeste had picked up on. He wondered where the real Patterson was—if he was even still alive.

"Don't waste your energy trying to speak." Vincent chuckled. He slipped Alec's sword back into the case and removed a large, silver-colored, semiautomatic pistol. Confirming that the clip was loaded, Vincent slapped it back in, checked to be sure the safety was on, and tucked the gun into the waistband of his pants beneath his jacket. "I gave you quite a hefty dose of tranquilizers, enough to knock out an elephant. In your case, it will merely take you down a few notches for several hours. Make you more . . . *human.* Which is fitting, I suppose, since you're acting more and more like one lately. Headstrong. Foolhardy. Throwing away everything for a girl you think you love."

Alec concentrated every ounce of his mental energy on his wrists, trying to command them to pull apart—an action that ordinarily would have been simple for him—but the wire that bound them only cut painfully into his flesh and held them tight.

"Stop struggling. You're just going to hurt yourself." Vincent closed the guitar case and leaned it against a bank of lockers, then glanced at his watch. "The drug should wear off around six a.m., just before the janitorial staff arrives."

Alec strained again to speak, but all that came out was a whisper. "You're . . . insane."

"No, *you* are. You refuse to deal with this Halfblood in the appropriate manner. I've been following this case for sixteen years, trying to do things by the book, but the rules don't work anymore. I try to convince the girl's father to be reasonable, then he tries to kill me—and vanishes. Every time I get a solid lead on him or his wife, it goes nowhere. When his spawn finally shows up on the grid, it's impossible to pin down. So I had to get"—Vincent lifted an eyebrow—"creative."

Alec stared at him. "The . . . scaffolding?"

Vincent shrugged. "Who else? I was desperate for an opportunity to force that boy to use his supposed speed talent, and when I overheard your gaggle was meeting him downstairs, I jumped at the opportunity. But instead of him swooping in and saving his friends, *you* did."

"Lucky thing . . . I was there," Alec managed.

"Hardly—if you hadn't interfered, the *real* Halfblood would've been contained weeks ago, and I wouldn't have had to pose as this idiotic teacher for the evening. Well, I won't let you screw things up this time. The world's equilibrium must be maintained, and you're so blinded by this disease of human emotion that you have lost sight of it." In a blink, the illusion was restored, and he was Patterson again.

"You've been . . . planning to kill her . . . all along, haven't you?" Alec gasped.

"Of course," Mr. Patterson scoffed, as he turned and left the room.

thirty-five

❧

C laire grabbed her bag and shawl, then hurried across the noisy gym toward the exit, hoping against hope that Alec would be waiting there. But when she emerged into the comparatively quiet entryway, it wasn't Alec she found, but Mr. Patterson.

He was rushing in her direction with a concerned look on his face, as if coming from outside.

"Miss Brennan, thank God! There's been a fight. Mr. MacKenzie was hurt. He asked that I find you right away."

Claire's pulse surged in dismay. "Alec's been hurt? What happened?"

"I don't know. By the time I got there, those three gate-crashers had fled." Mr. Patterson urged her to follow him out the door.

Without a second thought, Claire complied, hurrying outside with him and across the narrow street. "Where is he? Did you call 9-I-I?"

"They're on their way. He's just up the hill."

Claire hesitated. *The hill.* The very place where she'd seen a were-cougar attack her in the vision that had been burned into her brain. The very place Helena had warned her to avoid. But Alec needed her help. And she wasn't alone; she was with Mr. Patterson.

"Are you coming?" Mr. Patterson asked, looking back at her.

Claire nodded, catching up to him as they dashed up the central stairway toward the Upper Campus.

The grogginess threatened to consume him. *Stay awake,* Alec commanded himself. Using every ounce of willpower he possessed, he crawled, snakelike, across the tiled shower floor toward a bank of gym lockers. He was thankful that the locker he'd chosen for PE was on the bottom row. Propping himself up on one elbow, he raised his bound hands up to his combination lock and shakily turned the dial. His movements were slow, as if he were trapped underwater.

To his frustration, his hands slipped and he crashed to the floor, hitting his chin painfully on the concrete. *Bastard,* Alec thought. How could Vincent betray him like this? His own godfather. Alec had trusted him all his life. It sickened him to think of how blind and stupid he'd been—taking Vincent's word and leaving Claire so vulnerable.

He forced himself to try again with the lock. This time,

he succeeded. Awkwardly, he pulled open the thin metal door. His eyes fell on the black lockbox that lay inside—identical to the one in his regular locker. He dragged it out onto the floor beside him.

Through his brain fog, Alec tried to remember the combination. The lock refused to open telekinetically—his powers weren't strong enough. *Shite*, he thought, staring at the digital keypad in frustration, remembering how different it was to do things the human way.

Dropping onto his side, Alec struggled to input the series of digits with trembling fingers. His control was so off that he kept missing the buttons or pressing the wrong ones, and had to cancel and start over three times. Finally he got it right, the lock engaged, and the box opened.

Hurry the hell up, he told himself.

Inside lay his neatly organized array of emergency medical supplies. He grabbed a large, capped, liquid-filled syringe. Alec fell back weakly to the floor, struggling to remove the plastic wrapping. It was hard enough to do anything with his hands in such a weakened state, but even harder with them bound together like a trussed pig.

At last, he peeled off the cellophane wrapping, removed the cap with his teeth, and—with both thumbs on the plunger—stabbed the massive needle through his clothing, directly into his heart.

A rush of adrenaline shot like a rocket through his bloodstream. He sat up with a gasp and—with a single burst of restored strength—snapped the wires around his wrists and ankles.

Move, he thought, leaping to his feet. God only knew where Vincent was, and whether or not he'd already taken Claire.

"He's right up there." Mr. Patterson pointed toward the landing where the four stairwells met halfway up the hillside. The area was dimly lit by small lamps embedded in the low wall separating the walkway from the greenery.

To Claire's horror, she saw a figure lying on the ground, clutching his head. It was Alec, and his hands were covered in blood.

"Alec!" She rushed up and knelt at his side. His eyes were closed and he was unresponsive. Fear gripped Claire's heart. "What should I do?" she cried, glancing back at Mr. Patterson.

"He must be unconscious. Don't leave his side. I'll go down to wait for the paramedics." With a reassuring nod, he added, "I wouldn't worry. I'm sure everything will be all right."

Patterson disappeared down the hillside, leaving Claire alone with Alec on the landing. Blood seeped from a wound at Alec's hairline. Claire placed her gloved hand over the gash, trying to stanch the bleeding. "Alec," she said softly, "I'm here. Talk to me."

Still, there was no response. Claire gazed down at

him, overwhelmed by emotions. Love. Gratitude. Fear. Confusion. Why had he followed the trio all the way up here when they should have been parked in the lot below? Why wasn't he moving? Was he dying? His injuries didn't look that bad. But then she remembered Helena—also a Grigori with a head trauma—lying in a coma.

Her heart pounding with anxiety, Claire pulled back her gloved hand to see if she had stemmed the flow of blood. She hadn't. Strangely, however, when she looked down at her bloody glove, the bright red stain flickered before her eyes and then vanished, leaving the blue satin unblemished.

What the hell? Claire thought.

She heard a sudden rustling behind her. Turning in alarm, she glanced back into the dimly lit shrubbery and scattered palm trees that covered the hillside. There was nothing there. She turned back to Alec, and gasped in shock. He was gone. *Gone. Completely vanished.* Leaving not a drop of blood in his wake.

How was that possible? For a moment, Claire doubted her own sanity. Alec had been lying there, half-dead, just a second ago. How could he have disappeared like that? It didn't make sense.

She rose quickly, her mind whirling with confusion. "Alec?" Her voice was choked with panic. As she stared hard into the darkness, bewildered, something clicked in her brain. *The vision.*

She was living it, right here, right now, at this very moment—alone on the hillside, calling out for Alec, wearing the blue dress. How had she ever allowed this to happen? Was it possible that she'd been lured here? Then she remembered Vincent's power. *Had Alec ever really been here at all?* Had it all been an illusion? Could it be that Mr. Patterson was—?

Suddenly, she heard a thunderous growl directly behind her. She started to run toward the stairs, glancing back in horror to glimpse a tawny beast leaping from the bushes and hurling itself at her with claws and fangs outstretched.

The were-cougar!

Claire screamed in terror, stumbling in her heels, as it loped at her with deadly speed and pounced. Just as the creature's fangs and talons were about to sink into her neck and shoulders, another roar assailed her ears. Instantly, the beast was shoved aside in a blur of movement, as someone or something tackled it with great force.

Claire turned and froze. It was Alec.

Paralyzed with horror, she watched Alec battle the wildcat.

She'd never seen him fight before. At first, she was terrified for his life. But he moved with such incredible speed, strength, and agility, it nearly took her breath away. He hurled the cougar to the ground. The creature rolled and sprang at Alec again. As Alec writhed in the beast's grip, he seemed to anticipate his opponent's every maneuver, delivering the perfect counterattack, wearing the beast down. Claire gasped, too frightened and awestruck to move. A corner of her mind thought, No matter how smart and sensitive Alec was—no matter how much he wanted to live a normal, quiet life—*this* was what he was born to do—or at least trained to do. And he'd been trained well.

Anxiety hammered in Claire's chest as the battle raged on. Alec reached into his boot and withdrew a knife with a bright silver blade. For some moments, he continued to struggle against the huge creature's incredible strength. At last, he plunged the weapon into the animal's belly. The cougar roared in pain and flipped to its feet, backing off with a ferocious snarl.

But suddenly, to Claire's astonishment, it was no longer a cougar. It wasn't a man either. It was something halfway in between—half fur and half flesh, standing on two legs, with a mane of blond dreadlocks, human hands and feet, and a cougar's ears, eyes, teeth, and claws. With a low growl, the creature reached down and pulled Alec's knife from his stomach. The sight made Claire sick, but Alec appeared unfazed.

Alec leapt up, breathing hard, his suit shredded, bleeding from gashes in several places. In an instant, the man-cougar lunged at him again, the knife in one hand, claws bared on the other. Alec deftly dodged the wild swings and delivered a sharp kick to the creature's wounded belly. "Sword!" he cried.

Sword? Claire's eyes fell on Alec's guitar case, which lay on the stairs a few yards away. Could that be where he kept his weapons? She rushed to the case and opened it. To her surprise, a selection of swords and guns lay within. Before she could do anything, a long, thin, curved blade like the ones she'd seen in samurai movies rose out of the case and flew through the air into Alec's waiting hand.

The animal leapt toward Alec yet again. Alec quickly sidestepped the beast, extending his free hand with fingers splayed. The were-cougar froze in midair, flailing, caught in Alec's telekinetic grip. In its struggle, the animal seemed to summon all its strength, and before Claire's terrified eyes, it twisted and transformed back into a full-fledged wildcat. Alec's arm wavered now. The thing seemed about to break free.

Alec turned to Claire with a sudden, forceful look. "Close your eyes, Claire. You don't want to see this."

Claire put shaky hands over her face and waited for the sound of the blow she knew was coming. There was a horrific crunch of steel meeting bone, followed by a heavy thud. When she uncovered her eyes, the cougar lay dead on the ground in a pool of blood, its head severed from its body.

Alec breathlessly dropped his sword to the ground and ran to Claire. "Are you all right?" he asked, his eyes blazing with concern.

The tension that had gripped Claire's insides now

rushed like a hot wave into her head, and tears of relief sprang into her eyes. She threw her arms around Alec and hugged him tightly. "I'm fine. I'm alive." She heard and felt his wince of pain and drew back quickly. She saw now that his vest was ripped open and his shirt was soaked with blood. "Oh my God," she cried, horrified.

"Don't worry, I'll heal."

Tears ran down her cheeks. She had no idea how much time they had. There was so much she wanted to say to him, but all she could think of was, "Thank you for coming back."

"I never wanted to leave." Alec picked up his silver dagger, cleaned it on his pants leg, and slipped it into his boot.

"I didn't want to go to the dance," Claire admitted, her heart thundering.

Alec averted his eyes. The next sentence seemed difficult for him to articulate. "I'm glad you did, and that . . . Neil took you."

Claire was desperate for him to look at her again, hoping he could read the emotions she couldn't put into words. "I don't feel about him the way I feel about you, Alec. I never will."

Alec's eyes returned to hers then, overflowing with relief and a love he no longer tried to disguise. Claire wanted nothing more than to move into his arms again, to feel, if only for just a moment, the comfort she knew she'd derive from his embrace. But he quickly picked up his sword, wiped it on the bottom of his tattered jacket, and replaced it in his guitar case. "Come on. We can't stay here." Slinging the case over his shoulder, he took Claire's gloved hand and pulled her up the stairs toward the library, limping slightly.

"Mr. Patterson said you'd been injured," Claire explained as they hurried along. "That's why I came out here. But it was Vincent, wasn't it?"

"Aye." Alec practically spat the word out, trying to move quickly despite his injuries.

"Mr. Patterson's been at this school for years. He couldn't have always been Vincent."

"No, that was just Vincent's hoax for tonight."

"So where's the real Mr. Patterson?"

"Who knows? In Vincent's current state of mind, Patterson might be as dead as that wildcat."

"What?" Claire cried. "I thought the Grigori only killed the Fallen, not humans."

"Clearly, Vincent is operating outside the rules. He hired a Fallen to take you out. I think at this point, he'll do anything to get rid of you."

"But he promised! He said he wouldn't lay a hand on me!"

"No. When I look back on it now, he didn't actually say that. He chose his words very carefully. He promised that *no Elder* would touch you. And he's not an Elder."

"So you're saying he didn't actually lie?"

"Not really." They approached their locker. "If you'd been killed by that were-cougar, it would have looked like some random animal attack. No one could have traced it to him. He said what he needed to say to convince me to leave, so he could get to you without my protection."

"What an asshole."

"That's an understatement. You wondered how I could trust him. I wish I had listened to you." Alec pulled open their locker and took out the black lockbox from within. "Before he led you up the hill, he drugged me and tied me up in the locker room."

"Oh my God!" Claire said, shocked, as they moved to a nearby bench. "How did you get away?"

"An adrenaline shot. I have another box like this in my gym locker."

Alec rested his hand on the box, which emitted an audible click as it unlocked. Claire caught her breath in anticipation. Finally, she was going to see what was inside.

It was the last thing she'd expected. The top tray was like a first aid kit, filled with neatly organized supplies, including a syringe and several bottles of clear liquid. Alec lifted the tray and set it on the bench between them, exposing what lay below: various bundles of international currency and passports from a variety of foreign countries.

"Wow," Claire breathed in awe. "Who would have thought that someone like you would actually need a passport?"

Alec tore off his shredded jacket and shirt. "I don't have wings to fly on my own. I keep a bunch of these boxes, in case I need to skip town at a moment's notice from wherever I am." He glanced at her intensely. "I didn't want to take anything from my lockers when I left—any more than I could bring myself to report in."

At the look in his eyes, all the blood pumping to her heart seemed to change direction as it rose in a hot flush to her face. "You didn't report in?" she repeated breathlessly.

"Not yet."

Claire swallowed hard, uncertain what this would mean for his future—for *their* future, if they even had one. The thought so distracted her that she almost missed his next soft request.

"Help me, would you?" He handed her several packets of sterile gauze pads and a roll of adhesive tape, then held a pad over his largest wound, the one on his bicep. "And work fast—we don't have a lot of time."

With shaking fingers, Claire taped the pad in place, then moved on to bandage the worst gashes on Alec's chest, back, shoulders, and stomach. As she worked, she couldn't help but be aware of the beauty of his half-naked, muscular body. Her pulse beat so loudly in her ears, she had a hard time hearing what he was saying.

"I'm beginning to think that Vincent's been doing this kind of thing for years," Alec muttered.

"What kind of thing?"

"He routinely assesses Nephilim of all ages who are under suspicion of breaking laws. There have been countless incidents where he's reported them to be harmless—and then weeks or months later, they'd conveniently turn up dead in some accident."

"I guess he couldn't claim that every single one of the Nephilim he was assigned to had turned."

"Precisely. And he has more reason to take you out than anyone he's ever encountered."

"Because I'm a Halfblood."

Alec nodded, rolling up his pants leg to reveal a deep bite wound on his left calf. "And because you've been evading him ever since your birth. I think Vincent takes that as a personal affront. Plus, he said your father tried to kill him."

Claire bandaged the leg wound. Solemnly, her entire frame tense with apprehension, she said, "What happens now? Vincent's still out there. He's going to discover that the cougar is dead and I'm not. What should I do?"

"You and your mother have to disappear before he finds out. Go somewhere—anywhere—and stay under an assumed name."

"How long would we have to stay away?"

Alec gingerly slipped his ripped, bloody shirt back on. "I don't know. As long as it takes for me to find Vincent and bring him down."

"Bring him down?" Claire repeated, alarmed. "You mean *kill* him?"

"He's left me no choice. You'll never be safe until Vincent's dead."

"He's a master of illusion, Alec. That could take weeks. Or months. Or years!"

"It has to be done."

"But Alec . . . what if the Elders find out that you killed him?"

"I'll just have to hope that they don't—or find some way to explain what's going on without turning myself in."

Alec's last four words reverberated in Claire's brain. *Without turning myself in.* So Alec intended to stay AWOL! A wave of hope spiraled through her chest, wrapping itself around her panic. If Vincent was out of the way, was there a chance she and Alec could still be together?

"Okay," she responded quickly, "but you don't have to do this by yourself, Alec. We can get Helena to help us. Brian and I found her—she's stuck in a hospital in the city."

"I wondered where she was."

"I talked to her. She's an *Elder*. She can predict everything that I'm facing, and tell us what Vincent's next move is. Can't we use that somehow?"

Alec closed the lockbox and stood up, deep in thought. "We can try. But it's late. We won't be able to see Helena until tomorrow morning. And if you're dead before sunrise, her predictions won't do you much good."

Claire stared glumly at her gloved hands, which—after

tending to Alec's wounds—were truly bloodstained now, as was her dress. "I guess you're right."

Alec stowed the black box in their locker and shut it firmly. "We need to get you and your mother someplace where Vincent can't find you. Now. *This instant.*"

"What do I tell everyone downstairs? They must be wondering what's happened to me."

"You can explain it all later. You can't risk going down to the gym, Claire. Vincent might still be there, posing as Patterson, waiting for someone to find your body on this hill. Let him think you're dead. It'll buy us some time."

Claire heaved a frustrated sigh, knowing that Neil was going to hate her for disappearing without a word. And Erica and Brian would be sick with worry when they couldn't find her.

Alec helped Claire to her feet, his jaw tightening. "Come on. Let's go pick up your mom."

thirty-six

&

A lec parked at the curb in front of Claire's complex, where he traded his shredded suit jacket for his combat vest and leather jacket, then hauled his guitar case out of the trunk and slung it over his shoulder.

"What are you bringing that for?" Claire asked, discarding her ruined gloves.

"Insurance."

"Do you mind waiting out here for one second while I brace my mom for what you're going to tell her?" Claire asked as they rushed across the courtyard toward her apartment.

"Fine."

Claire unlocked her front door and hurried in. She'd only just stepped into the entryway, the door still ajar, when she caught sight of her mom on the couch. She wasn't alone. There was a man with her. And they were kissing.

Claire froze, shocked and mortified. "Mom?!"

Her mother broke from the embrace and instantly

leapt to her feet, her face turning red. "Claire! You're back already? I didn't——" She broke off, flustered.

The man turned to face her.

It was Mr. Patterson.

Claire's stomach convulsed with fear, disgust, and terror. Which Mr. Patterson was this? Was it the *real* Patterson? Her teacher? *Making out with her mother?*

Or was it Vincent? Already here. In her home. With all of them at his mercy.

Frantically, she tried to remember what the imposter had been wearing earlier that evening. She had no idea.

Whoever it was, he seemed to be just as surprised to see her as she was to see him.

"Mom! What are you doing?" Claire blurted.

Her mother looked embarrassed. "I'm sorry, honey. I thought you were still at the dance. This is Dennis. I told you about him."

"You've been dating *my history teacher*?" Claire cried, still uncertain.

Her mother's blush deepened. "I didn't know he was your teacher when I first met him. And then I didn't know how to tell you."

"I'm sorry, Miss Brennan." Mr. Patterson quickly stood. "We thought you might find it . . . awkward if you knew."

Claire stared at the pair in confusion. *Who was this man?* His gentle words of apology didn't match up with the sudden flash of anger in his eyes—anger that Vincent would certainly feel on seeing that she had survived the were-cougar's attack.

"Mom, get away from him," Claire cried, hoping her voice would reach Alec. "That's not Mr. Patterson. It's Vincent!"

"Who?"

"I told you! He's the Grigori who—"

With a crash, the front door behind Claire slammed fully open as Alec barreled through it in a blur, pinning Mr. Patterson to the wall with a dagger to his throat.

"What are you doing?" Claire's mom screamed at Alec.

Mr. Patterson's surprised expression turned to a wolfish smirk. "This makes more sense." He studied Alec calmly, as if ignoring the blade at his throat. "I wondered how she escaped without a scratch. You're heartier than I thought."

"You should've been honest with me from the beginning," Alec spat out with devastating calm. "Then I wouldn't have to kill you."

"No." Mr. Patterson chuckled. "No matter what, we would've ended up here."

"Take your hands off him!" Claire's mom shouted.

"Mom," Claire cried urgently. "You don't understand!"

Before their eyes, the image of Mr. Patterson flickered and was replaced by Vincent.

Claire's mom jerked back with a scream.

Vincent's eyes locked with Alec's. "Do you really have

the stones to kill me, boy? After everything I've done for you and your parents?"

"You've made all that meaningless now." Alec's eyes blazed with a fury Claire had never seen before.

Just as Alec's blade began to pierce the skin of Vincent's throat, the entire apartment shook as if rocked by a massive earthquake. Claire stumbled back a step, and Alec, in surprise, did the same. The earth beneath them rumbled. A horrible, buzzing sound assailed her ears, growing louder every second.

Claire gasped as a swarm of locusts burst in through the front doorway, circling Alec in a frenzy. His dagger fell from his hands as he batted away the flying horde. In seconds, to Claire's horror, the entire room was alive with the flapping insects. She and her mom ducked and covered their faces with one hand, trying to swat at them with the other.

Claire heard Vincent's chuckle mingling with the terrible hum of the swarm. Eyes still covered, she put her hand down to steady herself. But instead of carpet, she felt hot sand. Stunned, she looked around to find they were in the middle of an endless desert. A strong wind whipped past her ears, drowning out the buzzing of the locusts.

The insects concentrated in a swirling tornado around Alec. Her mother was a few yards away, staggering to her feet, screaming with bewilderment and terror. Vincent now stood above Claire, a confident smirk plastered across his face. He withdrew a large silver pistol from his waistband. Claire shrieked. Before she could move, Vincent pressed the steel of the barrel against her forehead.

Claire's pulse pounded in terror. Suddenly, her mother threw herself against Vincent, shouting, "Don't you touch my daughter!"

Vincent smashed the butt of the gun up against the side of her mom's head. Lynn fell to the ground, unmoving.

With a cry of rage, Claire leapt to her feet, some instinct urging her to bring her knee up hard into Vincent's groin. To her satisfaction he doubled over in agony, dropping the gun. Claire stared at the weapon, hesitating—she'd never touched a gun before—then frantically scooped it up and trained it on him. It was heavier than she'd imagined. Out of the corner of her eye, she saw Alec still surrounded by the horrible whirlwind of locusts.

Vincent fixed her with a malevolent glare. "Not comfortable holding a gun?"

Suddenly the pistol was gone, and in its place was a writhing rattlesnake.

Claire screamed and let it drop to the sand, where it reverted back into a gun. In one fluid motion, Vincent snatched it up and backhanded Claire forcefully across her face. She reeled away in pain, her vision blurring, tasting blood in her mouth.

"I have never relished violence," Vincent said calmly and rather ironically, adjusting a crick in his neck. "But you leave me no choice." He grabbed Claire by her hair and yanked her to feet.

"Why are you so afraid of me?" Claire cried, tears stinging her eyes.

Vincent looked at her coldly, still gripping her by her hair. "You are an abomination, and I will not have you destroy the world that I have spent my entire life protecting."

"You're wrong. I'm just a girl. I don't want to hurt anybody."

"But you *will*," he returned with conviction. He cocked the gun and pressed it to the underside of her chin. "I brought this to kill your mother. Now it will prove doubly useful. And it will have Alec's fingerprints all over it."

In a blink, it was no longer Vincent holding the gun to her head, but *Alec*, all the way down to the scrapes on his face, but overlaying his handsome features was Vincent's leering grin. Claire cried out in dismay, the illusion disorienting her as she struggled vainly to free herself from his iron grip. But it was a lost cause.

She was going to die.

There was a whizz of something flying through the air, followed by a sharp, wet sound. Claire heard Vincent's grunt of pain as her attacker stiffened, releasing her and the gun. She staggered back in astonishment. The swarm of locusts was dissipating, but the hot desert wind still blew harsh and strong. The real Alec stood with a broadsword at the ready, as his clone reached to yank the dagger out of his back.

Claire watched in a fever of panic and dread as the two Alecs engaged in battle. Vincent-Alec hurled the dagger with swift precision directly at Alec's chest. Alec batted the weapon aside with a swift tilt of his blade. Vincent-Alec raised his hands above his head, conjuring a broadsword identical to Alec's, and brought it down against the other's weapon with a mighty clang.

Claire ran to her mother's side and knelt down, calling to her gently. Her mom let out a low moan, but remained unconscious. *At least she's still breathing*, Claire thought with relief.

Spotting the pistol in the sand, she grabbed it. There must be some way she could help. But as she raised the gun on the continuing duel, she hesitated in confusion. In a flurry of blade and footwork, the two identical men were changing places so quickly that Claire had lost track of who was who.

She aimed first at one, then the other, then back again. Her heart hammered in her chest. Which one was the real Alec? What was she supposed to do?

Claire knew that Vincent's illusion was all in her mind, but that didn't make it feel any less real. A sudden thought occurred to her. *Her* powers involved the mind as well, and both Alec and Helena had told her that she was capable of far more than she knew. If everything she was seeing was

393 ∂୨

in her mind—in *all* their minds—maybe she could, somehow, peel back the layers of illusion to reveal the truth.

The men continued exchanging angry blows, the tip of a blade nicking the cheek of one Alec and drawing blood. She knew she didn't have much time.

Crouching down, Claire touched one hand to the sand. Weeks ago, when she'd touched her father's blazer, it had revealed its secrets to her. She knew that the carpet of her own living room lay somewhere beneath her fingers. Was it possible for her to connect with the truth beneath this mirage of sand in the same way?

Claire focused on her breathing, just as she'd done when she first contacted Helena, but this time she refused to close her eyes. She stared at the sand below her, concentrating on its warmth and texture as she pressed her fingertips against it. *This is not sand*, she told herself with certainty. *It's a carpet.* She looked up at the desert landscape around her. *This is not a desert. We are in my living room. Show me. Show me the truth.*

Claire sensed that she was doing something right when the sounds of the desert wind around her vanished. As she stared hard into the distance, the image began to flicker, the way the fake blood had flickered on her glove earlier that evening. The environment flashed back and forth between the desert and her apartment—illusion and reality—but she suspected that only she could see the difference. In between flashes, one of the fighting Alecs was revealed to her as Vincent. He was blocking the blows from Alec's sword with nothing but air!

Claire raised the gun shakily, aiming at the figure she could now see to be Vincent. But the combatants were moving so fast, she was still afraid to fire. Her aim might be off. She might inadvertently shoot the wrong person.

"Alec!" she cried, lowering the weapon. "His sword is in your mind! It's not really there!"

Alec wavered, his brow furrowing as if trying to process what she'd said, but the illusion was too strong to resist. He kept deflecting Vincent's blows.

Somehow, Claire thought desperately, *I have to get Alec to see what I'm seeing.* Was it possible? Did she have the power to transmit the truth behind Vincent's illusion to Alec— even if just for a second?

Setting down the gun, Claire placed both hands on the hot sand again and gazed intently at the two men fighting before her. The scene continued to flicker back and forth strangely between desert and apartment. *Show him,* she repeated in her mind. *Show him the truth.*

As she watched, to her horror, the two men erupted into flame! Claire gasped, but then she realized it was not real fire. In her effort, she must have inadvertently activated her aura vision. Both men's strength seemed to be waning, because the golden flames leaping off their bodies were sputtering. She had to act fast.

Summoning every ounce of her willpower and concentration, Claire struggled to connect Alec's mind to her own. The effort was so intense, it caused her head to throb, and she lost touch with the ground below her. A crushing pain speared through her temple, but she ignored it and pressed on.

Alec! she called silently. *Alec! See what I see!*

Alec wearily sidestepped Vincent's blow and swung into position to parry again. It was useless dueling the very man who'd taught him to fight with a blade—he knew every trick up Alec's sleeve. If only he could use telekinesis, he might be able to gain an advantage; but he'd tried and failed. He was nearly tapped out.

Just then, to Alec's amazement, the world before him flickered, revealing glimpses of the reality that lay behind it. In that split second, he caught a clear view of his opponent.

Vincent's hands held nothing whatsoever. Nothing but air.

Thank you, Claire, Alec thought. As Vincent swung at him with the imaginary blade, Alec ignored the attack, lunging forward with determination and stabbing him straight through the chest.

Vincent gasped deeply and crumpled to his knees. The entire illusion instantly vanished. They were in the apartment again. Alec turned—and caught his breath in astonishment.

Claire was several yards away, hovering two feet above the floor, illuminated by an aura of massive emerald flames.

She dropped to the carpet with a thud, moaning, blood dripping from her nose. Lynn lay unconscious on the dining room floor nearby. He heard Vincent wheezing, as if one of his lungs had been punctured, and blood seeped through his clothing.

Alec pressed his foot on Vincent's chest for leverage and pulled his sword free, then lowered it to Vincent's throat. "Any last words?" he asked dangerously.

"Yes. Don't . . . do this." Vincent inhaled weakly. "If I don't report back alive, they'll come looking for me. Which . . . will lead them to you."

"Let them *try* to find me. You deserve to die. You've lost sight of what's important."

"No, *you* have. No one is innocent, Alec. She will . . . *turn* someday. If I don't stop her, someone else will."

"Not on my watch."

"Mark my words," Vincent insisted. "Someone will have to kill her. It may even be you."

"*Never.*" Alec raised the sword, holding it above Vincent's neck, ready to deal the final blow. Then his eyes caught Vincent's and he hesitated. Could he really do this? Could he murder his own godfather?

"I told you," Vincent taunted, chuckling, "you don't have it in you."

Fury gathered like a storm in Alec's chest. He brought the blade down on Vincent's neck with a forceful swing. It connected. Vincent's broken body lay before him in a pool of spreading gore.

Relief spread through him. It was done. Claire was safe. That monster could never harm her.

Suddenly, to his dismay, the body on the floor in front of him vanished into thin air.

He heard Claire gasp.

A deep chuckle sounded across the room.

"Or . . . maybe you do." Vincent stood in the front doorway, still bleeding and grimacing in pain, but very much alive. "Be seeing you." He darted out, slamming the door behind him.

"Shite!" Alec cried, aghast, even as he glanced back in concern at Claire. "Are you all right?"

"Yes! Just go!" she cried.

Alec raced after Vincent, clutching his sword. Claire followed at his heels, her head pounding in agony, pressing her hand to her nose to stanch the bleeding. They dashed through the courtyard to the street, but it was dark and deserted. There was no sign of Vincent anywhere.

"Shite, shite, shite!" Alec cursed.

They stopped on the sidewalk, Claire's chest heaving as she struggled to catch her breath. There was no way to find Vincent now. He could be anything, anywhere.

Sudden tears welled up in her throat and blurred her vision, releasing her anger, disappointment, and relief all at the same time. Her nose, she noticed, had stopped bleeding, but her head was still hammering, and her cheek and jaw felt bruised.

"He'll come back." Alec's was voice tight with frustration.

"I know."

"But not tonight, I think. He was wounded. He'll need time to heal, to plan."

Claire exhaled a little, choking breath. Thank God for that. For right now, at least, she was safe. And she had Alec at her side. Tears fell down her cheeks as she looked at him, standing there at the curb—bruised, bloodied, and battered, his clothes in tatters, a look of fierce determination on his face. Their eyes connected, both relieved to be alive and together. Claire felt a rush of affection and gratitude so strong, she couldn't stop herself from wrapping her arms around his neck and kissing him.

"Thank you," she murmured in between kisses and tears, ignoring the pain in her jaw, her cheeks wet against his. "Thank you, thank you, thank you."

Alec responded with equal passion, pressing her close against him with his free arm. "Thank *you*," he said softly, kissing away her tears. "I couldn't have done it without you. You showed me the way."

"I love you," she whispered against his lips.

"I'll always love you," he whispered back.

His words infused her with joy. Their kiss deepened, and Claire felt as if she'd come home at last. She knew that this was where she belonged: in Alec's arms and at his side.

When their lips finally parted, Claire wiped her eyes and rested her forehead against Alec's chest. "Promise you won't ever leave me again."

He held her tightly. "I hope I'll never need to."

Claire heard a car approaching. She looked up to find Neil's Lexus pulling to the curb. Three doors flew open, and Neil, Brian, and Erica jumped out. Claire stepped out of Alec's embrace, glancing down at the bloody sword he still carried. They had a lot to explain, and she had no idea where to begin.

Neil strode up first, hurt and angry. "Where the hell have you two been?" As he drew nearer and caught sight of their appearance, he stopped short in dismay. "Oh my God. What happened?"

Claire's hand flew to her cheek, aware that she must be a bruised and bloody mess. "I—had a nosebleed," she said uncertainly.

"Are you guys okay?" Erica demanded, with a look that conveyed her frustration that they couldn't talk openly.

Claire nodded silently.

"Shit, Alec. You look like you've been through a meat grinder," Brian observed.

"I feel like it, too," Alec answered.

"Is that a real sword?" Brian added in awe.

Alec, Claire, and Erica all shot Brian a wide-eyed, silencing glare. Claire saw Neil pick up on their collective response. He frowned.

Erica instantly changed the subject. "Why aren't you answering your phone, Claire? Why'd you guys leave the dance? You promised you wouldn't go outside alone . . . with those weird kids around!"

"Yeah, well, Mr. Patterson told me that Alec was injured in a fight with them," Claire answered slowly. It was the truth, and Alec's appearance certainly supported her statement. But what else could she say, with Neil standing there? She hated to lie to his face, but what choice did she have? "So . . . I went out to help Alec, and then drove him to the hospital. He's okay now. We just got back."

Neil squinted at her, obviously not buying it. "How'd you get that bruise on your face?"

"I . . . tripped on the stairs at school."

"Bullshit," Neil said, angry again. "The police broke up the dance. A sophomore went up the hill for some air and found a dead mountain lion on the main stairwell, with its head cut off." Neil's eyes swerved to collide with Alec's. "So, MacKenzie. Did you and your sword have anything to do with that?"

Erica and Brian stared down at the ground knowingly, while Claire shot Alec a silent, desperate glance.

"Does it matter?" Alec replied quietly.

Claire felt the heat of Neil's gaze as he studied the four of them. "Something really weird is going on. You mind letting me in on it, Brennan?"

Claire swallowed hard. "I . . . can't. I'm sorry."

Neil shook his head in disgust and backed away, raising his hands in the air. "You know what? Screw you guys. I don't need this."

"Wait, Neil—" Claire began, racking her brain for some explanation that would smooth things over, but her head and jaw still ached fiercely, and nothing came to mind.

With undisguised pain in his eyes, Neil added, "The first half of the evening was really nice, Claire." He turned, climbed into his car, and screeched off.

Claire sighed. It hurt her deeply to see Neil leave like that. But no matter how upset she was, she knew that *he* felt worse. And it was all her fault.

"One of these days, you're going to have to tell him what's going on," Erica said.

Claire shook her head. "I hope not."

"Who says he'd believe it?" Brian muttered.

Just then, Claire heard her mother's frantic voice calling out from her front door. "Claire? Claire! Where are you?"

"We're out here, Mom!" she yelled. "We're okay! I'll be right there." To her friends, she said wearily, "She's got to be *so* freaked by what just happened."

Brian and Erica looked at the both of them. "What *did* just happen?"

Claire and Alec exchanged a glance. Then she sighed and turned back to their friends with a bittersweet smile. "It's a long story. You'd better come inside."

epilogue

At Alec's insistence, Claire and her mom spent the night at a hotel in West Hollywood, while he kept watch over them. It took a double dose of painkillers to stop the throbbing in Claire's head, which Alec guessed was due to the strain of putting her new powers to such a massive test. Nobody slept much. Claire and her mom were still stunned and afraid Vincent might come back any second, and they had a lot to talk about.

By early next morning, Alec's wounds were healed. Claire's mom called the real Mr. Patterson, and to their relief, he was fine. He hadn't even been on the faculty committee to chaperone the dance. He said he'd fallen asleep in front of the TV the evening before, which made them wonder if Vincent had drugged him to ensure that he didn't leave his house.

"He'll be very confused, come Monday, if anyone mentions seeing him at the dance," Alec commented with a shake of his head.

"I'm sorry I didn't tell you about us, Claire," her mom said, red-faced, after she hung up the phone. "I really like him, and I was afraid you wouldn't approve."

"That's okay, Mom." Claire hugged her. "There's a lot of stuff I didn't tell you, so I guess we're even. It's fine as long as you're happy."

After a quick breakfast, all three made their way to Twin Palms Hospital to visit Helena.

As they surrounded Helena's bed, Claire's mom stared down at her with compassion. "You're actually able to talk with her, even though she's in a coma?"

Claire nodded. "And today, I want to try something new. I'm hoping you'll both be able to see and hear what I do when I touch her."

She instructed Alec and her mom to hold hands in a circle with her and Helena around the bed. "On the count of three, I'll take Helena's other hand and complete the circle. If this works, it's going to feel really weird. Just relax and go with the flow. Remember, she can be kind of persnickety. Oh—and I hope you like English gardens."

Her mom looked puzzled and wary.

Claire took a breath. "One. Two. Three."

She took Helena's hand and closed her eyes. Instantly, Claire felt a jolt of energy pass through her. The sounds of the hospital disappeared, there was a flash of blank whiteness, and then the three of them were standing hand in hand on a great green lawn. It was the same English garden as before, with twittering birds, sunlit paths, and borders of colorful, fragrant flowers waving in the breeze. Claire spotted Helena nearby, sitting quietly on a bench in the shade of an enormous tree. She was no longer wearing her dark blue dress, but instead looked ready for a garden party in a stunning floral print dress and large, stylish hat.

"This is beautiful," Claire's mom said, staring around them in wonder.

They dropped hands as Helena walked over to them with a welcoming smile. "I see you've brought guests. How nice." She fixed her gaze on Claire's mother, who she seemed to find particularly fascinating. "So *you* are Lynn. The cause of all this trouble."

Claire's mom seemed taken aback by this unexpected remark but returned Helena's gaze with proud determination. "Yes. I am."

"Well, well. You're pretty enough," Helena mused, "but I hope there's more to you than that, considering a highly regarded Grigori left the fold on your behalf."

Claire's mom blushed in embarrassment. Claire felt her own temper rising. "Helena, can you try to be pleasant for five minutes, please? We're here because we need your help."

Helena shrugged. "Forgive me. It is our way to be blunt. Alec understands what I mean." Turning to Alec, she observed, "You are even more handsome in person, young man."

Alec's eyebrow raised. "In person?"

"A figure of speech. I am pleased that you heard my call and returned when Claire needed you. And you, young lady, your performance last night was impressive."

"Alec's the one who saved my life." Claire reached out a hand to him, and he took it affectionately.

"Yes," Helena agreed, "but he's had training, and has done such things for over a century. You, on the other hand, were operating on instinct alone. You opened your mind to the possibilities before you. You saw through Vincent's illusions, and—in spite of the pain it caused you—you managed to convey that truth to Alec. Quite a masterful feat."

"Aye, it was," Alec acknowledged, putting his arm around Claire and drawing her close. "But Vincent's still out there," he added grimly. "He could come back anytime. I've been thinking it over all night long. He's too powerful to take down on our own. I ought to report in and let the Elders know he's gone rogue."

"You can't do that!" Claire cried, her heart hammering in fear as she pulled away to stare at him. "They'll find you and make you go back!"

"It's worth it, if it means you'll be safe," Alec insisted.

"Such heroic sacrifices are currently unnecessary," Helena interrupted with an authoritative wave of her hand. "I wish I had foreseen Vincent's true nature sooner—but I summoned my strength and managed to report his actions last night."

"You did?" Claire asked in surprise.

"Thank God," her mom said quietly.

"I left out Alec's involvement, of course, just as I deliberately neglected to mention his ill-advised . . . *liaison* . . . with you, which we will have to hope they do not discover."

The color rose to Claire's cheeks.

"But wait," Alec added suspiciously, "there's no way you could have reported Vincent without telling them about Claire."

"Quite right, young man," Helena replied. "But that was inevitable. A Halfblood is a serious potential threat. There is no way the Council would rest until they found out who it was."

"What?" Claire cried, upset. "So how are you any different from Vincent?"

"Vincent's opinions are too black-and-white, and his behavior reprehensible. He rushed things just for closure on his old case. Whereas I—as the Council has decreed—am going to give you what no Nephila has ever had before. A mentor. Someone to teach and guide you."

Claire's eyes widened in surprise.

"Wait a minute." Claire's mom bristled. "I'm grateful that you intervened on my daughter's behalf. And I appreciate your offer. But it's my job to take care of her, not yours."

"I beg to differ," Helena returned with a tight-lipped smile. "You have done just fine nurturing Claire through the formative years of her human existence. But you do not possess the necessary life experience to train a Halfblood Nephila. Beyond her visions, she may have inherited the other half of her father's abilities, and will face difficulties you cannot begin to imagine. It remains to be seen what the Council will do about Vincent—if and when they find him. But as he so astutely noted, there are others who will either want her dead or on their side. And the Fallen's means of influence are so cunning, she may be unaware of what is happening."

"Even so, she needs *me*. I'm her mother. What gives you the right to step in all of a sudden, out of nowhere? Who the hell are *you*?"

Helena didn't respond. Instead she closed her eyes, as if summoning a deep, inner strength. To Claire's dismay, the connection between them suddenly ended. The garden vanished. The three of them were all standing once more around Helena's bedside in the hospital, staring down at the comatose woman's pale, motionless face.

They dropped hands as Helena's eyes suddenly snapped open. Fully cognizant, she smiled at Claire's mom and said emphatically, "I'm Claire's grandmother."

Claire gasped in astonishment and wonder. *"My grand-mother?"*

Lynn's hand flew to her mouth. Alec nodded, and Claire sensed he was thinking the same thing she was—that finally, Helena's part in all this made sense. "Why didn't you tell me before?" Claire asked.

Helena shrugged. "It wasn't important. And I knew if I told you, we'd never get down to business." To Claire's amazement, Helena immediately sat up and ran her fingers through her pale hair. "Now, will someone please find my clothes and get me to a hairdresser?"

"You just woke up! Shouldn't you be resting?" Claire asked.

"I've been resting for weeks," Helena answered.

"She's probably fully healed by now," Alec chimed in. "Remember? We Grigori—"

"I'll go find a nurse," Claire's mom interrupted. She left the room.

Helena grabbed the call button and pressed it repeatedly, muttering, "What does it take to get a cup of tea around here?"

Claire laughed. As she stared at this beautiful, feisty woman, this angel—*her very own flesh and blood*—she felt a rush of emotion so strong that her eyes welled up. Alec reached out and took Claire's hand in his, squeezing it with reassurance as his eyes met hers with a loving smile.

Claire returned his heartfelt smile as she wiped tears away. Admittedly, she still had a lot of problems. Her father and Vincent were MIA, she might be in danger, and her life might never be normal. But no matter what the future brought, she decided, she could handle it. She had her friends, her mother, and two angels to help her. She wouldn't have to face it alone.

acknowledgments

First and foremost, we'd like to thank Brentwood School, the inspiration for Emerson Academy, which has had a very lasting, positive influence on both our lives. (If we're ever lucky enough to make a movie of this, we hope you'll let us film it on campus!) Also, a special thank-you to the dedicated and nurturing faculty from the years Ryan attended, who provided such wonderful specifics for this novel—including Lynette Creasy, Robert Ingram, David Foote, Sarah Wallace, Paula Radomile, Mike Grasso, and in particular Dennis Castanares, Brian Vaughn, and Judith Lyons. We love and miss you!

Thanks and love to Bill, Jeff, Yakun, and especially Evey, for reading the first draft and giving us such valuable feedback.

Todah rabah to agent extraordinaire Tamar Rydzinski, for suggesting that Syrie write a young adult novel, and not balking when she decided to let Ryan in on the fun.

We owe a huge debt of gratitude to our brilliant editor, Kari Sutherland, for having such faith in this book at the outset, and then combing through our manuscript with such enthusiasm and attention to detail. It's not easy to engineer a brand-new, mythical reality and combine it with our own, but Kari made sure that the merger was seamless and consistent. And a big *¡gracias!* to the entire team at HarperTeen for all their hard work en route to publication.

Ryan would also like to thank Michael Scarpelli for introducing him to the concept of the Grigori all those years ago . . . and Vicious Brutal Overlord Roy Mumaw for helping forge an early rendition of Alec, and teaching him the arcane art of world-smithing.

Oh, and Ryan guesses he should say *xiè xiè nǐ* to Syrie, not just for being a great partner and mentor in the world of writing, but for the whole birthing him and raising him thing.

Lastly, Syrie would like to express her thanks to Ryan for sharing the fruits of his creative young mind, and making this one of her most enjoyable writing experiences ever.